STRICTLY
NEED TO KNOW

STRICTLY
NEED TO KNOW

by

MB Austin

2017

STRICTLY NEED TO KNOW

ISBN 13: 978-1-63555-114-3

THIS TRADE PAPERBACK ORIGINAL IS PUBLISHED BY
BOLD STROKES BOOKS, INC.
P.O. BOX 249
VALLEY FALLS, NY 12185

FIRST EDITION: DECEMBER 2017

CREDITS
EDITOR: RUTH STERNGLANTZ
PRODUCTION DESIGN: STACIA SEAMAN
COVER DESIGN BY TAMMY SEIDICK

Acknowledgments

Going from a story idea to first published novel was a long and sometimes bumpy ride. It would not have been successful, much less fun, without the help and company of a whole cast of characters. My eternal gratitude goes to those friends and family who indulged me in many conversations about how to give the "woman in danger" her own agency, what makes a hero, how to make reasonable force as cool as blowing stuff up, and other issues I had to wrestle with before I could get what I wanted onto the page. Huge thanks also to all the beta readers who gave me honest and constructive feedback, and to my critique group for helping me build on strengths and break bad habits.

Special thanks to my editor, Ruth, for being both kind and ruthless; to my military advisors, Lauren Osinski (Army) and Lt Colonel Bethany Ryals (USAF, retired), for their enthusiasm and great patience; and to my wife, Basha, for reading many alternate scenes and keeping version control in her head (for me), along with her opinions about which worked better (for her).

For Basha

Whither thou goest, baby.

Chapter One

Thwack! Maji's attacker slapped the mat and rolled back to standing as the next one moved in on her. *Thwack!* The dance continued. At the eye of the storm, Maji Rios conserved her movements, focusing on technique over muscle. After an afternoon of drills in the dojo, she'd sweated enough to feel washed clean. For long, delicious moments at a stretch, she'd had to concentrate on nothing but her body and her sparring partners. Tired now, she felt her attention wander. She dodged the next oncomer, clapped twice. Everyone halted, waited respectfully in silence.

"Thanks, everybody. This was just the welcome home I needed." She smiled at her friend Bubbles, now the head instructor, and bowed the two junior instructors out.

"That all you got?" Bubbles asked when the younger black belts had left. "You really all rehabbed?"

"I'm good," Maji replied, stretching. "Just jetlagged." She had gone directly from JFK to Oyster Cove via the Long Island Railroad. In her mind, she had left Sgt. Ariela Rios back at the airport and walked onto the train as her old self, Maji. She'd stopped at Hannah's house just long enough to drop her Army duffel in the living room and headed for the dojo without so much as hanging her clothes in her room upstairs.

But walking in the back door of the dojo erased the time gone by. The locker room smelled the same, and her locker waited for her as if she'd been there only yesterday, Rios on the nameplate, gi hung neatly inside. She hadn't felt any urge to poke her head into Hannah's office or the mat rooms but suited up first, knowing everything here would be as it had always been.

Standing across from her now, Bubbles seemed reassuringly the same. Except for the new stripe on her black belt. She'd kept progressing while Maji—well, Maji had taken another track, one with no kata but plenty of tests. It was reassuring today to see how much of Hannah's teaching came back, latent memory in the body like an unused language returning to the mind upon hearing it spoken again. A muffled clang of locker doors and laughter reached them from the locker room as the two junior instructors headed out to go swim at the pond, or sit down at their parents' supper tables, or whatever kids their age did these days. Kids? She'd been their age when she enlisted, Maji reminded herself as she racked the staffs onto the wall.

"Hey," she said with a frown, "we skipped gun drills. Knives, too."

Bubbles shrugged. "It's your first day back. Hannah said keep it simple."

Did she now? Maji glanced over her shoulder at the two-way mirror between Hannah's office and the mat room. *Hannah certified trumps Army field certified, then. Well, I wouldn't trust me with a prop gun, either.* "What else did Sensei ordain?"

"Don't be a brat," Bubbles replied. "It's been a rough time for all of us, you know."

The guilt over missing Ava's last months wiped any lingering self-pity from Maji's mind. "Yeah. Sorry. So, what else, then?"

Bubbles sighed. "No questions about the Army, the Fallujah thing, where you've been, all that."

"Fallujah? Who's asking about that?" Maji could guess, but she needed to hear it out loud.

"Lots of people around here got theories, *hermana*. They don't care you don't look like Ariela Rios in the news shots. Nobody trusts the government not to lie to them." Bubbles half smiled, an apology for the world at large. "But you know Hannah. She makes sure if you want somebody to know your story, you get to tell them yourself. Okay?"

"Okay." Maji nodded and leaned against the padded wall, all the travel and pushed-down memories catching up at once.

"Whoa, you gonna stay awake through supper? You need to go crash, Rey can wait to meet you."

Maji pulled herself together and gave her friend a wry smile. Rey was a vet. He'd know what to say, and what to leave alone. "Hell if I'm going miss dinner at the Dive with you two. It's high time I checked this guy out for myself."

"Don't believe a word that joker says," Bubbles objected, suppressing a smile in that way that dimpled her cheeks. "He'll try to win you over, but you remember you love me best."

"*Nunca puedo olvidarlo,*" Maji promised.

Bubbles grabbed her and hugged her tight. "God, it's good to have you home."

Hannah stepped out of her office and put her head around the corner, a smile on her face. "If you're all right to ride, your bike is in the garage."

Maji extracted herself from the hug. "Sweet!" To Bubbles she added, "Meetcha there."

Maji rinsed dried salt and the last of her homecoming anxiety down the drain in the dojo's showers, hung her gi up to dry out, and pulled on her traveling clothes. Jeans and sneaks were fine for Mona's Dive-In, their favorite hangout. But once she got settled, she'd let Bubbles take her thrifting, get something nicer to round out her three-outfit wardrobe.

Only a few blocks from the dojo, Hannah and Ava's big old Victorian looked exactly the same as always, down to the wrought-iron fence and the neatly tended flower beds. Who had trimmed back Ava's roses this spring? Maji wondered. Probably Bubbles. She thought about going in, unpacking, and changing, but the thought of being in the house with Ava's absence pushed her back. So she headed to the garage out back and checked over her bike. It stood ready, tires full and dust wiped off. Nearby hung a new jacket, with a note. *Welcome home. Ride safely.—Ava.* Blinking back tears, she wished for the hundredth time she'd been able to come home in time. Tomorrow she'd see how Hannah was coping. Really.

Angelo Benedetti slipped into the gay bar not far from Wall Street, blending in with the young brokers who frequented it. Scanning for one guy in particular, he picked him out, sitting alone at the bar. Fair-haired and slender, midthirties, the second-generation Russian was rumored to have a soft spot for traders. Angelo took the stool next to him and made a fuss about getting a drink, pronto. He looked to Sander and made a face. "Is it always like this?"

"Pretty much. You new here?"

"New?" Angelo gestured to the scene in general, the men, the action. "Do I look new?" Actually, he hadn't been in gay bars much before. Could have got him discharged from the Army. Or in high school, killed. But pretending? Nothing new there.

Sander looked unamused. "No, no. To Wall Street. To trading. You are a broker, yes?"

"Oh, hell no. I don't work on the floor. I come in here for the obvious, and to pick up any insider tips floating around. I day-trade." Angelo waited for the skeptical look. "I know. Everybody thinks that's a pipe dream. But if you're good with algorithms, you can clean up. I write my own."

"Really? I'm in tech support for a finance operation." He pulled a business card from his inside jacket pocket, handed it to Angelo. "Sander. You look so familiar."

"Angelo. That really the best line you got?" He shook Sander's hand, held it a beat too long for custom. "Sorry, I don't have a card. But I could give you my number."

"I would like that." Sander pulled out his cell phone. "Last name?"

"Just Angelo."

Sander's eyebrows arched, and his mouth turned down. "No last name, no phone number, no date."

Pity. Getting close to him would be more pleasure than work. "You not going to stalk me, are you?" Angelo said, laughing. No laugh from Sander. "Fine. Benedetti. *B-E*—"

"I know how it's spelled. No wonder you are Just Angelo."

Angelo shrugged. "I tell people my last name, and from there it's all either family biz or questions about being a hostage, or both. I'd like to skip that tonight, please, just be two guys having a drink. Can we do that?"

Sander hesitated, wary. "No, that's not likely. Sorry."

"Hey—we don't pick our families. Yours is so perfect?"

Sander closed his eyes, swallowed. "Look at the card."

Angelo read the glossy embossed type: *Aleksander Khodorov.* "Oh, crap. That is awkward." He leaned over the bar, grabbing for the bartender. "Where's my fuckin' order?" As soon as it appeared in front of him, he downed it. "One more. Please. And whatever he's having, on me."

"What are you really doing here?" Sander asked, not touching the new drink.

Angelo shrugged again. "Gettin' laid. Committing suicide. Changing history—you tell me."

"Melodramatic much?" Sander laughed, shook his head, took a sip.

"Are you sayin' it's not a risk, just you being here? What if one of your father's crew sees you?"

"Then they hope I meet a nice a guy, settle down, stop cruising joints like this. Such a bunch of old hens."

"Wow. You shittin' me here?"

"It's the twenty-first century, Angelo. You're really not out?"

Angelo laughed bitterly. "In my family, it's more like 1946. Especially with Gino as capo. Hell, I was more out in the Army." He hesitated, looked down at his drink. "They just let you…be you?"

"Look. I'm not saying it's paradise. I could get bashed leaving here. But not by my own people—I'm the boss's son, and I'm valuable in my own right. I may be a fag, but I'm their fag."

"Hey, watch your mouth!" Angelo flared.

Sander smiled wryly, looking for the first time like his father. "Little sensitive, in the closet?"

"I spent my whole life hearing that crap from idiots. I got no use for it around here."

"Well, good for you. Now make yourself essential, and maybe you could be yourself one day, too."

"Nah, not within the Family. What I'm good at they don't want. Took me months to get Gino to let me set up offshore accounts for him. Wasn't for me, he'd still be hiding cash in a mattress."

"You're into banking?" Sander asked, a bit too casually.

Angelo smiled impishly at him. "You say that like, *Are you into leather?*" He chuckled at Sander's blush. "Yeah, you could say I'm into it. Not like you guys, owning banks, dodging regulators. You own the racket. Tech support, my ass. You probably run a division."

"I couldn't say. You understand." Sander said it lightly, but without a smile.

"I understand completely. But what I'm good at, you would be very interested in."

"You have a truly odd way of flirting, you know that?"

Angelo shrugged and smiled affably. "I'm Italian."

Sander smiled, finally. "Let me buy you dinner, and we'll see if I'm interested."

"Go out? Together?" Angelo's smiled faded.

"My place, then. You can show me how good Italians really are in the kitchen."

"Baby, I'm good everywhere," Angelo bragged.

Angelo made a call to Frank, who was already on his way to Mona's Dive-In with Rose. "Give her my apologies, and make sure she stays for supper, okay?" Maybe she'd bump into Maji, even without him there to make the introductions. Assuming Maji showed up to meet her best friend's husband, as he'd been promised. Frank passed the phone to his cousin before he could stop him. "Hey, Rose. Look,

I'm sorry. I'll make it up to you. Stay and try the mocha shake for me. I hear they're legendary. Okay. Love you, too."

Sander was on the phone, as well, speaking faster Russian than Angelo could keep up with. He closed the phone and said with a smile, "Papa looks forward to meeting you. Our ride is on its way."

Angelo swallowed. Infiltration was moving faster than expected. But that was good, right? "Great."

CHAPTER TWO

Humming along the waterfront on her Zero DS electric motorcycle, Maji passed joggers in tank tops, kids swimming in the chilly waters of Long Island Sound, and picnickers lounging in the shade of leafy giant maples. She marveled at how cool the Kevlar air mesh jacket felt, light and porous yet snug and reassuringly rigid in all the places reinforced to protect bones and joints.

If she overshot the restaurant by a few miles, she could track down the neighborhood of stately spreads where Angelo grew up. Should she? Another night. Hard to believe they'd spent so much time in the same part of Long Island for so many years and never met. But then, his family didn't grace places like Mona's Dive-In. They went upscale and expected to be comped wherever they were recognized.

Mona didn't comp anyone she wasn't actually friends with, and she didn't have any friends in their circles. At any rate, Angelo would be anywhere but the House that Death Built. And without him in it, his family's estate would be just another overpriced property by the water. Once she got unpacked, she'd track down Dev and Tom, and catch up. They'd know where Ang was.

Maji pulled into the parking lot at the restaurant and smiled up at the sign reading Mona's Dive-In, with its illustration of a 1940s poster girl in a bikini poised to dive into a milkshake. *Mmm...a mocha shake.* Home.

The sound of a couple arguing drove the reverie away. Maji spotted them standing on opposite sides of their maroon town car and pulled into the space next to them, on the driver's side where the gray-haired guy in a sport coat couldn't see her, but the woman on the passenger side could. A quick scan showed her to be much younger than the man, late twenties to midthirties. She was looking directly at the driver, hands pressing on the car's roof as if to shove the man on the far side away from her, along with his vehicle.

"Go home, Frank. I'll call you for a pickup," she insisted in measured, crisp tones. Not in danger, then. Still, Maji kept an ear open while she stowed her helmet and gloves and zipped open her new jacket.

"He said to stick with you," the middle-aged man protested. "That's all she wrote." *Wiseguy?*

"You're old enough to be his father. You could make up your own mind." Dark eyes glinted with frustration, offset by the olive skin and curly wisps of black-black hair that suggested the woman was Italian. But she didn't dress like a Family girl; and she didn't sound local.

"He's a captain now. I'm just his lieutenant." Oh, yeah. Definitely a wiseguy.

"Well," the woman responded with obviously waning patience, "I am the commander-in-chief of my one-woman army. And I don't need a babysitter. I don't even need a driver."

Startled to hear the nod to Ani DiFranco from an elegant woman chauffeured by a body man, Maji just stopped and watched the drama unfold. The woman noticed her standing by the bike, taking in the exchange, and gave Maji an almost sheepish half smile. In return, Maji gave her a sideways head bob with a bare twitch of a smile, as if to say, *Better you than me.*

The Frank character just shrugged, not picking up on the silent exchange. She could almost hear his Lawn Guyland tough-guy dismissal in that shrug: *Whaddaya gonna do?*

Maji skirted the town car and headed for the front entrance, keeping one eye on the woman, who slammed the car door and strode off toward the restaurant without looking back. Maji sped up to reach the door first and held it ajar for her. She caught herself. *What are you doing, Rios?* But before she could answer herself, the mystery woman reached the door and gave her an appreciative once-over.

"Thank you," she said, with a slight incline of her head and a hint of a smile. If Gina Lollobrigida and Audrey Hepburn had produced a love child, she couldn't have managed to be more fetching.

Ouch...don't go there. Not tonight. She swallowed and nodded her politest, most noncommittal military nod.

Frank reached the door as his charge turned to check on him. He tried to take the door from Maji, but she held her place, gesturing for him to pass.

"After you, I insist."

Frank hesitated, flummoxed. "Uh…"

The mystery woman's face softened, tickled by his dilemma. "The word you're looking for is *thanks*, Frank," she coached him, one side of her mouth pulled into a smile that managed to look amused without smirking.

"Uh, sure. Thanks." He gave Maji the cool-guy up-nod and strolled through.

Maji's coconspirator winked at her, looking pleased by the unspoken inside joke they shared. *Too late, Rios.*

Inside, Maji let her eyes adjust, peeling off her jacket and enjoying the light breeze from the overhead fan. She caught sight of Bubbles waving to her from a table near the bar, and approached the not-so newlyweds.

"Maji, Rey," Bubbles said, her excitement endearingly transparent.

Rey glanced fondly at his wife and extended a hand to Maji. With an old-school buzz cut and muscles hinting from under his polo shirt, he looked every bit the off-duty cop. But his open smile and Nuyorican accent gave him away as a long-lost brother from the city.

"Feel like I know ya already," he said.

Maji grasped his hand in both of hers and returned the warmth. "*Mucho gusto.* Sorry I missed the Big Day," she replied. "*Felicidades.*"

Rey took his hand back with a shy smile. Not all tough guy, then. Good. Bubbles needed tenderness more than anything.

"And…thanks for Christmas," Maji added. Their first as a married couple, and Bubbles had spent it in an Army hospital with her. No *stille nacht* in Landstuhl, despite the snow outside. Having her best friend there had made it bearable.

"La Bubbles would do anything to get out of Midnight Mass with the whole Martinez *familia*," he joked. More seriously, he added, "You know how she is about churches."

The way Rey said both facts told Maji everything she needed to know. The darkness of Bubbles's past hadn't scared him off. He really was family, and she had some catching up to do.

From back behind the bar, out of the depths of the kitchen, Mona bustled toward them, apron spattered and hands fluttering as if to clear a path to the prodigal child.

"Majida Rios!" she exclaimed. "I thought you'd never come home! Welcome back, sweetie." Maji stood to let the older woman wrap her in a fierce hug. When Mona let her go, mascara smudging, she held her at arm's length and confirmed Maji's wholeness for herself. "That looker in the back bought you a beer," she said, adding a cheesy wink. "Whadda you want to go with it? Anything—my treat. Ribs?"

Maji shook her head, flushing slightly under her tan. "I'm on the bike, Mona—zero-T." It had been Mona who taught her the zero-tolerance rule for motorcycle riding and alcohol. Seemed like another lifetime now.

Mona gave her a squeeze. "Anything you want, sugar. Mocha shake?"

"Now you're talking." Maji turned her head toward Rey. "You want the beer?"

He half inclined his head, a done deal.

Maji looked back to Mona. "And, um, veggie burger?"

As Mona headed back to the grill, Bubbles smirked skeptically at her lean friend. "Veggie burger?"

"Maybe I'm watching my weight," Maji replied, glancing away.

"With fries and a shake? Your idea of a diet is the see-food diet."

Maji sank into her chair and ignored the bait, turning instead to Rey. "Does she give you grief like this, or is it just my welcome home present?"

Rey chuckled, then sombered a touch. "Guess she missed you. *La Bubbles siempre me molesta* when I been gone a few days."

"Days?" Bubbles retorted. "Sometimes weeks."

Maji gave Rey a quizzical look. "Business travel? I thought you were a cop."

He lifted one shoulder in a half shrug. "*Claro*. Lotta undercover time, though."

"Special Agent Martinez to you," Bubbles clarified, emphasizing the *special*.

Rey rolled his eyes, and Maji restrained herself from asking which agency his was with. FBI? DOJ? DEA? Please God, not the CIA. She took his cue and steered them to small-town catch-up talk. Bubbles filled her in on who had moved away, gotten hitched, gotten divorced. And died, besides Ava.

When Bubbles left them to check on their order, Maji surprised herself with a personal question for the other vet. "Were you Special Forces?"

Rey shook his head. "Nah. Just an MP. But after my tour, the day-to-day same-ol', same-ol' just felt so flat. *Tu sabes?*"

"*Claro*," she affirmed, oddly relieved. Everything in civilian life seemed to move in slow motion. "You missed the adrenaline?"

"More than that," Rey answered, leaning forward. "Being part of something that mattered." He looked at her, thinking. "Knowing who had my back. *Tu sabes.*" Not a question, this time.

She nodded.

Bubbles returned and was halfway seated when Mona's voice rang out, "Order up! Three burgers, fries, and a shake!" Maji rose, motioning the blonde to sit.

Maji smiled at the sight of the loaded tray on the bar. The sound of a man two stools over, speaking loudly into his cell phone, distracted her from thoughts of supper. She slowed to listen in, noticing the tattoos on his knuckles. Not good.

"Pull to the back door when the old guy lights up out front," he instructed in Russian.

As he spoke, Frank walked past her toward the front door, his oblivious image in the mirror over the bar already fishing in his sport jacket for a pack of smokes.

She grabbed the tray, giving the Russian an indifferent glance as he stood, still on the phone. "We'll only have a minute to take the girl. Be ready for me."

Maybe they were the mystery woman's rescue squad. But Maji's gut said no—and to get backup. She dashed for her table, leaning in and speaking sharply while abandoning the tray to her friends. "Call 9-1-1. Female hostage out back, two gunmen—plus me."

Maji left them staring at one another as she jogged toward the back hallway in search of the Russian and the woman. She spotted them almost to the back door already, in the hallway by the restrooms. The beefy man muscled his frightened hostage toward the exit, one hand clamped over her mouth. *Slow him down, don't alarm him.* Maji changed posture midstride, nearing them. "Yo, drink lady!" she bellowed good-naturedly. "You're not leavin' without me?"

The big guy pivoted neatly for someone of his bulk, revealing a pistol pressed into his captive's ribs. "No trouble. Buzz off."

No room to maneuver here. Maji raised both arms, looking alarmed, and took a step back. "Chee-zus!" she exhaled. "None of my business!"

The Russian shoved his resistant victim through the door ahead of him, scraping his shoulder on the jamb to keep his grip on her. As it started to close, Maji reached out to push through on their heels.

"Maji?" Bubbles squeaked behind her. Maji turned halfway back, waved her to stay away.

"Sirens," her friend blurted, their old shorthand for police on the way.

Today, the cops coming was good news. "Thanks," Maji replied, disappearing through the door.

In the back alley by the dumpsters, a black SUV sat idling, diesel fumes mixing with the sickly sweet odor from the trash and compost. The driver watched edgily as his partner struggled to open the back door while grappling with the feisty woman in his arms. *So only one of you is in this to win it.*

"Back off," Maji barked in full command voice, drawing both men's attention to her. "Cops are coming. Let her go—now!"

As she marched toward him, the captive-wrestler stopped fussing with the door and turned partway toward Maji. He took in her five-foot-four frame as she looked up at him, her empty palms raised as if to placate him. "We go," he responded flatly. "You back off, or I shoot you."

Finally coming to his partner's aid, the driver started to open his door. Maji slammed it on his hand, barking out in Russian, "Stay inside."

He seemed inclined to comply, but she left a hand on the car door in case, pinning his hand. Keeping just enough awareness to act if he moved, Maji directed her main message to the armed man towering mere feet from her. The one still holding the civilian. "Losing the girl will make your boss mad, but not as mad as if you go up for murder," she said slowly and clearly in Russian. "She's not worth that."

The big man snorted, masking his surprise at her use of his language. "Prison doesn't frighten me, little girl. American prison is summer camp."

Definitely a Vor, and proud of it. *Work that.* She sneered at him. "Oh, you like prison, *suka*? Then you can kiss the cops hello, *suka*."

The carefully targeted barb did its job. He looked startled, then irate, pushing his captive behind him and raising his gun abruptly.

Maji tracked the gun's arc and shifted sideways slightly while stepping in toward the Russian, grabbing his wrist, and sweeping his feet out from under him. The gun skittered off toward the restaurant door as sirens erupted at the far end of the alley. The driver gunned the SUV and screeched out, not bothering to close his door completely after pulling his mangled hand inside.

Rey, Bubbles, and Frank spilled out of the back to find the police cruiser bouncing to a halt beside Maji, her knee on the Russian's back, his arms twisted behind him. The intended target climbed to her feet, using the cruiser's hood for support, pale and shaky. Rey and Frank hung back, Maji noticed. But Bubbles beelined for the woman as the uniformed officers emerged, hands on holsters. *Guess we got a gun drill after all.*

❖

When Maji walked out of the office behind the empty reception desk inside the Nassau County second precinct station, Frank was waiting on a wooden bench, worry written all over his face. She lifted the hinged wooden counter, and he rose.

"She okay?"

"I'm sure she's fine. The medic cleared her. They just have a lot of questions." Maji started to walk past him.

"Where you goin'?"

"Home. I've had enough fun for one day."

"Hang out with me, I'll give you a lift after," he offered.

Maji didn't pause. "S'all right, really. Thanks."

"You can't just leave her like that," Frank blurted.

Maji stopped and turned halfway, tilted her head in disbelief.

"I mean," he tried again, "she bought you a drink. She likes you. She'd wanna say thanks herself."

"Look, that was very sweet, I'm sure. But I don't take drinks from women dating guys. It's a strict policy."

He smiled. "You really gotta meet her. Rose don't break your policy, I promise."

Rose, huh? That fits. Maji hesitated.

"Please," he added, more puppy dog than wiseguy.

So she sat quietly with him on the wooden bench, just to be polite, looking toward the exit rather than the offices.

Frank jiggled his knee and fidgeted with his pack of cigarettes. "If you don't mind my askin'," he started in, asking, "where'd you learn all that?"

"All what?"

"That commando shit—takin' down some chucklehead with a piece on him."

"Mostly in the service." *Let's drop it there, okay?*

"Iraq?" He pronounced it *eye-rack*. "I heard they sent girls now. Thought they couldn't do combat, though."

She took a breath, looked straight ahead. "When you're downrange, the front line keeps moving. Pays to be prepared."

"Huh." He paused to reflect. "All the girls in 'Nam was nurses. Great girls, don't get me wrong, they just didn't do all that, back then."

"Yup." *One more step down that path, dude, and I am out of here.*

"Well, you saved my ass tonight. I owe ya."

She picked up his pack of cigarettes and made a show of reading the warning label. "Shoulda read the warning." Seeing his puzzled look from the corner of her eye, she continued, deadpan, "See? Says right here they're hazardous to your health."

He looked sideways at her, then laughed. She would have laid money on his saying *You're all right* next; but the office door opened, saving them both from that. Frank hopped up at the sight of Rose. Maji remained seated.

As he walked her to the hallway, holding the counter up for her, Captain Andrews gave Rose his card and the usual send-off. "Thank you for your cooperation, Ms. diStephano. If you think of anything else, my direct line is on the card."

He was a lot nicer to Maji than the old captain had been. Of course, he hadn't worked here when she was a teenager. Even the old-timers were nice to her, though, treating her like a grown-up thanks to her tour of duty. It felt odd, frankly. She was all grown up, but the kind of stunts she'd pulled a decade ago tended to stick with you in a small town. Oh, well, as Ava always said, never spit at kindness.

Captain Andrews caught sight of her. "Ms. Rios, not home with an ice pack? Did you think of something to add?"

"No, sir. Just seeing things through." So easy to snap back into formation. Comfortable.

He nodded in approval. "You ever need a job, I'd like you to consider the county. Vets' preference, good benefits, and we always need more women in the field."

"I'm not looking for a new uniform." Too harsh? "But thanks."

During the exchange, Frank had gone for the car, but Rose diStephano waited by the door for her. "I hear we're giving you a lift home." Her eyes sparkled. God, they were…beautiful.

"If you don't mind." Maji took care to keep any hint of flirtation from her own voice.

"Not at all, I'm delighted. But I owe you supper, at least."

"There's nothing open around here this late, but thanks."

"Then let me cook for you—it's the least I can do. Please?" She held the door open for Maji.

"No, I insist. After you."

"No, no—after you."

Maji smiled, and waltzed through the door. *It's just supper.*

On the landing, Maji asked to borrow Rose's phone. She got Hannah's machine, left a message that all was well, and not to wait up.

"You have someone at home? I should have asked." Chagrin clouded Rose's face.

"Just my aunt." *And good for you for caring.*

The captivating smile returned. "That's settled, then. A good meal, and a good night's sleep." She nearly skipped down the stairs to the waiting town car.

Maji hesitated. *Slow down, Rios.* Then her feet started down the stairs of their own accord.

The back of the town car felt intimate but exposed at the same time. Periodically, Maji caught Frank peeking at them with the rearview mirror. The wide leather bench seat seemed a broad expanse, until the VIP extended her hand.

"I'm Rose, by the way. And you're, is it—*Mah-gee*?"

Maji felt momentarily exposed, having a stranger call her by her real name. *Roll with it, Rios. Just part of being home.* She took the proffered hand and grasped it lightly. "Close enough."

"No, really," Rose insisted, squeezing Maji's hand. "How do you say it?"

Maji pulled her hand back, taking a slow breath to settle the butterflies. "If you're a Spanish speaker, it's *ma-hee*. If you're American, it's *madg-ee*, more or less. If you're Middle Eastern or French, it's *ma-zhee*, like *je ne sais quoi*."

"Wow. Three chances, and I missed them all. Which do you prefer?"

Any one you say. Your voice is like a samba in the moonlight. "The third. But I'm used to every variation, really. It's not a big deal."

"Sure it is. Maji. Better?"

"Perfect will do. *Parlez-vous?*"

"*Mais oui.* Some book learning, and a little culinary tourism. You?"

"Not so much."

"Well, your accent is very good. They say that's the hardest part."

Sooner than Maji expected, the town car's wheels left the streets and shushed over a long driveway. From what she could see in the dark, it was a large house, almost stately. Inside, Frank flicked on lights—a formal dining room with heavy, dark wood furniture, a sitting room with beige carpet and overstuffed sofa and armchairs, both tidy but ready for use.

Chapter Three

Offered anything in the kitchen, Maji asked for eggs. Rose whipped up an omelet, letting her guest play the sous-chef. It was relaxing, just chopping while Rose hummed from fridge to stove, in her element.

"Are you a chef?" Maji asked, admiring her efficiency and grace.

"No." Rose kept with her task. "I teach cultural anthropology, with a focus on food. And you're…let me guess…a superhero?"

"What?" Oh, she was flirting again. "No."

"Hmm." Rose sounded unconvinced, but kept her attention on the eggs.

While they ate, Maji ventured again. "You're not from here. But you live here."

"I visit family every summer. Swim, read by the pool, get in touch with my roots."

"Ah, summer girl."

"And what are you, detective? You don't sound so Long Island yourself."

"Brooklyn, actually. It's a retreat for me out here, too."

"Well, I'm glad you're here. I was terrified earlier, and now I almost feel like nothing happened."

Maji gave a small shrug. "Helps to get back to somewhere you feel safe."

"I'm sure that's part of it," Rose agreed, meeting Maji's eyes with a steady gaze.

Maji looked away and excused herself. She locked the door and splashed water on her face, looking in the mirror. Since waking up in the hospital, she'd been looked at with unwanted sympathy, with clinical interest and professional courtesy, with empathy a few times, and more recently, with desire. But not gratitude mixed with admiration. She didn't deserve that, and she wasn't about to dump a truckload of baggage on a stranger explaining why. *Just eat, say thanks, and get out.*

On her return trip from the bathroom down the hall, Maji noticed the mirror draped in black. She couldn't bring herself to ask Rose about the family's loss, to see the pain in her eyes. Not tonight, not with the trauma so fresh and the house nearly echoing with emptiness.

The night air was soft on the skin as they sat eating by the pool. Their plates cleaned and cups empty, Rose sat back, contented. The pool lights flickered in the water. If she wasn't so drained, a swim would feel magnificent. Especially a skinny-dip, she thought, eyeing Maji's well-defined arms and shoulders, speculating on the parts covered by the tank top and jeans. She felt herself flush. "Breakfast for supper," she exclaimed. "Perfect comfort food."

"Works every time," Maji agreed, with a satisfied smile.

"Every time? Do you risk your life for strangers routinely?"

"It's a bad habit. I keep trying to break it."

"But you're not a cop."

Maji rose, reaching for her plate and glass. "I just teach self-defense. You could pick some up this summer, when you're not in the pool." She sounded tired.

The lights in the kitchen blinked out, leaving them in semi-darkness. Rose turned toward the dark house, pulse racing.

"Frank? Yo, Frank!" Maji called out.

The lights blinked back on, and Rose exhaled loudly. Frank's head popped out the back door.

"Sorry! Didn't know you was out here. You need me anymore?"

Rose responded for them. "We're fine, Frank. Sleep well."

"'Kay. G'night."

Rose turned toward Maji. "He's not a very competent bodyguard, is he?"

"Not so much," Maji conceded.

"But he's like one of the family." Rose smiled ruefully, glad Frank had not been hurt earlier. "Maybe I should take your class."

Back in the well-lit kitchen, Maji started rinsing dishes. She felt wide-awake again, and restless.

"You don't need to do that," Rose protested. "I'll take care of them tomorrow."

Maji continued, not turning. "S'all right."

"Maji?" Rose asked, sounding tentative.

"Mm-hmm?"

"About tonight. There's something you should know—"

Maji held up a hand to interrupt, and turned. She wiped her hands on her jeans, then spoke. "Let's stick with a don't ask, don't tell policy on this one, okay?"

"But you don't understand—"

"Sure I do." Maji cut her off more decisively this time. "You're connected to someone the Vory would squeeze with a kidnapping. Why is none of my business."

"Vor v Zakone?" Rose seemed genuinely alarmed. "And you spoke to them in Russian!"

"Eh. Really rusty, basic Russian," Maji admitted. "Not my best language." In fact, if she'd been quicker on the uptake, she might have taken him down right there in the entry. But then the accomplice might have grabbed Rose...

Rose blew out a long breath. "Sorry. My imagination is in overdrive."

"Too much adrenaline all around," Maji replied. "Don't be so hard on yourself."

Rose rewarded her with shy smile. "So which language *is* your best?"

"English and Spanish tie for first." Maji ticked them off on her left hand. She skipped over her mother's native tongue, Farsi. "Then Arabic. I'm decent in French, Italian, and Portuguese, when I can keep the Spanish out. But my Russian's strictly colloquial." Seeing the incredulous look on Rose's face, she put her hands back down and added, "I'm a linguist. It's what I do."

Rose laughed her infectious laugh, and Maji felt like she'd won a prize.

"A linguist. I didn't guess that one." Rose moved close to Maji, nearly backing her into the counter. She put her hand under Maji's chin, tilting it up to look into her eyes, and brushed Maji's lips gently with her thumb. "Nothing beats a woman with a versatile tongue."

Maji felt the pull of those soft brown eyes, and the thumping in her temple. *She's still a stranger, Rios. Leave her be.* She blinked and stopped Rose's hand, moving it aside but not away. "I should go. I have an early morning."

"I promise to set you an alarm. And give you a great night's sleep." Rose leaned in and kissed Maji softly, an invitation rather than a demand.

Maji closed her eyes and let Rose nibble lightly around her ear.

Abruptly, she stiffened and opened her eyes. "I should go. Unless you're uneasy alone. I could take the couch."

Rose backed off slightly, their faces inches apart. "I know I'd feel better if you stayed. I hope you would, too."

Rose brushed Maji's lips with hers, tantalizing.

For a long second, Maji felt frozen in place. Then with a small sound escaping her lips, she turned Rose and wedged her against the counter, one hip driven into the taller woman's crotch. They kissed fiercely, Rose grinding into the pressure between her legs, until she arched back and gasped. Maji trailed her lips tenderly down the pulse in Rose's neck.

"Upstairs," Rose breathed.

Before the sun was fully up, birdsong reached Maji's ears. Mourning doves. She yawned and tried to shift, but one arm was pinned under Rose. How long since she'd woken up tangled with someone else, dead to the world? Years. Rose had whispered, "Sweet dreams," and the next thing, daylight. No dreams, good or bad, no hyperawareness, ready to spring up at the slightest sound. Even drugs had never knocked her out like that. Had she been drugged? No. She was oriented, clearheaded, and able to remember every moment before sleeping. Every touch, every taste, every sound, every…Damn. Another night like that, and she'd know what addiction felt like.

She should get up and slip out, catch a shower and change at home, have breakfast with Hannah. Instead, Maji carefully brushed the tangled mass of her own hair, long since freed from the french braid, off her face, and breathed in the mingled musk and clean scent at the nape of Rose's neck. She wanted to brush the hair off Rose's shoulder, to run her fingers over that silky olive skin again, but it might wake her. So she laid her free arm over Rose's torso, slowly and carefully. Rose stirred, murmured, grasped for Maji's hand and pulled it in to cup her breast. She snuggled back along the length of Maji's front.

An hour later, Rose woke curled inside the spoon of Maji's frame. She rolled and faced Maji, gazing into her already-open eyes. "What a silver lining you are." She traced Maji's cheek with her fingers. "You have beautiful eyes. Green, not brown."

"Surprise." Maji's lips twitched slightly, too languorous still for a full smile. Staring back into the deep, warm brown of Rose's eyes, close enough to notice the golden flecks in her irises, Maji felt oddly at home. Even without the telltale crinkles by the corners of the black-lashed lids, she could tell Rose was smiling. No fear, no anger, not even desire muddying the pleasure that radiated toward her. It reminded her of the easy laughter that had bubbled up from Rose at several points last night, a pool of sunshine she could bask in all day. All day? Damn. She'd better call Hannah.

Maji closed her eyes, breaking the hold of Rose's gaze. "Could I borrow a phone?" She started to sit up, and Rose matched her movement, rising and leaning in to kiss her. Maji let the world beyond Rose's mouth, her skin, her scent, slip away. She let her prop arm sink back onto the bed and felt Rose's weight press into her, the silky length of one leg sliding up by her waist. She ran both hands down Rose's back as Rose pulled back and sat up, arms holding her torso suspended over Maji, hips straddling her thighs. Maji opened her eyes.

"It's downstairs," Rose said, and smiled at Maji's confused look. "The phone. You might want a shower first. There's room for two."

Maji shook her head. "Not yet." She curled up from her center, meeting Rose in midair and turning her as they kissed, one hand sliding from Rose's low back around the curve of her hip. She pressed it into the soft spot between hip bone and thigh, eliciting a gratifying hum from Rose, who pulled her close.

Just as Rose found Maji's ear with her mouth, the door swung open.

"Rose, you up? Frank told me about last night." Angelo stopped short, blushing, and spun around to face the hallway. Over his shoulder he said, "Well, clearly not about all of it. My bad. You come down in a few and see me, okay?"

"Angelo?" Maji pulled the sheet toward Rose and stood, naked and unaccountably furious.

"Rios!" He turned back around. "This is how you keep in touch? You don't write, you don't call—you just show up in my house? Points for style, babe." He tilted his head toward Rose, one eyebrow arched. "You okay?"

Rose just stared back.

"This is the House that Death Built?" Maji glanced from Rose's stunned face to Angelo's, noting chagrin warring with his pleasure to see her. "What the hell are you doing here?"

He grabbed her jeans from the floor and handed them to her, answering in Arabic. "I'm working—flying solo till you finally got here. Sorry about last night—nice work, as usual."

"That wasn't work. I'm on leave, and great as it is to see you, I have other commitments here." She answered in Arabic, aware of Rose and thinking they should step outside for this reunion. Where was her shirt, anyway? She started pulling her jeans on, not caring where her underwear had ended up.

"Seriously, that was your mission kickoff. You would have been off the clock until today, if you didn't always grab trouble by the throat. Hell, if you'd kept your head down in Spain, I could have had you back months ago." He plucked her shirt off the floor and handed it to her.

Maji swore, and pulled the T over her head. She spared a sideways glance at Rose. "You really telling me I have to deploy again?" His look was all the answer she needed. "Fuck. I haven't even unpacked. And Hannah…" Having to leave again, just like that, hit her like a sucker punch in the ribs. She sank down onto the bed, eyes on the open doorway.

Angelo perched beside her, one hand on her shoulder. "The firewall is down, babe. You get to see your godmama, and I get you here where I need you. It's a win-win."

She turned her head enough to catch his eye. "Here, here?" She couldn't work under a cover in this town. "Everybody knows me, Ang. Including Rose. Who is…?"

"My cousin. I knew you two would hit it off."

Maji stared at him. Those eyes. How had she not seen the resemblance? A terrible idea occurred to her. "Was this a setup? If this was a setup, I will hurt you."

"No. I would never put Rose in harm's way. Hannah said you'd be at Mona's, that's all. I was just going to suprise you with a welcome home and introduce you two like normal people do."

He sounded sincere enough. Maji relaxed, and glanced at Rose, who looked perplexed by the flow of Arabic in her bedroom. "Sorry," she said in English. "You can kick us out anytime."

"Speaking of which," Angelo said in Arabic, standing, "Hannah will brief you." He switched back to English at last, calling over his shoulder, "See ya at breakfast!"

The door clicked shut behind him. Rose and Maji looked at it, then at each other.

"What on earth was that?" Rose demanded.

In reply, Maji only asked, "You're really a Benedetti?"

Chapter Four

O ver the breakfast table, Angelo made a show of formal introductions. "Sergeant Ariela Rios, Dr. RoseMarie diStephano. Rose, meet my best friend. As you've discovered, there's nobody you'd rather count on to have your back."

Frank's chuckle announced his entry into the dining room. "Anybody need a warm-up?" he asked, holding the coffeepot toward them.

"Thanks," Angelo said, accepting a top-off of his cup. "Settle in a minute, Frank."

When Frank sat, Angelo continued, including him in the conversation. "This is the soldier who got me out of Fallujah. I owe her my life."

Frank openly appraised Maji's features. "Those bastards rearrange your face for you?"

Rose paled. "Frank!"

Maji waved her objection away."S'all right. Actually, they did me a favor. I look enough like the old me not to scare my friends, and different enough that strangers don't think to ask." Seeing the compassion in Rose's eyes, she felt guilty at the half-truth. How much of the truth was Angelo entrusting them with? Generally they protected civilians by telling them less, not more.

"Keeps the media off your ass, too," Angelo added. "A mess of reporters went looking for Ariela Rios in Brooklyn, and not a one of them found you."

So Iris had been on her trail. Message received.

Angelo turned back to Rose and Frank. "Anyway, get into the habit of calling her Ri, like I do."

"Ri?"

"Short for both Ariela and Rios," Maji explained with a weary note in her voice. "But Ang, nobody around here calls me that. They all know me from before the Army."

"Well, my family don't. So now the Army way is the Benedetti way, babe. The less they know about the private you, the better for you."

Maji watched Rose and Frank nod in comprehension. She didn't care what most people called her, but she was going to miss hearing Rose say her name.

Rose reached across the table and lightly touched the hand Maji had around her coffee mug. "Okay. Ri it is."

"Call me anything but late to dinner," Maji joked and was gratified to see the sparkle return to Rose's eyes.

"Right. Dinner's at six," Angelo said. "Come a little early, so we can talk first." To Rose and Frank, he added, "I'm going to ask Ri to help me with my little project here."

Rose frowned, leaning back and crossing her arms. "Will that put her in any danger?"

"Not any more than she can handle. I promise."

Maji wondered what line he'd fed Rose as his cover story. She stood to leave, anxious to go get a full briefing from Hannah.

Rose cleared her throat and waited until she had Maji's attention. "Good luck with your big day. *Ri.*"

Maji met her gaze. "Thanks. You be around later?"

Rose's eyes twinkled. "A pack of wild Vory couldn't drag me away."

When Maji opened the screen door to Hannah's kitchen, her godmother paused in putting away her breakfast offerings. "Have you eaten?"

"Yeah, I'm sorry, I—"

"No need." Hannah waved the apology away and turned toward the espresso maker on the counter. "Coffee?"

A cappuccino right after breakfast? I must look like I was up half the night. Fair enough. "Yes, please."

Maji sprinkled cardamom over her foam and noticed Hannah's wistful smile. The spice was a habit they'd both picked up from Ava. "So, I'm on the clock." She stirred and sipped. "Angelo deferred the briefing to you."

"Yes. I had planned to fill you in after your evening of reunions and introductions. We both wanted to give you a few hours to put your feet on the ground before breaking the news. In retrospect, perhaps I should have picked you up at the airport and briefed you first thing."

Maji shrugged. "It was a very nice day off, all things considered." It was surreal hearing Hannah's thoughts on a mission, after years of being forbidden to talk shop. "Ang says the firewall was lifted. Are we really cleared to talk?"

"Angelo made a strong case that the situation warranted an exception. So, for the duration of this assignment, yes."

Maji felt her stomach uncoil. She could handle just about anything, if Hannah was at her side. She recognized the caution in Hannah's voice. As a private consultant for the Joint Special Operations Command and also an ex-Mossad operator, her godmother had to be circumspect. If JSOC suspected either one of putting their personal relationship ahead of their commitment to US counterterrorism efforts, both would be discharged. Still, there were questions Maji had hoped to resolve while home this summer. "What about Fallujah?"

"As it pertains to this assignment, yes."

"They're connected? How?"

"Khodorov. He launders for al-Mashriki, as well as for the New York Families. And he has wanted a Benedetti alliance for some time."

The Banker. Everyone in Brooklyn knew of him. Even as a stupid, fearless kid, she'd known enough to stay off his radar. Maji fought the urge to get up and walk out. Instead, she stood by the screen door, breathing deeply the scent of fresh-mown grass. "Were those Khodorov's guys I jammed up last night?"

"I'm afraid so."

"I changed my mind about breakfast. Can I swipe a bagel?"

"Help yourself. There's cream cheese, and smoked trout, and some cut fruit as well."

While she made herself a plate, the worst of it sank in. "My real name's on the police report. By now, he knows who I am." And who her folks were, and where they lived...

"Have a little faith in us. Angelo took care of the digital trail, and I took care of what Captain Andrews needed to know."

"Look, send me someplace Khodorov can't connect me to my family, and I'll go toe to toe with him. But here?"

"I understand your concerns. But yes, here. Just for a few weeks. While you help me teach camp, as planned."

Well, that was comforting, but... "How are we going to infiltrate Khodorov's operation from Long Island?"

"You aren't. Angelo is already inside the Benedetti Family, as close to its center as he can get. And Khodorov will come to him, via the son."

Aleksander, if she remembered right. An out mobster, untouchable thanks to his father. "Quite a mark. Alek? Sasha?"

Hannah shook her head. "He prefers Sander. And yes, he is key. That's why Angelo missed supper, and why Yuri Khodorov sent his men to collect some insurance."

"What about Angelo's dad, though? I thought he hated Khodorov. Last night won't help any."

"Oh. Angelo didn't tell you anything at all?"

"No. He was too busy selling me as Ri and pushing me out the door."

Hannah frowned. "I suppose he couldn't say too much in front of others. Well, while you were still Mashriki's hostage, Angelo's father Max sent Gino to negotiate for his son's life. A few days later, both Max and Angelo's brother Carlo were killed. It was a well-staged accident, but the FBI has an informer."

Maji pushed her empty plate away. "Shit. Ang couldn't have seen that coming. Did his uncle take over the business?"

"Quite promptly."

"And the FBI hasn't moved on this?"

"No. They need more, especially for an international player of Khodorov's stature. But Angelo did sell the FBI on the idea that he could get them proof to indict Gino and Khodorov on conspiracy for murder, and bring the other Families in under laundering charges at the same time."

"He's been home all this time?" All she had heard was that he was deployed and couldn't be reached. "Downrange, alone, in effing Long Island?"

"You could put it that way. He put in a request for you, but I had JSOC delay until I was sure you were ready."

"And I didn't kill anybody in Spain, or flip out again, so I passed?" She rubbed her temples in the patient silence. "I'm sorry. It's a lot to take in."

"I realize you've never had a mission on home territory. They can be tricky, but you have my complete confidence. On the plus side, Angelo's plan is simple enough, and you only have the FBI underfoot, this time."

Maji nearly groaned. Well, the Feds were better than the CIA or

NSA, who never seemed to play fair with the Army's counterterrorism unit. "You call that the good news?"

Hannah smiled benignly. "Yes. The local FBI liaison is a good agent, and he has to play nice, since he married into my family."

Holy shit. Special Agent Martinez. "Rey." Maji set her cup down hard, spilling some. "Does Bubbles know?"

"That he's on this case, no. And she will not."

Maji sopped the coffee up with her napkin. "What does Rey think Ang and I are?"

"Well, you know how oblique JSOC can be about its covert operations. Rey assumes from what they don't say that Angelo is Delta, or at least Special Forces."

"And me?" They would never tell an FBI agent that Delta had started using female operators. No way in hell.

"He knows you were assigned to Civil Affairs, and that you served with Angelo at times. Of course he knows why the Army altered your name and image to protect your family. He's even met your mother—Bubbles invited Sal and Neda to the wedding."

Of course Bubbles had. And how convenient a cover for why Maji used two names, one for home and one for work. That would totally fly here at home, where so many people knew that Neda Kamiri was her mother. For the first time, a mission in her own backyard seemed almost feasible. Almost.

She would have to help keep Bubbles in the dark. And lie some more to Rose, too. Maji frowned at the last dregs of her cappuccino. She could have sworn the dregs frowned back.

Maji looked at Hannah. "All right. So where do I fit in?"

"As Ri, the woman who went through hell with her boyfriend in Iraq and has finally come home to look him up. That will work for Gino and the Italian side of the equation."

"And what will Khodorov see? He may think I'm Ri, but he'll know what I did last night. And I bet he knows by now that I'm not really Ang's type."

"Indeed. The Khodorovs will understand why Angelo needs you as his beard. And less obviously, as Rose's protector."

"So I'm at his house? Where Rose is staying?"

Hannah rose, kissed the top of Maji's head, and started clearing their dishes. "She's only here a few more days. Monday the family observes Memorial Day in style for Max and Carlo, and then she flies out for fieldwork in Peru. Surely you can manage that long?"

You haven't met Rose. "Yeah. I can keep it professional for a whole six days."

"No need to take a tone."

"What about the ramp-up for camp?" Starting tomorrow.

"Hmm. Best bring her to the dojo."

Rose floated in the pool, staring up at the drifting clouds through her oversized sunglasses. The sky was the perfect blue of New York in late May, not yet hazed by humidity, and the leaves on the maple trees nearby seemed to sparkle as the light breeze stirred them. The salt water supported and caressed her, awakening her body's recall of the night before. She wanted to bathe in those memories, to relive the delicious moments before Angelo and his brutal reality had barged into her room.

Rose felt a shadow fall across her. She opened her eyes behind the big sunglasses and looked up at Ricky Antonopoulos lazily taking in every line of her body. He was so much like Carlo used to be, right down to aping his mannerisms. Ricky had married his best friend's sister, his boss's daughter, and seemed since Carlo's death to be trying to replace him, one creepy word or gesture at a time. She suppressed a shiver, and the urge to duck under the water.

Cousin Carlo had made adolescent sport of Rose right here in this very pool, when she was a shy eleven-year-old. After two summers of ignoring her altogether, he had seen her swimming and made fun of her prepubescent breasts, obviously tiny under her one-piece. She had fumed and icily ignored him, until he tried to touch them. Catching him in the act, scrawny little Angelo had gone after his brother like a rabid raccoon. Carlo just laughed, until one blow caught him in the face and knocked him into the pool. He came up bloody, not laughing.

Rose avoided Carlo the rest of that summer, and the next. And Carlo went back to treating her like Gino's nine-year-old daughter, Sienna: too little to be bothered with.

By the next year, however, no one could overlook the signs of her being a young woman. Her uncles made oblique comments about her taking after her mother, until Grandpa Stephano loudly declared "*Basta!*" and all joking ceased. The silence made her more conscious that she was the reason for her unwed mother's exile to California, thirteen years before.

Carlo, with only one year left in high school, spent his days out with the wiseguys, learning the rackets like a summer intern at a corporation. He drove, he drank, and he hit people who didn't dare hit him back. Worst of all, he picked up groupies like Ricky Octopus, wannabe gangsters in muscle shirts and Air Jordans.

Rose managed to stay off his radar until the night he came home high, mixing drinks for his loudmouth high school friends in the living room. Hearing their laughter, she ducked from the pool down the back hall to the bathroom. As she came out, he reached for the knob to go in, and stood in her way with a leer.

"Hey, youse should come join us." He grabbed her wrist, and she pulled back, to no avail. "C'mon, don't be such a tight-ass. I got some blow'll loosen you up. Come do a line with us."

"I don't want to loosen up, Carlo—let me go or I'll—"

He laughed. "Loose as a goose!" He pulled her toward him and put a hand on her crotch. "Loose as your mama." He breathed on her, stinking of tequila.

She grabbed his long dark curls with her free hand and yanked hard. He jerked sideways, yelping and swearing, and she drove her knee into his groin. He doubled over, wheezing, as she shoved past him, tears streaming down her livid face.

Coming down the hall, Frank caught sight of her, and the man's back leaning on the wall behind her. He shot past before she could open her mouth to speak. Without pausing to see who it was, Frank lifted Carlo up and slammed him against the hallway so hard the plaster shuddered.

"Did you hurt her?" the big man bellowed. Carlo merely stammered. Frank turned his head toward Rose and asked almost gently, "Did he hurt you?"

Stunned, she stared at him. She'd never thought of Frank as dangerous before. "I'm—I'm okay," she managed. "Really."

Carlo had found time to regain his breath, and his attitude. "Get off me, you fuckin' idiot!"

His friends, drawn by the noise, gaped from the foyer. Ricky looked ready to step in, the rest unsure.

Still holding Carlo up with one hand, Frank reached under his jacket and pulled out a pistol. He didn't point it, just palmed it, and barked at the group, "Get the fuck outta here, all a'youse—now." They scrambled for the door.

He set Carlo on his feet, raised a hand as if to belt him. "Go. To. Bed. Now."

Carlo backed away, shaken. Frank turned and put an arm around Rose, who had started to shake lightly.

"I could have you killed, you fuckin' moron!" Carlo spat in their direction.

"Yeah, yeah," Frank replied and kept on walking.

Where was Frank right now? Probably home in his apartment over the garage, enjoying a few hours off. Not that Ricky was afraid of him anymore. Still, she wished she knew if Frank was within range of her voice, at least.

Dammit, anyway. She was a grown woman. Rose eyed Ricky back, trying to picture him as just another frat boy swaggering into her Introduction to Anthropology class, mistakenly expecting an easy A. She abruptly stood up in the middle of the pool, water cascading off her torso as her feet settled on the tiled bottom. "What do you want, Ricky?"

"I came for Ang, but I could make do with you." A light breeze carried both his voice and a funk of cologne. His gaze remained appraising, targeted down at the rivulets between her bikini-wrapped breasts.

"He's out," Rose stated, keeping her eyes on the chaise with her wrap on it as she walked calmly up the steps at the shallow end.

Ricky met her by the chaise, not obviously blocking her but close enough that she'd have to lean around him to get her cover-up. He wasn't as tall as the gunman at Mona's last night, maybe only five ten or eleven. But he was bulky, and used to taking up all the extra space around himself. She wondered for a second how Maji would see him. Surely her pulse would not be racing like this.

"Hand me that, would you?" she said, keeping her voice neutral with some effort.

He followed her hand to the wrap and slowly reached for it, pausing before holding it out to her. "Pity. Body like yours, going to waste."

She grabbed the wrap, trying to formulate a comeback through her anger.

"Ay, Ricky!" Frank's voice came from the kitchen doorway. "'Sup?"

Rose wrapped herself in the terry cloth as the two men exchanged a few words, and walked into the kitchen. She looked back through the screen door and knew from Frank's body language that he wanted Ricky gone as much as she did. She'd never seen that explosive side of Frank again, but she imagined with some satisfaction that Ricky had not forgotten it, either.

CHAPTER FIVE

Maji turned the motorcycle off the road and into the Benedetti drive, slowing to cruise up the long, straight path lined with Italian cypress. She frowned at the empty guard booth and open gates at the entrance. Well, that would change soon.

She took a good look at the property's layout for the first time. Angelo's family home off a path to the left, the Big House up the hill and back farther. Maji couldn't see behind it, but knew from Angelo's stories about the long sweeping lawn down to the boathouse on the shore of Long Island Sound. Somewhere off to the sides, hidden by the leafed-out deciduous trees, were eight-foot walls with security cameras. When Angelo said the House that Death Built, he meant the estate collectively. She could see why he called it a picturesque prison.

Maji cut the electric motor by the garage and propped the bike on its stand. She swung off the saddle and stripped off her gloves and helmet. The license plate holder on the sparkly, low-slung Corvette nearby caught her eye. *My Vette makes your girl wet.* She snorted.

The front door clicked shut, and the Vette's owner sauntered over. She took in his receding hairline, an excess of product giving what was left an unnatural sheen. He looked Maji over. "I heard Ang had a new girl over last night. No offense, but you're not his usual type." With a smirk and a nod to her bike, he added, "Nice ride."

Maji ignored the double entendre and gestured to his car. "Yours?"

"Got a V-8 with six hundred horses. Zero-to-sixty in four seconds," he stated proudly. "Wanna ride?"

"Oh, I don't think I could handle that," she responded, with a trace of a polite smile.

"How many CCs your bike got?" he persisted.

"None," she began, only to be interrupted by the jangle of his cell phone. He turned away without so much as a wave good-bye and began berating someone on the other end. With a slam of the driver's door and a squeal of tires, he was gone.

Maji raised her fist to knock on the front door, but it opened before she could tap it.

"Ay!" Frank greeted her. He looked around. "Where's the U-Haul?"

"What?"

"Lesbians, second date. What are you, new?" His eyes twinkled.

"Last night was not a date," she snapped. "Where's Angelo?"

Maji found Angelo down at the boathouse, which looked smaller than she had imagined. It was wide enough to hold two boats, with tall, open-raftered eaves for stowing boat gear, and a roll-up door, open now to let in the afternoon sun. Angelo was sitting on the platform on the far side, dangling his feet in the water that filled the empty slip.

"Who's the asshole up at your house?" Seeing Angelo's look, she narrowed the field for him. "Early-to-mid thirties, ex-jock, wannabe gangster clothes, hair slightly receding. Oh, and a Vette that makes my girl wonder what he's compensating for."

"Ah, Ricky. Ricky Octopus. Rickiopoulos. The Rickster. Married to my cousin Sienna, thinks he's the capo in training."

"Will I be seeing more of him?"

"Oh yeah."

Maji shifted on the platform next to Angelo. "Can't wait to meet the rest of them. Oh, I heard we're dating again. Why don't you ever believe me when I break up with you?"

"Benedettis are stubborn. We don't let go of a good thing." He took her hand and gave her a syrupy look. "Will you be mine, sweetheart?"

"Depends. This time you promise to treat me right?"

"Don't I always? Ow!" He rubbed his shoulder.

Angelo and Maji walked back up from the boathouse hand in hand.

"You look good as new, babe. How you doing, really?"

"Tip-top." Physically, anyway. "Lean and mean."

"I noticed this morning. Should I be worried?"

Maji tensed. "No. You should stick to your own lane for a fucking change."

"You are my lane, babe."

She stopped and looked up at him. "Then you should have been there last night, stopped me from repeating my mistakes."

"Whoa. Don't go comparing Rose with Iris. They are nothing alike."

"Thank God. But still, do you know how hard it's going to be to keep my distance from Rose now? We both need me to be a professional."

"So, I'm sorry. It does kinda suck to be you. She must have really got to you, that you told her your name right off."

She pulled away from him. "Not right off. After Mona and Bubbles and the police called me by my name. 'Cause why shouldn't they? They know who I am."

"Good soldier always has a Plan B. We'll make it work."

"Ang, even your hacking skills can't make me two people in one place."

He caught her hand, and she glared at him. Anyone watching from a distance, or on the estate's surveillance cameras, would have thought they witnessed a lover's quarrel. "So we just have to keep my family and your friends separate. Ain't like they move in the same circles."

A few months ago, Maji hadn't wanted to be herself, under any name. She wasn't who she'd always thought she was—that person wouldn't hurt people like she had in Fallujah. But then in Spain she'd saved a life again and resolved to come home. Where she might figure out how to live with herself, despite everything. Damn Ava for leaving her.

"Hey," Angelo said, giving her a quick hug before slipping one arm around her shoulder. "We do have your back. And you're an ace at improvising—look how great you did last night."

"My Russian was rusty, and it slowed me down. Rose could've gotten hurt." She tucked her hand into the back pocket of his pants and they started up the hill again. "Speaking of which, what do Rose and Frank think your little project is?"

"Turning state's evidence—informing for the Feds. True enough, and Rose gets it. She's the only one in the family who really understands how I feel about the family business. Knew that before she knew I was gay, and always kept both to herself."

"So she's trustworthy. But she's still a civilian."

"And she's like a sister to me. She gets a few days to say good-bye to her family before I blow this place up. I owe her that much."

Maji didn't like it any more than she ever liked having civilians involved in an op. But it was his call. "And Frank? How much do you trust him?"

"With my life. And he's on a CI agreement with the FBI, too. Don't tell Rose—she's worried enough about me."

"So you've got him scared silent? Can't rat on you without getting himself killed." Not Angelo's favorite ploy, but he'd resorted to it before.

"No, it's not like that. He really wants to help. This guy, he'd take a bullet for me or Rose."

"Sooner we get her to a safe house, less likely it'll come to that. I guess I should thank you for introducing us, even if you did fuck it up."

He laughed. "I knew you'd love her. She's beyond fabulous. And I really needed for the two of you to meet, to know that you would have each other when I'm gone."

Angelo's tone scared her more than his words. Operators might go off grid for a bit, when things got too hot, but they didn't start new lives under WITSEC. "Gone how?"

"Look at my ear. The one they broke." He brushed his curls away and leaned toward her.

"What's to see?" There was no visible scar, no bruising where she'd last seen blood.

"Cochlear implant. Nobody here knows. But I'm washed out for fieldwork. And besides, I burned myself in Fallujah, huh?"

She nodded. "For Khodorov. Is he really worth it?"

"Khodorov's not just one target, Ri. He's a gateway. And I'm willing to gamble it all on him. But when I'm done here, I'm done. I've got to be good and gone. No ties, not even to you."

Maji hugged him and wrapped her arm around his waist, inviting his arm over her shoulder for the rest of their walk. She thought of him leaving everyone behind for a life alone, in hiding. His house, the home of his childhood, came into sight. "Fuck you, Ang."

He gave her shoulder a squeeze. "I love you, too, babe."

As Maji and Angelo entered the kitchen from the pool area, Rose walked in from the dining room. She smiled upon seeing Maji. "Welcome back. Ri."

Maji took in the bare feet and drying curls, the casual elegance of white shorts and a gauzy silk blouse. She allowed herself the most fleeting of fantasies, an unformed vision of spending days by the pool and nights upstairs with this woman. *Who needs to get the hell out of Dodge*, she reminded herself.

Rose looked uncertainly between Maji and Angelo. "You are staying? Ang says you've been his cover before. You two have a plan, right, to keep him safe?"

Maji worked consciously to keep her face blank. Angelo was going to break her heart, the asshole.

"She's staying," Angelo said. "You're under her protection until you get on that plane to Peru. But as far as anyone else knows, Ri's just the girl of my dreams."

Rose nodded seriously. "And I only want you to be happy, of course."

Maji relaxed. Rose was bright, and honestly devoted to Angelo, that was clear. Maybe for just a few days...

"I'll be so convincing, no one will know who's really with whom."

Dammit. She's still a civilian—what did you expect? Maji pulled herself to her full height and looked Rose coldly in the eye. "There is only one story. If you're in, you live it," she drilled. "If you slip out of your role, someone will see, and there will be casualties. I am not your girlfriend. This is not a game. Are we clear?"

Rose looked as if Maji had slapped her, but she spoke with her usual poise. "Quite."

Maji looked at Angelo, who had followed the exchange with quiet interest. He nodded once.

Maji exhaled, stood down a notch, but still didn't smile. "Here's how it works. I advise you to go to a safe house, now. But if you stay, you stay under my protection. You go where I go, you do what I do, you follow my directions without discussion."

"Well."

"Can you live with that?"

Rose looked at Maji steadily. "I'm a grown-up. I can do as I'm told, whether I like it or not."

Maji nodded and walked past them without further comment. She grabbed her duffel and took the stairs two at a time.

Rose looked after her, then turned to Angelo. "Does she hate me?"

"No, hon," he answered softly. "But she's good and pissed at me, and right about the stakes, too. If you change your mind, wanna catch the next flight out, nobody'd blame you."

"I'm all in," she responded, crossing her arms. "Now what?"

An hour after sunset, Maji told Rose to set an alarm for six a.m. Rose looked up from her copy of Vandana Shiva's *Monocultures of the Mind.* "Oh six hundred? Yes, ma'am."

Maji didn't laugh, or even smile. As she started to turn away, Rose reached out and touched her arm. "I hope I won't be underfoot. At your dojo, I mean. I'll bring a book, entertain myself."

"Don't bank on that," Maji replied, with a flicker of a smile. "You're in training now."

Rose went to bed shortly after Maji left the room, then woke with a start. She couldn't think what had disturbed her; but she scanned the outline of furniture shapes in the near dark of her room, ready to cry out if anything moved. Then she heard a sound, a murmuring voice outside her door. As quietly as she could, she slid out of bed and padded toward the sound. She pulled up short, realizing the voice was inside her room, at the base of the door itself. She froze, listening, ready to whirl and dash for the window.

Her eyes adjusting to the scant light through the curtains, she peered at the figure curled up on the floor. Maji. When she'd said she would be right by the door, Rose had assumed Maji meant outside, in the hall.

With just a sheet covering her middle, and a pillow under her head, Maji twitched and mumbled with some urgency, strands of hair loosed from her braid falling across her face. Rose knelt on one knee and reached out to brush the hair back. When her hand was nearly to Maji's face, however, Maji snapped awake, grabbing her wrist and pulling her forward. Rose fell, while Maji scooted backward and away, catching her before she hit the floor.

"Jesus!" Rose floundered to roll over and sit up.

"Sorry," Maji mumbled, brushing the hair from her own face.

"You were dreaming." Rose spoke haltingly, her heart pounding. More than anything, she wanted to kiss that face before it lost its soft, unguarded look. Instead, she said, "You can't be comfortable down here. Why don't you take half the bed?"

Maji's eyes glowed in the dimness just inches away. "No, thanks," she said softly. "Better this way." She slid back down to the floor and rolled with her back to Rose, the pillow clutched under her head.

CHAPTER SIX

When her alarm went off at six, Rose looked to the spot on the floor by her bedroom door. It was empty. She washed her face in the private bath attached to her room and slipped out to peek in Maji's room. The door was ajar, the sheets rumpled. She smelled coffee and heard Angelo laughing downstairs.

Rose walked into the kitchen wearing her best guess at appropriate gear—yoga pants and sneakers, with a sports bra and T-shirt on top. "Will this work for training?"

Maji gave her a quick glance and answered without meeting her eyes. "That's fine."

For six or seven miles, Angelo and Maji jogged, chatting away in a mix of English and Arabic, while Rose pedaled her bike alongside them. As casual as it seemed, she could tell that Angelo was familiarizing Maji with the layout of not just the family estate but all the homes and roads around them. The tour ended in the back of Angelo's house, by the pool and the kitchen door.

"Frank!" Rose said as she walked into the kitchen, raising her eyebrows at the sight of him, up and dressed at 7:10, and frying bacon with an apron over his polo shirt and chinos. "Is it my birthday?"

"Not till October, hon. But I heard you needed a ride early today. Thought you might want some fuel to run on, too."

"Pull up here a minute, Frank," Maji instructed from the backseat, as they reached the block with the dojo. The building looked like the other houses on the residential street. "We'll be in that one, with the wraparound porch. See the front door?"

The deep porch wrapped most of the way around the left side of the house and ran the length of its front. The picnic tables were the only indication it might not be a large single-family dwelling. The little walkway from the sidewalk to the front door was lined with flowers, and gauzy white curtains hung in the windows looking out on the street.

Frank gave the whole place a quick scan. "Sure. Drop you here, then?"

"Never. You see anybody at that door besides the mail carrier, assume they're a threat. Now, take us down that drive to the right of the house."

Frank pointed the town car toward the garage at the end of the drive. As they neared the smaller wood-framed building, the drive's left turn appeared. "Oh," he said, and turned into the parking area behind the house. With just six marked spaces and another drive connecting to the alley between the houses on either side of the alley, the lot was invisible from the side streets. A six-foot wooden fence blocked the view from the normal backyards nearby.

"Here, then?" Frank pointed to the back door, which stood ajar at the top of a ramp that had clearly replaced the original set of stairs.

"Here," Maji said. "Stay put a sec." She got out, and Rose moved to follow. "Both of you."

Less than a minute later she returned and gestured for Rose to come in. Maji crouched down by Frank's open window. Rose heard her quietly instructing him, "Go out the alley. When you come back at three o'clock, come back in that way. And pick another route to get here. Every time, a new route. Clear?"

"Gotcha."

When Rose stepped through the back door, she saw the homey kitchen on her left, with its round wooden table in the center of a linoleum floor. She glanced to her right, into the laundry room. "I thought dojos were a kind of gym," she said, hearing her own voice rise at the end, turning the statement into a question. She hadn't sounded so unsure of herself since she was a teenager. How annoying.

Maji turned to respond, but stopped at the sound of a voice full of quiet certainty.

"Some say that dojo means *place of enlightenment*," said the slight woman standing in a doorway just down the hall. "Welcome, Rose. I'm Hannah Cohen."

"Thank you for having me. I'll try not to get in the way of your training."

"Oh no, thank *you*. Our two younger instructors will benefit greatly from having you as a student for a few days. A gentle warm-up before the teenagers descend next week." Her accent was subtle, just a slight thickening of some of the consonants, paired with the precise way she pronounced each word. "Maji, why don't you set up while I give Rose the tour?"

"Oh," Rose said. "Does everyone here call you Maji?"

Maji looked to Hannah, who answered. "Ri is only for your family, and those…connected to them. If that gets too confusing, you may call her Ri here as well, to ensure consistency at home."

"She'll manage for a few days, Sensei," Maji said and left them in the hall.

The locker room was plain, but immaculate. Rose stopped by a locker with her name on it and found a pair of white pants and jacket hanging inside. "How thoughtful."

"Your workout clothes are fine for now," Hannah replied. "But you may want the gi later on. Someone will show you how to tie the belt."

Back in the hallway, Hannah motioned to the doorway next to the kitchen. "My office."

The hall ended in a larger long room that ran the full width of the squarish house, floored with a dense mat. One wall was covered in full-length mirrors, the one opposite it with a plethora of neatly stacked or racked items. Some Rose recognized as weapons, like the wooden staffs. Others she could only guess at.

"Will I get to see how you use those?" Rose asked, pointing to a set of what looked like a cross between sawhorses and Tinkertoys.

Hannah's eyes crinkled. "I think we can work some parkour basics in. Yes."

The picture windows on the street side let in plenty of natural light, despite the gauzy white curtains. The inside of the door had a bar across it.

By the far wall, Rose noticed Maji moving one of six putty-colored torsos on heavy stands. She had it tilted sideways and rolled it several feet out from the wall, into a line with the others. Rose walked to the dummy closest to the windows, farthest from the one Maji was muscling alone. It looked like a heavy task, but apparently one Maji had done five times on her own already, and nearly silently at that.

The male figure pinned to the post had no arms. His torso muscles were outlined in the rubbery skin, as were a pair of trunks below his navel. He looked menacing, with a crew cut and square jaw, and eyes the same putty color as his skin.

"Does he look angry because people punch him, or to encourage them to do so?"

"A much-discussed paradox," Hannah answered, with a smile in her voice. "But you'll soon discover that a sparring partner you can never injure is a real asset to your training. You may even develop a fondness for Bob's surly attitude."

"Bob?"

"Body Object Bag."

"We can name one Ricky, if you want," Maji offered.

A smiling, curvy woman with a head full of blond curls announced her arrival at 8:20 by running across the mat toward Maji, near the spot where Rose was stretching by the windows. Rose watched Maji register the footfalls behind her, turn partway, and extend one arm back toward her attacker. The blonde grabbed her wrist, and Maji led her through what looked suspiciously like a swing dance twirl, but ended with the blonde sprawled on the mat, laughing. Maji gave her a hand up, and they hugged.

"Show-off," the blonde said.

"I didn't start it." Maji nodded toward Rose. "Bubbles, Rose. Rose, beware La Bubbles."

Rose stepped forward, having backed herself up to the door while the two women were playing. She put out her hand and was pulled into a hug. Released a few instants later, she stepped back with a laugh. "Beware, indeed."

"Hey," a young black woman said as she and a redhead bowed and stepped onto the mat, dressed in their gis.

"Hey," Maji replied. To Bubbles, she said, "Go suit up, already." Then she introduced the two junior instructors.

Tanya and Christy looked barely out of their teens. Maybe she could help give them confidence, and even gain a little herself, in the process.

Frank was waiting for them as promised, the town car idling. Rose gave Bubbles a hug good-bye and slid into the backseat, followed by Maji.

"How'd it go?" he asked, looking at Rose in his rearview mirror.

"It was…fun. And quite a workout." She leaned her head back on the plush seat and closed her eyes.

After a few minutes, Rose opened her eyes. She did not recognize the street and remembered Maji's words to Frank that morning. "Wouldn't you have a better view from up front?"

Maji switched her attention to Rose. "No. Protocol says ride with the protectee. I can see enough from here."

"Oh." So, she wasn't staying close just to be close. Rose sighed. "Should I hold my questions until the house?"

"About the dojo?" A smile flickered briefly on Maji's face. "No, go ahead. I can multitask."

"Yes, I noticed you were doing that earlier." Maji had spent most of the day inside Hannah's office, or sitting against a wall with a laptop over her knees. "Don't you need any practice teaching, like Tanya and Christy?"

"Nope. This is their first camp. But the girls will love them. They teach teens here all the time."

"So how is camp different? Other than the intensive setting."

Maji looked at her, as if weighing what to say. She lowered her voice. "Camp is for young women who will be leaders in their communities and need a special skill set to protect themselves at home, so they can make a difference there. They don't get everything they need in six weeks, but they get a lot. It's very intense. And fun, because, you know…Bubbles."

Rose thought about the homey dojo, the mysterious camp, Hannah the sensei. The composed older woman with the close-cropped salt-and-pepper hair, who moved like a dancer and spoke with quiet authority, made Rose feel honored to be invited into her private domain.

"Was Hannah ever a dancer, professionally? She moves so gracefully."

"Not to my knowledge." Maji did not stop her visual scanning of the neighborhood.

"Meaning what?"

"Not everyone who moves well has been a dancer. You haven't."

Rose found herself distracted by the compliment, then annoyed. "That's a dodge. What do you mean by *not to my knowledge*?"

Maji leaned toward her, speaking even more quietly. "Hannah was Mossad. You know, the Israeli intelligence service?" She waited for Rose to nod. "So who knows what jobs she had as a cover."

"Oh. And how do you know that I haven't? Been a dancer."

"I've read your file. You've worked as a lifeguard, a teaching assistant, and a professor. You have not cha-cha-ed for cash. Though I'd guess you social dance quite well."

Rose ignored the flattery. "I have a file? Like, an FBI file? Just for being related?"

Maji smiled ruefully. "Yeah, you probably do. But that's not it. Angelo makes his own."

Rose let that sink in, finding it made her angrier than the thought of government surveillance. "Well, I think it would only be fair for me to see yours, then."

"Mine belongs to the Army. They don't release personnel files." Maji straightened up and resumed scanning the outdoors.

Irritated at being dismissed, Rose asked, "Would they explain why you have one name at home, and another in uniform?"

Maji's face hardened. "Yep."

"I'm sorry—I can't seem to resist overstepping. It's just...I had really wanted to get to know you."

"Don't beat yourself up." Maji sighed. "Look, when a person who might receive special treatment, or threatening attention, signs up, the Army can at its discretion let them serve under a different name."

"Oh. Like the heir to a fortune, or something. Or a senator's daughter. I see."

Maji broke a smile at last, complete with a dimple. "Well, I'm not rich or powerful. But it was nice to have some privacy after Fallujah. Complete with the Photoshopping."

"Really? I thought Angelo said surgery. Or Frank did."

"I was pretty banged up. But if you look at the photos of me in the dojo, you'd recognize me, not that woman in all the media shots. So no need to feel sorry for me."

"Why would I?"

"Well, she's more conventionally pretty than I am."

Rose laid a hand on Maji's thigh, getting an inquiring look in response. "Conventional is overrated. Whoever she is, she's got nothing on you, *chula*."

Maji's blush was so gratifying, Rose stopped while she was ahead.

CHAPTER SEVEN

A Mercedes coupe pulled in behind the town car on the drive into the Benedetti estate. Maji recognized Angelo driving.

The large sedate sedan and the sporty smaller car lined up in front of the three-car garage. Frank pulled two bags of groceries from his trunk and started for the house.

Angelo pulled an oversized paper shopping bag from the coupe. "Got some toys in the city," he said to Maji.

Maji ignored him and called out, "Frank! Hold up." When he stopped and turned, she instructed, "Put those down, then go in first to confirm."

Frank nodded. "Right." He set the bags down by Rose and headed for the front door.

"Who trained him?" Maji asked Angelo.

"You think there's a school for Mafia bodymen?" He let out that annoying bark of a laugh. "But he does take instruction well, and I told him you're in charge of security down here. So have at it."

"Can't wait."

A minute later, Frank rejoined them. "All clear."

"We'll be right in," Maji said to Rose and Frank, and waited with Angelo, leaning on the Mercedes's trunk, until the front door closed behind them. Then she turned on him. "You drove to Manhattan and back by yourself?"

"Had to meet with Sander on his turf. No danger to me. They want to partner, remember?"

Maji spoke through her teeth. "Or they could have just taken what you had to show and tell, killed you, and dumped you. Because you had no backup." She sighed. "Rose would have been safe at the dojo. I could have gone with you."

"Hey, no harm, no foul. And the sitdown is set for Saturday, so we're all good."

She stood down a notch. "You need me for that?"

"Nah. Can't risk surveillance, and girlfriends aren't welcome in the boys' club. I'd love to have you in line of sight, though. Just for insurance."

"Let's plan it in, then."

"I will. You know how to sail, right?"

They unpacked the pile of small boxes Angelo had dumped out onto the spare desk in his basement office. He laid out two pendants on chains, a large watch, three sets of earbuds with transmitter packs, a charm bracelet, and a cell phone.

Maji scanned the offerings. "No gun?"

"Don't sound so optimistic. It's on order, with your carry permit."

In response, she just picked up one earbud and fitted it snugly out of sight in her right ear. "Transmitter?"

Angelo handed her an ungainly looking watch. "His and hers," he said, showing off the matching one on his wrist.

Maji slipped it on, then listened while he showed her the transmit and listen-only options. "I can figure out the stopwatch and alarm clock on my own."

"It's got a tracker, too," he said. "And it's waterproof to a hundred meters."

"Great. I'll try not to drown too far offshore, then."

He chuffed at her dark humor. "What do you think for Rose, necklace or bracelet?"

The bracelet was too cutesy for Rose, but a better-disguised device, resembling actual jewelry. The pendant, in contrast, looked like a high-tech fob on a heavy nylon cord. "Let her decide. By now she'll need to have some say over something," Maji noted. "Even a little thing, like this."

"You're not still fuzzy around her, are you?"

"My judgment's crystal clear, asshole. I just remember what I was like under protection."

Angelo snorted. "You were a teenager, Ri. And hell on wheels, from the sound of it." He got only a hard stare in return for the verbal poke. "Rose is a full-grown woman. As you may have noticed."

"Yeah. So let's respect that."

They brought Rose the choices. Not surprisingly, she took the pendant. "Should I take this off at the dojo or in the pool?"

Although it was waterproof, and durable, Maji nodded. Being able to remove it sometimes would add to Rose's sense of control. So she added, "If we get separated, it could be vital. But you can take it off in low-risk spaces where you've got help nearby."

"Dojo, pool." Rose's eyes twinkled mischievously. "Shower?"

"I'll have the door."

"Like you do at bedtime?"

Maji felt herself blush. "No, on the outside of the door."

"Just where exactly you taking night watch?" Angelo asked.

"Inside, floor. She sleeps with the window open." Maji fixed him with a level gaze, daring him to suggest they lock the windows down. The place was enough of a prison as it was.

Angelo went over the entire house with them, confirming how the doors and windows were alarmed and how to cancel the alert if it was tripped accidentally. A moment after the test, Frank appeared, breathing hard.

"Just testing," Angelo said by way of apology. To the women he added, "There's a monitor at Frank's, and one in my office."

"You want I should start dinner?" Frank asked, apparently not fussed at all to have run over for nothing.

"Thanks. 'Bout an hour, for us."

They used the time to run Rose through evacuation plans, including where to meet outdoors if they had to flee the house and became separated. Maji demonstrated how to climb out Rose's bedroom window and reach the ground using the reinforced downspout and a series of brackets hidden in the English ivy. Finally, Angelo had Rose draw a map of the house and lock it in her mind's eye.

At nine p.m., Angelo came upstairs and found Rose and Maji in the living room, Rose stretched out on the couch with a book and Maji in an armchair with headphones and her laptop, silently mouthing words toward the screen. She clicked the keyboard when she saw him, and removed the headphones.

"Italian?" he guessed.

She shook her head. "Russian."

Rose recalled that Maji had had an Italian textbook open at the dojo, during one of the sessions where she had watched the self-defense instruction from a distance. She glanced out the window and noticed the dark blue sky had turned to black. "Bedtime already?" she asked her cousin.

He shook his head slowly. "Time for a drill. You can sleep when the adrenaline wears off."

Rose's stomach clenched, and she looked at Maji, who was laying her computer and headphones aside. "What kind of drill?"

"Just an exercise to put in your body what your brain already knows about the house." Maji gave Angelo an annoyed look before continuing. "Think of it like a fire drill. Just practice."

"I wanted to run it when you were asleep, but Ri told me to fuck off," Angelo told her, letting his suppressed grin escape at last. "Let's go."

They turned off all the lights in the house and switched off the security lights outdoors as well. Standing in the kitchen, Rose could barely make out the unlit pool outside in the hint of moonlight. She heard Angelo from the doorway to the dining room. "Walk to the front door. Don't open it."

She found her way there cautiously, touching the doorjamb and walls lightly as she passed, managing not to bark a shin on the entryway table. Easy enough. She took a breath, and let it out slowly. "Next?"

"Through the dining room, down to Angelo's desk," came Maji's voice from a few feet away.

Rose gasped, and nearly swore. "Fine." She found her way through the dining room, into the kitchen again, and to the top of the basement stairs. The inky darkness below gave her pause. "Ang?"

"Come on down," he said, his voice carrying from below. She wondered how he had gotten there before her without a sound. And also where in the dark Maji might be. She swallowed, and walked down cautiously, feeling the coolness of the basement as she descended. In her mind's eye, she saw where she knew the desk should be and felt her way to it.

"Nice job," Angelo said and took her hand. He placed it on his shoulder and added, "Now, follow me back up."

They walked swiftly back to the kitchen, into the entry hall, and up the stairs to her bedroom.

She heard Maji's voice from over by the window and made out a dark shape there. "Almost done now. Ang? Give us sixty."

Angelo detached Rose's hand from his shoulder and slipped away. Maji's voice came again. "This one is an actual fire drill. Lie down, and when the alarm sounds, crawl down the hall and out the back door by the pool."

Rose found her bed and stretched out, just in time for the first piercing shrills of the fire alarm to sound. Her pulse skyrocketed, and she rolled off the bed onto the floor, oriented herself toward the door, and crawled rapidly toward it. She paused to feel for heat, wondered at herself, and turned the knob. She paused at the top of the stairs and tried to think through the noise that relentlessly assaulted her ears and nerves. Head first, or feet first? She chose to lead with her feet, skittering down with her arms under her torso. At the bottom she dropped into a crouch and ran through the living room into the kitchen and out the back door.

Angelo stood in the moonlight by the pool, one eye on his watch. "Good time." Inside the house, the alarm stopped abruptly, leaving a palpable quiet behind.

"Thanks," she panted, hands on her hips. "Are we done?"

"Yeah. You can go to bed anytime. You want a glass of wine or something?"

The kitchen door shushed open and clicked shut. Rose glanced at Maji's form in the shadows. "No," she told him. "Water, and a towel." Rose stripped off her top and started to shuck her shorts without waiting for his reply.

As she prepared to dive in, she heard Angelo say to Maji, "I'll go fetch. You're on watch."

Maji watched Rose rest in the back of the town car, her head back and her eyes closed. Thursday's training had been physically intense, and Rose had started the day looking tired. Maybe they should have skipped the house drills last night, given how short a time Rose had left in town. But better to waste training than skip it and need it later. In Peru, even.

Not that they could teach Rose that much before her flight out on Monday. But for only her second day in a dojo, Rose picked up the basics remarkably well. Maybe Sunday Maji could show her some advanced moves. *You just want an excuse to get close.*

Maji had hung back at the dojo. So Bubbles had stuck by Rose, offering encouragement and a supportive touch now and then, drawing a smile from Rose with her warmth. The more distance Maji kept, the harder Bubbles worked to make Rose feel at home. La Bubbles probably thought Maji was being a jerk. Who could blame her?

Frank looked into the rearview mirror and caught Maji's eye. "Ang had me pick up a bunch of stuff today. I feel like Santa."

Maji thought of the gun on order and wondered what else there might be. "Well, keep out of chimneys, Frank. If you don't get stuck, somebody'll shoot you at the bottom."

He laughed, but Rose only winced.

"You okay?" Maji asked softly.

Rose did not open her eyes. "Just tired."

An hour later, Rose slipped on her swimsuit and tried to pull her hair back into a ponytail. It wasn't long enough anymore. She ran her hands through the curls, uncertain how she felt about the new crop. Angelo said it gave her a gamine look, but was that a good thing? Angelo's ideals of feminine beauty seemed to have been set from watching movie classics with Grandpa Stephano. She wondered if Ang had made Maji sit through his favorites, on some base in Iraq during their downtime. Before the I-am-not-your-girlfriend lecture, she would have asked.

As she reached the top of the stairs, Rose saw Maji at their base, ready to head up. In running shorts and a T-shirt now plastered to her front with sweat. They looked each other over, awkwardly.

"Swimming laps?" Maji asked.

Rose turned to the hall closet and grabbed a towel to cover her self-awareness. "Every day—I'm addicted." She turned back around, a spare towel in hand. "Why don't you join me, this time?"

Maji blinked twice, and Rose almost felt guilty about her skinny-dip the night before. "No suit." Oh, the mischievous glint in those eyes. "I better send Frank for one. What's in style these days?"

"You want Brooklyn, Long Island, or tasteful?"

Maji laughed and started up the stairs, pausing at the halfway point landing. "Not what Angelo would order up. Something that stays on."

"I'll give Frank instructions for you," Rose offered, smiling conspiratorially.

As Rose reached the landing, Maji added, "I'll be out as soon as I wash the funk off me."

Rose stood close to her for a few breaths, inhaling the scent of clean sweat and something extra, something indefinably Maji. "Not the word I'd use," she said softly. She quickly padded down the remaining steps, before she could get herself into real trouble.

By the time Rose came up for air, the household had migrated outdoors. Angelo, still in Dockers and a crisp button-down shirt, set up his laptop on the patio table, a gin and tonic close at hand. Maji took the chaise next to him, an advanced Italian course book on her lap and headphones over both ears. Frank came out and fired up the grill. Maji sniffed and looked at Angelo, who raised an eyebrow. She shrugged and went back to her book.

Maji closed the book and let the sounds of the language fill her head as she gazed across the pool. Rose stroked smoothly through the water, clearly at home there. Angelo touched Maji's shoulder, drawing her attention. He smirked and motioned for her to wipe her mouth. Maji responded with a bit of Italian not found in the course book, along with a suitably rude gesture.

She had just opened the book again when Angelo leaped up and dashed to the edge of the pool. Maji tore the headphones off and was by his side in an instant. She saw that Rose's face was twisted in pain as she clung to the side of the pool.

"It's just a cramp. I'll be fine," she gasped.

"Yeah, yeah," Angelo replied. "Can you get to this end?"

As Rose worked her way gingerly to the pool's end, Maji waded in and wedged one shoulder under her arm, supporting her up the underwater stairway. She helped Rose to a chaise lounge. Angelo laid the chair flat and ordered his cousin to lie down, ignoring her protests. He motioned Maji to Rose's feet, and rolled his sleeves up, going to work on her shoulders.

"Whadda ya doing in that place, beating her up?" Angelo asked over her head.

"Eff you," Maji retorted. "We've done basic falls, escapes, a few throws, and some parkour warm-ups. Nothing heavy."

Rose flinched as Maji dug into her calf, and the two stopped bickering momentarily.

"You don't have to actually train her, you know," Angelo pointed out. "She only has to go where you do, not do what you do."

Maji held his gaze. "Thought you wanted her to be able to take care of herself."

If Angelo had a comeback, it was lost to Frank's arrival. "I got us steaks. Now, I know Rose likes it medium, Angie's a rare—how you want yours, Ri?"

"I'll just have a salad, thanks."

"You off red meat?" Angelo queried.

"Uh-huh," Maji replied casually. "Since September."

A look passed between them, and Angelo nodded twice, slowly, then turned toward Frank. "Put that halibut on for her." He stood and looked down at Maji. "Lemme grab you a towel. You're dripping on the patient."

Maji reached over to Angelo's table and grabbed his drink, handing it to Rose. "Lime juice," she said by way of explanation. "Electrolytes."

Rose sipped through the straw, and made a puzzled face. "This has no gin. But I could swear he smells like it."

"Surprise," Maji said. "Roll over. Please."

Maji's hands worked their way down Rose's spine, searching out the knots along it that caused her flinches. Finding a particularly bad one in the right side curve of the low back, she instructed, "Just breathe." As Rose took a deep, slow breath, Maji placed two fingers on the troublesome spot and two on the back of Rose's right knee, and held them simultaneously. Rose cried out.

"Breathe." Maji leaned over by Rose's ear and breathed steadily in and out, like a birthing coach.

Rose followed, her body relaxing. Then she rolled her ankle and flexed her shoulders. "Wow," she exclaimed, rolling onto her side to face Maji. "Where did you learn that?"

Angelo interrupted, returning with the towel. He tossed it to Maji, who stood and started to blot her soaked shirt. "I got her now. Why don't you go change?"

"I wasn't planning to come to dinner wet," Maji replied with a prickle in her voice.

"Me either," Rose said quietly.

Angelo's head whirled toward her, then tilted back and let out a sharp laugh. Maji just wrapped herself in the towel and padded toward the kitchen. As she passed the grill, Frank opened it to turn the steaks and she stopped, caught by the wafting aroma. Feeling the heat radiate toward her, she stood watching the flames lick at the meat.

"Going to hide upwind, Rios?" She heard the echo of Angelo in Iraq, chiding her by the piles of trash they had to burn routinely, long before the nightmare of Fallujah. *Was that out loud?* She turned, and he was behind her, watching attentively.

"Stick to your own lane, Benedetti," she snapped as she brushed past him into the kitchen, leaving him frowning thoughtfully behind her.

CHAPTER EIGHT

At the end of training on Friday, Rose closed her locker and sighed. "Got you hooked, didn't we?" Bubbles teased, leaning against a locker nearby.

Rose smiled. "I learned so much. Thank you."

"Nothing like what you'd get out of camp." Bubbles paused. "You are coming to Shabbat dinner, aren't you?"

Rose knew it was Friday, and assumed that Hannah was Jewish, but Maji hadn't mentioned anything. "Not that I know of. Is it a family thing, like Sunday suppers at the Big House?"

"It was, when we were all here." A shadow passed over Bubbles's face. "Hang on." She left the locker room, only to return a moment later with a wide grin. "It's a family thing. See you at six!"

Maji touched the mezuzah by Hannah's front door, then let herself and Rose and Angelo in with a key. *"Bienvenidos a casa Cohen.* And *Shabbat shalom."*

Inside, she threw the bolt on the door behind them, inhaling deeply. The house was filled with savory aromas of the promised dinner. Rose felt transported.

Maji looked disconcerted. "Papi?" she called out.

"Aquí, mija," came a rich voice from the kitchen.

Angelo and Rose followed Maji into the kitchen, where a handsome man in his midfifties stood wiping his hands on a towel tucked into his apron. He smiled warmly, the corners of his mouth lifting a bushy mustache of the same coarse black as his hair, sprinkled with hints of gray.

"Papi!" Maji hugged him fiercely. "You didn't have to come all this way."

"Hannah said you couldn't come to the city for a while," he said, kissing her forehead. "So the city comes to you."

"Mom too?"

"*No puede*. A prior commitment."

Maji nodded, and let him go without further comment.

After introductions, Maji left Rose in the kitchen with her father and took Angelo upstairs to speak with Hannah.

Angelo screwed up his courage. Telling Hannah was a risk, but he didn't see pulling his whole plan off without her. "If I could deliver more than what I've promised, would you back me?"

"That would depend. What more, and at what risk?"

He had to admire how much nothing her poker face revealed. "Sirko." Still nothing. If catching Leonid Sirko, the world's second biggest money launderer, didn't impress her, he was fucked. "For the balance of power. I mean, if we take down Khodorov, Sirko will just step into the vacuum, right? Interpol might not care, but I sure as hell do."

"Of course you do. And I agree. But I have two concerns."

There it was. Hannah's famous *concerns*. Well, her ability to think through the downside of any mission plan had saved the team members' lives enough times. "I look forward to exploring them, ma'am."

She smiled for the first time. "The colonel's not here, Angelo. Please relax. And yes, you may call me Hannah, if you don't forget yourself when we do have oversight again."

His bark of a laugh brought Maji to the open door frame. "Am I missing happy hour?"

"Your godmother's a pistol," Angelo admitted, sorry he'd assumed Maji had gone downstairs already. "What are you skulking around for?"

She raised a hand and backed out into the hallway. "Just passing through."

"Bubbles should be here anytime," Hannah noted.

Maji gave a little faux-salute and turned toward the stairs. "See ya at supper."

Angelo waited until his friend's footsteps had faded. "First concern?"

"Ah, yes. When Justice freezes the Italians' accounts, there will be some shuffling in this region. Nothing too disruptive. But when Interpol ties up business for Khodorov and Sirko, the fighting among the second tier of major players who want to take over will hurt a great number of people, and in the end just put new leaders on the same field, possibly a syndicate or two. Have you thought about this?"

"For years, Hannah. For years." Since he was eight or nine, in point of fact. Mob politics were woven into Grandpa Stephano's chess lessons. "What's number two, then?"

"The obvious. How do you plan to reel Sirko in without Khodorov knowing? Because if he does find out, you know what he'll do."

Angelo frowned at the reminder. The thought of Khodorov having every member of his family killed slipped into his mind whenever he slowed down too much, relaxed too much. "I'm thinking Sirko needs to steal the program. But not until it's ready."

"Naturally. We can manage the timing, I'm sure." She paused, her brow furrowing. "But destroying both major players will only break the monopoly. So many would rush forward to try and take their place."

Angelo smiled wryly. "Yep. We'd still be playing Whack-A-Mole, like we do with terrorist cells. I'm worn out on that."

"Well, it is the nature of organized crime. A hydra, with no head to cut off."

"Skip the head. The beast eats money. Cut that off, it dies." He noted with satisfaction that Hannah seemed intrigued, not skeptical. "I'm working on a sleeper virus, to suck all the funds from their accounts, then go do the same to every account they've ever done business with."

Now Hannah looked worried. Did she think he couldn't pull that off? "The collateral damage could be enormous," she said. "Have you thought about how to prevent an economic collapse? Or even just the likely damage to honest citizens who may have unwittingly done business with them?"

She was right. There were trillions of dollars, euros, yen, whatever, involved. Thousands of fronts that provided real services, real jobs. Millions of people could be hurt. Angelo sighed. "So you can see why I'm not floating this idea to JSOC."

"Indeed. I don't know whether to be flattered or offended that you shared it with me. You understand the position it puts me in."

Angelo nodded. "If I can't convince you that I can do it, and address your concerns, you won't have to blow the whistle. I'll drop the sleeper virus and just stick with stinging Khodorov and Sirko. I promise."

❖

Rose found herself oddly at home with Maji's father. While she poured herself a glass of white wine, he hummed to himself, tossing salad in a large wooden bowl. "What smells so heavenly, Mr. Rios?"

"Sal, *por favor*. Come, taste." He lifted the lid off a large pot and held a spoonful for her.

Savoring the creamy stew of squash, beans, corn, and tomatoes, she closed her eyes in pleasure as she recognized the dish from her last fieldwork trip. The Quechua women of southern Peru had taught her to make it. "*Porotos granados?*"

"*Claro!* A favorite of all true Chileans—and Maji." He beamed at her. "*Y aquí...*" He lifted a second lid with a flourish. She leaned over it, inhaling deeply.

"*Mazamorra*? Can you get *choclo* here?"

"*Pues*, if you know somebody in the city." He waggled his eyebrows and Rose giggled.

Bubbles and Maji appeared in the kitchen doorway together, playfully shouldering each other to reach Sal first. Maji gave way and Bubbles torpedoed into Salvador Rios, wrapping him in a tight embrace before he could stumble from the force of her enthusiasm. From the way he chuckled fondly as they separated, Rose guessed the friendly ambush was a tradition.

"No Rey?" Rose asked, peering through the doorway to the empty dining room beyond.

"Had to work tonight." Bubbles frowned. "He wanted to meet you, too. But maybe when you come back."

Bubbles showed Rose how to set the dining table. In addition to the place settings, they set out little candles in candleholders, and small glasses for the Kiddush wine. Rose counted the chairs.

"Who else is coming?" she asked.

"Nobody. That one's for Ava." Bubbles's face crumpled, and Rose enfolded her, letting her cry. "Sorry," Bubbles said, pulling away after a moment. "This would have been our first Friday night all together again." She looked around for a tissue, pulled a handful from a box nearby, and blew loudly.

Sal emerged from the kitchen and put an arm around Bubbles. "He gives and He takes, *mija*," he said, his tone tender.

"Well, He can just...go to hell!" Bubbles sobbed, and ran into the kitchen. The back door slammed.

Sal looked mournfully at the empty chair.

"Who's Ava?" Rose asked him.

"Hannah's wife," Sal replied. "She was like a mother to Bubbles."

Maji stepped out of the little powder room tucked under the stairs. "Something up?"

"*Tu hermana. Le duele su corazón.*" He tilted his head toward the back door. "*Afuera.*"

Maji passed them briskly, slowing only to give her father's arm a squeeze. The screen door banged a second time.

As they filled the serving plates, Rose could hear Maji and Bubbles on the back porch, their voices rising and falling, punctuated by more nose blowing. They came to the table red eyed, holding hands. Hannah led the group through the candle lighting, the Kiddush, the hand washing, and the blessing of the challah.

After a brief silence while everyone tasted the stew, Angelo asked, "Aren't you supposed to crack the door for Elijah?"

Hannah broke out laughing, wiping her eyes as the outburst subsided. "Oh, she would have liked that one. You're thinking of Passover, dear. That seat's for Ava, my late wife."

"Oh, I'm sorry." Angelo looked uncharacteristically nonplussed. "I never heard of that tradition."

"It's new to our family," Hannah replied.

"How long after do you do it?"

"I don't know yet," she answered, tears again welling in her eyes. "Until I can bear to stop, I guess."

Over dessert, Rose asked Hannah about her particular interpretations of the kosher edicts. They exchanged thoughts about fair trade, organic farming, humanely raised animals, and the like, ignoring the rest of the table as they delved into the intersection of traditional food cultures, modern agribusiness, ethics, and theology. When the rest of the table fell silent, they finally looked to their four companions.

"Sorry," Rose said with a sheepish smile. "Occupational hazard."

"Guess where Rose did her fieldwork," Sal said to Maji.

"Peru," Maji responded, digging her spoon into the cobbler as if it might escape if she paid it less attention.

"And I'm going back next week," Rose said, ambivalence creeping into her tone. "Maybe you'd like to join us for brunch tomorrow," she said to Bubbles, "at the Harborview."

"Um," Bubbles said, looking questioningly at Maji.

Maji and Angelo started a debate in Arabic.

Rose glared at them. "Both of you, cut it out."

Bubbles snorted. "She'll drive you nuts like that," she assured Rose. "You don't know the half of it."

"Knowing anything would be a start," Rose grumbled.

Bubbles gave her a wink. "I'll tell you whatever you want to know."

"I know where you sleep," Maji warned Bubbles, crossing her arms.

"Girls..." Hannah said.

Bubbles mimed holding a phone to her ear and smiled at Rose, who couldn't help but smile back.

CHAPTER NINE

Bubbles came waving and smiling toward their table at the Harborview, dodging busy waitstaff at the popular restaurant. As she approached, Frank asked Maji, "You want me to take the door?"

"Nope. Stay with us."

Rose stood and hugged Bubbles, who whispered, "She's the boss of him?"

Rose inclined her head as she stepped back. "Frank, meet my friend Bubbles. From the dojo."

"Right." He extended a hand and they shook briefly. "Rose says all kind of good things about you."

"You always fool the nice people," Maji said to Bubbles. "Even the smart ones."

Bubbles bumped Maji with her shoulder. "You could too if you practiced. You know, fake it till you make it."

Seeing the concern on Frank's face, Rose reassured him, "This is how they show affection, Frank. Like you and Pants Sarcone."

Maji and Bubbles stopped pushing against one another, stunned into a momentary halt.

"Oh. Sure." Frank nodded at them. "You two come up together?"

"No," Maji answered. "But we go back a ways."

"Maji scraped me off the sidewalk, back in Brooklyn," Bubbles added. "And pushed me out into the 'burbs."

A smiled quirked at Maji's mouth. "You were bringing down the neighborhood."

They ordered, Maji keeping one ear on the conversation and her eyes on the Glen Cove Marina's docks. Right on schedule, Uncle Lupo DiVincenzi, Gino's consigliere, arrived and opened up his motor yacht, the *Lucky Lady*. Angelo arrived next, followed a moment later by Gino. This section of the marina was private, accessible only to members with a key code for the gates at the top of each dock ramp.

Maji watched Angelo confer a moment with his elders in the Grand Bank's spacious cockpit. When he hopped back down onto the dock and started heading back to the gate, she picked the binoculars up off the tabletop.

"What are you looking at?" Bubbles asked.

"Shh," Maji replied. She watched Angelo greet Yuri and Sander Khodorov, and argue politely about the three men with them. The one she recognized as Sergei, the FBI's informant, followed them to the boat. The other two turned and walked away. She recognized one from Mona's, and worried for a moment they might decide to come into the Harborview to keep an eye on the *Lucky Lady*, too. Maji sighed as they turned and headed for the parking lot.

"Are you working?" Bubbles asked as Maji laid the binoculars back down. She didn't try to keep the disapproval from her tone.

"Just a little surveillance," Maji replied.

"And you brought her with you?"

"Nothing's going down in here."

"Great." The mimosas arrived for Bubbles and Rose, along with coffee for Frank and Maji. Bubbles lifted her glass, eyeing Maji. "You sure?"

"Yes. Go ahead. You driving?"

"I know my limits. Unlike some people."

"Watch it," Maji said with a hint of a smile quirking the corner of her mouth. "Rose still thinks you're the nice one."

The server set a lovely omelet in front of Rose and moved back to the tray of entrees for the others. Before her plate had touched the table, Maji pushed back, swearing under her breath. "Excuse me," she said to the table at large.

Frank looked out the window. "Crap." He fiddled with something inside his jacket, while Maji simply pressed her watch once.

"Everyone stays here," Maji said, then wove her way rapidly through the tables and disappeared out the front door.

Rose saw the Grand Banks puttering away from its slip and picked up the binoculars. She saw Maji punching buttons on the gate's keypad and shoving through. After a quick scan of the finger docks, she jogged down one and crouched by a small sailboat.

"What's she doing?" Bubbles asked.

"I think she's stealing a sailboat," Rose replied. She handed Bubbles the binoculars. "See?"

As Bubbles scanned the marina for her friend, Frank said, "Maji says no worries, please enjoy brunch. It's all good."

Bubbles turned toward the sound of his voice, caught sight of him magnified, and startled backward. She lowered the binoculars and looked from Frank to Rose. "What?"

"They have ear things," Rose said. "Comms."

"She's really okay out there?" Bubbles asked Frank.

Frank gave her an earnest look that Rose didn't entirely trust. "She's just keeping Ang in sight. Nothing to worry about." His expression faltered. "She can sail, right?"

Bubbles relaxed and almost smiled. "Yeah. And of course she picked a nimble little boat to steal. She can dodge and weave with the best of them."

The Hobie catamaran zipped out toward the basin, quickly catching up with the leisurely progress of the staid motorboat. On a beautiful Saturday morning in late May, there was plenty of small boat traffic to dodge. Fortunately, most of it was heading toward the marina's breakwater.

The Grand Banks didn't seem to have its mind made up, ambling first toward the open water outside of the marina's protection, and then making a turn inside the basin. Maji tacked to keep from sailing toward it on a collision course. Without any bugs or comms inside the *Lucky Lady*, the best she could do was guess their intention. Obviously they had left the dock to avoid the possibility of electronic eavesdropping. But now they seemed to be compromising on how far from other boats and humans was far enough.

A little yellow ski boat zipped between her catamaran and the motor yacht without warning. The cat pitched and nearly changed course on its own. Holding the tiller lightly in one hand and the mainsheet in the other, Maji turned and yelled after the oblivious stinkpotters. Not that they could hear her over that motor. Idiots.

To keep a better eye on the *Lucky Lady*, Maji came about, jibing to set a new course that would look like she was just dinking about inside the harbor. No need to get too close to the motor yacht, which was slowing almost to the point of losing helm control as it neared the inside of the breakwater.

"Oh," she said out loud, as Angelo and Sergei worked together to throw out light anchors from the bow and stern. "They found a spot for the meeting, Frank. I'm just going to sail around casually for a while. All good in there?"

"Yeah. They're taking turns watching you through the binoculars."

"Tell Bubbles I said, *Dinner and a show*."

There was a brief pause, and then he said, almost apologetically, "She called you a brat."

Maji started to laugh, enjoying being on the water again, even if she was missing a nice plate of eggs and hash. With a homemade biscuit. And coffee. Well, maybe the Benedetti-Khodorov alliance would be a quick deal.

The little yellow ski boat passed by again, slowly this time. The two men inside didn't look relaxed, or dressed for a day in the sun. One had a suit jacket on, and the other a polo shirt but also a large white wrap around his left hand. The hand she had smashed in the car door behind Mona's. Dammit.

They recognized her as well, and Maji thought about tacking again and making a run for the channel. No—if they raced after her, there could be a collision, harbor police, unwanted attention. And if they didn't, she'd be too far away if the meeting went south and they decided to board the *Lucky Lady*.

So Maji gave the two men a polite wave, one boater to another, and pretended not to notice as they crept up on her. Just to buy time, she tacked a couple more times, forcing them to change course to stay as close as they clearly wanted to. "Frank," she said, "I might be out here awhile, making friends. Keep everyone cool until I get back, okay?"

"Sure, hon."

Maji led the ski boat toward the breakwater, close enough to the shallows to anchor it. They were such good followers, she was tempted to zip toward the shoals she knew were nearby and let them ground themselves in pursuit. Now that would be fun to watch. But again, likely to piss somebody off. And this was Play Nice with Others Day on the big white boat with all the important players onboard.

Maji sighed and pointed the Hobie at the ski boat, letting the main luff as she got close, to slow it down. The two Russians looked alarmed and reached for their pistols. "Friends," she called to them in Russian, showing both her palms even while one held the tiller. With her empty hand, she grabbed the coiled docking line, held it up for them to see, and tossed it across the gap between the two boats.

"What the fuck?" Bubbles said.

Rose resisted the urge to grab the binoculars from her. "What?"

"She's, um…rafting up with the yellow boat."

"Let me see." Rose put the binoculars to her eyes and scanned until she found Maji. Who appeared to be holding a friendly conversation with two strangers, perched on the edge of the ski boat's small cockpit.

"There's nothing to worry about," Frank said. "Hon…?"

Rose tore herself away from the far view long enough to glance at him. "What?"

"She's fine out there. She wants us to just hang out here till she comes back in. Okay?"

Rose looked to Bubbles. She knew Maji better than anyone, even if she didn't know what was going on out there, either. "Should we try to help? Somehow."

Bubbles asked her in Spanish, without looking toward Frank, "How much do you trust this guy?"

"Completely," Rose answered, also in Spanish.

Bubbles shrugged. "Then do what she says. 'Cause apparently she's the boss of all of us today. Have another mimosa."

They finished their plates off while watching Maji chat with her new boating pals. "She looks relaxed," Rose said. "Can you tell what they're talking about?"

"Nah. They're talking Russian." Frank motioned the server over. He gave her a charming smile and three hundred dollars. "We'll give you the table back just as soon as we can. Don't want to be any bother."

"No bother at all, sir." She offered more mimosas and graciously took their orders for coffee and tea instead.

Rose pushed back from the table. "Excuse me. I'll be right back."

Frank looked worried. "Um, I should—"

"No, you really shouldn't," Bubbles said, nearly rolling her eyes. "I can escort the lady to the ladies' room."

As they washed their hands, alone for the moment, Rose asked, "You really aren't worried about her, out there with those…men?"

"Mysterious are the ways of the Maji. If she needed help, she'd have sent a message by now."

Rose toweled her hands off. "So we shouldn't slip out, steal another boat, and go save her?"

Bubbles laughed, and gave Rose a squeeze. "I wouldn't dare."

Nearly an hour later, Frank succumbed to the bottomless cups of coffee in his system, promising to be back in a flash. Rose passed the binoculars to Bubbles, who scanned back and forth between the two boats quietly for a moment. Then she sat back with an "Ooh!"

Rose took the binoculars. Both boats were pulling anchor. She looked around for Frank and spied him working his way back between full tables of diners.

He gave her a wink and a smile. "They'll be back in a minute. Says to meet her at the car."

Rose didn't wait for any more permission. She headed for the dock.

At the top of the ramp, Rose realized she didn't know the code. What would she do if she reached Maji, anyway? She stepped back, torn between the desire to see for herself that Maji was safe and the instruction to meet at the car instead. A family of three with a dock cart arrived, punched in the code, and held the gate politely for her. *I'll beg forgiveness later.*

Seconds later, Rose heard Frank on the dock behind her, calling for her to stop. She ignored him, her only thought to reach Angelo and Maji as quickly as possible. *Ri*, she corrected herself. *Call her Ri.*

She turned onto the connecting dock that led out to the yacht slips and caught sight of Angelo. Next to Gino and Uncle Lupo, he smiled and shook hands with three men Rose didn't recognize. She slowed her walk, uncertain now. Angelo was clearly fine. But where was Maji?

Angelo spotted Rose, and waved cheerfully. "Hey, how was brunch?"

"Delicious."

"Told you you'd like it. Can't beat the view, huh?" He turned to the men cluttering the dock behind him. "Where are my manners? Rose, this is Yuri Khodorov. And Sander. And their guy, Sergei."

Rose exchanged the required pleasantries, one eye behind them, on Maji and the two men who had captured her.

"We're heading home," Angelo said, with a gesture for her to clear the path. "I'll meet you there, okay?"

Frank, at her elbow now, gave a little tug. "Will do."

Rose had no choice but to back up and turn the corner, stepping back onto the larger dock again. She waited as the men made a single file, walking toward her. From behind them, she heard, "'Scuse me. 'Scuse me. 'Scuse me."

Maji looked irate as she reached Angelo. She rattled off some angry-sounding Spanish, one finger pressed into his sternum.

"I'll make this up to you, I promise," Angelo replied, flicking a glance toward the men waiting behind him. "But right now, I gotta…"

"I don't give a fuck what you gotta." She flicked his chest and started off toward the parking lot.

Angelo took a few steps after her, then looked back at his business associates. He stopped by Rose and Frank. "Don't let her take off alone," he instructed, his voice pitched for all to hear. "Get her home and cooled down. I'll be there in a bit."

Angelo stopped Sander as they were about to split up into two groups to leave the marina. "Hey, I got that thing in my car for you. Can I borrow you a minute?"

Sander looked to his father, got a noncommittal look, and said, "Sure."

Angelo opened the Mercedes's door and reached inside, then turned back to Sander.

"What thing are you—" Sander started. "Oh. Having a moment, are we? Fine, go ahead."

"You think it's funny? Ri could've been hurt. What were you thinking?"

"Same as you, apparently. That we should have someone nearby, just in case. I have better someones, that's all."

If only you knew. "Well, it worked out. But still. You can't pull something like that again. It'll set Gino off."

"Not to worry. We're partners, now, right?"

"Right." Angelo simmered himself down. "Actually, that went smoother than I expected."

"Yes. When your uncle Gino listens to Uncle Lupo, things go well. We should keep Lupo dialed in."

"Count on it."

"Okay then," Sander said. "I wish I could kiss you. Right now."

"I wish you could, too."

"Well, see you Tuesday."

"I'll be ready."

Maji waited until Rose closed her door to speak. "Did Bubbles at least stay out of sight?"

"Went out the back, like you asked," Frank replied. "Sorry I let Rose—"

"Skip it." Maji looked at Rose, who appeared to be fuming quietly. "Just take us home. I'm starving."

After giving her the silent treatment for several minutes, Rose looked ready to burst with some withheld thought.

"What?" Maji asked.

"Were those the same men who tried to kidnap me?"

"Just the one. With the…" Maji pointed to her hand. Where were her words? "Bandage. That's Vlad. He hopes you don't hold that against him, by the way."

Rose laughed incredulously. "Now he's my friend, too?"

"Yep. One big family now. That's how these things work."

"But you didn't know that when you just…handed yourself over. What if the meeting didn't go well?"

Ah. She'd frightened Rose. Got it. Maji sighed. "Then I'd have been where Angelo needed me—as close as possible."

Rose blanched visibly. "Well, thank goodness it went well, then. And…I'm sorry for not staying out of sight, as ordered. I was worried about you."

"I know. But if you can't let me do what I'm here for, there's always the safe house."

Rose glared at her for the full length of the long driveway. Maji felt pinned in place, and she didn't want to look away. As Frank pulled the car into its space, Rose leaned toward her. "Don't you dare," she said, and flung her door open.

Maji hung back while Frank let Rose into the house, then followed them inside. Rose angry was a force to be reckoned with. That was good. Better than frightened, and taking foolish chances. Or trying to protect her, and getting someone hurt, like… *Lighten up, Rios. She's not Iris.*

Maji shook off the thought and headed for the kitchen to rustle up some food. She stopped short at the doorway. Rose was tossing ingredients out of the fridge and thwonking items on the counter with barely contained force. Still angry, then.

"You don't need to cook for me," Maji said.

Rose kept moving, not looking at her. "It's the least I can do. You're giving up your vacation, putting yourself in danger—"

"Hey," Maji said, catching a head of lettuce before it bounced off the counter island. She stepped between Rose and the counter, careful not to touch her but close enough that Rose had to look at her or move away. "I'm sorry you were scared. But I need you to trust me, my decisions. I promised to keep you safe."

"I wasn't thinking straight," Rose acknowledged. "You were out there so long, and I couldn't do anything, and I just wanted to make sure…" She closed the little distance between them, leaning her forehead against Maji's.

Maji felt Rose relax, with their heads touching, like they could figure this out together, if only they tried. She put her hands on Rose's hips, intending to push her back a step, give herself room to think again. Instead, she pulled her forward, tipping her face up to meet Rose's.

The second their lips met, everything that was not Rose—the feel of her against Maji, her scent, her taste—faded away. The time between their first night and this moment disappeared. Rose's hands found her face, cupping her jaw gently as the kiss deepened. All thought stopped, Maji's brain and senses taken over by feeling, until the front door slammed.

"Hey, Frank," Angelo boomed. "You seen Ri?"

Maji jerked back to the kitchen, panting. She caught Rose's eye, and they both took a step back. It hurt, like a bandage pulled off a healing wound.

"In the kitchen," Frank answered. "But don't go in—they're making out."

Maji swore under her breath and slipped around to the end of the counter island. How could she be so out of it she didn't even know Frank had seen them? "I'm sorry," she said.

Rose had responded to Frank's words with a charming blush and a hand over her impish smile. Now she curled it into a fist under her chin, the fire in her eyes banked but not extinguished. "I broke a rule, you broke a rule. Let's call it even."

"Sounds fair to me," Angelo said from the doorway. To Rose, he added, "Give us a minute?"

Rose nodded, and stepped toward the doorway. As she passed Maji, she paused and said quietly, "And if you expect either of us to follow your rules, don't be in my room tonight."

CHAPTER TEN

Maji clipped along up the hill behind Angelo in her awkward chunky heels, struggling to keep up. Add the tight jeans, hoop earrings, makeup, hairspray, and push-up bra to the ensemble, and Maji almost missed the missions that only called for the head-to-toe drapery of the abaya, or even a burqa. They were a hell of a lot quicker to get into, at least. She touched the fake piercing on her belly button, one last check to make sure it wouldn't fall off.

"This is a little over the top, Ang. What kind of women you been bringing around?"

"None that wanted to stay and meet the folks. But trust me, one look and Gino will have no worries about you. First impressions, right?"

"Well, let's dial it back soon. Ricky's already seen me in riding gear, and we could've been seen on our run, too."

"So they'll see a scrappy kid from Brooklyn, trying to fit in. Speaking of which, bring on the moxie but remember not to push too far. Specially with Gino."

Maji grabbed his wrist before he could open the Big House's front door. "I *was* that kid, you asshole. So whatever comes out, roll with it."

Angelo led her by the hand into the dining room, where the family was already assembled. Maji recognized the women from the photos in their files. Gino's wife Paola, dressed expensively if not in particularly good taste, had added highlights to her hair recently. Nonna RoseMarie Benedetti had aged some; Sienna looked about the same, a twentysomething with the same black-black hair as her cousin but little resemblance otherwise. The slight orange cast of Sienna's spray tan clashed with her yellow top.

"'Bout time," Nonna announced. All heads swiveled toward them, looking Maji over.

"Sorry, Nonna," Angelo said, as Maji headed for the matriarch. "Everybody, Ri. Ri, everybody."

Maji leaned in toward the matriarch, extending her hand. "So nice to meetcha, Mrs. B."

The elderly woman just looked at her, owl eyed, ignoring the proffered hand. She squinted at Maji's bejeweled navel. "Your midriff is showing." She gestured toward the piercing. "Why would anyone do that to themselves?"

Angelo grabbed Maji's hand. "We'll be right back."

Behind them, Sienna's voice rang out. "Nonna!"

Angelo led Maji up the stairs to Ricky and Sienna's suite of rooms and started planting bugs. "Grab something to put on." He plucked a dress shirt off the back of a chair and flung it at her. "Here."

She sniffed it and frowned, holding it at arm's length. "Does he bathe in that crap? I'll find something else."

"No time, babe," Angelo replied, tugging on her free hand. "I gotta hit three more rooms, bing, bang, boom."

Rose looked up as the couple reentered the dining room. Maji wore a slightly sour expression and a starched white dress shirt, open down the front so that her décolletage still showed, but tied at the bottom over the offending bare skin. The smell of Ricky's cologne reached her from across the table. This woman, Rose realized, she would not have flirted with at a diner. Or invited home. Rose could almost imagine Maji as an entirely separate person than this Ri.

Gino pulled the cork on the wine bottle in his hands. "Sit already! Supper's getting cold." He bowed his head and the family followed suit, while Nonna spoke a brief prayer in Italian. All heads bobbed up at the *amen*, and for a few minutes chaos reigned, as plates circulated and competing discussions sprang up.

"Can I have some more manicotti, please?" Maji asked during a lull in the conversations. As she helped herself from the platter Angelo held, she took a moment to praise the cook, the farmers, and the house, all in Italian.

Oh, thought Rose, *there she is*. Under the tacky clothes, overdone makeup, and attitude, Maji peeked out at her.

"You speak Italian?" Nonna questioned.

"*Solo un po*," Maji replied sheepishly. "I got that line from TV. You like cooking shows?"

"No," Nonna replied, turning her full attention back to her plate.

"She loves Julia Child," Sienna said in a faux whisper, leaning across the table toward their guest.

"But you do talk Russian, right?" Gino asked. "Made some points with Khodorov."

Maji looked at him a moment before answering, then gave a half shrug. "I picked some up in Brighton Beach. Turns out Vlad and me know some people in common."

"You're from Brooklyn, huh?" Ricky asked.

"Born and raised. You?"

Sienna made a noise that Rose took to be a stifled laugh. "He's from Syosset."

Rose recalled Carlo making fun of the town as a teenager. Apparently Sienna had picked that up from him.

"I spend a lot of time in the city now. For business." Ricky sounded defensive.

Angelo smirked. "Is that what you call it?"

Ricky opened his mouth to argue, but Gino cut him off. "Where your people from, Ms. Rios?"

"I go by Ri, sir." She paused. "My folks moved to New York from Guatemala."

Rose was sure Sal Rios was from Chile. Interesting. Also, she noticed that Ri pronounced the country's name like a native, *wha-tay-mala*.

"Where?" Ricky asked.

"Guatemala," Angelo answered, using the typical American pronunciation. "You know, in Central America."

"I know where it is, smart-ass. She said it funny."

Maji gave him a look. "I said it right. Everybody else says it funny."

Gino chuckled. "Where'd you get this one again?"

"The Army, Dad," Sienna said, sounding for all the world like an adolescent. "You know, from the news."

Gino gave barely a flicker of recognition at the reminder of Fallujah. "'Course. Right. Glad you made it home okay."

Ricky openly surveyed their guest's makeup and revealing outfit. "You don't look like no GI Jane. No offense."

"She cleans up good," Angelo agreed.

Maji turned on him, but held her peace at the sound of the front door opening and closing again.

"Hello?" Angelo heard his mother call from the foyer. Frank must have made great time from the airport.

"Ma!" He stood and dashed into the living room, picking up his mother in a hug. He whispered in her ear as he set her down. "You're gonna meet my girlfriend Ri, Ma. Don't act too surprised, okay?"

She frowned, but nodded.

Angelo walked her into the dining room, arm around her shoulder. Jackie made her way around the table, giving hugs. She paused when she reached the unexpected girlfriend.

Maji extended a hand. "A real pleasure, Mrs. B—I've heard so much."

"Jackie, hon—only Nonna is Mrs B." Jackie took her hand, but pulled her in to touch cheeks, then pulled back and took a look at her. "So, I finally get to meet you."

Frank pulled out a chair for her, and she sat. He settled into the last empty spot at the long table. "Sorry we're late. Plane got delayed."

Rose passed the tray of homemade manicotti down. "I think there's a little left."

Frank chuckled, and Jackie gave her a wink.

"Wine, Aunt Jackie?" Rose asked, reaching for the bottle.

Jackie patted Rose's hand. "You are a saint, hon. And now I know where you get it."

"Aunt Bobbi cooks?" Sienna asked.

"Only if you count salads. Lots of salads," Jackie replied, wiping her mouth. "No, she showed me all about real estate, went over all the rules with me. Gonna help me get my license."

"You moving to California?" Gino asked, with a studied neutrality not lost on Angelo.

"God, no—no offense, hon," she added to Rose, taking the glass of red wine from her. "But who do I know there? I'd be starting from scratch."

Angelo gave her a skeptical look. "Ma, you gonna make a career selling houses to wiseguys?"

"Why not? I know how they think, and they got cash. They shouldn't have nice houses?"

"No, sure, I just"—Angelo paused to weigh his words—"worry about your safety, that's all."

"She's a Benedetti," Gino stated with finality. "Anybody messes with her, messes with me."

"Do me a favor, Gino?" Jackie gave him a crooked grin. "Don't do me any favors." At his affronted look she added matter-of-factly, "If I can't stand on my own feet here, I might as well move to California, am I right?"

He acknowledged this with a scrunch of the face, then raised his glass. "To the Benedetti women. The backbone of the family."

Everybody drank, while Jackie and Frank dug in.

"Frank says you've got big news," Jackie said to Gino. "What's up?"

"Just business stuff," he answered, sparing a glance at Frank. "Nothing you need to worry about."

Angelo would have preferred to tell her at home, in private, in his own way. Too late now. "She's gonna hear tomorrow, Big G. Your guests here after the memorial are sure to be buzzin'."

Gino nodded, frowning. "Suppose so." He looked at Jackie. "We've got a partnership with Khodorov. Just on the one thing, though."

Angelo suppressed a smile. Everything Gino referenced was *this thing*, or *the thing with that other Family*, or something equally oblique. It was a wonder wiseguys ever knew what they were saying to each other. Not that his mother needed anything spelled out, from the look of her. *Better duck, asshole!*

"Well, that didn't take you long. Eight months Max is gone, you're turning the business upside down." She looked ready to throw her glass of wine in his face. "One thing today, sure. Tomorrow he'll run the whole goddamn show."

Nonna tsked. "Watch your language."

"That you care about? And this is okay with you? Going against Stephano's wishes like that?"

The clock on the sideboard ticked while everyone at the table held their breath. Finally, Nonna shrugged. "It's not our worry anymore."

"The hell it's not. For all we know, it was that man killed Max and Carlo."

"Ma, the police ruled it an accident," Angelo said, taking her hand.

"Well, guys like him can buy a police report," she said. "Maybe he wanted somebody new in charge here."

"Hey," Gino said. "When you lost your husband, I lost my brother, my best friend. And Carlo, he was like the son I never had." He dropped his head briefly, a fierce look in his eyes when he lifted it again. "I find out that Russian took them from you, from us, I will make him pay. You have my word on that."

Angelo worked hard to look impressed with his uncle. *Yeah, G. He'll pay. And so will you.*

❖

Maji sat quietly at the breakfast table, sipping coffee with Frank. She'd risen early, as usual, and gone for a run. Then there'd been nothing to do but clean up and slip into the modest black dress and low heels Angelo had procured for her. She stood to put her cup in the sink and noticed Rose in the doorway from the dining room, looking elegant in a fitted black linen dress and sandals.

"You look great, hon," Frank greeted her. "Too bad you can't wear that to something happy, huh?"

Rose responded not to Frank but to Maji's puzzled look. "I got this dress for Grandpa Stephano's funeral, a few years ago. And then wore it for Max and Carlo's service last fall. Is it gauche to wear it again, so soon?"

Jackie answered from the doorway into the living room. "Anybody plays fashion police at a memorial don't deserve to be there." She swept her hands over her own outfit. "Still, whatta you think? Your mother helped me pick it out."

"It's perfect, Ma," Angelo answered, laying his hands on her shoulders, behind her. "It says, all you wiseguys, fuck off. I'm not on the market...yet."

He squeezed past her, heading for the coffeepot, pressed and polished in his Army dress green uniform.

"Oh, my," Rose gasped. "You look just like your portrait photo."

Frank stood and took the car keys from the tabletop. "Should I have worn mine?" To Maji, he added, "Max and me served together."

"No time to change now," Angelo said. "Besides, Dad never liked being reminded of 'Nam."

"Then what's with the Class As?" Maji asked. When he glared at her, she just held his gaze.

"'Cause if it was me in the ground," he said finally, "I'd appreciate the nod." Angelo pivoted on his heel and strode toward the door. The others followed.

Maji sat in the middle of the town car's wide backseat, aware of Rose to her right. In the front, a subdued Jackie rode in near silence, while Frank drove.

"You look very nice, too," Rose said softly.

Angelo responded. "Anybody asks, you helped Ri pick out her clothes."

"And tone down the makeup," Maji added.

"Who's going to ask?" Rose protested.

"My money's on Sienna," Maji replied.

"What about Sienna?" Jackie asked from the front.

"Nothing nice, Ma," Angelo confessed. "We'll cut it out."

Jackie turned in her seat to look her surviving son in the eye. "You better. And for once in your life, be civil with Ricky. Carlo was his best friend, after all."

"For you, Ma. A one-day special."

The cemetery was crowded with solo mourners and families making their Memorial Day pilgrimages.

Still, Maji was surprised at the size of the crowd around the Benedetti crypt. At least sixty men, women, and children stood in the sun on the cemetery lawn, sweating in dark clothing while the priest spoke interminably, his bald pate glistening.

Back at the Big House, the visitors spilled through the front parlor to the dining room and out the kitchen to the expansive patio. Angelo walked Maji around on his arm, introducing her as Ri to all the Family heads and their key crew members. She smiled politely each time someone trotted out the same quip about there being a quiz later.

Aunt Paola noted her more demure behavior, and commented to Jackie, "Thank God Rose took that Ri girl shopping." Her voice almost too low for Maji to catch, she added, "She could almost pass for one of us."

"Mm-hmm," Jackie agreed, reaching out to snag a glass from the passing server's tray. "I think Rose helped with the makeup, too."

Maji retreated to the kitchen, only to find Sienna already there, fishing in the freezer for ice cubes. She tried to walk quietly past, to find a moment of solitude on the patio.

"Hey," Sienna said. "Nonna's out there already."

"*Carajo.*" Maji peeked through the window and saw three white-haired heads around the patio table, backs to the house. "So, who's that with her?"

"The old guy's Arnie somebody, he used to run with Grandpa and the other guys back in the day. The other one's Gina Lucchetti. She and Nonna been friends since God was in short pants."

"Sienna!" Jackie cautioned, coming in from the dining room, Rose behind her. "The window's open."

Sienna's face didn't hide her scorn. "They're practically deaf anyway. Especially Nonna."

"Since when?"

"Since she got those new hearing aids and started turning them off all the effing time."

Jackie looked skeptical. "Well, she hears fine whenever you don't want her to. Anyway, I need a drink."

"Me, too," Rose agreed as she joined them. "You hiding out in here?"

Maji gave a weary look. "I been arm candy all I can take. You'd think Ang never brought a girl home before." Seeing the hesitation as the other women looked to each other, she asked, "What? It's okay, we broke up before Fallujah. I'm just here on, let's say, a trial basis."

"Oh." Sienna smiled at her. "Well, between you and me, he went through a few right after he got home." She stopped as if just realizing Angelo's mother was there. "Um, I think he was a little messed up there for a bit, you know, losing his dad and brother and all."

Jackie took Maji's hand. "I'm glad he's got somebody he can really talk to, finally. I hope you'll stay awhile." She took the glass Rose offered her. "Thanks, sweetie."

Rose handed Maji a glass, also. "It's just Coke. You can add rum if you want."

"Thanks. This is fine."

Rose paused, looking uncomfortable. "Maybe you could talk to Ang about his drinking?"

Nice play, Rose. Maji gave a half shrug. "Maybe me, and you, and Jackie, too."

The three clinked their glasses in solidarity, while Sienna looked on as if she didn't get it, but wasn't going to cop to that. Maji wondered how many hours would pass before Sienna found an excuse to mention it to Ricky.

Maji stripped off the little black dress and pulled on her worn blue jeans and a T-shirt, feeling more like herself by the minute. Three hours of playing Angelo's girlfriend for an audience of Mafia men and wives was about two and half hours too many. She inserted the earpiece and strapped on the clunky watch, turning the transmitter on.

There was time to clean off her makeup, too, before they had to escort Rose to the airport. As she restored her face to its normal clean look, she indulged a moment in speculating on the future. They'd wrap the mission up shortly after the Fourth of July party, and not long after that Rose should be back from Peru. Then camp would wind up, too, and…what?

Maji stared at her own face in the mirror. What Rose saw in her, she didn't know. Maybe it was just the roller coaster that had started that first night at Mona's. Maybe normal life would kill the spark. Maji watched her mouth curl at the thought. Even as a Reservist, she couldn't offer anyone a normal life. *Let her go, Rios.*

She padded down the steps and noted there were no bags by the door yet. Nobody downstairs, either. Maji went back upstairs and found Rose sitting up on her bed, reading.

"You're not packed?" Maji asked, leaning on the door frame. "Is your flight delayed?"

Rose looked embarrassed. "I won't be on it. Ang didn't tell you?"

No. Because I would kill him. She rocked back on her heels and smacked the wall outside the doorjamb. "You're staying. Here?"

Rose winced at her tone. "I'm sorry that inconveniences you. But putting holes in the wall won't help. Ang said he'd be in the basement if you wanted to talk to him."

Maji spun and jogged downstairs, slamming the door at the top of the stairs to the basement. Nobody wandering into the kitchen should hear what she meant to say to Angelo. She clicked her transmitter off, too.

"Hey," Angelo said solemnly, pushing back from his spot at the desk as she reached the bottom step.

"Are you drunk for real?" Maji spat. "It's not getting any safer here."

"I know. It's not going to be safe anywhere, soon." He paused, as if weighing how much to tell her. "I'm working with Hannah on a plan to let Sirko steal the program, without Khodorov tumbling to that fact."

Crap. Obviously, once word was out about this mythological moneymaker, Sirko would hear. And intel said what he couldn't take, he would destroy. If that made her bait, fine. "Your mother and Rose, at the very least, should go to a safe house."

Angelo shook his head. "Look, I pulled the plug on Peru because no matter how remote that village might be, Sirko could get somebody there. And even if I had the resources to protect her down there, I couldn't sleep with her so far out of reach, you know?"

"I know." The idea had made Maji a little queasy, too. But Rose here for the duration made her too scared to think straight. "But a safe house is different." Maji had hated her time in them, when her mother was under direct threat. But she'd lived to remember hating it. "Safer."

Angelo came around the desk and leaned back on it. "If we use a safe house, we have to tell the FBI."

"So? Rey is solid." She took a seat halfway up the stairs, where she could look Angelo in the eye. And watch his body language, check for what he wasn't telling her.

Angelo crossed his arms. Not a good sign. "Rey is great. But he still reports to a team, not just our folks. And you know Sirko works way too much like we do, with all those ex-Spetsnaz guys on his payroll. An FBI safe house could be an easy target."

"So use Hannah. I'll ask her!" This was his mission, and his call to make. But she had to try.

"Don't put her in that position. I already got her out on a limb, with the firewall down. Plus, she's invited Rose to camp."

"Bullshit." Rose was way too old for camp. Even if she had been a teen, she didn't fit the profile Hannah looked for.

Angelo finally smiled. "Tell me that tomorrow, after class. Now look, I got work to do."

Maji wasn't ready to be dismissed. And as much as she hated to admit it... "I can't protect her, Ang."

"Yeah. We're way too thin on the ground here. I put in a request—Dev and Tom will be here in a couple days. You can rotate watch, and they can handle Ma while you and Frank cover Rose."

Maji sighed with relief. Having the team back together—minus Palmer—would make a world of difference. And she could handle having Rose at the dojo, if that's really what Hannah wanted. But at home? "I need you to put them on Rose at home, Ang. I'll cover Jackie."

"At home you can tag-team, hon. But I'm not taking you off Rose just because you two got chemistry. I trust you to act like a professional."

"Ang," she said, irritated to feel herself flush, "don't."

"Hey, you slipped. It happens."

"Not to me. Not like that. I didn't even know Frank was in the house, much less close enough to see us." She saw from his shift in posture that he was finally really listening. Might as well come all the way clean. "And I can't promise that if we spend time alone, it won't happen again."

Angelo unfolded his arms, the better to talk with his hands. "I hear you, babe. Do your best. And be prepared to give up the rest of your privacy."

That would have to do for now. "Thanks." She stood to go, started up the stairs.

"Hey. You two really click, huh? That's kinda awesome."

Maji didn't walk down to where he could see her face. Angelo knew as well as she did why a romance now was dangerous, and would be unworkable later. "No, Ang. It's just kinda cruel."

Chapter Eleven

Camp began formally with a bow-in, all of the new students in their fresh gis. Maji had glimpsed Rose in the locker room moments before, teaching a few of the girls how to tie the stiff white belts.

After everyone was seated in a circle on the mat, Hannah gave her spiel about dojo etiquette and safety, and the daily schedule. After the instructors introduced themselves, Hannah impressed on the girls her *What's said here, stays here* rule, along with the patented answer when asked for gossip: *That's not my story to tell.*

For a moment, Maji felt thirteen again, scanning the faces of a handful of girls from exotic-sounding places and watching the black belts for some hint about what was to come. Looking around the circle at the girls today, she saw a familiar apprehension in them. Rose alone looked calm, eager to begin. Maji admired her openness. Maybe being the only adult, and having been the test student the prior week, was helpful. Or maybe she was just a great sport, in addition to being beautiful, and smart, and nice. *Move on, Rios.* Maji refocused her attention on the kids.

Maji observed while the first few students introduced themselves: Dimah, from the United Arab Emirates; next Valerie, from the Couer d'Alene Tribe; then, also from Idaho, Amber, a slight blonde whose mother "married this white supremacist creep."

Something about Amber made Maji recall Siobhan, the first girl she'd done more than kiss. Who'd gone home to Belfast after camp to help secure the Good Friday Agreement, only to lose a leg a few months later in the Omagh bombing. What price would these kids pay for the risks they'd take on, full of youthful optimism?

Maji shook the thought away, tuning back in to hear the last three girls: Martine, as dark as Amber was fair, and "proud to live outside the binary"; Bayani, a willowy youth from the Phillipines clearly trying to fit into the female binary box; and Soledad, whose family organized farm workers in California. Each of these kids would have to act as her own bodyguard, Maji thought.

As if hearing her thoughts, Rose raised her eyebrows and smiled. "I'm Rose, and I wish I'd been here at your age. But I'll do my best to keep up. I've taken a couple little self-defense classes, but never anything like this before."

Maji nodded, appreciating the relieved looks on the teens' faces. Rose had fessed up to the insecurities they all felt as strangers and first-timers there. As Hannah had noted last week, in a private moment, Rose would be an excellent student and a good example.

The rest of the morning, they worked on fighting techniques. Before beginning, Hannah illustrated on one of the Bobs some key disabling strikes—a hammer fist to a clavicle or temple, a kick to a kneecap, a hard stomp over the foot. Moves that would keep an attacker from using a weapon, hitting, grabbing, or running after them.

"The human body is surprisingly easy to break, and just knowing that you can, if you must, will change how you respond to a threat." With a nod to the instructors lined up in the one-kneed kneeling position, Hannah added, "Your body can also function as a shield."

On cue, the instructors stood up and demonstrated several techniques in slow motion, while Hannah narrated. Maji threw a punch at Bubbles's head, and Bubbles put her into a standing arm bar. Tanya grabbed Christy by the lapel, walking her backward with a menacing look on her face. Christy remained calm, and with her hand, pinned Tanya's to her chest. She made a tiny bow, and Tanya dropped to her knees, no longer able to attack. Next, Christy stood over a cowering Bubbles, pretending to punch at her head while Bubbles shielded her face from the blows. Maji walked up behind Christy and caught her arm as it rose to strike the next blow. Maji turned Christy away from Bubbles, taking her to the ground and pinning her arm behind her back. Then Bubbles handed her a prop knife, and Maji became the aggressor, moving toward Tanya and raising the knife to stab her. Christy sprang into action, entangling Maji's knife hand while she applied a choke hold to Maji's throat. When Maji slumped in mock unconsciousness, Christy kicked the knife away and pulled out a cell phone, saying, "9-1-1" as she dialed.

Rose began to clap, and the girls joined her. Hannah nodded to the instructors, who took a knee again in a silent row.

"Try to have fun with your fighting skills," Hannah said as the students settled back down. "Soon you may come to see them as the easiest ones to master. We will also develop skills at escape and evasion, verbal deescalation, creating allies, and—most importantly—how to employ sound tactical judgment."

Angelo pushed back from the kitchen table with an apologetic look. "Thanks for lunch, Ma. Wish I didn't have to get back to work."

His mother looked unimpressed. "It was bad enough, you working back office for Gino. If I'd had any sense, I'd have sent you packing after we laid Max and Carlo to rest."

Angelo put an arm around her. "I needed to be here with you as much as you needed me. And I gotta do something for a living, now I'm outta the Army."

She pulled away from him. "You left here once. You could do it again. And Gino? Jesus, how can you work for a man who would kill you if he really knew you? Hell, I can barely sit through supper with him."

"He's just a means to an end, Ma. I've done good work for Gino, and that got me connected with Khodorov, right? Next thing you know, I'll be out from under Gino for good."

"Like you're gonna be safer in Brighton Beach."

"Think bigger, Ma. Wouldn't you like to see Europe?"

She squinted up at him. "Whatever angle you're working, just promise me you'll be careful."

"Speaking of which"—he leaned down and placed a kiss on her forehead—"I gotta stop up at the Big House."

Angelo walked up the hill alone, enjoying the sunshine on his face. As he approached the formal front entry, Ricky emerged, jingling the keys to his Corvette.

"Going to work?" Angelo asked. If you could call bouncing work. Ricky would hit all the clubs, drop in on the wiseguys while they took care of actual business, and collect Gino's share of each crew boss's take for the week. Perks included free drinks and hookups with women who thought anybody that close to the *capo di tutti capi*—the boss of bosses—was sexy. Ang shoved that thought aside.

"Somebody's got to. We can't all sit on our ass playing Mr. Alco-rhythm."

"Algorithm." Angelo motioned him to move aside so that he could enter the house. "Well, don't let the door hit you on the way out."

Ricky remained a one-man blockade. "Whatcha need?"

"A word with Gino. Nothin' to concern you."

"All his business concerns me, Alco."

Angelo almost smiled, wanting to ask which smarter wiseguy Ricky had stolen the wordplay from. Instead, he pulled his best fuck-you face. "Really, Little Dick? Who promoted you to consigliere? Marrying the boss's daughter don't make you anything but Gino's bitch."

"Who the hell is it?" Gino's voice came from inside the house, before Ricky could digest the nickname or the insult. Ricky turned to answer him, and Angelo slipped by. Ricky followed on his heels.

In the parlor, Gino sat reading the paper, a short-haired tabby curled on his lap. Nonna Rose dozed by the picture window, snoring softly.

Sotto voce, Angelo asked him, "Can we talk someplace? Your office, maybe?"

Gino laid his paper aside, careful not to disturb the cat, whose ears he rubbed absentmindedly. "Ma took her hearing aid out. Here's fine."

Angelo took a seat on the edge of the couch, facing him. Ricky flopped down at the other end of it.

"Khodorov's son is coming out here to work on the program in a couple days. And he can't drive back and forth from the city all the time. So—"

"All what time?" Gino interrupted.

"While he's helping me with debugging and testing. Gonna be a lot of work, all kinds of hours."

"You ain't done already?" Ricky interjected. "You don't even know if it works?"

Angelo ignored him and spoke directly to Gino. "It will be ready. It will work just fine. The distribution deal you made with Khodorov is solid, and he knows I need the kid to give me a hand."

Gino nodded. "So what are you asking?"

"Can you spare him a room up here, in the Big House?"

Ricky sat up abruptly. "I don't want one of them under my roof!"

"Whose roof?" Gino said in his dangerously quiet tone.

Ricky looked down at his hands. "Why can't you put him up?" Ricky asked Angelo, looking at him sideways.

"I got two friends coming in, and my house is not so humongous as *yours*, Rickiopolus. Plus, I'm gonna need some downtime when Sander's not looking over my shoulder."

"More like breathing down your neck." Ricky shuddered. "Don't know how you can work with a fag."

Angelo turned to look Ricky in the eye. "Grow the fuck up, already. You think there weren't any in the Army? I can take care of myself. It's Mom's feelings I gotta respect here."

"She don't like fags, either?" Ricky asked.

Angelo sighed loudly. "No, you idiot." He looked to Gino again. "She don't want a Khodorov in her house when nobody's got an eye on him. And this is already tough on her, you know?"

Gino picked up his paper again, done with the discussion. "Send the kid to me when you want him outta your hair." He looked to Ricky. "And you—watch your mouth. Word gets to Khodorov that you're bad-mouthing his kid, it could screw up our thing with him. And I'd hate to see my daughter become a widow so young."

Ricky nodded sullenly and looked down at his overpriced sneakers.

Gino looked to Angelo as if he expected him to be gone already, having been dismissed. "You want me to talk to your mother for you?"

Angelo blushed and stood to go. "Nah, I'll handle her. Thanks, Big G."

Rose slumped in the back of the town car. When the adrenaline from her first ever scenario finally wore off, somewhere halfway through the group debrief of all six of the scenarios they had run that afternoon, she had just wanted to curl up and sleep. Drilling a technique was so much different than being thrust into a situation and having to decide how to respond, and then keep improvising until Hannah clapped for the break. Even in gis, with familiar faces all around her, it felt nauseatingly real.

"You okay?" Maji asked.

"Depends. Are we doing scenarios like that every day?"

"Nah. We'll do different scenarios. Every day." Maji paused. "It gets better. And you did fine."

Rose chuffed. "Liar. Everything I practiced went right out the window. If that had been real…"

"Yeah. You would get hurt, or break somebody, or get arrested. A stress test lets you learn about yourself with no permanent consequences."

"I learned adrenaline makes me stupid. Yay."

"Rose, we taught you how to hit in just a few days. Learning how to not hurt someone when you should be scared or angry, that takes lots and lots of practice." Maji laughed ruefully. "Hell, my first year I defaulted to hitting every fucking time. I was like Hannah's object lesson in…well, I had adrenaline and an attitude, I guess."

Rose opened one eye and squinted at her. "You? I just can't see it. How old were you?"

"That year, thirteen. Had to repeat camp three times before Hannah would let me assistant teach."

Rose sat up, smiling. "You flunked three times?"

"Bubbles is starting to rub off on you." She sounded disapproving, but her cheeks dimpled with the effort not to smile back.

"What's it like to come back now? After...everything."

Maji looked out the window for so long that Rose thought she wouldn't answer. "It's good to remember where I come from. Who I am."

True to his word, Angelo made sure Maji and Rose were not alone together at home. Not by the pool, not in the kitchen, and not in the living room after supper. He brought his laptop up and worked quietly while his mother used the dining room table to take a practice exam. When Frank left for his own apartment over the garage, Angelo excused himself, kissing his mother on the head.

"Where you going?"

"Living room. Keep Ri and Rose company."

"What, they need a chaperone?"

"Basically, yeah."

"Ang, they're grown-ups. A little kissing never killed anybody. Hell, they can't even get knocked up."

Angelo figured Rose and Maji had heard the exchange, so he answered for Rose's benefit. "Ma, Ri's my beard. Anybody but you caught them together, how would that look for me?"

She snorted. "Nobody in this family pays attention to women, Ang. You should worry more about who's watching you and that kid."

"Me and Sander? What's to see? He comes here, we work."

"Don't insult me, Ang. Go on, let me work here."

While he settled into the open armchair in the living room, Maji ignored him, and Rose glared at him silently. Undeterred, he set his laptop on the coffee table and gave her a warm smile. "So, how's camp?"

Rose blinked twice, and looked to Maji. Then she cleared her throat.

Maji finally looked up from her Russian textbook. "Tell him whatever you want, within Hannah's rules."

Rose smiled, finally. "It was amazing. I actually knew more

about striking, blocking, and falls than some of the girls. I guess I just assumed they came from martial-arts backgrounds."

"Better they don't, sometimes," Maji contributed. "No bad habits or attitudes to unteach. A clean slate like you is easier. Especially a fast learner."

Rose flushed slightly, and Angelo felt for her. After that last girlfriend had chipped away at her ego, she could use some building up. And the hot-cold treatment from Maji had to be rough. He looked to his best friend and most trusted teammate. "She's doing okay, then?"

Maji kept her face neutral, but she couldn't hide the sparkle in her eyes. "Rose fits right in." The corner of her mouth twitched with a suppressed smile. "And she has a right cross like a freight train."

"It was very nice of Hannah to make a place for me," Rose demurred. "Especially now I understand where the girls come from— who they are, and why their success matters."

Maji gave her a long serious look. "You belong at camp as much as they do. You're welcome to train as long as you want."

Rose met Maji's eyes across the room. The spark in her eyes was almost mischievous. "Good. I hadn't planned to stop."

This time, it was Maji Angelo felt bad for. He'd never seen her so affected by a woman, or trying so hard not to be. He'd thought for years that she'd like Rose. And this summer they were finally both free. He hadn't counted on them needing a chaperone, but at least he knew they clicked. And neither one would be alone when he was done here.

CHAPTER TWELVE

Rose rode home with her leg across the town car's width, her foot in Maji's lap. She fussed with the ice pack on her knee. Thursdays seemed to be the day her body cried *basta*. She grimaced when they hit a bump.

"Maybe you should take tomorrow off, hon," Frank said from the front.

"Or you could just take Thursdays off," Maji joked.

A ninja and a mind reader. Rose shook off the thought. "No way. I'd have hated to miss today."

"Yeah? What'd you learn?"

"How to scale an eight-foot wall, and then get back down—on my own." Rose said. "If I can just learn to land properly, I might actually become a ninja like Maji. I mean, Ri."

"S'okay," Maji assured her. "Nobody's got a bug in the car. Right, Frank?"

"I'm still checking every time I get back in. Promise."

"Thanks." Maji turned partway, the better to look Rose in the eye. "If you need a day off, Dev or Tom can cover you."

"And give you a break. No, don't be nice, everyone needs one sometimes. But you'll have to take yours on weekends, because I'm not missing a minute of camp."

"If the swelling's not down by morning, you will. We'll get you an MRI. Wouldn't hurt to have Dev look at it when he gets in tonight."

"He's a doctor?"

"Field medic. Next best thing."

"Dammit, anyway. I had a special meal planned to welcome them."

Maji frowned. "Look, the last thing I need is you waiting on those two—you'll undo years of effort on my part. No, we'll cook for you tonight. Right, Frank?"

"Damn straight."

"Anyway," Maji continued, "you should put your leg up. I promised Hannah to keep you off your feet."

Rose raised an eyebrow at the double entendre, and Maji flushed.

As the town car pulled up in front of the garage, Rose goggled at two Humvees that dwarfed it.

"Looks like we got company," Frank noted.

Maji shook her head. "Oh, for God's sake." Apparently, this wasn't what she'd expected her friends to arrive in.

"Wow," Rose breathed, as they passed the giant hunks of steel and chrome with rugged-looking tires as tall as her waist. "There's no other word for it. They're obscene."

"Mmm," Maji concurred.

Inside, they followed the low murmur of deep voices down the hall and into the living room.

"Hey! You parked in my spot," Maji announced to the back of the couch and its occupants.

Two men, a study in contrasts, popped up from the couch with a whoop, whirled, and beelined to her. The short one, built like a fireplug, took the land route. The other, a full head taller and slender with the wide shoulders and narrow hips Rose found quite attractive on a man, simply stepped over the back of the couch. He got the first hug in, only to be elbowed aside by his counterpart.

"Jesus, Mary, and Joseph," the fireplug with a crewcut muttered, rocking Maji from side to side with him. "You promised to eat more, Ri."

"Good to see you, too, *akhi*." My brother.

The tall, dark, and handsome one waited for Maji to extract herself, his feet planted shoulder-width apart and hands clasped loosely in front of him. He smiled politely at Rose.

Rose extended a hand to him. "Rose diStephano. You must be Angelo and Ri's friends." She caught the relieved look in Maji's eyes and her hint of a nod, before Mr. Runway responded.

"Devadutt Goldberg." He shook Rose's hand politely.

"And this one's Tom Taylor," Maji said, her arm now around the stocky man's waist.

Tom stepped forward with a hand extended. "Ma'am."

"Rose," she corrected him warmly and found herself pulled into a hug. When she stepped back, her knee shot pain up and down her leg, and she flinched.

Frank moved from the doorway. "I'll get you some ice, hon." As he went through to the kitchen, he said to the newcomers, "Name's Frank. Thanks for coming, guys."

"You break another one, Rios?" Dev asked with a deprecating look.

Maji glared up at him. "Don't go there, dude." She looked at both men. "Let's get you oriented."

Maji took Tom and Dev on a jog around the compound, pointing out security features and weaknesses of the property. They asked appropriate questions about wall heights, blind spots, adjoining properties, video monitoring, other guards. She was pleased to see they could hold a conversation at a reasonable trot.

"Mrs. Benedetti looks to be a handful," Tom noted, when Maji asked how they planned to split their detail on her protection.

"We should just about keep up with her, with two of us," Dev agreed.

"How's that Frank guy for backup? You need us to rotate in?" Tom asked.

"Nah, Rose is cooperative. I got her covered."

"How come Ang always assigns the single ladies to you, Rios?" Dev asked. "We all know they're safer from my charms than yours."

"Oh, I bet he's counting on your winning ways to soften Jackie up. You are more her type."

Tom laughed. "I'll remind her you're married, big guy. I got your back."

As they headed downhill from the far side of the Big House and the Hummers came into view, Maji slowed to a walk. "What are we, fucking Blackwater? You couldn't get a Jimmy, a Tahoe, a Navigator? An effing Escalade, even?"

"Nope. It's what we sell, dude," Dev responded.

"We?"

"Mira's folks, and now me, I guess. They have a dealership in Jersey. Hummers, Fords, and VWs."

"How eclectic."

"And we rent out the up-armored models. Got a fleet of six."

Tom added, "Anyway, they were available on short notice. Like us. And Ang liked the idea."

"'Course he did." The paramilitary vibe, the high visibility. Like wannabes, taking themselves too seriously to be real professionals. "Has he got uniforms for you, too?"

"Not so far as we know," Tom replied. "And don't you dare suggest it."

They finished the welcome tour with a cooldown walk around Angelo's house. Maji pointed out the perimeter security, including the upstairs escape routes and the bars on the basement windows.

"Ri, that consultant, the one who JSOC tapped into all your missions?" Tom asked.

"Cohen, yeah. What about her?"

"Angelo says she's in town for this one. You think that means we'll finally meet her?"

"Maybe. Rose is taking classes with her."

"The classes you're teaching? Then you've met her already. What's she like?"

Maji glanced sideways at him. "Quiet. Nice enough, I guess. Short."

In the world of elite security services and private military contractors, Hannah's firm was one of the best regarded. The kind of outfit where a Special Forces vet would want to work. And a covert ops specialist? Well, working anywhere else in the private sector would be a waste of their skills.

Dev stopped, looking at her skeptically. "Short? Like, shorter than you?"

Tom shot him a warning look. "So, maybe you could introduce us sometime? If we happened to drop by class, or something."

Propped up by the kitchen window, keeping Frank company, Rose heard the question and listened for the answer.

"You here for the mission, or here to audition?" Maji's voice replied, sharp and clipped. Rose could imagine the hard look her face took on when she was pissed off.

"Hoo-ah," the duo responded quietly, in unison.

"Then cut the fanboy crap," Maji said.

The kitchen door opened, and the three traipsed in, shirts sticking to their torsos.

"Hey." Maji nodded at her. "We'll be back in ten to help down here." To the guys, she said, "I'll show you where the showers are. Then we're on KP."

Rose caught the two men grousing as they walked toward the stairs. But it sounded playful, and so did Maji's tone. She wondered what it was like to hold your own in the Army's boys' club. Maybe camp would give her a chance to ask. The more she knew, the more she wanted to learn.

❖

Angelo paced in the kitchen, checking his watch as if he could make it change time.

"I'm sure he's fine," Tom said. "Probably caught in traffic."

"On a Friday morning? No, he shoulda been here by now."

"Who?" his mother asked, making a direct line for the coffeepot as she joined them.

He considered waiting to answer until she'd had her first cup. What the hell. "Sander Khodorov. He's going to be working here with me."

She set the pot down by her cup, with her ready-to-fight face on. "He's a nice kid, really."

Angelo watched the wheels in her head turn as she drank down half her mug of coffee in a hostile silence. Tom sat silently at the table.

Finally she spoke again. "He's not staying the weekend?"

"No, Ma. Just getting set up today. Next week he'll stay up at the Big House."

"Don't tell me that was Gino's idea. Not if he knows the kid is... you know."

"The whole world knows." Angelo considered telling her about him and Sander. No, too soon. "I asked him to put Sander up, as a favor to me. Give us both a break sometimes."

Her face lost its hard edge. "You sure that's a good idea? We could make space down here if—"

A rattle of the knob on the front door, followed by an impatient knock, interrupted her. Tom stood and turned to go answer it, looking briefly to Angelo.

"If it's Sander, let him in," Angelo instructed. The rest went unspoken.

Tom opened the front door, while Angelo listened from the kitchen, shushing his mother. "You Ricky Antonopolus?"

"Who wants to know?" Ricky sounded, as Angelo expected, deeply annoyed.

"Tom Taylor," Angelo heard Tom say, and pictured him politely offering his hand, a human blockade with manners.

"Who is it, Tommy?" Jackie called from the kitchen.

"Ricky, ma'am. To see Angelo."

"Hold on," Jackie yelled toward the foyer. She glared at Angelo, whispering, "Why do you always mess with him?"

Ang kissed his mother on the cheek and shrugged. "Can't resist."

Tom and Ricky stood in the foyer, watching each other silently.

"Thanks, Tom," Angelo said, with a toss of his head toward the kitchen. Tom nodded and walked through the door, out of sight.

"What?" Angelo asked.

"I need their IDs. To run backgrounds."

Angelo crossed his arms over his chest. "They're my friends. I vouch for them."

"Gino don't know them. Just give me three IDs, for God's sake. Why you gotta bust my balls over every little thing?"

"Because you waste my time on stupid shit. You wanna know who they are? Go check your Google. *American soldiers held captive in Fallujah.* Then run whatever you want. I'm going back to work."

Angelo turned to leave, but stopped when Ricky said, "Hey. I already did that. Your girlfriend don't look right."

Angelo spun back and smacked Ricky on the back of the head, enough to sting. "She spent months in the hospital, you asshole. She may not look like she did before, but she looks just fine. I hear you say anything around her, I will break your fucking jaw. We clear?"

Ricky opened the door with one hand, rubbing his head with the other. "Shit. I didn't mean it like that. She just looks different, that's all." He stepped out, then stuck his head back in. "Ang?"

"What?"

"Is the other guy gonna show up? The blond one?"

Angelo saw through the open doorway the towheaded Russian getting out of his car. "Who? Sander?"

"No, you idiot. The other guy that got took with you."

Angelo sighed. "No, Rick. Palmer was killed. Next time, read the words that go with the pictures."

"Hey," Sander said and beeped his car lock with the key fob.

Ricky flinched. "Jesus! Don't sneak around like that." He backed away from the door, leaving Sander ample room to enter the house. "You could get hurt."

"I'll keep your razor-sharp reflexes in mind," Sander said, a smile in just his eyes as he glanced at Angelo. "Ready to work?"

"Yeah. Let me show you the office, and then I'll take you up to the Big House," Angelo offered. He looked at Ricky. "His room's ready, right?" He took the shrug as a confirmation. " ' Kay, then. See ya."

As the door closed behind him, Sander asked, "What's with him?"

Angelo rolled his eyes. "He's not allowed to hit you. And he's afraid to like you. It hurts his brain."

❖

Rose tied on an apron and started pulling supper ingredients from the fridge. Her knee felt fine, thanks to ice and an easy day at the dojo. Each of the teens she partnered with had reminded her to be careful, and Hannah herself had checked for swelling and range of motion at lunch. Rose had promised to rest and recover all weekend.

If she tried, she could imagine tonight as just a Friday evening at home with friends. Practically normal, except for the armed guards at the gatehouse. And in the driveway, those ridiculous Humvees. As nice as Tom and Dev seemed, it was hard to forget why they were here.

"Hey," Maji said from behind her.

Rose nearly dropped the bundle of asparagus. She swore and spun around. "Do you have to do that?"

"Do what?"

Rose sighed. "I'm sorry. I guess I need a weekend off from play danger in the dojo and real danger at home."

"Yeah. Me, too." Maji looked weary. "You really want to cook for a crowd tonight? We didn't poison you last night, we could do it again." Some sparkle returned to her eyes.

"No, I need this. It helps me relax."

"Well, your sous-chef's lounging around with your lazy-ass cousin," Maji said with a little up nod toward Angelo and Frank by the pool. "May I help?"

Rose gave a passing thought to Maji's language. She had perfect, polite academic English whenever she chose, and a tendency to slip little words or phrases in that connected her with whomever she was speaking with. Without seeming like she was mimicking them. Was that part of being a linguist? Or was it uniquely Maji? She brushed the distraction away. "Sure. Start by picking some music."

Maji plucked Rose's iPod out of its speaker base and scrolled through the offerings. "Nora Jones Prozac soothing, or Buena Vista Social Club?"

"Not that mellow, and not Cuban, please." Rose didn't want to think about the big party coming up. Not tonight.

"Okay. Brazil it is."

The playful rhythms and silky sound of Portuguese being sung while they worked quietly together unwound the tightness in Rose's chest. Maji chopped in time to the music and softly sang along, seeming to taste the words as they left her mouth. Rose realized with a little tremor that if this were a normal summer, and they were alone tonight, dinner would never make it into the oven. Maji looked up and smiled, and Rose wondered if she was thinking the same thing.

"So," Rose said, more brightly than she meant to, "Ang says you two are going out tomorrow night."

The private smile vanished. "Date night."

"Ouch, *cara mia*." Angelo spoke through the screen door, before letting himself in to join them. "Don't sound so excited."

"At least take her somewhere nice," Rose said. "Like Brio." The little hidden gem of a restaurant on the North Fork served only seasonal fare from the local farms and fish caught from the Sound that same morning. She pictured sharing a table for two with Maji, looking out at the water together, knees touching under the tablecloth.

"Not Ri's speed," Angelo responded. "Anyway, nobody's watching where we go. All that counts is we do."

Maji cut him a sideways look. "And you get out of going bouncing with Ricky."

In reply to Rose's questioning look, Angelo explained, "He wants to drag me around to the clubs to brag about the great deal with Khodorov. I told him I had to take my girl out, keep her happy since she's stuck here. So he thinks I'm pussy-whipped, but so what?"

"I hate that expression," Rose said. "So where to, then?"

He grinned. "I was thinking Mona's Dive-In. You want to join us?"

Maji stood to look him in the eye and fired off a string of guttural sounds that could only have been a series of objections in Arabic.

Angelo put a hand on Maji's shoulder and said gently, "Babe, let her go out while she still can. We'll take security." To Rose he added, "'Course, it would look better if you had a date, too."

Bubbles sprang to mind. "I think I can manage that."

Maji looked around the table at the odd new normal. Her team—what was left of it—hanging out in a suburban kitchen, joking and enjoying a great meal. Two nights in a row. It reminded her of dinners at Dev's house on Fort Bragg, passing platters of his wife's amazing Ayurvedic dishes. She wondered how Dev felt about being on assignment here, out of contact while so close. "How are Mira and the girls doing?"

Dev looked up from his plate. "Great. They love Jersey."

Rose jumped in. "Angelo says you're in the Reserves now."

"Yep, a weekend warrior. Sweeter than I could have guessed."

Maji blinked in surprise. Dev was a top operator. "Regular Reserves? Really?"

"Really. Finally got to move back to New Jersey. Mira was sick of living on base, and now the girls have their grandparents right next door."

Well, maybe now he'd go to med school. "How long you been out?"

"Twenty-six days." Longer than either of them had ever spent at Fort Bragg between ops. "Don't worry, I'm still in fighting shape. Ma'am."

Maji bet he would rather be with his family right now, catching up. But any one of them would have dropped everything and come, for Angelo. A look passed among the four surviving teammates.

Rose looked to Tom. "And what about you? Are you in the Reserves now, too?"

"Me? No. I'm just on leave. I always wanted to see Long Island. The way Angelo talked it up, I was expecting surfer girls and clambakes on the beach." He laughed, and the rest of the table smiled with him.

"Classic bait and switch," Jackie said, patting Angelo's hand as if she was proud of him for it.

Rose turned to Maji. "And you?"

"Select Reserves," Angelo answered for her.

"Same-same, only different," Dev offered.

Rose looked quizzically at him. But he simply looked at Maji. *Thanks, dude.*

"Same idea," Maji said. "One weekend a month of training, plus two weeks once a year."

"But they can call her up at any time," Tom added. Maji cringed inwardly.

"Any time? As in, they could just call you tomorrow, while you're here? No matter what you're doing, where you're working? No matter that you have commitments?"

"Theoretically," Maji admitted. When she had been on the team, they had often deployed with just a few hours' notice. She hoped to get the luxury of a few days' notice once she officially started in her new status.

Angelo smiled at Rose. "Don't worry, babe. She'll be here."

Rose frowned at him, looking annoyed. "That's not what I meant. It's just…that's a lot to ask, isn't it? People have jobs, and families. Why be a Reservist at all, if you can't count on being at home?"

"Free baggage check," Maji deadpanned.

"What?"

Tom smiled. "Select Reserves get active duty perks."

"Half off at Great Adventure," Maji added.

Dev rolled his eyes. "Second Tuesday of every month."

Tom puffed up, suppressing a grin. "Thank you for your service."

"We support our troops!" Angelo proclaimed, with air quotes.

Jackie shook her head. "You kids."

Chapter Thirteen

Mona showed the party of four past the *Closed for Private Party* sign into a room with tables, but no patrons, and a jukebox. "You expecting anybody else, sweetie?" she asked Maji.

"No. But Tom on the front door and Dev out back could use some supper. Thanks." Maji paused. "Mona, this is Rose DiStephano, from the other night."

Mona covered her mouth, then beamed at Rose. "Of course! Thank you for coming back here, hon."

"We promised her a mocha shake," Bubbles offered.

Maji rolled her eyes. "And this is Rose's cousin, Angelo."

"Hey," he said, offering his hand. "Thanks for hosting us. I know it's a lot to ask on a Saturday night."

"For these two, anything," she said, then turned back to Maji. "Thank God you're home safe." She stepped back, blinking hard, and cleared her throat. "Lemme grab some menus."

After they ordered, Angelo fed the jukebox, and the sound of "Bad Moon Rising" filled the room. Bubbles paced over to the jukebox, gave it a bump with her hip, and punched in a new selection, "La Bamba."

She sat back down and said to Rose with a smile, "That's better. Thanks for inviting me."

When Mona came back with their orders, she rolled the cart of plates and pitchers up to the table. Bubbles and Maji got up to help, handing out plates. When the cart was empty, Mona gave Angelo an odd look and shook her head. "I'm sorry, hon. I just keep thinking I know you from somewhere."

Angelo scrunched up his face as if caught out. "I'm a Benedetti. I hope it doesn't bother you, my coming around your place." Surprised, Rose felt a little sorry for him.

"Oh, sweetie. My mother's a Mormon, married a Hell's Angel.

Everybody's welcome here." She rounded on Maji. "But if you two served together…"

Maji held up one finger to pause her. She clicked her watch's listen-only function, and waited while Angelo did the same. "Go ahead," she said. "Fallujah, right?"

"I hate to even ask. I been dying to know, but I didn't want to ask Hannah, add to her worries."

Maji took her hand. "It's okay." She breathed in, and let it out. "It was me. The Army played with my name and photo to give me some privacy and keep Mom out of the headlines."

"Oh, honey!" Mona pulled Maji from her chair, into a hug. When she stepped back, she wiped both eyes. "Your poor parents. I can't imagine. How they doing?"

"Really good. I'll give them your best."

Mona excused herself, and Maji looked around the table. "Sorry."

Before Rose could reassure her, Angelo threw his hands up in frustration. "Jesus, babe. Why even have a cover?"

"I told you, Ang." Maji's eyes were cold. "People around here know my name, know my family. From before."

"Before the Army?" Rose asked, sure she was missing some vital piece.

Bubbles shook her head. "Before those jackasses put a price on her mom's head."

"Hey!" Angelo looked almost frightened.

Bubbles scowled at him. "Rose is bound to hear. And it's nothing to be ashamed of. Besides, we look out for them. Maji is safe here."

Maji shrugged, at Angelo. "Bubbles is right."

Angelo leaned back, his arms crossed. "And you want her to know."

"It's not classified," Maji said, coloring. "And if she keeps coming to the dojo, she'll hear it from someone else."

When Angelo finally nodded, Rose asked, "Well?"

"My mother is Neda Kamiri," Maji said simply.

A faint buzzing filled Rose's ears. Bubbles took her hand. "Hey, you okay? Drink something."

Rose drank, thinking of Nobel Peace Prize coverage, Dr. Kamiri's picture on the cover of *Time*, the excitement on campus when the renowned professor came to speak to a packed hall of admirers. The security teams and local police struggling with crowd control. And that story about the attack on the UN, alleging Dr. Kamiri was the target.

Maji's mother must be in danger all the time, thanks to her high-profile work. "I'm so sorry," Rose managed at last.

Bubbles sprayed soda across the table, hitting Maji, who caught her friend's eye and burst out laughing. While the two dissolved in giggles, Rose and Angelo looked across the table at each other.

"Worst fangirl ever," Bubbles gasped, tossing napkins to Maji, who patted herself dry with them while she caught her breath.

"Oh, I didn't mean..." Rose started. "That is, of course I admire her work. It's just—"

Maji waved her apology aside. "S'okay. Refreshing, actually." She lifted her watch wrist and nodded toward Angelo. "We can move on now, though."

"Wait!" Rose blurted. "The guys don't know?"

Angelo shook his head. "Nope. It's not a state secret or anything, but it's private, you know?"

"Of course," Rose said, and turned to Maji. "Your story to tell, as Hannah would say."

Rose settled into a shaded spot by the pool and surrounded herself with the Sunday *Times*, two research papers she'd been asked by colleagues to peer-review, and two paperback romances she'd packed on a whim.

Maji appeared in flip-flops, cutoffs, and a large man's shirt tied in a loose knot at the waist. She picked the chair on the other side of the café table, and laid her laptop and Russian textbook down. "You want anything? Iced coffee? Water?"

"Water, thanks." Rose gave her what she meant to be a polite smile. "Will you swim today?"

"Can't," Maji answered, and drew back the left side of her shirt to reveal a handgun tucked into a stretch band over her ribs. "I'm packing."

Before Rose could respond, she saw Maji wince. Then she looked away and spoke to someone unseen. "Yeah, hilarious. Now, grow the fuck up, all three of you." She gave Rose a long-suffering look. "Now they're explaining the joke to your aunt."

Which meant Frank was hearing the guys' snickering explanation of the double entendre, too. Rose flushed.

Then Maji laughed and broke into a grin. "Jackie told Dev, and I quote, *Only in your wettest dreams, hon.*" She waited for Rose to smile back, then went inside for the drinks.

Maji returned in record time and handed her a sweating glass of ice water. "Frank'll be at his place, if we need him."

Rose nodded, relieved he'd chosen not to carry the drinks out himself. She was mildly surprised when Maji sat and said, "Guys, I'm going listen-only," then frowned at the reply. "You wanna listen to me practice Russian the next couple hours?…Thought not. Rios out." She pressed a finger to her watch and relaxed into the lounge chair. "Summer with the boys. How'd we get so lucky?"

Rose was pretty sure the question, spoken toward the sky, was rhetorical. There were questions she wanted to ask Maji about her mother, her childhood, everything. But just because she'd shared the secret didn't mean Maji wanted to indulge her curiosity. Or did she? Feeling cowardly, Rose held the paperbacks toward Maji. "I haven't read these, but there might be some hilarious packing in one of them."

"It's not so hilarious in real life, just awkward. But maybe it was the whole drag thing. I've never been able to take myself seriously in drag."

Rose blushed. "You've gone out as a man? Complete with the…" She swept her hand along her thigh.

"That was a special case. I very briefly dated a woman who was really into it. Didn't hurt to try, but I couldn't keep it up, pardon the pun." Maji looked a little sheepish. "Just wasn't me." She paused. "You?"

"Me?" Rose squirmed under Maji's direct gaze. *And she's not even flirting.* "Um, no. Never really saw the point."

Maji shrugged. "I hear you." She looked over the book titles and handed one back. "This one's good. Given enough suspension of disbelief."

Rose blinked. Maji never failed to surprise her. "Doesn't the genre rely on that?"

"Not more than most. Maybe the happily-ever-after part. But what I meant was, this one has a smoking-hot thirty-five-year-old virgin."

Rose laughed. "Okay, that's a stretch. Unless you mean, didn't figure out she was gay until then. I've met women who swear that was true for them. I can't imagine it myself, but you have to take people at their word, don't you?"

A cloud passed over Maji's face, and she opened her laptop without responding. Rose surmised the strange, frank discussion was over. She watched Maji log in, then reach for the companion textbook, and notice Rose watching her.

Rather than look away, Rose asked, "We're off air, right?"

"Listen-only. Yeah." Maji looked at ease, her face neutral.

"Was there more you wanted to say about your mother last night?"

A shadow of Maji's amusement at supper peeked out. "Not especially. You curious about the real woman behind the hyperbolic headlines?"

"Yes," Rose admitted. "But…I don't want to intrude."

"Well, she buys the designer suits off the rack, and they're never gifts, despite what the tabloids say," Maji started. "And it pisses her off that what she wears makes the news more than what she says, publishes, or stands for."

"Wow. Is that what fangirls want to know?"

Maji gave a half shrug. "Now you see why Bubbles said you weren't good at it. Seriously, though, whatcha got? Ask now, because this isn't casual talk for home or the dojo."

"I do understand." Rose pulled her thoughts together. "Okay. She must travel a great deal. Was that hard on you?"

"As a kid? Not really. She always kept her teaching schedule at Columbia, only did speaking tours during school breaks. And the UN's right in town."

"I heard her talk once, when I was an undergrad—*Farming as Feminism*. Actually, that had a lot to do with my decision to focus on women's role in food production and the preservation of traditional foods." Maji seemed to be waiting for another question, so Rose asked, "What about you? Why linguistics? It seems a little arcane for someone who got expelled from several schools. Or was Bubbles pulling my leg?"

Maji chuckled. "No, Doc. Bubbles doesn't play games, any more than you do. I had to get my GED before I could enroll in college."

Hearing Maji use the girls' nickname for her made Rose smile. "So? Linguistics? I don't know much about the field, except what one hears of Noam Chomsky."

"He's a generativist, I'm more a congnitivist. Ask me about that when you can't sleep sometime. All that came later, anyway. Mostly I just kept learning new languages because they didn't bore me."

Rose laughed. "Okay. How so?"

"Well, to really absorb a new language, you have to get inside the head of people who speak it. You pick up geography, history, food of course, and how they think about the world. It's so much more than vocabulary and grammar."

Rose found herself momentarily speechless. Maji was so much more than she seemed. "Your mother must be very proud of you."

Maji's expression clouded. "She'd rather I was an academic, like you." She grimaced. "I'm sorry. Teaching is cool. You might just inspire the next Vandana Shiva. Or be the next wave yourself."

Rose flushed. "I doubt that. But thank you."

For her second Sunday supper with the family, Maji toned her Ri look down a bit. Not so much as the tasteful memorial outfit, but enough to show she was trying to fit in.

Sienna, at least, was sold. "Gawd, I love that top!" she exclaimed, grabbing the fabric on Maji's sleeve. "You find it around here? I can't find anything in the Hamptons that isn't for, you know, the golf set."

While the antipasto steadily disappeared, Sienna tried several times to get Maji and Rose to go out with her—mani-pedis, the spa on Montauk, maybe shopping in the city. Maji dodged each idea, giving Angelo a more pointed look each time. Finally, she said, "Ang? A little help here?"

"What?"

"Your cousin's gonna think we don't like her," she said to him. "Which isn't true," she assured Sienna. "This just isn't a good time to be going out around town, with Ang's thing heating up. Right, Ang?"

Angelo looked uncomfortably between his girlfriend and his uncle. "We don't talk business at the table, babe."

"What you're doing on that computer all day and night, who cares?" Maji shot back. "I'm talking about you saying we can't go out." She gestured to Jackie and Rose and herself. "When clearly everybody in *this* house can. So?"

Maji noticed Jackie training her attention on Gino, and Gino's color rise from under the collar of his dress shirt. Ricky's face took on a familiar smug cast as he said, "Your boyfriend's just overestimating his importance, as usual. Thinks his thing is bigger than all our normal things put together."

"For a guy with a nickname like Little Dick," Maji said slowly, "you really leave yourself open, you know?"

Sienna snorted again, and Rose just stared.

"Enough with the pissing contest," Gino growled. "Ang's Army buddies are welcome here, if they make him feel better."

"So, what's with the muscle at the gate?" Jackie asked Gino. "I thought everybody was happy, now you and that Russian are tight."

Maji watched Angelo pass a look to Gino, who lifted one shoulder and an eyebrow—permission to speak. "Khodorov's not the issue,

Ma. Except, he's kind of a big deal, with big-time competitors. And they don't play by the rules we're used to." He paused and gave an unconvincing smile of reassurance. "Dev and Tom are combat vets, Ma. They've seen action our guys aren't used to. I just feel better having them watch your back. Okay?"

"Daddy," Sienna whined, "even my girlfriends are talking about Ang's thing." She caught herself, and blushed. "So why don't Mom and me have bodyguards?"

"Who's talking business with your girlfriends?" Gino demanded.

Sienna looked at him from under lowered lids. "They don't know any more than I do. They're fishing." She turned to Maji and explained. "Wiseguys are the worst gossips. 'Course they got their girls asking me. Like I know any more than you."

Gino sighed, and turned to Ricky. "Pick a couple guys and reassign them. Starting tomorrow."

Chapter Fourteen

Shouldn't I be with the bicycle gang?" Rose asked Maji, looking past her to the girls on their bikes by the SUNY Stony Brook student union. It was empty of students now, just as the big upper campus parking lot was empty of cars—except for Frank's town car and the county patrol car, a white sedan with blue and orange stripes down its length and a rack of lights on its roof.

Maji looked at her quizzically.

"Well, when am I going to be behind the wheel of a car here, with you and Frank always chauffeuring me around?"

Maji tilted her head and adjusted the holster under her left arm. "If Frank and I were both down, you might need the kind of driving we're going to train on today." She smiled and added, "Or it could be handy any normal day around LA. Even for a California driver like you."

Rose appreciated Maji's attempt to divert her from the first, chilling possibility. But she couldn't bring herself to joke back. "I see."

Maji turned toward Frank and a tall, walnut-brown woman wearing the police uniform of black shoes and slacks and short-sleeved shirt.

Rose couldn't see the officer's eyes through her dark sunglasses, but she seemed at ease, her hands lightly clasped in front of her, away from the bulky utility belt with its gun and radio and God knew what else.

"Frank and Officer Barnwell will be assisting you today," Maji said. "Frank, tell us about your car, please."

Frank nodded to her. "Well," he started, "it's a standard model Lincoln, with some mods. V8 engine, tweaked for quicker takeoff from zero. Shocks and struts are souped-up, brakes get changed out at fifty percent. Inside's reinforced for rolling, so's it don't crush anybody. And all compartments got airbags, except the driver. I gotta be able to hit something and still keep going."

Barnwell nodded thoughtfully. "A more comfy equivalent of my Interceptor."

"What else, Frank?" Maji asked, patting the roof of the sedan.

"Oh, um. It's up-armored. Anything under fifty caliber'll just make a dent. You could still blow it up, but bullets aren't worth much against it."

Rose noticed Officer Barnwell's eyebrows lift above the top edge of her shades, and that she made no more comparisons to the patrol car. At least not out loud. She took off her sunglasses to look Rose in the eye. "Ever been in a high-speed chase before?"

Rose shook her head.

"You will not be asked to drive like this," Maji said. "But it will make what we teach you feel easier."

Frank opened the front passenger door for Rose and handed Maji his keys.

"How long will this last?" Rose asked, swallowing hard.

"Couple minutes, max," Maji reassured her. She showed her how to brace against the passenger door and started up the engine. Sliding her window halfway down, Maji put her left hand out and gave Barnwell the ready signal. The patrol car sprinted off as Maji's window slid back up, and with a lurch the heavy car tore off after it. Maji wove between the cones, swerving without braking, following the lead car closely, fishtailing on the corners. Rose tried to relax and breathe as the car's g-force pinned her to the door and then let her loose, then pinned her again, the view through the window streaking by. Now and then, a sound escaped her, somewhere between a squeak and a grunt.

"All right?" Maji spoke loudly over the roar of the engine, keeping her eyes on the course.

Rose nodded dumbly, then tried her voice. "Just great."

Maji's smile was kind. "Almost done."

Barnwell's patrol car pulled smoothly off the course, and Maji decelerated at last, then braked hard and threw the car into a tailspin. She rolled both windows down and turned to Rose. "You okay?"

Rose heard the concern, with not a hint of patronizing. She nodded. "Give me a minute."

Maji came around and held the door for Rose, offering her a hand. Rose accepted the help and stood with a hand on the hot roof of the town car to steady herself, feeling queasy. Frank came trotting over with a cold bottle of water, twisted the cap off, and handed it to Rose.

❖

From behind the wheel, Rose found the town car heavy, but eager to leap forward and solid on the hard stops. Maji talked her through the basic drills, clear and direct with the instructions, and quick with a word of encouragement. Rose struggled to overcome the instinct to brake when approaching an obstacle, to instead swerve around it while maintaining control of the vehicle. But, with repetition and Maji's assurance that she really was getting the hang of it, Rose came to enjoy the maneuver.

After a particularly good run, Maji joked, "Look out, California." Rose laughed with her, giddily triumphant.

In comparison, hard stops felt easy after that and backing up at preposterous speeds was actually fun. Rose found herself surprised when lunch break was called. "Already?"

Maji grinned. "Just like that. How's your stomach?"

Rose realized she had stopped feeling queasy as soon as she took the wheel. "Fine. Ooh, and hungry!"

"Excellent. Get plenty to drink, too—you're going to be on a bike next."

But instead of putting her into the bicycle group, Hannah walked Rose to a cool spot under a big-leaf maple where Maji's motorcycle and one almost its twin stood parked in the shade.

"Oh no," Rose protested. "I don't even like being a passenger."

Hannah *hmm*ed. "Still, I would like you to experience what it is like to be the one in control. Will you try?"

How could she say no? "Please tell me there won't be a high-speed chase."

Maji laughed behind them, approaching with Frank, each of them with a jacket and helmet in their hands.

Rose put the jacket on, surprised by how light it felt. The hard pads in the elbows and back made her feel like a gladiator, but she didn't swelter as expected. Hannah showed her how to secure the helmet and made sure the built-in radio was working.

Astride the bike, Rose's sneakered feet just touched flat on the ground. Learning to power-walk was simple, a matter of controlling the anxious throttle. With all the controls at her hands, following Maji smoothly around the course was easier than she expected, and stopping much like being on a bicycle. As they worked up to slaloms and turns, Rose forgot her anxiety. The quiet machine followed her body as she looked and leaned, as instructed, wherever she wanted to go next.

"Where the head goes, the body follows," she said to herself in quiet wonder.

A chuckle in her headphone startled her. "Just like in the dojo," Maji agreed.

"Sorry," Rose said. "I forgot we were on radio."

"No worries," Maji said. "More fun than you expected, huh?"

"I will admit to that only if you promise never to tell my mother."

"Deal."

Angelo could hear Frank chatting with Hannah, through the comm. He got up and stretched, asked Sander if he needed more coffee, and went up to the kitchen. Switching the master controls so that only Frank could hear him, he asked, "Frank, you and Hannah alone there?"

"Yup."

"Okay. Ask her, did she get to listen to my message." Angelo had sent a brief recording with Frank, explaining how the sleeper virus would redistribute the funds sucked out of the targeted bank accounts. Millions of ordinary citizens and hundreds of nonprofits would wake up to find money from an untraceable source in their accounts, like a surprise lottery win. It was simple, and elegant.

"Hold on," Frank said. Angelo heard murmuring, then Frank's rendition of Hannah's words. "She says, can you really write code that complicated, on your own."

Angelo smiled. She was in. "Tell her I wrote it, tested it, and know it works."

"She says you have the green light to continue. And she'll arrange to meet with you in person soon."

"Great. Thanks, Frank. I'm gonna go back to open channel now. And this little talk never happened, got it?"

"Oh, okay. Wait—she's got one more thing. Oh, wait. She wants my earpiece."

Uh-oh. What could Hannah not say through Frank? "Hello, Angelo," Hannah said.

"Hey. You got a concern?" He'd been so close.

"Maji."

He breathed again. "I know how to keep her insulated." Keeping Gino and Khodorov from assigning any blame to her would be fairly simple. And they had already discussed how to keep JSOC from coming down on her.

"That's not my concern," Hannah said. "When she realizes the cost of this mission to you, she will want to stop you." He started to object, but she cut him off. "Don't underestimate her. Be prepared."

Of course she was right. Even though he'd let Maji think that he planned to go off grid, at some point she would recognize it for what it really was—a suicide mission. "Understood, ma'am."

"Very good. I'm giving the comm back to Frank now. It appears that Ricky has decided to spy on class today."

Angelo opened the channels back up, so that Maji and the guys could hear him, too. "Frank, go see what bug Ricky's got up his butt. I'll be online with you."

Maji glanced to the spot where Frank was in discussion with Ricky, on top of the rise at the edge of the lot. She'd listened to Angelo coach Frank as he approached the asshole. It was probably for the best she was on the helmet headset with Rose as well and needed to stay quiet to keep from distracting her.

Now she pulled off the helmet and stripped off her gloves, listening to the two men almost out of her sight.

"Rickster!" Frank said. "What's up?"

"The fuck's this about?" Ricky sounded irritated.

"Driving school, for Rose and Ri. Cool, huh?" Frank paused. "You need me?"

"No. Gino sent me to find out where you been going every day."

"Here. There. Why?"

"You always take the girls someplace?"

"Just when Ang says to. So?"

Maji wondered how long this dance could go on.

"So where you take them?"

Frank hesitated, while Ang repeated his instructions. Then he answered, "Ang can tell you. Why don't Gino ask him?"

"He's asking you. Through me."

"Whatever. But I'm not playing telephone here."

"Huh?"

"That game, where one person whispers to the first person, then the next repeats, and when you get to the end of the line, it comes out all funny?" Neither one laughed. "Didn't you ever play that? At a party?"

"What are you, a hundred?" The sound of Ricky spitting— hopefully on the grass—filled Maji's earpiece. "Fuck it. You gonna talk to me, or not?"

"Nope. I'm gonna stay out of the middle. That's how you make it to a hundred around here."

❖

When Ricky came to fetch Angelo on Wednesday, all he said was, "Gino wants to see you guys."

Maybe, Angelo thought, Gino wanted to meet Dev and Tom in person. "The guys are out with Ma," he answered.

"Not your rent-a-cops. You guys."

Oh. Maybe Gino wanted to tear him and Frank a new one, at the same time. He was efficient that way. "Frank's out, too. I can call him, have him skip the groceries," Angelo offered.

"Jesus, you're an idiot. He wants you and the...Russian kid."

Angelo stifled a laugh. *That's Mr. Faggot to you, Little Dick.* "His name is Sander. Hold on." He left Ricky at the doorstep, closing the door in his face.

Down in the basement, Angelo took a few seconds to enjoy just looking at Sander, so engrossed in programming he didn't even look up. He did everything with that intensity. It was a shame to hurt him, really. "Hey," he said at last. "We got a summons to the Big G. Like, now."

Sander stretched up and back, rolling his shoulders to undo the hunch from typing. "Well, I hear daylight is healthy in small doses. I could use a break. What's he want?"

"Dunno." Angelo envied Sander's ability to be curious about Gino without any accompanying apprehension. What would it have been like to grow up feeling insulated from harm by your father's protection? Carlo had, flaunting the Benedetti name like a badge. But not him. "Let's go find out. Maybe Nonna will make us lunch."

Sander looked skeptical. "I don't think she likes me."

"She say that to you, direct?"

"No, but—"

"No buts. You'd know."

They walked silently behind Ricky, who ushered them into Gino's office. The man cave of polished wood and leather furniture had been Angelo's grandfather's until his death, and then his father's. It still smelled like it did when Grandpa Stephano would let him sit quietly by the corner bookcase, soaking in every word while he conducted business.

Today, Angelo knew, Gino dressed himself in the room to give Khodorov's kid the right impression—a big man in the center of command. As they entered, he nodded from behind the big desk, inviting them to the leather chairs across from him. They sat, and Ricky stood awkwardly to the side.

Gino had his genial face on. "Boys. How's it going down there? I hear you got quite the setup."

"We're well equipped, thank you," Sander said. Such a polite kid.

"How you feeling about the schedule?" Gino asked Sander. "This Fourth of July thing gonna work?"

Sander tilted his head briefly in consideration. "Yes. Turns out Angelo's not full of shit when he calls himself a genius."

Gino laughed, with an undercurrent of discomfort Angelo picked up from years of reading his uncle's tells. "Okay, then. We better get the party lined up now. I'll put my wife on it. If that's okay with your people?"

"It's your house," Sander acknowledged. "Any help you want, of course, just name it."

Angelo dug in his back pants pocket. "Here, G. Give this to Aunt Paola, okay?" He handed him a business card for Cuba Libre, the FBI's front. "They're local, and I hear they do food and music, both."

"Fine," Gino said, slipping the card into his jacket pocket without a glance.

Angelo stood to go. "Great."

Gino motioned for him to sit again. To Sander he said, "Something happened last night—I wanted your take on it."

"Okay."

Gino looked to Ricky, who stepped to Gino's side of the desk in order to face Sander. "Ricky visits certain places on my behalf, stops in to check on things, see people. You understand."

Sander nodded and looked to Ricky. "Where, when, and who, please. Be as specific as you can."

"Dusty's," Ricky started, looking half chagrined to be dictated to by Sander and half proud to be in the spotlight for once. "Maybe one, two o'clock this morning. I was getting ready to wrap up the bounce, so I hit the john before driving back home."

Angelo hoped to God they weren't about to hear a tale of how the Rickster had bashed one of Khodorov's men by mistake. Any guy so much as looking at Little Dick in the men's room would regret it. "And?"

Ricky looked annoyed to be interrupted. "And this guy comes in, stands at the pisser next to mine. Just stands there. So I say, *You got a problem?* And then I see he's holding a pistol with a silencer, flat against his abs, pointing at me. And I'm in there by myself, no backup."

"What did he want you to tell him? Did you tell him about this project?" Sander asked.

Ricky shook his head. "No. *He* told me. He told me who I was, who I work for, where Sienna and my folks were all day, where they live. He said the project at my house was drawing attention, and not everyone interested had been invited to the party."

Sander leaned back, crossing his arms as he looked up at Ricky. "What words did he use for the project at your house?"

"That. The project at your house." Ricky looked genuinely concerned. "And not everyone interested has been invited to the party. Those words exactly. 'Course, I didn't say nothing back to confirm, or give anything away."

Angelo watched Sander digest that. "So what *did* you say?"

"I said, *You want me to deliver a message or something?* And he said, *No. You will wait for instructions. And if you tell anyone about this meeting, we will know.* Then he just walked out. I didn't even get to ask, *Who's we, motherfucker?*"

"No need," Sander said. He switched his attention to Gino. "Classic Sirko."

Chapter Fifteen

The second week of camp ended early on Friday, with Hannah sending them all to Winston's Dairy in recognition of their hard work. The move had seemed spontaneous until Rose saw the line of host-family cars in the parking area, ready to caravan out toward the North Fork and ice cream. Bubbles rode out in the town car with them, in the back with Rose while Maji took shotgun for a change of pace.

"Does camp always come with ice cream on the second Friday?" Rose asked.

Bubbles grinned. "If we've been very good. And we always are."

"Something good today?" Frank asked, looking at them in the rearview mirror.

Rose thought of Bayani bringing the workout to a hushed halt when she knocked one of the boxing dummies to the floor. "A ninety-eight pound girl laid out a Bob with one hard kick," she offered. "That was impressive."

"Bob? You got guys in there, too?"

Rose shook her head, deciding not to share her theory about the willowy Filipina's original gender assignment. If Hannah accepted Bayani as a young woman, so would the rest of them. "No," she told Frank. "We have six Body Object Bags. Bobs."

"Huh. No Joe or Dino. Not even a Ricky?"

As Rose and Maji had helped Bayani right the dummy, Maji had asked the teen who she'd been thinking of. *Tariq* was the answer, the name spat out with half chagrin, half defiance. And Maji had shared the names she'd given the Bobs—Efran, Skip, Gus, Lalo. And a girl's name—Sheila? Rose gave him a wink via his mirror. "Maybe we'll have a Ricky this year."

The girls got their cones to go, heading off with their host families to play tourist for the weekend. Bubbles caught a ride with the other instructors, anxious to spend an evening at home with Rey. Maji checked in with Frank and left him posted up on the little road into the farm, enjoying a cone in the town car. She and Rose sat at a picnic table, watching the cows graze in the field.

Maji allowed herself a moment to just enjoy being out in the open, with no walls or alarms. Frank could watch the drive up to the farm. She had her earpiece in and her gun pressed into the small of her back. They were secure enough, and the ice cream was as fantastic as she remembered.

"It's so bucolic," Rose said next to her, leaning back against the picnic table, taking in the rolling hills of grass and scrub. "I'd come here even if they didn't make the best ice cream on Long Island."

"You've sampled all the competition?"

"I've had a lot of summers to explore this area. And I really like homemade ice cream. Isn't that in my file?"

Maji laughed. "No." She turned partway toward Rose, wishing she could see her eyes behind those big sunglasses. "If you were free to roam this summer, where would you go?"

"Oh, the usual. The beach, window-shopping in East Hampton, the arboretums, maybe a Gold Coast estate. And the farmers' market, of course."

Maji would have loved to tag along, hand in hand, if this summer had been the vacation she had planned for herself. "Next summer, maybe." There would be life here after Angelo, wouldn't there? Rose would come back to see her grandmother, at least.

"Maji?"

"Mm-hmm." It was so nice to hear Rose speak her name.

"Was the girl in Bubbles's story the Sheila-Bob you mentioned to Bayani?"

Maji sat up straight but didn't turn to look at Rose. The afternoon's discussion session had gone from the importance of looking out for each other, to roofies, to Bubbles's disclosure before Maji had had time to prepare herself for the memory of that terrible day. And while she was impressed that Bubbles could talk about it, finally, so matter-of-factly, Maji wasn't sure she could. The whole time Bubbles had been telling the story, she could feel Rose watching her. She exhaled slowly. "Yeah."

"Was Sheila a friend of yours? Before she set Bubbles up, of course."

Maji didn't try to hide her bitterness. "A junkie can't be your friend. They can pretend to, but underneath that, everything is always about the next fix. I learned that years before Sheila."

"I'm sorry," Rose said softly and laid her hand on Maji's. When Maji pulled hers away, Rose didn't object. Instead, she handed Maji a bottle of water and a napkin.

Maji washed the stickiness off her hands in silence, grateful for the moment to pull herself back together. She'd been holding the memories at bay since the afternoon, locked behind her blank-slate face.

"I can't believe you took on four guys by yourself. I mean, I can believe it, but...you could have been killed." The quaver in Rose's voice gave away the horror behind the words.

"I was lucky," Maji conceded. "Lucky I got her out without killing anybody."

Rose took her hand. "Nobody could have blamed you if you had."

"I would have." And how she would have lived with the aftermath at fourteen, she didn't know. It was hard enough as an adult.

Rose turned Maji's face toward hers. "You can't know that," she said, her warm brown eyes liquid with caring so sweet it hurt to look at them.

"Yes. I can."

Rose's eyebrows shot up, her hand rising to her mouth. "I'm so sorry. I can't believe I forgot."

Maji looked away. She stood and turned toward the road, clicking the transmitter back on. "Frank, let's roll."

No reply came back.

Maji slipped the gun from its holster with one hand and pulled Rose off the bench seat with the other. "Stay behind me."

Rose opened her mouth to ask what was wrong, but no words came out. She sprinted after Maji, barely keeping up. When the town car came into view, Maji stopped short and Rose had to dodge to keep from running into her. "What is it?"

"Don't know," Maji answered, scanning the area between them and the car, and the road beyond. "Stand by," she added quietly. Rose realized she was speaking to her team via the comm.

They approached the car at a cautious jog. When Rose saw Frank slumped over the wheel, she gasped and surged forward. She felt herself knocked aside, then steadied by Maji's hands on her shoulders. "Get behind the wall, and stay down until I say so. Clear?"

Rose followed her glance to the stone wall across the drive, with the Winston's Dairy sign propped against it. She nodded and went, fighting the urge to run to the car and yank the door open instead. When Maji opened the driver's door, Frank didn't move. Maji briskly checked him over, talking all the while. Rose couldn't tell from her hiding spot whether she was speaking with Frank or the team. When Maji hefted him out of the car and onto the ground, Rose headed over to help. The sight of Frank on the dirt road, clammy and pale, made her light-headed.

"Not yet!" Maji barked, waving her back. When Rose retreated, she slid into the driver's seat. Only when Rose complied with her gestured command to duck behind the wall did Maji start the engine. Then she stepped back out and waved Rose over.

As Rose ran over, she realized with a shudder that Maji had protected her from the possibility of the car exploding. The thought gave her a surge of adrenaline, and with it the strength to help Maji wrestle Frank's deadweight into the backseat.

"You drive," Maji said, climbing in over Frank and pulling the door shut behind her.

Rose got in and clicked her belt without thinking, slammed the car into drive, and started down the road. "Where?"

"The VA. Ang, you got it called in?" Maji said, then paused. "No, VA is closer. Yes, they can. Call it in!" And then, "Stand by."

At the two-lane road, Rose braked. "Which way?"

"Right." From there, Maji guided her turn by turn, rubbing Frank's sternum and speaking words of encouragement to him. At the parkway entrance, she told Rose, "Go as fast as you can, safely."

Rose took a deep breath and hit the gas, the car bouncing onto the wider roadway. Maji's head hit the roof as she leaned over Frank. "Sorry!"

"Just drive," Maji said, her voice steady but dead serious. From the front, Rose heard her steady patter continue. "Stay with me, Frank. Hang in there."

He just gurgled in response, drool running from the corner of his mouth as his head lolled. Rose pulled her eyes off the scene in the rearview and back to the road. She changed lanes without signaling and shot past a car moseying along at the speed limit.

A siren wailed behind them, a patrol car appearing on the town car's tail. "Shit," Rose spat. "We don't have time for this."

Maji's head popped up, turned to take in the cruiser. "Slow down and wave him up." She smiled tightly in Rose's general direction, which Rose took as reassurance. "Window down. Ask for an escort."

Rose drove half in the right lane, and half on the shoulder. The patrol car pulled alongside, cutting its siren as it straddled the lanes. The look on Rose's face stopped the driver before he could speak. "We have to get to the VA," she pleaded. "He won't wake up!"

The patrolman nodded, and with a booming, "Follow me, ma'am," pulled ahead of her, relaunching the sirens while accelerating. Rose stuck as close to his bumper as she dared, barely registering the traffic that pulled over to let them by and halted at the intersections they sped through. In what seemed both a flash and an eternity, they pulled under the ER marquee. A team in scrubs with a gurney and oxygen waited, pouncing forward as she came to a stop.

Maji lifted herself out of the way inside the car, then followed Frank's limp body out as they hoisted it onto the gurney. She exchanged rapid-fire data with the team, jogging alongside them as they disappeared through the sliding doors.

Rose meant to open her door, stand up, and follow them, but a wave of light-headedness washed over her. "Ma'am?" she heard vaguely. "Ma'am?"

She looked up, and the patrolman was opening her door. She let him give her a steadying hand out and seat her in a hospital wheelchair.

The double doors slid open, and Maji emerged onto the sidewalk, looking concerned. "You have to move the car, ma'am," the patrolman said to her. Maji glanced anxiously from the car to Rose, and back. "I'll get her hydrated," he added, and she nodded to him.

Maji crouched and squeezed Rose's hands, looking steadily into her eyes. "I'll be right back."

In the waiting room, Rose listened while Maji talked to Angelo on a cell phone, like any normal person in an ER. The words didn't make sense to her; and for a minute she thought perhaps she needed more water to counter the shock. But then she recognized the Arabic and knew they were not talking normal-people talk. When Maji hung up, letting her hand go, Rose asked, "Is he coming?"

Maji shook her head. "But Tom and Dev will be here soon to pick us up."

"But—" Rose protested, then caught herself. She got up and walked over to the admissions clerk. "He's conscious," Rose exclaimed on her return. "They want to keep him overnight, but we can see him." At Maji's doubtful expression, she explained, feeling sheepish, "I might have called him Dad instead of Frank."

Frank looked, if possible, even worse than he had on the drive to the hospital. But at least he was breathing, alive. Rose approached his bedside and started to grasp his free hand. At her touch, he jerked and gasped, jangling the IV attached on his other side. She flinched and stepped back.

"Some wake-up call, huh?" Maji quipped, laying a hand on the small of Rose's back.

Frank tried to smile, but grimaced instead. "Swore I'd never be here again," he whispered hoarsely. Maji passed a cup of water from the bed-foot table to Rose, who gingerly held the straw for Frank.

He sipped and closed his eyes. "Owe ya again," he said to Maji.

Maji shook her head, her hand back on Rose's back. "Not this time. Rose tore the tires off the car to get you here."

Frank looked at Rose, and his eyes filled with tears. Blinking them away seemed to hurt.

A nurse appeared in the doorway. "Sorry, ladies. He's due for a sedative." To Rose she added, "You can pick your father up in the morning."

As she nodded her consent to the nurse, Rose noticed the look that Frank shot Maji. She winked at him and said, "Just rest, Frank."

Chapter Sixteen

In the morning, Maji felt like she'd been the one shot up with heroin and then brought back from the brink with Narcan. Everything ached, and her eyes felt gluey. Thank God for two days off from camp. Maybe she'd just float in the pool, staring up at the sky the way Rose sometimes did.

Rose's gentle snoring prompted Maji to check her watch. Six a.m. She carefully rolled up her mat and sheet, tucked her pillow and bedroll under her arm, and slipped out of Rose's room. No rest for the wicked, but maybe there was coffee.

As Maji walked into the kitchen, Tom looked up. "Wanna go for a run?"

"Nuh-uh," she said and poured herself a cup of coffee. It tasted flat. She eyed the rarely used espresso machine but couldn't work up the energy.

"How you sleeping these days?"

"Okay." Though her sticky eyes told her she might have cried while sleeping. Still, at least no nightmares. The look on Tom's face showed he wanted to ask more, but was holding back. "Well, as normal as on alert can be."

"You really sleeping on her floor every night?" He blushed. "Ang said you're by the door, asked if I knew why."

Sweet Tom. Last thing he'd want was for her to think he was prying into her love life, or questioning her tactical decisions. She wondered which intrusion would bother him more. "Yes." She peered into the fridge. "Why is there no half-and-half?"

"Frank missed the grocery run yesterday, in favor of that trip to the ER. He's stable, might get released today."

"Good. We know who did it yet?" Her money was on Ricky.

He shook his head. "Not yet. We got ears set up, but so far just the cops have been in. 'Course, Frank swears he was alone, and he can't explain where the drugs went given the car was clean."

"So it was a mean SOB who Frank will protect, even though they clearly fucked him up on purpose. That narrows it down."

"Hey, you want some breakfast? I'll make you something."

She shook her head, and sat. "Not yet."

"You need the calories, Ri." To blend in as an average woman without all her muscles on display, he meant. "You were doing good there for a while."

"Yeah, till I lost my appetite." When she'd learned of Ava's death, the high of being able to perform in the field again, having her strength and will back after months of recuperation, had vanished. "I'm working on it."

"She eats all day long at the dojo," Rose offered from the doorway. She had a light cotton robe on over the long T-shirt she wore to sleep in. "The host families rotate who brings snacks, and Hannah stocks the kitchen like she's expecting a natural disaster."

Maji realized she was staring and pulled her eyes away. Keeping the walls in place took too much energy, and her face was likely to telegraph how seeing Rose tousled and sleep kissed made her feel. She rolled her neck, stretching the tight tendons until a twinge made her wince.

Rose moved toward her, but Tom laid a hand on Maji's shoulder before she was in touching range. "I got this," he assured her. "Set up, Rios."

Maji sighed. It was pointless to argue. "Fine." She stood and flipped her chair around, then sat straddling the back, her forearms resting on the table. There were worse ways to start the day than a massage. "Just, go easy."

"Right, then," Rose said. "I'll get the crepes started."

Rose watched with satisfaction as Maji and Tom polished off an entire batch of crepes, with sausages and fruit and cheese sauce for fillings. She'd almost burned a few, keeping one eye on them as Tom worked his wide, powerful hands down Maji's spine. The involuntary sounds Maji made as he released knots and found trigger points brought back memories Rose had worked hard to suppress. And if she didn't know better, resentment. But that was ridiculous. Rose set two lattes before her guests—plain for Tom, and Maji's with a sprinkle of cardamom.

"Thanks," Maji said in her unfailingly polite way. But when she lifted it to sip, she frowned and set it down, looking almost alarmed.

Rose gaped. Were those tears? "I'm sorry," she said. "Angelo said you liked cardamom." She reached to take the mug back.

"No, it's perfect. Really." Maji squeezed the bridge of her nose, sniffing as if she could pull the tears back. Then she read the watch face under her wrist. "Shit. I gotta call Bubbles and cancel."

"Don't you dare," Rose said before she had time to censor herself.

Tom gave her a look of approval. "We got things covered here," he agreed. "Catch a break while you can, dude."

"Maybe next weekend." Maji sipped the latte calmly, her game face back on.

Rose's temper flared. "Maybe," she said, "you need a friend today. Maybe you are human, and last night was horrible. Maybe you *want* to be ready every minute for the next horrible thing." She paused and steadied herself. "But I'm sure you'll handle whatever it is better if you let yourself catch that break today. Dude."

Based on the look that passed between Tom and Maji, Rose had only managed to amuse them both. Tom said something to Maji in Arabic, and her hint of a smile faded.

"You want to say that in English, *akhi*?" She looked at Rose. "Sorry. You're probably right, but I can't just waltz out the front door on my own today. It would look bad."

Tom smiled conspiratorially at Rose. "I said we got you covered. I moved your bike off the grounds last night, to a spot you can reach without the cameras picking you up."

"Sounds like another parkour lesson," Rose said. Maji didn't smile at that, but at least she didn't argue.

Maji caught her breath in the boathouse. Following Tom's directions brought her to the cool, dim interior in only a few minutes. She'd not realized how easy it could be to circumvent the security cameras, if you thought about it from an infiltrator's perspective. And she'd do just that later today, sneaking back in. Then have a chat with Angelo about tightening up security. For now, she took stock of the building. It was uninsulated, just a wooden shell to keep rain or snow off any boats and gear inside. Neatly coiled lines lay by the cleats closest to the pulled-down garage door that stopped two feet above the waterline. Miscellaneous boating gear—life jackets and spare line, predominantly—hung between the support beams that tied the roof and exterior walls together. And overhead, crossbeams with an occasional square of plywood. If you put a ladder up, it would be a handy place to store larger items. Maji wondered if the building had been used for more than an occasional visit from Uncle Lupo and his motor yacht, back when the Benedetti family was intact.

Making sure not to get her riding boots wet, Maji swung herself around the outside edge of the chain-link fence at the property's edge. She landed next door, still shielded from the security cameras by the boathouse. Much too easy. They should put a perimeter alarm in the area.

She found her bike in the underbrush, her helmet and a spare clipped on. Who did Tom think she would take with her? Rose came immediately to mind, and Maji mentally praised her teammate. Push came to shove, this would be an excellent extraction route. She started the electric motor and drove nearly silently to the property's back entrance to the road, escape scenarios flowing through her mind.

On her approach, Bubbles's place looked exactly as it always had—cozy, and well-kept by the estate's owners, old friends of Hannah and Ava. The little guest cottage tucked out of sight of the road enjoyed easy beach access and a water view. But strangers would never find it, and it didn't exist as a separate address. Maji wondered if Rey, like Bubbles, would have his mail delivered to a PO box in town. Might be a wise choice for an FBI agent.

Inside, the house looked the same, only slightly cluttered now with the addition of Rey's belongings. Maji sat next to Bubbles on the little slipcovered sofa, paging through three photo albums of Rey's family, the four *abuelos* and five sets of *tíos* and *primos*, Rey's brother and two sisters, and so many of the siblings' and cousins' children that Maji lost count.

When Maji yawned, Bubbles asked, "Are you bored? We can stop."

"No, it's great. Just a rough night." Maji thought about telling her friend about Frank, but decided against it. She was already worried enough about Rose. "I'm happy for you. Looks like your dream family."

"And they all live close enough for holidays together," Bubbles agreed, a note of wonder in her voice. "They have these huge, buffet-style meals where they run out of chairs—it's crazy."

"And you, the poor *gringa* in the middle of the chaos. They make you sit on the floor? No, wait, I know—they fight over who gets to fuss over you."

Bubbles bumped her playfully, sitting shoulder to shoulder on the couch. "Brat. How'd you know? The *tías* are the worst. They drag me into the kitchen to roll tamales and make me eat all day long. Even you would gain weight."

"Viva tamales! But I'd have to sneak outside, go look at the *primos'* low riders." She'd been fussed over this morning almost more than she could handle. A houseful of loving aunts and grandmas would be overwhelming in about five minutes. "What about Rey? Does he join you? You said he's gone a lot."

Maji felt her friend's shoulder lift. "He is. Sometimes he works holidays, and a lot of weekends, too. But when he's home, he's a hundred and ten percent. And he won't be a Fed forever."

"No?"

"He's got some feelers out. Other kinds of work. I just don't want him to grab something easier to make me happy, and then feel stuck in some boring cubicle land, or something."

Maji remembered what Rey had said about the day-to-day feeling...*flat* after his tour of duty. She nodded. "Smart to not push him."

Bubbles snorted. "You trained me." She jumped up and pulled Maji after her by the hand. "C'mon. I'll show you the patio we put in."

By sundown, they were pretty much caught up. Watching the sun turn the undersides of the clouds over the Sound pink and orange, feet dangling off the dock, they sat quietly.

"Thanks for coming," Bubbles said, looping one arm through Maji's and scooting closer to her. "I half expected you to cancel. Not that I'd blame you wanting some alone time with Rose."

"We avoid alone time." Maji wished like hell she could tell Bubbles the whole story. "And Rose insisted I come see you." She paused. "Don't tell her, but I won't risk coming back here."

"Your friend Angelo's in some serious shit, huh?"

Maji chuckled. "Yeah. You could say that."

"But you've got his back."

"Best I can. There's only so much I can do."

"You know, Rey might be able to help. I could ask him."

"No. Seriously, Bubs—no."

The silence stretched out, and the deepening blue of the sky turned to purple. It was cooling off, but Maji didn't want to move. Behind them was Bubbles's little hideaway, now a home for two, and their grown-up lives. Out here they could still be fourteen, sixteen, eighteen. For just a few more minutes, she could hold on to the feeling of peace, and forget the changes 9/11 had wrought.

"Maj?"

"Mm-hmm."

"Don't get yourself hurt again, okay?"

The spell broken, Maji pushed up from the dock and offered Bubbles a hand. "I'll do my best."

Bubbles rocked herself up by their clasped hands and looked her in the eye. "Rose will be okay, right?"

"I'd rather she was off in some safe house. But, you know."

"That she's got you whipped? It's pretty obvious." Bubbles smiled and danced back, out of Maji's reach. When Maji just stood stiffly, she dropped the act. "Oh, come on. It's about time somebody got to you. Hell, if I was sleeping with her, I'd be whipped, too."

"It's not like that. We're not even dating."

"No, you're just living together." Bubbles searched Maji's face. "And didn't you...you know, that first night?"

Maji sighed. "I went home with her, yeah. Now it's different. All that counts is keeping her safe."

"Safe from who? Them, or you?" Bubbles's look reminded her how pointless it was to bullshit her best friend.

But both were true, really. "From any and all threats. I can keep her alive, but I can't make her happy." Maji pushed past a worried-looking Bubbles and headed for the cottage.

Inside, they found Rey standing at the kitchen counter, eating the rest of the dinner that she and Bubbles had thrown together earlier. He didn't look pleased to see Maji.

"Hey," she said. "Don't worry. I was careful getting here, and I won't be back."

He nodded. "Good call." He smiled at his wife, in the doorway behind her. "Hey, *guapa*. Thanks for supper."

"You're home!" She gave him a hug and a kiss. "Can you stay awhile?"

"I got tonight and tomorrow off. Didn't know you had company."

Maji gathered from his tone that Bubbles still didn't bring friends home. Or maybe it was just disapproval—he couldn't know how careful she'd been to ensure no one tailed her. "Well, I gotta scoot. One of these days we'll all hang out, yeah?"

"Yeah," Bubbles echoed, squeezing her husband as she looked up at him. "And you have to meet Rose, too."

"I'll try, baby." Rey kissed her by the ear, apparently unfazed by the stink eye he got for not agreeing outright. "You know I want to."

But, Maji thought, that could blow his cover. *When Rose meets you, best she has no idea that you're mixed up in the mission, too.* Her respect for Rey rose another notch. And with it, a touch of envy. He could work undercover, come home to his wife, and manage to keep her safe. And happier than Maji had ever seen her. She looked away, almost embarrassed to intrude.

Bubbles pushed away from Rey and shook her head. "You two are so alike. Can't live with you, can't shoot you."

"You missed another fabulous meal, courtesy of our private chef," Tom said to Maji as she entered the living room.

Rose looked up from her book. "I made them prep and clean up, promise. No spoiling the crew." Barefoot, with her legs stretched nearly the length of the couch, Rose looked content.

"Good."

"You're glad you went, aren't you." Rose delivered the nonquestion with a pleased look, and Maji felt herself color. Damn Bubbles for being right—Rose did get to her. And she liked it.

"Well, I'm going up," Tom announced, rising and heading for the stairs. "Gotta get some rack time in before my watch."

Rose laid her book down and drew her long, tanned legs up on the cushions, leaving room for Maji to sit.

Maji glanced at the armchair Tom had just vacated, then took the open spot on the couch. She draped an arm over the back of the plush cushions, making the cotton of her T-shirt stretch across her chest. Suddenly self-aware of her braless breasts outlined so clearly, she put her hand back down. It came to rest on Rose's foot. "So, what'd you make? For dinner."

As Rose described the meal, Maji stroked her foot lightly, almost absentmindedly. Rose's breath caught and Maji froze. "Sorry, I wasn't—"

"Censoring yourself?" Rose looked wryly sympathetic. "I never asked you to. So stop or go, but don't tease me." She lifted her foot and placed it in Maji's lap.

Maji looked at the foot, up the bare calf to Rose's top and shorts, and finally at her face. It didn't hold any recrimination, and no challenge. She wasn't being played. *What the fuck are you doing, Rios?* "I don't know how to do this," she admitted, feeling as scared as she sounded.

"Why should you? It's a ridiculous situation, playing pretend every day." Rose pressed her instep into the denim on Maji's thigh and gave her a friendly nudge. "You should have a few minutes now and then to just be yourself. For sanity's sake."

Maji exhaled and gave her a crooked grin, then started kneading Rose's foot. "Who said I was sane?" She worked the tiny muscles under her fingers on autopilot. "I left my family and my friends, a nearly finished master's degree, and a job offer from the UN. All because the Army convinced me that I could help people. Uniquely *fucking* qualified."

Rose blinked, looking like the profanity cut through the pleasure of the foot rub. "And did you? Help people?"

Maji thought about the ops she'd worked, the dozens of individuals she had extracted from places and situations that would surely have killed them. She could remember all their faces, all their names. Right up until that last night in Fallujah. Her hands kept moving of their own accord. "Yes. I did."

"Because you can," Rose said, with Hannah's words but also, what? A tinge of sadness? Or understanding?

Maji set Rose's foot back across her lap and met her eyes. "Because I could."

"If you're not sure you can anymore, you should talk to someone. Maybe Hannah?"

Maji's eyes prickled, and she looked down, noticed Rose's other foot, and placed a hand on it. "I was counting on more time with Ava." She shook her head to clear her fugue and gave Rose an apologetic half smile. "Other foot?"

Rose gave her a teasing look, half sultry, half playful. "You make this one feel as good as the other one, and I'll show you where I hid the last piece of tiramisu."

"You made tiramisu? From scratch?"

Rose smiled again, eyes twinkling. "Baked the cake, brewed the espresso, whipped the mascarpone. I did not milk the cow, I admit. Don't tell Martha Stewart."

"Oh. My. God." Maji closed her eyes and waved her fork like a conductor. "You get tired of teaching, you could be a chef, you know."

Rose sipped a glass of red wine, shook her head, the smile in just her eyes. "Too much work, and takes all the fun out of cooking. I'd rather only feed people to show my love, like a good Italian mama."

Maji looked at her speculatively, no quip to keep the banter light. Rose blushed, and blinked. "Speaking of which, how's Bubbles doing? I know Ava's loss was hard on her, but I hate to bring it up at the dojo."

"Yeah. It's been a rough ride for her and Hannah both. I wish I'd come home sooner."

"Well, you're here now. You'll be here when Bubbles needs Aunt Maji on hand, right?"

Maji nearly dropped her fork. "What?"

"Oh, I'm sorry. Bubbles said something about having to take a break from teaching when she gets pregnant. I got the impression they were trying. I may have misunderstood, of course."

Maji looked pensive, ran her fork around the plate and licked it clean. "No, I bet you're right. It just didn't come up." *Why? Because I'll be gone again by then?*

"Do you think they'll name it Maji," Rose asked, "if it's a girl?"

Maji twisted around to look at her. "Why? Did she say something?"

"No, sorry—I was joking. I get a little silly about babies. Seems like all my friends are having them."

Maji cocked her head. "Did you hear that?"

"What?" Rose followed Maji's gaze, wariness clouding her features.

"I swore I heard a loud ticking." Maji gave her an impish look. "Could it be a biological clock?"

Rose straightened up on her kitchen stool, set her wineglass aside. "I'm not your girlfriend, remember? Let's stick to safe ground, like Bubbles and Rey." She slid smoothly off the stool, walked her wineglass to the dishwasher, then paused. "I forgot. Angelo asked me to tell you. See him in the morning. Something about Hannah contracting with a reporter. Does that sound right?"

Maji's face went blank. "No, it doesn't. Are you sure?"

Rose thought a second, brows drawn. "Maybe it was *bringing that journalist on board*. Could he mean the one you all got captured trying to rescue?"

"Definitely not."

CHAPTER SEVENTEEN

Rose woke, not sure what had jarred her out of sleep. *Crack!* Swearing. Voices hissing, muffled but audible. Her heart began to race. Where was Maji? She hopped from the bed, crossed the space where she'd finally grown accustomed to finding the bedroll and its occupant. She eased open the door, and listened. Arabic. Dammit! Ang and Maji arguing—at one a.m., no less.

She tiptoed to the top of the steps and stopped there. If they wanted her to listen, they wouldn't be using their private language. Then she heard English.

"Why are we using Arabic? I'm fucking exhausted." Angelo sounded on his last legs, indeed.

"Because we've got civilians upstairs."

"Ma takes pills. She'd sleep through a nor'easter."

"Great. You carry her if we have to evacuate."

"Yeah, yeah. Seriously. Just calm the fuck down, sit, and talk to me, Rios."

Rose slid quietly down onto the top step.

"You trying to kill me here, Ang? See if you can push me completely over the edge? Watch me snap?" The ragged edge in her voice made Rose hurt for her. "'Cause that went so well last time."

"You saved our lives. And…I know it cost you."

"You don't know jack. Or you wouldn't ask that…woman…here. After what she did."

"Iris didn't kill Palmer." Ang sounded more level, serious, and reasonable than she knew he could. "She didn't do anything to us. Mashriki did it all—and we got him, right?"

Maji was silent a few beats, then flat toned. "If she'd stuck to the plan, it wouldn't have gone down like that."

"It wasn't her plan. How was she supposed to know?" He paused.

"All she ever cared about before was getting the story. That's why we picked her."

Rose realized they must be speaking about Iris Fineman, the journalist.

"So what makes you think she won't screw us over again?"

"Hannah." Another pause, before Angelo continued. "She and Iris's editor go way back. Hannah got him out of Serbia in '92. He'll keep Iris on script."

Maji's controlled exhales filled the brief silence. "Your op, your call. But keep her the fuck away from me."

"Look, I get that you're pissed—"

The stairwell shuddered as something large thumped against it. "You don't get anything. This isn't Baku Bay, or Ciudad del Este, or Iran. I can't be anybody you need me to be. This is home." Rose heard the anger shred into raw pain. "This is where people know me, my family, my name."

"Aw, jeez." Rose heard sobbing, muffled by what she guessed was Angelo holding Maji. There was shuffling, and a nose blown. Then Angelo's words came, soft but firm. "Maji Rios, you and I have been downrange our whole lives. And so have our families and friends. They just don't know it like we do."

"They used to know us, at least. Now we can't even give them that."

"Babe, look at me. Please." A brief pause. "Maybe they don't know what we *do*," Angelo said, "but the ones who count know who we are."

"Iris isn't one of them." A touch of bitterness gave Maji's voice some of its strength back.

"I hear you. I really do. But we absolutely need Fineman to pull this off. I'd explain why, but it's better you know less. You'll understand later, I promise."

Rose listened hard into the silence, then realized with a start that they were headed upstairs together. She stood and saw them looking up at her looking down at them.

"We wake you up squabbling?" Angelo sounded neither angry nor embarrassed. Something in Maji's face, however, hardened.

"It's okay," Rose offered, trying not to look guilty. "I'll see you in the morning. I promised Jackie waffles before her golf game."

When they reached the top, Rose moved to let Angelo pass by on his way to his room. Then Maji followed and went into Carlo's room without a word to either of them. Well, Rose thought, she deserved a real bed. And some privacy for a change.

Maji was already awake when Rose pushed the bedroom door open partway. The heavy drapes Carlo had liked kept the bright sun out, but couldn't turn off her internal alarm clock.

"Hello?"

"I'm up." She stretched under the sheet, propped herself up on both elbows, and inhaled deeply. "Coffee. Hallelujah." Seeing Rose reach for the light switch, she blurted, "Don't. Please."

"Are you hungover?" Rose asked, sounding incredulous.

Maji shook her head, loose hair falling in her eyes. She squinted at the clock. "'Course not. I'm just not used to sleeping so long. My body's confused." *And I bet I look like hell.* She took the cup of coffee, rolling onto one elbow to free up the other hand.

Rose slid onto the bed facing her, her back to the door. With her free hand, Rose reached out and tucked a loose swath of hair back behind Maji's ear. "Sorry about last night. I didn't mean to eavesdrop."

There was no subtext that Maji could see in Rose's eyes, which shone with their usual intelligence even in the dimness of the stuffy room. "What did you hear?"

"Something about a reporter. Did you mean Iris Fineman?"

Might as well be as honest as you can. "Yeah. Ang wants her help, I think it's a bad idea. But it is his call."

Rose's hand brushed Maji's ear as she tucked another strand of hair behind it, then pulled back to rest on the bed between them. "Can I ask you something? And you can tell me to go away if I'm out of line."

Maji blew on the coffee, buying time. The discussions Rose initiated always felt intimate, and she should be pulling away, not helping her get closer. *Fuck it.* "Go ahead."

"Back when you gave me that *I am not your girlfriend* lecture, you said that if we broke the rules, there would be casualties."

"Good recall. And?"

"Were you her bodyguard?"

Oh. Huh. "No. I was assigned as her interpreter. Free to fraternize, if that's what you're asking."

Rose blushed, but didn't look away. "Even under Don't Ask, Don't Tell?"

"A forward operating base is a small town. Lots of people breaking rules, lots of looking the other way." Maji didn't add that her team wasn't stationed at the base and didn't answer to the chain of command there. "Still, the guys were worried she might try to out me."

"Why?"

"She was against the war, against US policy. She's a Canadian. We argued a lot."

Rose looked unconvinced. "But that's not why you're so angry. She did something."

Maji looked past Rose, fixing her eyes on a point on the wall. She weighed what she could say, and could not. "Fineman was supposed to go into the camp to interview refugees, under our escort. Those were the terms of her embedment agreement." Well, that much was true. The rest was off the record, but not actually classified. "The night before the scheduled visit, she slipped off base without us, to go in alone. Well, with a local driver as interpreter. They killed him right off."

"Oh God. Why wasn't that in the news?"

"Because we weren't authorized to go in after her." Not on paper, anyway. None of their missions came with a paper trail. "Hostage rescue isn't really a Civil Affairs thing. But it takes a while to mobilize strike teams, and we couldn't just wait while Mashriki held her, knowing what he did to most hostages."

Rose gave a little shudder. "Of course you couldn't. But I'm so sorry you lost your friend. No wonder it's hard to trust a civilian to behave."

Maji reached out and put her hand on Rose's. "You'd never put Ang in danger, not on purpose."

"Or you," Rose replied, turning her hand to match Maji's and lacing their fingers together. "I'm sorry for suggesting you might be using the rules to let me down easy."

Maji laughed, incredulous. "Seriously? That would even be in your head? You really underestimate yourself."

"Thank you. I didn't so much, before Gayle. It was a bad breakup, but overdue."

Maji hesitated to ask. "Was she cheating on you?" Hard to imagine, but then, some people were idiots.

"Nothing that dramatic. Or simple," Rose conceded. "More like death by a thousand cuts. Insidious, corrosive."

Maji worked to keep her voice calm. "Abuse?"

"Not like that." Rose's eyes dropped to their entwined hands. "I'm not sure I can explain."

"You don't have to." Maji rubbed her thumb on the back of Rose's hand.

Rose looked up. "But I want to. It might help me figure out how I got there."

Maji waited, not prompting, just being available. She gave Rose the barest hint of a smile.

"Gayle is gorgeous. There's no picture of her in my file, is there?"

"No." *The only gorgeous one in there is you, and you don't seem to know it.*

"Well, take my word for it. She's always very styled, dressed like a rich artist—she teaches art history. I was really flattered when she asked me out." Rose's eyes lifted to the wall beyond Maji and focused on something far away. "And before she moved in—long story—she was very supportive, very complimentary. But then the suggestions started. *Here, doesn't that look better? Oh, not that color, really? You look so much better in red.* And so on. It just inched down this slope, and I hardly noticed. Then one day I realized that I'd stopped being at ease with her, ever. Everything had to be her way, which means fancy—food, clothes, cars, furniture, you name it. She passed herself off as a connoisseur, and at first I liked that, admired it even. But eventually I realized she just didn't know how to be happy with any simple, good thing. Not a homegrown tomato, not a nice meal of leftovers, not me without makeup."

Maji shook her head. "Then she's an idiot. A pretentious idiot."

"Thank you. It took me a long time to realize that, though. Finally, one day, I asked myself, who watches their girlfriend come out of the shower, drop her towel, and give her the Look, and then has the gall to say, *Wouldn't you like to put on that teddy I bought you? You look so nice in it.*"

That movie clip ran through Maji's mind, with herself in a supporting role and a very different ending. She blinked, at a loss for words that wouldn't put her way over the line. "Um," she tried, then gave up. Swallowing hard, she handed the mug to Rose and slipped out from under the covers, onto the floor with a graceless thump.

"Are you okay?" Rose asked, mercifully not following to check.

"Fine," Maji answered, her voice not as steady as she'd hoped. "Just trying to remember I'm a professional."

Maji listened to Rose roll off the bed, and her steps reach the door. "I'm going to go back down to the kitchen, then. Would that help?"

"Yes, thanks."

"If you make that cold shower quick, I'll save you the last waffles."

"Deal." Maji waited until the door clicked shut before standing up. *You are so whipped, Rios.*

Maji reclined on the one chaise by the pool that didn't have to be moved to find shade. It also afforded a view down the hill toward the Sound while she kept an eye on Rose. The afternoon was dimming fast as clouds moved in from the south. No rumbles yet, though. And unless there was an actual flash in the sky, Rose would keep slicing through the water in her easy, methodical rhythm until all her laps were done. Relentless as a long-distance runner, and equally graceful.

The screen door banged closed behind Angelo, who jogged over to Maji and handed her an iPod and earbuds. "Frank's home from the hospital. Take a listen, courtesy of Rey."

Maji pictured Rey slipping into the hospital room in scrubs, never looked at twice.

Rose stood up in the shallow end, water sluicing off her upper half. She removed the goggles and said loudly, "Ang! You taking a break finally?"

"I wish, hon. No Marco Polo today." He sounded genuinely regretful.

Rose swam toward them and tried to hoist herself out, then looked frustrated. "Give me a hand."

Ang leaned toward her, his arm outstretched. He nearly pitched in when she yanked on his hand. "Hey! No fair! I got clothes here, a watch."

Rose gave no ground, still clinging to his hand at the center of their tug-of-war. "Promise you'll get your suit and come in for twenty minutes, and I'll let you go. Twenty minutes, Ang."

"Fine. I'll be right back. Finish your laps."

She smiled beatifically at him, resettled her goggles, and resumed her swim as he turned back to Maji, shaking his head.

Maji slid an iPod earbud into the ear without the comm. She watched Tom and Dev come out in their matching khakis and blue button-downs, the hired-security uniforms Angelo had crafted for them. Jackie must be close behind. Sure enough, Angelo's mother appeared next, in a coverup and sandals. They settled in across the pool, in the sun. Maji gave them all a small wave and gestured to her ears. Tom gave her a nod in reply, while Dev leaned over and spoke quietly to Jackie.

"She's working," Maji heard through the comm.

"When isn't she?" Jackie replied. "Best fake girlfriend Ang ever had."

Maji shut off their voices in her ear with a single click, and pressed play. She heard the hospital room door, then footsteps and Ricky's voice: "Wow. You look like shit." He sounded more smug than sympathetic.

The bed creaked. "You're lucky I can't move fast," Frank rasped. Then, "Why?" in a wounded tone.

"That you gotta ask that, Frank, troubles me." Gino sounded indulgent, almost patronizing. "Max always said what you lacked in smarts you made up for in loyalty. Like a fucking Irish setter."

"Whatever I did, Mr. B, I'm sorry. I would have stopped if you'd told me what it was." Frank's plaintive tone and undisguised fatigue hurt to hear.

Gino sighed. "Frank. You been with the family what, thirty years or something?" There was a pause. "Who took you in?"

"Max."

"No, Frank. Max might have got you home from 'Nam in one piece, and got you clean, but he wasn't capo. It was Pop cut the deal with the Lucchetti family, made you a Benedetti."

"I'd never hurt the Family," Frank pleaded. "I haven't talked to nobody about Ang's thing."

A smack sounded sharply, and Maji flinched. "There's the problem in a nutshell, Frank. It isn't Ang's thing. It's mine. He's mine, you're mine. All of this is mine now. Am I getting through to you? Am I?"

"Yes, Mr. B. It's just…I thought looking out for Ang was my thing. I promised Max, and—"

"You see Max here?" Another pause. "Nobody you answer to lives in that house anymore. You can go fetch for the kid, and drive those girls around, run whatever the fuck errands he says. But you remember this…everything you do for him, you do for me."

"I thought I was. Honest."

Gino cleared his throat. "I'm going to give you the benefit of the doubt. This one time. From now on, Ricky says I want something, you give it. You hear something I should know, you don't wait. You fucking tell me. You're my eyes and ears down there, Frank."

"What do you want to know?"

"Anything. Everything. Don't decide what I need to know or don't. Just tell me. Well, tell Ricky…he'll decide what's important. You can do that."

"Without letting Ang know?"

"Yes, you retard!" Ricky interjected.

"*Basta!*" Gino spat. "Frank, let me make this as simple as I can. Who owns you?"

"Only you, Mr. B," Frank answered. "Only you."

The recording clicked off, and Maji took the earbud out. She clicked her comm back on but didn't speak. The guys looked relaxed, sitting quietly on either side of the reclining Jackie. Angelo was splashing Rose, who tried unsuccessfully to get behind him and into dunking position. Maji let the recorded conversation filter through her brain. Frank would be reporting to Gino now, that much was clear. Would they need to cut him out of their daily lives? As if they could. No way to do that without tipping Gino off.

Gino was smart enough to figure out what scared Frank more than death, and mean enough to give him a taste of it. How could he do that to a guy whose only fault was looking out for his brother's and sister's kids too well? Some reward for thirty years of giving up having a family of his own to live over their garage, always on call. Maji pictured Frank the last moment she'd seen him in the hospital, the flash of panic in his eyes when the nurse had called Rose his daughter. Those sweet brown eyes, so tender like hers. *Fuck.*

Angelo must know. Maybe that was why Frank was planning to turn state's evidence, risking his own life to help Angelo take down Gino. And why Angelo was sure they could trust him. *Like one of the family.* Rose's words came back to her, infused with irony.

Standing and stretching, Maji felt the familiar dissonance that always hit her at some point in a mission. On the surface, the six of them were just relaxing on a cloudy Sunday afternoon, alert to no threat greater than a thunderstorm. At the first rumble, they'd gather up their towels and traipse inside for drinks before dinner. But Maji would go in and gear up for another performance as Ri, sitting at the table with boyfriend Angelo, both of them chatting with Gino and Ricky like they had no idea what mendacious *pendejos* they really were.

A distant boom sounded, more like a jet than thunder, and Maji squinted at the horizon, out toward the cloudbank shadowing the Sound. Something larger than a bird, just visible at this distance and up too high for the security cameras to capture, hovered in the sky. A remote-control plane?

Maji picked the binoculars off the café table and zeroed in on the object. Then she waved at Ang, getting his attention without yelling.

"Drone five hundred meters out," she said into the comm, at the same time giving Ang hand signals. "Move!"

Angelo grabbed Rose, speaking low and moving quickly. Dev hoisted Jackie from her chair, while Tom drew his sidearm and covered the four of them, scanning in all directions while moving toward the house. Maji ran for the tree line, heading toward the water under cover of the leafy branches.

CHAPTER EIGHTEEN

Maji zigzagged down the yard just inside the tree line, trying to keep out of view of the drone without losing sight of it. "Coming into range, under cover," she said.

"Hold your position," Angelo ordered over the comm. "I got nothing from the ground cameras. Is it weaponized?"

Maji couldn't be sure yet, but it looked as though only a camera hung from its lattice of support bars and rotor arms. "Negative. Eighty percent." Which were not the best odds that it wouldn't shoot her.

"Dev?"

"Eyes on front of property, nothing in the sky or on ground."

"Tom?"

"Rear view from second story clear." So wherever the operator was, they probably couldn't see him or catch him once he realized they were hunting his very expensive toy.

In a few seconds, the nearly silent baby helicopter would glide by her, if it held its course. "Preparing for takedown," she spoke in a near whisper. If it had audio on board, no point giving her position away.

"Scrub if you have to," Angelo replied. She nodded, preparing to step out for a clear shot as soon as the drone had its camera pointed safely away from her. Of course, he couldn't hear the nod. "Rios, confirm."

"*Shhhh*," she breathed, stepping out from under the branches with her pistol trained high.

Five shots from the semiautomatic, and at least one connected. The drone spun down onto the lawn, digging up grass where it collided with the earth. "It's down. No weapons visible."

"Sending backup," Ang replied. "Rios, approach with caution."

"Roger." She skirted around behind the big black metal spider on the grass, keeping out of line of sight of the camera suspended underneath. Tilted awkwardly where it had crashed, the golf-umbrella-sized flier sat motionless, its eight rotor blades still. "Anybody miss it yet?"

"Negative. Disable feed, but watch your six."

Maji nodded, still not willing to put her voice on its audio feed. As long as the big bug had power, it was still transmitting—sound, images, location. The camera whirred, turning on its axis via remote control. She placed herself in the machine's six o'clock position, where the camera lens couldn't point. She hoped.

Before Maji could dig out her penknife, Angelo's voice halted her. "Wait! Scan for an IED."

"None," Maji breathed. Since the thing had no gun mounts, explosives had come immediately to mind. But apparently this drone was for surveillance only. She clipped the cable to the transmitter and then, for good measure, gave the camera lens a sharp smack with the handle of her gun. The crack was satisfying. Maji peeked over the top of the drone carefully, and sure enough, the lens was fractured. She sighed and took her voice back. "Disarmed. Where's my sherpa?"

"Close enough," Tom answered in the comm.

Maji took a knee and watched Tom jog down the hill, carrying his rifle with scope. She had indeed been close enough for him to pick off when he'd answered her, before Maji could spot his approach. As always, she was grateful they were on the same team.

Tom gave the downed machine a careful once-over, then slung his rifle over his shoulder and prepared to hoist it up off the ground.

"I'll carry, you cover me," Maji said. If unwanted company appeared, he was better able to handle it from a distance.

"Negative," Angelo's voice countermanded. "You're on the house cams, Rios. Act a little girly, for once."

Knowing her stealth run and sharpshooting had probably been caught on the security feed, Maji snorted. "Dream on, lover."

She and Tom walked up to the house, each with one hand holding an arm of the drone, their other on a weapon.

Rose watched over Jackie's shoulder from the kitchen doorway as the three guys dismantled the center of the odd machine taking up the entire kitchen table. Maji leaned against a counter, arms crossed, watching them as well.

"This guy's starting to irritate me," Angelo said. "And you." He pointed at Maji with the needle-nose pliers. He continued the thought in Arabic.

Maji shrugged and replied in kind. Then Dev said something, and Tom gave him a little shove. Angelo snapped at them. Although Rose had heard Maji and Ang speaking in Arabic, it surprised her to hear the incomprehensible language from Dev's and Tom's lips, too.

"What the hell?" Jackie said, almost to herself.

"I keep telling Ang it's rude," Rose said. "Isn't that right, *akhi*?"

Tom nudged Angelo, and he looked up from the guts of the machine. "What? Oh, sorry." He looked over his team and seemed to come to a decision. "I have to tell Gino, sooner the better. But unless I say otherwise, when Sander gets back Monday, none of this ever happened."

His teammates each gave him a nod. When Angelo looked to Rose and Jackie, Jackie answered for them both. "I hope you know what you're doing."

"Thanks, Ma." He pointed to Maji and Rose. "You two drop in on Frank, let him know he's not feeling well enough to come to supper at the Big House."

"He's not?" Rose asked, then felt stupid. "Oh. All right." To Maji she added, "Just let me go shower and change. I'm not dressed for cloak-and-dagger."

Rose felt sheepish going to Frank's apartment, after all these years. She'd only been inside twice before, once when she was twenty and he had the flu. More recently, she'd gone in to pull him out for Max's and Carlo's funerals, finding him bandaged from the crash and suffering from a bad case of survivor's guilt. Rose climbed the stairs on the side of the garage and let Maji knock on his door. Something thudded inside, and Maji opened the door, motioning Rose to wait. Seconds later she was back.

"He's wobbly," Maji said. "Leave the lights off."

They entered into the dim living room, where Frank reclined in a battered Barcalounger. At the sight of Rose, he fussed with his robe. "I shoulda cleaned up," he said weakly.

"Nonsense," she replied, not raising her voice more than necessary. "Let me freshen that up."

Rose took the TV tray by the lounger, with its half-finished sandwich and empty cup, and headed for the kitchen behind him. As she re-emerged with a tall glass of ice water, she saw Maji crouched down by him, holding his hand. Not branding him a junkie and turning her back on him, then, she thought with relief.

"Thank God," Frank replied to whatever Maji had said. "I couldn't have looked Mrs. B in the face today."

Rose recalled Frank's version of a just-say-no lecture on drugs, delivered as an anecdote when she was a teen. The tales of hash smoked on the front lines, trying heroin the first time, and the agony of withdrawal. And the fact that he'd sworn to Nonna on his life to stay clean. She couldn't believe he would start again of his own accord. Yet Angelo wouldn't give her an explanation for what had happened.

"You want the music back on?" Maji asked.

Rose noticed for the first time the album jackets on the floor by the stack of vintage stereo components. Billy Joel's *Cold Spring Harbor*, the earliest of the scattered collection, sat on the record player, hissing softly as it spun. How many times had she heard that on the cassette players of his cars, over her summers here? Music forbidden in California, now nostalgic as part of her adolescent rebellion.

"No!" Frank snapped. "I got a headache," he apologized. "Just gonna doze a little."

Rose set the cold water by him and gave him a kind smile, taking her cue from Maji. Not that she would have berated him, but there were questions she was dying to ask.

"I'm so sorry, hon. I let you down again, and—"

"Stop, it Frank." Maji popped up from the crouch in her effortless way and stood back where she could make eye contact with both of them. "Lie to whoever else you're supposed to, but not Rose. She's too smart, and she needs to know she can trust you."

"I can't," he protested, looking even more dejected than before.

Maji looked unconvinced. She turned her attention to Rose. "When Frank picked us up, did he have coffee in the car?"

Rose couldn't recall. She shrugged.

"Well, he didn't. But there was a take-out cup in the holder when I parked at the hospital." Maji turned her gaze back to Frank, as if to pin him to his recliner with it. "And whoever brought it to you put your cigarette out in it. Somebody you never thought would slip you a Mickey and shoot you up."

"No," Frank said, shaking his head. "I—"

"You're right-handed," Maji interrupted, poking her left hand inside her right elbow. "But the needle went in here. And not too smoothly, either. Not like someone with plenty of practice."

Rose watched him close his eyes, a tear squeezing out from under one lid. "I knew it," she breathed. "But why?"

"Because he doesn't have family to threaten, and getting hooked again scares him more than dying," Maji said.

She swore softly in Spanish, the expletives aimed at…whom?

"Sirko?" Rose asked. "No, you wouldn't let a stranger bring you coffee while you were on watch. So…?"

Frank gave Maji an anxious look, and Maji answered with a wry smile. "Too smart by half. And Frank, you won't let anybody get to you, will you?"

He shook his head. "I'd die first. But they don't know that. And, Rose?"

"Yes?"

"You don't know none of this. I can't help Ang if they don't think they got me good, and that I'm keeping their secrets. You understand?"

She couldn't honestly take it all in, but she nodded. "I'm getting pretty good at acting. I can pretend to be mad at you, and disappointed—whatever makes sense, I guess—as long as you know the truth."

He blinked back tears, nodding silently.

It was frightening to see him so vulnerable. Rose looked to Maji. "Thank you."

Maji left Rose in the Big House kitchen with Nonna and went to find Angelo.

"Ay, Annie Oakley!" Ricky called from the living room.

So her marksmanship was now on record. Great. It looked like they'd been meeting, the snacks untouched on the coffee table between the armchairs Angelo and Gino occupied and the couch Ricky dominated.

"Scoot over, will ya?"

Ricky made room for her. "We should go to the range sometime."

"Ri don't need the practice," Angelo said.

Maji shrugged. "Took me four, five shots."

"Yeah, but it was moving, and way up high," Angelo countered. "Anyway, don't tell Sander. Gino's call."

"Okay." She looked to the boss of bosses, staying in character. "What about Frank?"

"He'll keep his mouth shut," Gino said.

She nodded. "He gonna keep driving us? 'Cause I got some reservations."

"We got that covered too, babe," Angelo replied. "Gino's bringing more of the crew in."

His crew. Ang couldn't possibly let that fly. "No offense, Mr. B," Maji started, "but I'm not comfortable out and about with guys I got no history with."

Ang grimaced. "Then you're gonna be stuck in the house a lot, you and Rose both. Dev and Tom got their hands full with Ma."

"We'll make do," she said. "It's just a couple more weeks, right?"

"Three," Ang answered. "And I can't be entertaining you. I got work to do here."

"She gets that," Ricky said. "We all get how busy and important you are."

Gino raised a hand to wave off Angelo's comeback. "Both of you, shut it. We'll see how it goes. Besides, I get the feeling Ms. Rios can take care of herself."

Maji didn't hide the surprise she felt. "Thanks, Mr. B."

Chapter Nineteen

Rose was excited to start the third week of camp outdoors. She watched the Humvee pull away from the waterfront park's playground. There, the rest of the students were already warming up, their voices light and playful.

Rose noticed Maji restlessly scanning the sky, as if expecting another drone to appear. "Nice of Dev to drive us," she said.

Four cars had left the estate, Frank driving the town car as usual, but without them in it. When the three decoys had split off, Maji's full attention went to scanning the road for signs of trouble.

Here in the park, Maji seemed equally consumed by the task, though Rose caught her bare nod of acknowledgment.

"What are you looking for?" Rose asked. Their classmates were nearly the only people in the park at eight fifteen on a Monday morning. The smart runners and dog walkers had already made their circuits, before the humidity began to creep up along with the temperature and the sun's intensity.

"Anything out of place," Maji replied, finally giving Rose her attention. Well, most of it. She touched her watch and said to someone at the other end of the comm, "Going radio silent. Rios out."

After confirming that the tracking pendant Rose wore was functioning properly, Maji let her join the others while she stood a little apart, maintaining watch. Rose saw Hannah take in Maji's positioning and give her a tiny nod before issuing a final safety reminder to the students.

Indoors, the parkour drills felt safe, like a gymnastics class. All the rolls they had practiced so far made landings second nature, and if they missed their grip on an underbar or got sloppy on a pop vault, kong, or balance walk on top of the prop wall, the mat provided a forgiving cushion. Outdoors, with real concrete, solid walls, and hard metal railings, Rose hesitated to try some of the moves that seemed plausible in the dojo. She noticed a few of the girls in their follow-the-leader drill adapting the sequence to accommodate their own fears, as well.

Or perhaps it was the weather dampening their spirits. Rose could feel the humidity in every breath and had to keep wiping away a trickle of sweat as it tried to sting her eyes. The yoga pants and stretch top she'd worn to protect her arms and legs against scrapes clung to her skin. A simple catwalk across a park bench made her pant. Thunder rumbled off to the north, and the leaves on the trees stirred fitfully.

Rose stepped away from the line of students and looked for Maji. Appearing drier and more composed than the rest of them, Maji spoke into her comm, her expression darkening to match the sky. A flash of heat lightning lit the sky, and she turned her head until she caught sight of Rose watching her. Standing transfixed, Rose watched Maji fish a bottle of water from the cooler, drain half of it, and briskly stride over to her.

"Finish this, and follow me," Maji said, her eyes flitting from Rose to the horizon. "Act casual."

Rose chugged the water down and tossed the bottle into a nearby trash can. "Ready."

Maji led her at a jog across the park toward a neighborhood of tree-lined streets and modest houses. At the edge of the park, they paused, Maji listening and then replying, "No, we're better on foot. Is it a rental?" She paused to listen briefly. "Just make sure it stays there, and let me know if anyone else is on the move. Out."

They dashed across the street and into the grassy, graveled alley that ran through the middle of the block, behind the houses. Once out of sight of the street, Maji looked back and slowed to a walk. Rose fell into step with her, asking between gulps of air, "What are we—"

"Watch for a little white car. Or anything else cruising around." With that, Maji led her on an extended game of follow-the-leader. They crouched low behind hedges to peek at cross streets and flipped themselves over chain-link fences to cut across a parking lot.

The first sprinkles of the imminent thundershower did little to cool Rose off. Instead, they made surfaces slick. When she slipped on a grating, Maji steadied her, and the touch made Rose's pulse sing. Or was it just the adrenaline?

"We're almost there," Maji assured her, stepping back. "You're doing great."

Rose flushed. She wasn't about to admit it—not with Maji genuinely concerned for their safety—but she'd been enjoying herself.

They crossed a narrow street and jogged up the side of yet another modest two-story house. As they approached the six-foot fence at the end of the driveway, Rose recognized the dojo just beyond it. The fence loomed taller in Rose's overheated eyes, too high to scale even with Maji's help. Inside the house, a dog barked, and they both turned, following the sound of a window sliding open.

A white-haired head poked out. "What do you think—" The annoyed look on the old woman's face turned to wonder. "Maji?"

"Hi, Mrs. Altadonna," Maji replied, blushing. "Sorry to set Figaro off."

"Nonsense," Mrs. Altadonna said. "Figgie remembers you. Come on in and say hi."

Maji glanced up at the sky and held a hand out for the drops of rain beginning to come down. "Another day. We gotta get back to class before it really opens up."

"Well, come back soon." Mrs. Altadonna was already sliding the window shut as Maji smiled and waved her good-bye.

"I could use a secret tunnel right now," Rose sighed as Maji looked through a hole in the fence.

Holding up one finger to pause the discussion, Maji said into the comm, "Roger that. Stand by." She reached her right hand to the small of her back and withdrew the gun, then gave Rose a hint of a smile. "No tunnel needed." She flipped a latch between two boards, and a small section of the fence hinged open.

Maji slipped through sideways, and Rose followed. At the back door, Maji keyed in a code and entered first, motioning Rose to wait against the wall just inside the laundry area. "Back in a flash."

In under a minute, Maji returned, holstering her gun as she spoke. "All clear. Area secured. Sit rep?" She frowned, but nodded. "Okay. Out."

"No bad guys after all?" Rose asked.

Maji looked less than convinced, but her voice was neutral. "False alarm. Sorry."

"It was a great parkour lesson," Rose said, giving her a weary smile. The relative cool of the dojo, with its dehumidifiers humming quietly and the ceiling fans moving the air gently, was immensely refreshing. And the showers were only steps away.

❖

Bubbles greeted her with a cup of coffee as Rose emerged from the locker room in a fresh T-shirt and her gi. "Ready to play indoors, huh?"

Rose laughed. "Ready for clean clothes." She accepted the coffee, realizing that she was also hungry. "And a snack?"

Crunching on celery sticks with peanut butter while she arranged the tray of snacks, Rose saw a large van pull up to the back door, Tanya and Christy in the front. The girls spilled out the side door, squealing and giggling as they dashed between raindrops. Soledad hopped out last and stood with her face upturned, catching the rain in a posture of gratitude.

"Amen," Maji said from beside Rose. At Rose's startled reaction, she added, "Sorry. I like rain. You?"

Rose thought of all the times she'd run outside with Angelo into a summer downpour to revel in it. "Yes." She took in Maji's fresh gi and still damp, neatly rebraided hair. "Summer thunderstorms were part of the magic here. Exotic, like lightning bugs."

The cacophony of girls headed for the locker room and snack tray forestalled Rose asking Maji about her own experience, her own feelings. Did she find the buildup to a storm stirring, the release when the dark sky finally broke open cathartic? In those moments, Rose always wished she was sharing her summer on Long Island with a lover. Maybe when Angelo was finished, and safe, a simple luxury like this would be theirs.

Maji rotated among the paired students as they worked on striking drills. They'd gone back to the basics while the din of rain on the roof made talking too difficult. When the showers let up, Hannah would have them switch gears again. She had more delicate topics and some trigger-inducing scenarios planned for the afternoon. The kids might as well get their ya-yas out now.

She noticed Rose standing frozen in place, then searching the room for her. Maji caught her eye and moved toward her. As she neared, Rose yelled, "On the porch!"

Maji turned toward the porch and froze as well, but not in fear. With one hand on the doorknob, Iris Fineman stood looking determined to enter, the hair matted to her head, gone dark with the soaking she'd taken between the little white rental car at the curb and the sheltering overhang of the porch. So much for the *Please use back entrance* sign on the locked door. Maji turned back toward Rose. "That's Iris," she said, leaning in close to Rose's ear to avoid yelling. "Wave her around back."

Maji strode down the hall, her pulse pounding in her ears, and pushed the door of Hannah's office open. "Fineman's here. Now."

Hannah raised an eyebrow. "With a white compact car?"

"Yes. Probably the one from the park."

"Then she followed us back. Not Sirko's people, at least."

In the rational part of her brain, Maji knew that was more important than how Iris had found the dojo. But if the rational part was trying to say more, the rain was drowning it out. "So you didn't tell her to come here?"

"I did not," Hannah replied. "I told her six p.m., at my house."

Maji let out her breath. "Yeah, well, we know how well she follows the rules."

"Look who's talking," came a rich, slightly raspy voice behind her. Too close, and way too familiar.

Maji pivoted toward the sound and looked up into the blue-gray eyes of the woman dripping on the floor not two feet away. No words came to mind, just a buzzing in the back of her head.

"Since I'm early," Iris suggested, "let me take you to lunch. To catch up."

Maji blinked and swallowed down bile. "I have nothing to say to you," she bit out at last. Then she stepped around Iris and headed straight for the back door.

Rose looked up from the kitchen counter just in time to catch Maji striding toward the door, still barefoot from working on the mats. "Wait," she started, as the door banged open and then shut again. "You don't have any shoes."

"Rose," Hannah asked, poking her head into the kitchen area, "would you get our guest a towel and something dry to put on?"

"Sure, but—" Rose began, looking out the window at Maji's retreating form.

"She'll be fine," Hannah assured. "Please stay inside until she returns."

While the students and instructors ate on the porch, Rose waited with her back turned for Iris to strip off her sodden clothing.

"If you're modest, fine." The journalist chuckled. "But don't be polite on my account. I gave up that luxury a lifetime ago."

Rose turned back toward her and looked past the nude stranger to the washer and dryer combo in the corner. "You can throw your things in the dryer." She held out a stack of folded clothes.

As Iris entered the kitchen dressed in the borrowed T-shirt and sweats, her hair toweled dry to a rusty red, Rose looked up from the table, where Bubbles had joined her.

"Thanks," she said, extending a hand. "I'm Iris." She pronounced her name, as Maji had, *ee-rees*.

"We need to eat," Bubbles said, not introducing herself. "Hannah will be here for you in a minute."

Rose gave Iris's hand a perfunctory shake. "Drink?" She gestured toward the shelf full of cups. Given Bubbles's uncharacteristic coldness, she decided not to offer anything more.

"Thanks again," Iris said, opening the fridge. Seating herself, she asked, "You two teach here?"

Rose looked to Bubbles, who had just taken a bite. "She does. I'm just a student. And you're the reporter."

Iris looked surprised, which gave Rose a twinge of guilty pleasure. "Has Ri been talking about me?" Her eyes drifted to the window and the yard beyond, then back to Rose.

"No," Bubbles answered. Rose made a mental note to never, ever get on her bad side.

Hannah appeared in the doorway, and Iris rose, asking, "Shall we begin?"

"We'll meet as arranged," Hannah replied, eyeing the borrowed clothes. "I'll have your things at my home at six p.m." She stood aside, sweeping her hand toward the back door.

The sting of pavement on her soles barely registered as Maji loped down the block. "Fuck. Fuck. Fuck. Fuck. Fuck," she spat, one outburst for every stride forward and away. Away.

She'd had months to run through a thousand conversations, all one-sided, in her mind. And she'd never planned to have them in person. Just because Iris had managed to track her down didn't mean she had to now, either.

Maji crossed the street at the corner, headed into the park with its rain-soaked lawn, and opened into a sprint. "Fuck, fuck, fuck, fuck, fuck, fuck, fuck!" she belted out.

Panting up the grassy knoll, she looked out over the water as she crested the peak. Starting down the other side, her feet slid out from under her. Maji slapped the hillside, chin tucked, as she landed on her back. She looked up into the slanting rain, now a gentle shower as the storm tapered off. "What the fuck?" she yelled at the sky. "Are you fucking kidding me?"

Only the rumble of retreating clouds replied, and Maji laughed mirthlessly, rolled over and pushed herself up, careful not to skid down the hill on her face. She sat on the knoll and looked out at the inlet, the last of the clouds scudding southward, the intermittent drops hitting the water. Her feet stung, and she gingerly crossed each over the opposite knee, inspecting the soles. Pretty scraped up, but no gashes. She should go back and tape them up. Would Iris still be there?

Maji stood, then doubled over and left the remainder of breakfast in the wet grass. "That about sums it up."

As she straightened back up, Maji caught sight of the silver Humvee cruising through the park. She thought for a New York minute about running again, then sighed, giving up the fantasy of escape for good this time. She waved and waited.

Dev pulled up, took one look at the mud coating her gi, and said, "Wait." He hopped out and opened the back, pulling out a beach towel and first aid kit while speaking softly into his comm.

Maji laid the towel on the passenger seat and got in, crossing her right foot over her left knee. "Save me the lecture." She didn't need to hear how stupid and irresponsible it was to expose herself that way.

"Not my lane," Dev agreed. He frowned at her dirty sole. "We need to wash those."

"You can't come in the dojo," Maji replied. "Just drop me off—I'll take care of them."

Dev shook his head. "I've seen you treat yourself." He pulled the key from the ignition and crossed his arms. "Point me to a wash station. Anyplace secure."

A few minutes later, they pulled into Mrs. Altadonna's drive. Maji rolled down her window and listened for Figgie's yippy bark. Dev was not fond of small dogs, she recalled. "If my friend doesn't show in two minutes, we'll borrow the hose."

Dev looked from the house to her again, and shrugged. "So, Fineman tracked you down, huh? I heard she'd been digging. Guess that's what happens when you embed an investigative journalist."

"War correspondent, dude. Whatever." She looked toward the window, willing Mrs. A to pull back the blind and open it again.

"So she found you, so what? Just say thank you and send her on her way."

Maji goggled at him. "Thank you?"

"For cutting your little Rambo episode short," he said, as if stating the obvious.

Maji's vision wavered. She remembered grabbing the rifle and opening fire. And waking up with a blinding headache, three days after they medevaced her. "She hit me?"

"Somebody had to," he said matter-of-factly. "I couldn't get around behind you. Okay, I'll thank her."

The house window slid up on Maji's right, and she accepted Mrs. A's offer to come inside.

Ten minutes later, dressed in an old terry cloth robe and slippers from the late Mr. Altadonna over well-cleaned and bandaged feet, Maji slipped through the little secret door in the fence for the second time that day. She'd send them back with a nice card and a gift, tomorrow. As Dev called to her from the back door of Mrs. A's house, she gave him a jaunty wave and snicked the fence boards back into place. *Extract yourself, dude.*

Angelo sat Maji down on the bed in Carlo's room. "When you said you wouldn't work with Iris, this isn't quite what I pictured."

He watched Maji square her shoulders and train her eyes on the wall beyond him. Good soldier Rios, prepared to accept whatever discipline he called for. That thousand-yard stare worried him more than her breaking protocol earlier. She was always in danger of beating herself up over relatively small stuff. And he needed her back on her game. "This is where you tell me it won't happen again, Staff Sergeant."

"Dev said she knocked me out."

He'd been passed out in Mashriki's tent when the women of the camp, led by Iris, had risen up. But he'd gotten a thorough briefing from JSOC during his layup at Walter Reed. From the sound of it, if Iris hadn't cold-cocked her lover, the heroic Sergeant Rios would have earned a medal for taking dozens of enemy combatant lives. And every one of them would have torn Ri to shreds inside. "I heard that, too. Not so pissed at her now, are you?"

"Doesn't make it any easier to look at her." Maji shifted her gaze down. "She asked me to lunch, for fuck's sake."

He chuckled. "Sucks to be you, babe." Her glare in response only served to reassure him. "Some point, you gotta talk to her. But today we got bigger worries."

She gave him a skeptical look, but took the iPod and earbuds he handed her.

On the audio, Ricky showed Uncle Lupo to the door at the Big House. Then his high-tops squeaked back over the foyer floor to the carpeted living room, and he phumphed down on the couch.

"How come you didn't tell him about the drone?" Ricky asked.

"Lupo talks to Khodorov," Gino answered, sounding vexed. "And I don't want that asshole thinking we don't have things covered here. I'm with Ang on that."

"But this guy's sending hovercraft onto our property. And feeding me instructions. He's creepy."

"Since when are you afraid of a messenger boy? You're making me rethink your place in my organization now."

"I'm not afraid. It's just, he keeps showing up from nowhere and telling me things, like what's on the daily specials at my folks' restaurant."

"You think I can't stand up to some Russian fuck who doesn't even have the balls to come to me directly?"

"'Course you can, G. It's just..."

"Rick! Look at me." Gino paused. "Who do you answer to?"

"You."

"Okay, so try and pay attention for once. Just because a guy scares you, and you play along a little, doesn't mean you have to give him anything of real value. You keep telling me what they ask you for, and I'll keep telling you how to handle them."

"What if Khodorov finds out?"

There was a smacking sound. "Goddammit! I worry about all the Russians, got it? There is a reason I run this organization and you run around collecting the vig for me. Do you even know why you put Frank in the hospital?"

"You said to. And I do what you say."

"Jesus," Gino swore. "First off, you nearly fucking killed him. And then who would I have down there for eyes and ears on that Khodorov kid? Second, Khodorov gets wind that anybody here told Sirko anything, even the crap we're feeding him, somebody's gonna go down for that. You want that to be you, or Frank?"

"Oh," Ricky replied. "Oh. Gotcha."

Maji handed the iPod back to Angelo and lay back on the bed. "Double-dealing runs in the family, doesn't it?"

His wry smile said yes. "Gino's a Benedetti, for sure. More ambitious than Grandpa or Pop, and greedier than both put together. He was smart, he'd tell Khodorov and ask for protection. But he's just not wired that way."

"But you're going to get the program to Sirko somehow, aren't you?"

"That's outside mission parameters," Angelo answered. "And more than you need to know."

"Does Hannah know?" As Angelo's support she should, but then as JSOC's consultant she'd also be bound to tell Command.

"She's on board." He didn't explain further.

"And Tom? Dev?"

"I'm keeping them insulated. Like you, if you'd stop asking questions."

She let that sink in. It wasn't the first time the team had chosen a course of action that would make them unsung heroes if they succeeded and hang them out to dry if they didn't. "Does JSOC know you're bringing Iris in?"

He paused long enough that she knew he wished he could rewind the whole conversation. "No. And I'm sorry that I had to tell you. But when they debrief you later, at least you can say you didn't know why."

Maji doubted the addition of Sirko as a second high-value target was Angelo's only secret. Or that he really planned to sit in a black-ops prison, taking the blame for going off mission to keep the rest of them out of hot water. Which only left one real exit strategy—and it wasn't going off grid. Her stomach knotted. *Hannah must know.* She looked at him levelly, careful not to reveal her suspicions, and reminded herself to breathe. "Hell," she lied, "I can honestly tell Command that I didn't want to know."

Chapter Twenty

W hat do you mean, we can't go?" Rose demanded. After realizing she had overslept, and rushing down to the kitchen, this was the last news she had expected. When had they decided this, without her input, as usual? Rose reminded herself she had promised to bend her own desires to fit their safety needs, but…she had been looking forward to another week of camp. Besides, if they didn't show up, the girls would worry. Bubbles would be disappointed. And worst, she'd fall behind, maybe lose what she'd already learned.

"You started to like it, then?" Angelo asked.

Rose bristled at his surprise. "Did you really think that I was just tagging along, trying to stay close to Maji? Dammit! *Ri*. Give me a little credit."

He ignored her slip, and her ire. "Okay, so you're actually learning stuff. That's great, but—"

"Don't you patronize me, Ang. You have no idea what it's like to walk through this world as a target, to always weigh what you want to do against your fears. I'm not getting banged up and worn out in the dojo for fun, you know."

"I'm sorry, hon. At least a day or two, you gotta show your face around here." He paused. "Rios, will you get down here already?"

Dammit to hell—had they been having this argument with an audience? She sank into a kitchen chair and leaned her face in one hand. "When do we get our lives back?"

"Fifth of July, babe," Angelo answered.

"Or you could opt for the safe house." Maji sounded like she'd been up long enough for coffee. Rose watched her stride across the kitchen and open the fridge like she owned the place.

Why even dignify that with an answer? "What are you doing in there?"

Maji stopped rummaging and laid an egg carton on the counter. "*Desayuno*." Breakfast.

"Really? And what can you cook?" Rose cringed inwardly at her snippy tone. What was wrong with her today?

"Pancakes, scones, crepes. Quiche, strata, scrambles, omelets, hash. Also, *migas* and *chilaquiles*. What do you feel like?" Maji's offer came across as a peace offering.

This isn't her fault. "I feel like an ass." Rose sighed and stood up, eyeing the coffeemaker. "Did you say *chilaquiles*?"

"Yeah, but we're all out of ass," Maji answered, giving her a wicked grin.

Sander came in, followed by Frank, while they were finishing breakfast.

"You're hungry, grab a plate," Maji offered.

He gave her a perfunctory smile. "No thanks. Nonna fed me."

"Mrs. B cooks for you?" Frank looked like he'd been slapped. "She likes you?"

Sander shrugged. "I guess. Or maybe she's just old school. Keep your friends close, your enemies closer."

Or maybe, Maji thought, *maybe she wants to check the secret boyfriend out for herself.* She exchanged a look with Rose.

"Ang is working downstairs," Rose said. "Take some coffee?"

Sander shook his head and looked at his watch. "By now he's overamped. I'll take him water and make him use that weight machine."

"Oh," Rose said. She sounded like the thought of someone taking care of Angelo surprised her. But then, Rose had no idea how Ang worked his targets. "Well, we're going up to the Big House—Ang wants us to help with party planning."

Sander looked directly at Maji. "For the Fourth? Talk to me later about security."

"We're strictly food and music," she protested.

"We'll need to vet the contractors before any arrangements are approved," he countered.

Maji headed for the doorway to the dining room, and then upstairs to don her daytime Ri apparel. "Whatever. But first we get to taste the free food samples."

❖

As soon as she heard Sander's and Angelo's voices murmuring from the basement, Rose closed the door at the top of the stairs and gave Frank a hug.

"Missed you, too, hon." He stepped back from her embrace. "But why are you home? It's Tuesday, right?"

Rose sighed. "Apparently Gino is worried for our safety, so we're locked in."

"'Cause of that drone thing?" Frank's face registered the surprise Rose showed. "Ang had me show the guys where to stash it."

So. He still trusts you. Rose went to the refrigerator and added salsa to the grocery list. She paused before adding tampons to the list.

"If we're going to the mattresses, best to put down everything you can think of," Frank said. "I'll do a big run this afternoon, lay in supplies."

"Going to the what?" Rose asked.

"The mattresses—you, know, like in *The Godfather*," he elaborated. "You still haven't watched those? Not one, two, or three?"

"No. Not *Scarface* or *Goodfellas*, or any of the others either." She leaned one hip against a counter. "What does it mean, Frank?"

"Well, in the movie there's a war between the Families, and all the guys bunk together and don't go nowhere alone. All the food gets brought in, and one guy cooks for all of them." He shrugged. "I haven't done it since '77, when Mickey Spillane got whacked and all hell broke loose. Also, *Star Wars* came out."

Rose laughed. "What's that got to do with anything?"

"Your mother was just a kid then. All her friends were going, and she drove Max nuts bugging him to sneak her out to see it."

"Uncle Max?"

"Yeah. She knew Mr. and Mrs. B would never go for it. Anyway, I helped." His face betrayed an internal struggle before he spoke again. "You really miss camp so much?"

Rose touched her ear. "Are you on the comm?" *And privy to my arguments with Ang?*

"Yeah. But I'm listen-only right now. This here's private."

Rose resisted hugging him again. "Well, yes then. But…if this Sirko really is such a danger, I don't want to cause problems by being selfish."

"Ain't your fault you're a Benedetti," he reassured her. "You didn't pick this family."

Rose thought of her mother's similar words, and a startling

thought occurred to her. "Frank. You must know who my father is." His immediate reddening only confirmed her suspicion. "You do!"

"Nah, hon. I got theories—everybody does. But only Mrs. B knows for sure. And I don't bet you wanna ask her."

"I did," Rose said. That summer Carlo had put his hands on her, and she had stayed in the Big House the rest of her visit. Nonna had tucked her in that night, and Rose had summoned up the courage to ask, "Did you send Mom away because you were ashamed of her? For getting pregnant."

Nonna had turned around and stood square in the open doorway, backlit by the hall light. Rose couldn't see her face, but she sounded hurt. "Is that what she tells you?"

"No, I just guessed."

"Well, don't guess about other people's lives, their feelings. Always ask." She sounded so stern, but Rose had learned already to see past Nonna's brusqueness.

"So?" she had prodded.

"Every teenager in history wants sex, hon, and most of them find it. I was disappointed she wasn't smarter about it, but I was never, ever ashamed of her. If she'd stayed here, she'd have married some wiseguy, and she deserved better. I sent her away to get a life."

And with that, Nonna had turned and firmly closed the door. Rose never asked again.

"Um, what'd she say?" Frank didn't sound certain he wanted to know.

"That it was better for me to not know, I guess." Rose felt bad paraphrasing, but the actual words her grandmother used were insulting to Frank.

"Well, there you go then."

Maji scanned the sky as she and Rose walked back from the Big House.

"Were drones common in Iraq?" Rose asked her.

A loaded question. The team knew surveillance drones from using them, in many countries that did not include Iraq. "No," Maji answered. "In Iraq, UAVs—unmanned aerial vehicles—are usually bigger, fly up out of range of ground munitions, and announce their presence by launching a missile."

"Oh." Rose walked silently beside her. "I probably shouldn't ask about the war, anyway."

"If you don't mind my not answering sometimes, I don't mind your asking." Oddly enough, that was true.

Rose's hand brushed her arm lightly. "Thank you. And I'm sorry about earlier. I shouldn't have blown up at Angelo like that, or sniped at you. Would it be very unfeminist of me to blame it on PMS?"

"One, if that's a blowup, you may just be a saint, like your mother. Two, I'm glad you like camp that much. And three, you don't need PMS to be wound up by the last few days. Hell, you've heard me melt down, and I don't have that excuse ever, anymore."

Rose stopped and looked at her. "You don't have...?"

The worried look on her face, combined with the hands genteely circling her abdomen made Maji laugh. "Not like that. Uterus yes, period no. Happens to a lot of female soldiers. By now I thought, maybe. But, no."

"Wow. I guess that's a good thing when you're...downrange?"

"Yeah, it's handy in the field." Maji started walking again, and waited for Rose to fall in beside her. "Anyway, I probably need to gain some body fat back."

Rose opened her mouth and shut it again, no doubt thinking better of her reply. "Which caterer's food did you like best?"

Five businesses had brought samples. Three were clearly Mexican, one sort of generically Latin, and the third served actual Cuban fare. "The Latin fusion stuff was okay. But Cuba Libre won hands down, for me." Plus, it was the FBI's cover business, headed by Rey. Maji knew who the contract would go to.

"For me, too," Rose agreed. "I was impressed with how you handled Aunt Paola and Sienna. I didn't know Ri had such finesse."

Maji chuckled. "Civil Affairs is all about diplomacy. Which is code for getting others to play nice."

"That's like camp," Rose said, wistfulness creeping into her voice. "I love the scenarios where we get to use words instead of fighting."

Maji held her peace. Rose was a natural in scenarios. If she kept her cool like that in real life, she'd do fine.

"Don't you have some obligation to Hannah to teach?" Rose asked.

Was Rose playing her? Compliments followed by a request... Well, hard to blame her. "She understands."

"But you're really good with the girls," Rose pressed. "And I can tell it's important to you. If it helps, I can stay here and you can go solo."

Shit. Rose really didn't play games. In Maji's experience, that made her rare. And nearly impossible to outplay. "Well, I missed four whole years in a row for the Army. I can miss a few days or weeks for this."

As they approached Angelo's house, Maji noticed both Humvees were back. She wondered what excuse Angelo was using with Gino to account for Jackie's outings for lunches and golf and her real estate classes.

"But how can you just give up what you love doing, being with the people you care about?"

Maji saw the sympathy in Rose's eyes and put up a wall inside to block it. "Practice."

Rose didn't know which surprised her more—how they got to the dojo the rest of the week, or that Angelo had approved it.

"Whose car did you hotwire today?" Bubbles asked with a cheeky grin.

Rose objected, "She doesn't hotwire them." Each morning, they had left the estate in the usual parade of cars, all decoys except the one Maji drove. Then in one quiet neighborhood or another, they'd park the Benedetti car and change to another, *borrowed* from a driveway or shady street.

Maji walked into the locker room, empty now but for the three of them. "I do know how."

"Sure you do," Bubbles replied. "And someday you'll show me."

"Your car's a *P-O-S*, why don't I demonstrate right now?"

"Because I need my piece-of-shit car. To get places without stealing."

Neither of them was smiling now, Rose noticed. Why they'd fight, she couldn't imagine.

Maji's eyes flitted to the clock on the wall, and back to Bubbles. "You coming to Hannah's?"

"No. She said not to." Bubbles's expression softened at last. "But I could crash it."

Maji shook her head. "Nah. Thanks."

They hugged briefly, and Rose smiled. Bubbles wanted to protect Maji, and Maji knew it, but neither of them would say it outright. Real sisters, blood notwithstanding.

Bubbles let herself out of the dojo, while Maji stopped at the door of Hannah's office, Rose waiting in the hallway behind her.

"What time tonight?" Maji asked her godmother.

"Let's say seven," Hannah replied.

"Hooah," Maji said, adding a curt nod.

"I beg your pardon?"

"Heard. Understood. Acknowledged. *Hooah.*" Maji's back stiffened. "Ma'am."

"I know what it means." Hannah's voice hardened. "Don't ma'am me."

Maji bowed herself out. "Yes, Sensei."

Rose could tell from Maji's tone she was still trying to bottle up whatever bothered her. And it was still leaking out on whoever got in her way.

CHAPTER TWENTY-ONE

Maji let Angelo into Hannah's house, touching the mezuzah in the door frame as she followed him in. Inside, she spotted Iris Fineman standing stock-still in the center of the living room, watching her. For a second, she wondered if Iris would assume she was Jewish, just from that one gesture. Well, let her guess. Or ask.

"I'll let you two get caught up," Angelo said, giving Maji a pat on the back. "Where's Hannah?"

"Kitchen," Iris said, never taking her eyes off Maji.

Maji watched him disappear through the swinging door, wishing she could follow.

"God, Ri," Iris said, her voice scratchy with emotion. "You look fabulous."

Maji raised one eyebrow. "Um, you, too." Well, she looked the same as always. And there'd never been anything wrong with that. Maji crossed the room to claim the only armchair.

Iris perched herself on the love seat, barely shifting her gaze from Maji as she settled. "I was so worried," she blurted.

"About how I would look?" Maji deadpanned.

"About whether you'd recover," Iris corrected, letting the hurt show in her voice. "I saw them carry you out of there." Maji looked down at her hands, and Iris continued more softly, "They wouldn't let me see you. I couldn't even find out which hospital you were in."

"Well, I'm fine now, thanks."

Iris ignored her tone, pressed on. "I thought you would want me to find you, want to see me again." Her face clouded with stored-up hurt. "If you were alive, you'd find me." She rolled her eyes. "Abso-fucking-lutely meshugganah."

"You're not crazy," Maji relented. "I'm just not the person you thought I was." She stared at a point on the love seat next to Iris.

Iris laughed. "Hell, I was starting to wonder if you existed at all.

All I could get out of the Army was the same bullshit they fed all the media. So I dug and dug, and I found some good leads that matched all your stories. Remember those stories? The ones you told me while I stood watch with you in the dark? Well, now. You'd think that a determined enough person, say a very talented journalist, could take those bits and pieces and find a neighbor, a school friend, a relative— *somebody* who knew you. Want to guess what I found?"

"Not really."

"I found a decrepit old apartment building, with not a soul who remembered the world-famous female soldier from her pre-Army days. Nobody at the corner store, your bodega of myth and legend, who remembered banning you for shoplifting."

"So?"

"So, Ri, people move, and sticky-fingered kids might all look alike. But then I found an actual Ariela Rios still living in Brooklyn. Tracked her down by going to every public high school in the borough, and I have to admit she looked kind of like you, and kind of like those pictures the Army PR machine pumped out. And you know what she said?"

"Nope."

"She said if I ever found you, to give you a piece of her mind. Said she never served in the military, she was sick of reporters bothering her, and you owe her for having to change her phone number five times."

Maji shrugged. "Sorry for the inconvenience. We left Brooklyn for New Jersey when I was twelve. I just always thought Brooklyn sounded cooler. Same shit, different neighborhood."

"And you expect me to believe that?"

"My home life's not really any of your business. Your story was the camps, the refugees, the vultures like Mashriki. And you got it. In fact, I'd say being a hostage really boosted your signal. Did you plan that?"

Iris looked oddly satisfied, relieved even. "There's the Ri I know. You give as good as you get."

"Quit dodging. Did you plan to get taken hostage by that fucking psycho?"

"Of course I knew he'd try—I'm a Westerner, a journalist, and a Jew. But you weren't supposed to come in after me. Not you."

"You had to know we'd send a rescue squad."

"That's what SEAL teams are for, Ri. Not Civil Affairs, for fuck's sake."

It was starting to feel too familiar, their voices rising, the connection growing even as they clashed. But instead of heat building in her core, Maji felt cold setting in. "SEALs die, too. You had no right."

"The story needed to be told. I was willing to risk my own life for it." Iris's eyes blazed with the same righteous fury as before. But Maji felt no spark. "War correspondents and soldiers know the risks. We're the same that way. Except of course, *we* can't defend ourselves."

"And you don't have to kill anyone," Maji spat back, nearly choking on the words. She put her hands over her eyes and temples, trying to shut out the memory. Iris's hand pressed against her shoulder, the shoulder Mashriki's man had burned with the branding iron. Maji flinched. "Don't fucking touch me."

Iris stumbled backward. "I'm sorry." She sank to the floor by the armchair. "Oh God, Ri. I am so sorry."

Angelo popped out of the kitchen, followed closely by Hannah. By the looks of it, the reunion wasn't going so well. Painful, and he hoped for Maji's sake, worth it. As for Iris…well, he needed her in one piece.

Both women looked up at them.

"Maji, give me a hand in the kitchen please," Hannah said.

Angelo offered Iris a hand and helped her stand. "Can we talk upstairs?"

"My office is available," Hannah answered.

Iris didn't speak until she was seated behind Hannah's desk, looking across it at him. "Did the head injury mess with her, you know…emotions?"

"As fucked-up vets go, she's very high functioning," Angelo replied. The sarcasm seemed to help steady her. "Were you really expecting to kiss and make up? Just like that?"

Iris rubbed her face. "No, I suppose not. At least she's physically okay. Isn't she?"

"Far as I know. Can we switch gears now?"

"Business. Of course. For you, that's the whole point of all this." She looked around the office. "God, I could use a drink. And a cigarette."

"You can't smoke in the house. But I'll get you a drink." He laid a folder on the desk. "Read up. What do you want?"

"Anything with vodka, gin, or rum." She opened the folder, already shifting gears. "Oh, and I gave up smoking."

"Really?" He paused in the doorway. "When?"

"Right after my editor told me I was finally going to get to see her."

Maji chopped in silence while Angelo mixed a drink for Iris. Hannah had set her up with the Israeli salad makings and left her to work in peace. Angelo was smart enough to follow suit.

As the door swung shut behind him, Maji looked up and caught Hannah watching her. "What?"

"Once in a while," Hannah replied, "I want to turn back time." She smiled. "But only once in a while."

"If I had a coupon book full of free do-overs, I'd have used them all up by now."

Hannah glided over with that dancer's walk Maji couldn't miss since Rose had pointed it out. She planted a kiss on Maji's brow and smoothed the hair down the back of her head. "You haven't done so badly as you imagine. I only wish Ava were here to tell you so. You'd believe it then."

"Maybe." Now was the right time to ask, not to chicken out. Maji took a deep breath and let it out slowly. "I need to know something. About the mission."

"Something Angelo has not decided you need to know?"

"Things he hasn't told JSOC. Like using Iris again. And taking down Sirko in addition to Khodorov and the big Families. More, maybe." She couldn't figure how he'd pull that big a sweep off, but it felt true. "Things he said you're on board with."

"What is your question, exactly?"

Maji breathed some more, her mind finally centering down. "Are you helping him go way beyond mission parameters? At risk to your own freedom?"

"Yes." Hannah looked and sounded as calm as ever, her hands folded on top of the counter, perched on a stool on the other side of the island. "I can take these risks now. And the potential for good, for *tikkun olam*, even, is too great to pass up. I have pledged all my support."

"Jesus." Ang must have a true game changer in the works, to inspire that kind of promise from Hannah. To Hannah, *tikkun olam* wasn't everyday acts of kindness that anybody could perform. It was repairing the world through big shifts, big changes that restored order. And when it came to billions of hidden dollars fueling the arms and training and technology behind modern terrorism, there was a lot of order to restore. "Jesus."

"Yes. You keep saying that. Here, have some water."

Maji drank and felt sadness wash down her throat, into her belly.

"There's only one way to pull off something that big and not expose your whole family to a hornet's nest of payback."

"I told him you would figure this out, sooner or later. And, Maji?"

Maji looked at her godmother, feeling but not caring about the tears running down her cheeks.

Hannah reached out and took her hand. "I am very sorry."

At five a.m. on Sunday, the sound of mourning doves woke Maji. For a few seconds, she was back in Rose's room that first night, curled around her, waking full of gratitude and wonder. But then cool air from the vent overhead caressed her face, and reality slammed her. She opened her eyes to Carlo's room, full of loss.

There were a lot of hours between dawn and another command performance at the Big House family supper table. She'd make it through that, of course. But the time between now and then? She couldn't spend another day hiding out in Frank's apartment, staring up at the stains on the ceiling.

Twice yesterday Maji had ignored knocking at the apartment door. As Frank's albums spun, she had walked through all of her time with Angelo. From that first day when he'd introduced himself and announced that he wanted her for his team, right up until they left Fort Bragg for the last mission in Iraq. Every time Fallajuh tried to creep into her memories, Maji pulled up a successful op to focus on instead. She couldn't let what she'd done there wipe out every life they had saved until then.

The third time, the knocker gave up and just came in. Angelo's face moved into her line of sight, blocking the ceiling from view. "You eat anything today?"

"Maybe." What did it matter?

He came back with a protein shake, got her up and into a chair, and made her drink it. Satisfied, he took both her hands in his and waited until she met his eyes. "Why aren't you pissed at me?"

"Wouldn't change anything." Looking back, she could see the pattern. Ang took the wins they could get, one small victory at a time, and raised his glass after debrief like the rest of them. But in between he looked for ways to do more, to kill the virus rather than treat the symptoms. And when he said they had to follow the money, he didn't just mean to track down a terror cell or its backer.

Maji looked out the window, registering lush greens outside with a peaceful pale blue above the trees. It shouldn't be so beautiful out there. It was gorgeous the day she got the news about Ava, too. So wrong, somehow. "What's the difference between Osama bin Laden and your average religious nutjob?" she asked, still not looking at him.

"Three hundred million dollars," he said, in a voice ready to crack. It was his punch line, practically a mantra. And he'd always maintained that if you could take those resources away, at least you could level the playing field.

"Can you really do it?" She fixed her eyes on him.

There was no shadow of doubt on his face. "I really can."

"And you expect me to let you?" A tiny flame of anger took hold. "Because of Rose."

He shook his head. "You'd protect my family no matter what. It's who you are."

"I'm not a killer." After Fallujah, that felt like a lie. But it was true. Had she been in her right mind that night, she never would have fired into a crowd. She'd cracked because she was human—and that was bad enough.

"I'm not asking you to pull the trigger. Just don't block me."

Right. Just stand aside and let someone else do it. Like that let her off the hook. "Fuck you."

"I love you too, babe."

Maji swung her feet onto the floor of Carlo's room. Yesterday memories had pinned her to the floor. Today she needed to move. Whatever today held, she'd face it better after a run. And she was missing the magic hour out there, the neighborhood still quiet, asleep but for the birds and squirrels.

The smell of coffee told Maji that she wasn't the first up. She pushed the comm earpiece down out of sight in her ear and listened. Silence—whoever had watch was on listen-only also. Maji padded quietly into the kitchen and saw Tom. "Been for a run yet?"

Tom turned and she caught the relief that flickered across his face before he slid his normal open look into place. Both of them did better when they didn't talk about how much he cared about her. "Waiting for Dev to un-ass his bed and take watch. But I've had something on my mind. Gimme twenty, and I'll join you."

"Cool."

"Taylor to Goldberg. You're on." Tom clicked the transmitter back to listen-only. "Coffee? Toast, fruit? You got time."

Did they all know she'd stopped eating? Didn't matter—Tom

always pushed the food, even when she was on the six-meals-a-day plan. "Sure. Thanks."

Maji set a relaxed pace, a little under a ten-minute mile. Enough to feel her muscles warm up, but not to interfere with conversation. She headed them out the front door, turning away from the main drive well before the gatehouse. They skirted the inside of the estate's perimeter walls, turning at the property's edge toward the water.

"You have concerns about the mission, Tom?"

"Hell no. It's right up Angelo's alley. Plus the Feds will look like aces—that never hurts." He took a few more strides. "Though I was surprised he brought Iris in. You okay?"

Fair question. First she'd done a runner from the dojo, and then walled herself indoors all of yesterday. Of course, he wouldn't know why she was actually upset with Ang. "Yeah. I wasn't happy to see her, but I think I can finally put that mission to bed now."

"Well, that's something." Tom left time for her to say more. When she didn't, he asked, "Mind if I switch gears?"

"By all means. What's on your mind, *akhi*?"

"I'm thirty-seven, Ri, and I'm not the operator I was at thirty. I've only got five more months on my contract, and well, I've been thinking about my options."

She glanced at him sideways, without breaking stride. "What happened to Tom *they'll get me out of the unit in a body bag* Taylor? You get in trouble after I left?"

"Nope. I'm getting the job done, and I always will. It's just… different."

Maji understood now why he had wanted to have this conversation while they jogged together. She wouldn't look him in the eye while he thought out loud, wouldn't see the expression on his face while he spilled the self-doubts he'd been holding inside, keeping private even from his other teammates. "Did they put you back on an all-guy team?"

"Yep. No openings on the other enhanced teams."

It tickled her a little to know that he'd requested assignment to another team with a woman attached. If they hadn't recruited and trained any more women yet, then they were down to six full-timers.

But at the same time, Tom had been proud of his work as a Ranger before being selected for Delta, and prouder still of the missions he had been a part of before she had been loaned from Civil Affairs to Delta. The stories he had told her of retaking hijacked planes, tracking down and recovering stolen nukes, parachuting into Panama, even of staking out Gaddafi as a sniper, were full of love for that demanding life. And the enhanced teams specialized, didn't give the Delta operators the same range of work. They relied heavily on covert techniques to insert the female operator into arenas where a man would be scrutinized, a woman overlooked, not given credit as a threat. And then she would obtain critical intel, or extract a high-value target, or pull off some small task vital to a larger operation. In the least successful ops, the targets knew they had been acted upon, but not by whom. In the best scenarios, they never knew anyone had targeted them at all.

"So what—they stick you on security detail for some ambassador's brats?"

He laughed. "No, I'm hardly pulling the short stick on assignments. Hell, they put me on the team that got to bag al-Mashriki."

She paused and jogged in place, forcing him to look at her. "I didn't take him out?"

"No. Didn't they debrief you?"

She shook her head, and started forward again, following the waterline toward the boathouse.

"Well, hell. Far as I know, you didn't kill anybody. You may be an expert marksman with a pistol, but with an AK-47 and blind rage, you just tear shit up. Anyway, you hit eight, maybe nine people, didn't kill a one."

She kept her pace steady, eyes sweeping the waterline beyond the boathouse, the far perimeter wall just coming into view. "What about the kid? The little boy?"

"They medevaced him on the same chopper as you, but sitting up, awake. Dunno after that. Probably put him in a bona fide refugee camp." When she didn't respond, he glanced over. "Ri? I would have told you."

"To the wall," she replied. "Sprint!"

When he caught up with her, Maji was sucking air in through her nose, and blowing it out through her mouth, hands on top of her head. He stopped and put his hands on his knees, huffing. "*Whoo*. God, I hate sprints."

She tapped him with her toe. "Tom." When he looked up, Maji looked him in the eye. "I didn't kill anybody. I didn't fucking kill anybody."

He straightened up, and smiled at her. "Nope. Can we walk back?"

She laughed. "Not a chance. But we can pace it slow, *viejo*."

They followed the east wall back toward the front of the property at a leisurely jog. Maji recalled where the conversation had started, why

Tom had wanted this run with her. "So, soldier, what do you want to do when you grow up?"

"Well, I've been thinking about applying to Paragon. For real, this time."

Two months back, they had both worked an op under the cover of Hannah's security firm, as contractors to a media mogul with a star getting death threats. It had let them show off some field skills without revealing their military status. And it was the kind of work he'd always scoffed at.

"Wow. Could have sworn you'd rather be a Walmart greeter than go over to the dark side." In war zones, private military contractors, or PMCs, earned huge money but often did more harm than good.

"Well, having the Mighty Cohen on our team hasn't hurt us any." He paused. "Besides, not all PMCs are the same. For all the Blackwaters, there's a couple good ones out there, too. And Paragon's more a personal security firm, anyway."

True enough—as far as the firm's public face went. "Really? Sounds like a lot of babysitting some ambassador's brats again. Could be a waste of your talents."

"Well, when you're an associate, you get to pick your assignments. I been collecting stories from anybody ever ran into Cohen or her operators in the field. Back in '92, they were the tip of the spear for a group Israel sent into Serbia to get the Jews out. Extracted over a thousand civilians."

Maji remembered that time only by Ava's worry. She'd learned about the Mossad connection years later. "So they're kick-ass humanitarians. What else?"

"Well, I hear over half the operators, or associates, whatever, are women. And their ops are strictly white hat. Did you know they protect a woman Nobel Prize winner?"

"Two, actually. I hear the nuclear physicist is a nice lady." *And then there's Mom.*

"Ri...you and I both know that you know more than you're saying. Cohen doesn't let just anybody teach at her dojo. You've got some kind of an in with her."

Maji thought about spinning him a tale about meeting Hannah through their recent op. But not telling him key things about herself—like her name, and her mother's—was different than lying. "Tom, you want me kicked out of the program?"

"'Course not. I'm glad they still get to use you, however that Reserves thing's gonna work."

"Then try to remember you don't know what I'm about to tell you."

From the corner of her eye, she could see his grin. "Things I don't know could fill a book."

Maji almost told him about Hannah saving her father's life, about her own rough childhood, and Papi bringing her to Long Island for some tough love. Time for that later, if he went to work for Hannah. "Hannah is my godmother."

"Oh my God." He pulled up short, and stuck his hands on his hips. "You're family."

"Guilty as charged. And after I got all the way through selection, JSOC freaked out about that. Nearly washed me out."

"Stupid. Typical." He fell into pace with her, walking the cool-down to the house. "But?"

"But nothing. They finally decided they wanted me as an operator, and her as a consultant. So they firewalled us. No personal contact from the day I started boot camp until the day I woke up in the hospital."

"Jeez."

"Yeah. And you know how much the Army loves security companies that try to poach its best and brightest? I mean you, asshole."

"Oh. Thanks. And yeah, I get your point. I'll make another plan."

"I didn't say that. Just, when you do go after that brass ring, if you do, don't go through me to get to Hannah. Clear?"

"Five by five, Rios. Five by five."

CHAPTER TWENTY-TWO

A ngelo hiked up to the Big House, climbed the wide, arching stairs to the patio, and peeked into the kitchen. To his surprise, Nonna was actually letting Maji help with dinner. As agreed, she had dialed the Ri persona back a little more. He wouldn't say she looked like her everyday self in training back at Fort Bragg, but she didn't look like an extra from *My Cousin Vinnie* anymore, either. The jeans were a little too tight, and the makeup still noticeable. But the running shoes and fuchsia tank top gave a relaxed feel, like she wasn't trying as hard now.

Angelo noticed Rose watching his friend, too, and wondered if she was struck more by seeing Maji's hair down or by the rippling of the muscles in her shoulders. Mostly Rose looked concerned. Of course she would be, after yesterday. Even he was not convinced his top operator was on her A game. But she was bouncing back, obviously. Something Maji said made both Nonna and Rose laugh. He took that as his cue to enter.

"Ladies. And Ri."

"Ha-ha." Maji pointed the long-bladed knife she held at him. "Get out of my kitchen," she said in an uncanny imitation of Nonna. "Some of us are trying to work here."

He skirted around her and attempted to give Nonna a squeeze. She fended him off, repeating Maji's message in Italian. But he could see the smile his grandmother tried to mask with gruffness. Must be the Rios magic. "Fine—I'm going. I gotta do my exterminator act anyway."

"You still do that?" Rose asked.

"Every Sunday since I was ten. Never could get Ricky to learn."

Rose looked incredulous. "But we've been on the mattresses all week. Who could possibly have gotten in and planted bugs?"

"On the mattresses," Maji said, and actually snorted. "She's so cute sometimes."

"Be nice, Ri." He turned back to Rose. "Not a chance in hell, of course you're right, hon. But still, it's best to know for sure that the house is clean. Right, Nonna?"

"You do a thing yourself, you know it's done right," Nonna agreed.

Angelo left them, pleased to hear music behind him as he went. He wished he could stay and actually spend some downtime alone with the women he loved. But it was time to yank out all the bugs he'd hidden around the house. If Sirko pulled any more tricks, Khodorov would be sure to run his own search. And he'd better not find anything.

Rose looked around the table at her family. At the end, Nonna seemed to be tuning the family out. She caught every word of conversation in the kitchen, but apparently in a crowd with multiple voices, it was hard for her to make out who was saying what. Nonna seemed to retreat inward at those times, and Rose could see how much she had aged since Max's and Carlo's deaths. Jackie was quiet, too, perhaps in anticipation of Angelo leaving.

At the side table, Frank opened the red wine and poured a glass for everyone except Maji. Rose gave him a little smile, pleased to see him back in the fold and looking himself again.

"How you girls doing?" Gino asked as the glasses were distributed. Rose wasn't sure whether he really cared or was just being polite. She hesitated to answer.

Maji saved her from having to respond. "Permission to speak freely, sir?"

Gino looked almost tickled. "Please do."

"I feel like I'm stuck on base, not allowed to go outside the wire, and just waiting for the mortars to come find me," Maji reported in a matter-of-fact tone. "Running helps, but it's not enough. I can only go so many loops inside the walls here before I want to hit somebody."

Angelo's bark of a laugh got even Nonna's attention. "She really does need to hit something, G. I know that sounds bad, but—"

"Oh no, I know what you mean," Rose contributed, on solid ground at last. "I took a kickboxing class on campus once, and it was great. Really helped my stress level that semester."

"A woman living alone should know how to take care of herself," Jackie added.

Ricky frowned. "I think we got all you ladies covered here."

"Yeah, you got us locked down, while Aunt Jackie's got two guys in Hummers to take her out every day." Sienna's tone veered toward whining. "Why won't my guys take me out? I just want to go shopping."

Aunt Paola gave Uncle Gino a pointed look. She would never speak up in front of others, but Rose guessed they'd had words in private.

Gino looked to Aunt Jackie. "You been going out? Every day?"

"I want to pass the Realtor exam, I gotta go to class," Jackie said. The look in her eye dared him to suggest that he could decide these matters for her.

"Max wouldn't like you taking chances," Gino grumbled.

But if he had known, via Frank, and not stopped her, Gino must like it. The thought frightened Rose.

"A widow makes her own decisions," Nonna said. All heads turned and looked at her.

Angelo took the opening. "We're taking measures. I send a bunch of cars out, only one has Ma in it. When they split up, anybody watching don't know which one to follow. And so far, no tails."

No, Rose thought. *That's how* we've *been going out. Has Jackie been staying in?* She drank half her glass of wine before catching herself.

"See?" Maji jumped in, elbowing her boyfriend. "Just put me in one of the other cars."

Angelo almost winced. "Babe, that's really not my call."

"Fine. Then I'll just move out."

Angelo started to object, but Gino stopped him with one raised palm. "I'd really rather you stayed here," he said slowly and clearly, directing his words and look to Maji.

Rose watched Maji pale as the message sank in. "I hear you."

As Ri, she bordered between insolent and deferential. Gino looked as though he was weighing whether to use threats or geniality in response.

Angelo didn't wait for Gino's reaction. "Look, let's get a bag and some gloves, set her up here. There's room downstairs, right?" he asked his uncle. "You should learn some moves, Sienna. Ri could teach you."

"What, like self-defense?"

"Then I'll need mats, and striking pads, too," Maji responded, as if Sienna hadn't spoken. "And a red suit for one of the guys to wear."

"Let's do it!" Rose said, looking to Sienna.

Sienna seemed torn between gratitude that the cool kids were inviting her to join them, and some deep reluctance. She peeked sideways at Ricky. "Well…"

"Oh, come on," Jackie said. "You do it, I'll do it. Teach us how to kick some ass, Ri."

Maji looked from Jackie to Sienna, and from Sienna to Rose, with a final glance at Gino, who gave her a *Why not?* look in return. She twisted in her chair to eyeball Angelo. "Fine. Order us a gym."

Rose noted that Angelo looked immensely pleased with himself.

The next morning, Rose was surprised when Maji woke her even earlier than normal and told her to dress for camp. Downstairs, Dev briefed Maji on the quiet night watch. They passed on Dev's offer of coffee, skipped breakfast, and hurried out of the house via the back door, jogging to the tree line.

"I thought we were going out in the decoy parade," Rose said, following Maji as closely as she could without tripping over her.

"Not anymore," Maji replied, her attention on their surroundings.

Of course, Rose realized—Gino would assume they were abiding by his wishes and staying inside the estate, waiting for self-defense equipment to arrive. And so would Sienna, who seemed more aware of their comings and goings than Rose had given her credit for. So much playacting to keep a few family members in the dark about their whereabouts. Angelo clearly didn't think they were all on the same side.

As instructed, Rose followed the odd meandering path that Maji chose. Their pattern of movement seemed almost random. Was this a drill, or could they really reach the boathouse this way without being caught on camera? Maybe they were going to sail to class.

Between the boathouse and the perimeter wall, a short stretch of chain-link fence extended into the water. High tide on the Sound. Maji was on the other side of it before Rose could ask, *Where now?* She coached Rose up and over and caught her when she wobbled on the hop down.

"Thanks," Rose said, almost sorry to stand on her own when Maji's hands let go of her. Then she turned and saw the motorbike. But..."Your bike is out front, isn't it?"

"Like a good decoy. This is Hannah's." Maji handed her a helmet and slipped her own on.

Rose smiled. Even without coffee, she felt wide-awake and ready for adventure. With Maji, she could sometimes forget how serious the game they were playing really was. "Do we get to steal a car, too?"

"Borrow." Maji gave her a hint of a smile and swung a leg over the bike, motioning for Rose to climb on behind her. "Not today."

❖

The day had gone so smoothly, it almost made Maji nervous. She recalled the bike ride to the dojo with guilty pleasure. Rose's hands pressed against her belly, her thighs against Maji's butt, were a distraction. But not a dangerous one. They had reached the dojo before everyone else except Hannah, who folded clean towels in the laundry room while Rose made coffee and Maji pulled the remainder of yesterday's snacks out of the fridge for breakfast. Rose had said something nice about the odd meal. What exactly? Didn't matter, it was classic Rose graciousness, served up with a twinkle in those eyes.

And then the kids had arrived as they finished eating, full of their usual exuberance. Everyone maintained their good mood, even during the sit-down debriefs and discussion of the scenarios, which had been scary for several of them. But their comfort zones had increased along with their self-confidence, to a girl. Bayani had lost her defensiveness, and Dimah had come out of her shell, even taken off her headscarf indoors, a sign she accepted the all-female dojo as home. Some changes on the surface; others Maji knew didn't show but were just as profound.

Hannah and Angelo could have decided not to let her return to camp this summer. And then she would have missed so much. She hoped the equipment Angelo ordered for training at home took a while to arrive. As Rose had pointed out, every day here felt like a gift.

Now, as they circled up to bow out, Hannah added to her standard parting the six words Maji always dreaded hearing. "Instructors, please stay and see me." Had she and Rose come in today just for closure?

Maji, Bubbles, Tanya, and Christy stood awkwardly in the hallway, waiting for the summons to Hannah's office. Rose seemed to be taking her time in the locker room, no doubt uncertain of her place with them.

"Come in," Hannah instructed the back belts loitering in the hall. "And please ask Rose to join us."

Bubbles reached the locker room door first and stuck her head in. "Doc! Sensei wants you, too."

None of them tried to sit in the little office, but stood shoulder to shoulder by the wall across from Hannah's desk. Maji watched Rose enter and notice that she could see through that wall, into the mat room. Rose masked her surprise admirably, finding a corner to stand in by the door, near Bubbles.

Hannah stood, looking up slightly at all five of them. "Off and on this week, we will have a visitor. As you know, I do not allow recording or photos in the dojo, and normally no observers. This will be an exception."

No. Maji's stomach clenched. Sharing camp with Iris would be worse than staying home. Maji wanted to slam out of the too small space, but four bodies stood between her and the door.

"Iris Fineman, as you know, was held hostage in Fallujah last fall, and freed by a small group of soldiers. She wants to do a follow-up story on the female soldier, Sergeant Ariela Rios."

"So?" Bubbles said. "Too bad."

A chunk of gratitude caught in Maji's throat. Even if it was too late. Arguing with Hannah was pointless.

"It's time, and this is a controllable environment," Hannah responded to the outburst, her voice firm and level. She looked at Tanya and Christy. "Ms. Fineman knows our Maji as Sergeant Rios, or Ri, as her Army friends call her."

"I knew it!" Tanya burst out, elbowing Christy. "You owe me twenty bucks."

Christy twisted to look at Maji. "Wow. Really?"

Maji nodded. "Yeah." Looking to Hannah, she asked, "So how's this going to work?"

"As simply as possible. Ms. Fineman arrives, observes, and leaves town. If she needs to stay on Long Island, she stays with me."

Where Hannah can see her, Maji thought. *Good.*

"In our room?" Bubbles sounded ready to pop. "With our stuff?"

Hannah tilted her head, a small tell of wearing patience. "Of course not. Everything there, as here, will be stripped of Maji's history. As far as she knows, only Ri exists."

"But…" Rose began and, when Hannah did not stop her, said, "we all call her Maji here."

"Yeah. So why doesn't the Army?" Christy asked.

Maji raised one brow. "Mom."

"Oh…right."

Bubbles leaned forward. "And no fucking way is that woman finding out about Neda."

"Hey," Maji said and wove her way over to her best friend. She put an arm around her and felt her take a shaky breath. "Everybody's safe here." Maji let her go and stood next to the desk, where she could see the others' faces. "I didn't want the kids knowing my history in Iraq, so you all call me Maji. That's all Iris needs to know."

"I have already explained this to Ms. Fineman. I gave her permission to use *Ri* as a nickname, if she must."

"Says Rios on my locker," Maji reminded them. "The kids will get it."

Rose raised her hand, and Hannah nodded to her. "What will the kids think Iris is doing here?"

"A story on women teaching self-defense to the next generation," Hannah replied. "With no names or photos used without their permission."

"Won't they be disappointed when the story isn't published?" Tanya asked.

Hannah smiled mysteriously. "Camp is pretty interesting, up close. Perhaps Ms. Fineman will get two stories for the price of one."

The price, Maji thought. Of course. Iris's price for helping Angelo was getting to be close to her. Well, if that's what she wanted, she wouldn't get paid much.

With eight for supper, Rose had Frank set the dining room table. Even with regular dishes and silverware, and simple placemats and paper napkins, it felt like a special occasion. Angelo was ebullient, and Sander seemed shy but happy to be included. Rose was pretty sure they were a couple, not just business partners. She should probably ask, except Angelo had never talked about any man he'd dated. And of course, if he was going to turn state's evidence and disappear into witness protection, their relationship couldn't last.

Rose thought about the end of this perilous charade coming in a few weeks. Angelo probably was keeping things as light as possible with Sander, since he had to keep the imminent end to their relationship a secret. Rose felt a little bad for Sander, but mostly she hoped that Angelo could protect his own heart.

"It is manicotti to die for!" Sander burst out, halfway through his plate of pasta and salad. He looked at Angelo as though he'd been tricked. "But you said that was your grandmother's."

"It's Nonna's recipe," Rose responded. "And I thought you were a big fan, too, Ri," she said to Maji. When Jackie, Frank, Dev, Tom, Sander, and Angelo all looked at Maji, who blushed, Rose regretted her words.

"Sorry. It's delicious. Just me that's off today."

Sander gave her a sympathetic look. "I heard the lockdown was getting to you. I'm sorry."

"Have a glass of wine," Jackie suggested, reaching for the bottle of red between Rose and herself, the only two with glasses. "It's working for us, right?"

"It does help a little," Rose conceded.

"A little helps a little," Jackie corrected. "A lot helps more. Frank, get her a glass."

"No," Angelo countermanded.

"He's right," Maji said. "Bring me a G and T, Frank. What? He makes them for you all the time. I'll take one of those." Frank rose and looked to Angelo. "Just one, sweetie pie," Maji said, raising her right hand in a half salute. "Scout's honor."

"Okay." Angelo sounded uncertain, but motioned Frank to go.

Maji sighed. "Really, Ang. I'm not going to bust up your mother's house. Or pick a fight. I'll make it until you're done."

"Thank you," Sander said. "For all you're doing to help Angelo." He looked to Dev and Tom as well. "You're good friends. It's important to have people we can trust around us."

"Amen." Angelo lifted his glass, and they all toasted the sentiment.

Maji dug in to her plate, pausing only to thank Frank for her drink.

When the cup was half empty, Rose gave in to curiosity and stole a sip. Sure enough, no gin—just like the ones Angelo drank by the pool. Still, she gave a little cough. "One would be enough for me."

Maji moved her drink out of Rose's reach with deliberation. "I feel a good night's sleep coming on."

"See?" Jackie said. "Don't knock what works."

CHAPTER TWENTY-THREE

Hannah introduced Iris to the students when they bowed in for morning drills. Rose noticed that everyone looked at Iris with interest, except for Maji and Bubbles. Hannah paired Iris with Rose to practice kicks.

"Oh!" Rose exhaled as a solid front kick shoved her backward, the striking pad pressed against her front. "You've done this before, then?"

Iris looked pleased with herself. "Level four, Krav Maga."

Rose handed the pad over. "That's a martial art?"

"No—it's actual self-defense. Hebrew for *close combat*. Hasn't Hannah told you?" Iris held the pad along her side, covering her ribs and thigh.

Rose lined up for a roundhouse kick and gave the pad a satisfying smack with her shin. "I must have been out that day." She popped several more kicks, taking care to pivot properly on her balance leg to avoid twisting her knee.

"Not bad for a beginner," Iris said. "Now once more, with feeling."

It wasn't hard to work up some feeling with this woman. Rose took a breath and concentrated on driving her shin not into the pad, but through it, clear to the other side of Iris. Iris winced from the impact, and staggered.

"Oh my God! Are you all right?" Rose gave her antagonist an arm to lean on.

Iris grinned at her. "Sure. Just need to walk it off." She flexed her leg and stood on it gingerly. "Aren't you a little old for this crowd? I heard it was a teen camp."

"Are you saying I can't pass for seventeen?" Rose crossed her arms in mock offense.

Iris's slow appraisal made Rose flush. "I'd say you'd pass for an instructor's girlfriend. I just wondered which one."

"None." Sadly, true. "I'm Angelo's cousin. Camp is my hall pass to get out of the house."

Hannah glided by them. "Less talk, please. Practice is participatory."

"Wait," Iris said. Hannah pivoted and looked expectant, so Iris went on. "She's never even heard of Krav. Do you at least teach them the handshake?"

Hannah's brow furrowed, and then a look of recognition passed over her face. She looked at Rose with a faint smile and explained. "Front rising kick to the groin. Naturally. But today," Hannah said, "work on the roundhouse." She moved on.

Rose picked up the dropped striking pad. "Okay. Go easy on me, Level Four."

At lunch break, Hannah asked Rose to join her in the kitchen, while the others ate out on the porches, as usual. "And you two," she told Maji and Iris, "can use my office."

Maji carried her plate into the office and took Hannah's chair behind the desk. It gave her a measure of confidence. She started on lunch without tasting it, swallowing extra gulps of water to get it down.

Iris settled in across from her and didn't touch her own plate. "Mind if I close the door?"

Maji felt her face heat, the memory of what a rare closed door in Iraq had allowed them to get up to. Clearly Iris remembered, too. "No reason not to." She noticed Iris had no paper or pocket voice recorder, her journalistic staples. "No notes?"

"I thought today we could stay off the record."

Maji took another bite of her sandwich and chewed, letting the silence speak for itself.

"So they're calling you Maji. What kind of name is that?"

"Lebanese. You never heard of Majida El Roumi?" She didn't mean to sound defensive. It would only encourage Iris.

"The singer. Sure. You don't look anything like her. So?"

"My grandparents used to play her records all the time. They thought it was really cute when I sang along."

"Aren't your grandparents Hispanic?"

"Latino. And only on my dad's side. Mom's folks were Lebanese."

"Were?"

"They're gone now."

"I'm sorry," Iris said, though there was no sympathy in her eyes. No time for trivialities, as usual.

Maji answered around another bite of sandwich. "S'okay."

"You never mentioned them before."

Maji swallowed and took a sip of water. "You never asked. You were pretty busy giving me your worldview, and picking fights."

"I seem to remember you finding our arguments...stimulating."

"Look, if you think we're picking up where we left off, I'm sorry. I hear from Angelo the story he's got for you is really big."

Several emotions crossed Iris's features. "Your friend's story is Pulitzer material. And it could get me killed. I could use a bodyguard. I was hoping you might be available."

"I'm not for hire. And I'd rather not know any more about what he's involved in than I have to. Your Pulitzer's not worth my life."

Iris's hand went to her pockets, searching in reflex for a cigarette. She caught Maji registering the gesture, and smiled sheepishly. "Old habits." When Maji didn't respond, she added, "I gave them up, finally. For real."

"Good for you." Iris's argument about her likely lifespan as a war correspondent had been a terrible excuse. "Planning to stick around, then?"

Iris smiled. "If the warlords and Russian mobsters don't get me." The smile faded and a rare look of vulnerability replaced it. "And if I found somebody who hated smoking but would spend forty weeks a year on the road with me."

Maji felt the first real twinge of sympathy. "Maybe you will yet. As for me, the Army still owns my ass."

"How?"

"Select Reserves. Anytime call-up status."

Iris's mouth twitched. "How are you so sure your Mafia buddy's up to anything good, if you don't know what he's really doing?"

"I trust him. Speaking of which, are you really doing a follow-up article on me? On the record."

Iris blinked at her, apparently thrown by the redirection. "Can I?"

"Seems to be what Hannah thinks. A fluff piece on teen girls learning self-defense isn't your style."

"See how well you know me?" Iris smiled again. "But you'd want to vet the content first, wouldn't you?"

Maji gave a half shrug. "I'd trust Hannah to work with your editor."

"Ouch." Despite the reply, Iris looked more engaged than hurt. "Another one you trust more than me. Well, Hannah did hook me up with Angelo. And my editor acts likes she's some kind of ex-Mossad Wonder Woman. So it'll go through them anyway."

Maji saw through the one-way glass wall the students filtering back onto the mats. "'Kay then." She stood, and moved toward the door. "Next time, bring your notepad."

By Wednesday evening, Angelo was dying to know how Maji was doing with Iris. She'd seemed fine at dinner the night before, but he couldn't ask. Sander had joined them again, and then worked until after midnight with him in the basement. Angelo had sent him up to the Big House with a smile on his tired face. But tonight the kid had needed some downtime, thank God. Angelo bet they left him alone up there, a luxury he'd never experienced himself.

The minute Maji walked in the back door, stripping off her motorcycle jacket while Rose did the same, he pounced. "Hey. Take a walk with me."

"Sure." She hung her jacket on a kitchen chair.

They walked hand in hand down to the boathouse, not talking on the way. Inside, she scanned the building quickly before plunking herself down on the dock and taking off her riding boots.

Angelo waited until Maji's feet were in the water, dangling off the dock. "So, how's it going with Iris? She behaving?"

"Other than trying to teach everyone the Krav Maga handshake, sure."

Angelo laughed, recalling Iris embedded with their team. After a few days, the guys covered their crotches whenever they saw her.

Maji gave his hand a light squeeze. "And yesterday she made it pretty clear she wants a partner in the field. You remember her whole forty-weeks-a-year thing?"

"Yeah. Can't blame her for trying." He looked at Maji's profile, her gaze latched to the distance, somewhere out by the horizon where the sailboats disappeared into dots. "And today?"

"Today she played reporter. Asked me bullshit questions about life after Fallujah, wrote down my bullshit answers."

"Hannah's gonna vet the story, right?"

"'Course. Iris won't piss anybody off if she thinks it'll cost her a Pulitzer."

"How's that?"

"Don't ask me. You're the one stringing her along. Whatever you've promised, she's hooked. And she seems legitimately frightened for her safety. Does she know you're taking on Khodorov and Sirko, both?"

"Yeah. All background so far. She'll get the rest when I'm gone." Hannah would see to that.

She shifted her weight, twisting slightly to see his face. "Speaking of which...you're not going to ask Tom or Dev to help with that, are you?"

It was an inevitable question, one that he and Hannah had talked through at her house. "Well, I don't want you anywhere near, when it goes down. But I'm going to need insurance, make sure I don't just get knocked out or something. So, yeah, I need at least one of them."

"How could either of those guys say yes? Especially when you can't tell them why."

He braced himself and said as calmly as he could, "Tom would if you asked him to."

She leaned back as if he'd struck her and stared at him. For a second Angelo thought Maji was going to shove him off the dock. Then she settled back, her feet dripping on the dock between them, her arms wrapped around her knees. "This must be a record for you, a personal best." Her voice was cold and flat with suppressed anger.

"It's not like that," he protested. But in truth, he had treated her like a mark, worked her step by step.

"It's just like that, Ang. Right out of the fucking training manual. Step one: ask for something little. Like, say, a few days protecting your cousin. Step two: up the ante—just a little." She stroked her chin, indicating the ask to act as his beard to protect him from Uncle Gino's homophobia. "Wait until I've shown full commitment, and then—only then—ask for something way outside the mark's normal mores."

"I got no defense but necessity."

"And you think now I'm a made man, I can live with not just your blood on my hands, but on Tom's, too?"

He could see the pain hiding right under that anger. But it was too late to undo. "Tom's a seasoned operator, Maj. He can take it. So can you—you've proved it." He let the made man reference go. This was not the time or place to compare first kills in the Mafia to war.

"*Cabrón!*" She swore at him. "You knew they didn't tell me what really happened in Fallujah. You let me think I'd killed those people."

Oh, shit. Well, no way around it but through. Angelo reached for her, thought better of it, and pulled his hands back. "I didn't know at first, what you'd been debriefed on. Then later I did hear, but I thought, well, she's back in the saddle, so it didn't kill her."

She just watched him, with that hurt and anger burning in her eyes, rocking a little in the space it took to gather his thoughts.

"Every time we sent you in someplace," Angelo explained, "I never worried if you'd pull off the mission. And only a little that you'd get hurt before the extraction. No, I worried about the day you finally fucked up. That you'd do great so long as you thought you could be perfect, only ever save lives and never take any."

Maji had stopped rocking and sat still. Angelo needed to say the rest—it was way overdue. She might not like what he was saying, but she needed to hear it. From him, with all the tough love he could muster.

"Most of us go into the field like we're going into a knife fight," he continued. "We're prepared to get cut. Then we see the gash, it hurts like hell, but we keep going. Day comes you can't keep going, you better step out of the game. After Fallujah, I was waiting to see which way you'd go. I wouldn't have blamed you for washing out. But thank God, you didn't."

"So that now I can do something even worse."

He sighed. Of course the only thing worse in her eyes than killing someone herself would be choosing to let someone come to harm when she had the power to stop it. "You're no worse than a sniper. Is Tom a bad person? Does he not deserve to be happy?"

"Don't fuck with me like that. I know we need people who can do what he can. And you know I'm not one of them. You knew that when you picked me for your team."

"Yeah, and it was the right call, too. Another operator would have left a body behind so many places that you managed not to. No echoes, no footprints, no retribution."

"That's a lot to expect this time. Even if the whole team cooperated. Even with Hannah's help."

"Well, the stakes have never been higher."

"Yeah," she agreed, with a bitter laugh. "I fuck up my part, Khodorov will come after everybody I love, too."

"Don't think I don't know it." Angelo reached out for the hands wrapped around her knees, and when she didn't flinch, tucked his hand into them. "We plan this extraction to protect everybody from the blowback. Even Hannah gets a shield. I promise."

"I get to help with the plan."

"'Course. You're at the table."

"Ang?"

"Yeah."

"This isn't an extraction. You taught me the three ways to exfil. Option four's not in the playbook."

"Doesn't have to be. We always know going in that if we can't swing one, two, or three, we're not coming home. You got your will and advance directives on file, same as me."

"Yeah, but I don't go in planning to get killed. This is different."

"You go into the knife fight same as the rest of us. Over and over, and you got some scars to show for it. Don't tell me you wouldn't take the bullet, or stay with the bomb, or whatever it was on that particular op. We both know you would."

Angelo knew she couldn't argue with that. They sat in silence a long while, watching the sky change as evening came on. *Finally*, he thought, *she gets it.* Angelo was about to stand up when Maji spoke again.

"Remember that dissident we extracted right off the streets of Tehran?"

He smiled at the memory. It was a brilliant op. They went in as Basij, the Islamic Revolutionary Guard's morals police, which routinely harassed women for violations of their extremist version of sharia— wearing the headscarf so that too much hair showed, daring to polish their nails, carrying books that might be—gasp—banned. Precisely because their HVT was a known dissident, the neighbors assumed she had been taken to jail. And the authorities? They found the suicide note she left in her apartment, angrily declaring they had driven her to take her own life. "'Course I remember."

"If we could pull that off, we could extract you from this."

Alive, she meant. Clearly it was going to take a little longer for her to get her head around his plan. "Don't think I haven't considered it. But you grew up with a frigging parade of refugees in your house. So you know how hard never getting to see your home or family and friends again is. Would you wish that on me?"

"Fuck you. At least they got lives. Your way makes me a murderer. You wish that on me?"

"Last thing I want, babe. I know what it'll cost you. But I got my family to think about, and so do you."

The stubborn look in her eyes was reassuring. Better than the pain. "If Hannah helped, and you agreed, we could make it real enough to protect them. Then you could do something worthwhile still. You're not even thirty-five, for Chrissake. You can't be done, Ang. Hell, even if you stayed out of the game for the rest of your life, at least you'd have a life."

He shook his head. "Nobody's good enough, babe. Gino can't

poke my cold, dead corpse, he'll be suspicious. And Khodorov? He'd better be ready to stand up and tell his whole effing network that I'm cashed out, beyond even his reach. It's zero retribution, or—"

"We could try it my way," she cut in, "and fall back on the real thing if that doesn't fly."

"And see who they take out between Plan A and Plan B? No way. We only get one chance, and it has to be seamless."

The tears in her eyes, and the silence, told him she understood. Still, they had to seal the deal. "On your word, soldier."

She looked away from him. "Fuck me. On my word."

CHAPTER TWENTY-FOUR

By Thursday night, Angelo had enough placeholder IDs set up to start distribution. Now he just had to find time to finish the virus subroutine when Sander wasn't around to check his work on what he was now thinking of as the Robin Hood subroutine. Well, virus, really. He typed faster, trying to finish today's work before it was tomorrow already.

"I have to go back to the city in the morning," Sander said.

Angelo didn't look up. He was nearly done with this section. "What?"

"I said, I'm going back to New York in the morning."

Angelo looked at his watch. Twelve thirty a.m.—already morning. "A day early?" He let disappointment show, then tried to look understanding. "Well, Friday night traffic does suck. And we are ahead of schedule. You can afford to."

"You could use a break, too. Why don't you come with me?"

Angelo stretched and reached for the right response. "Other than the obvious security issue with me stepping out of here, I got some areas I should polish up."

"But the meeting is about you. Sort of." Sander held out his hand.

Angelo took it and was pleasantly surprised to find himself pulled into a light embrace. Instead of telling him more, though, Sander just slipped one of his iPod earbuds out and put it in Angelo's ear. They swayed slowly together to an old Billy Joel song. Sander kissed him seductively, as if they had nowhere to go and all night to get there. Angelo let himself pretend for a moment that it was true.

When the chorus of "Vienna" sank in, Angelo leaned back in Sander's arms. "Austria's a very friendly country for our kind of work. Would be a great base of operations."

Sander smiled, and kissed him on the tip of the nose. "Papa has a network there already. The Vienna head of operations is coming to discuss distribution of our product."

"Sweet."

"And I'm going to pitch the idea of moving you there. As part of our organization."

Angelo stepped back from him. "Whoa."

"You said you wanted out of here."

"Wow. Yeah. I mean, I do. But…I'd be out, wouldn't I?"

"You say that like it's not a good thing. Would you not like to live openly? Perhaps with me."

Angelo felt himself tear up. Nobody had ever proposed more than a few nights together, before. Words wouldn't come, so he just grabbed Sander and kissed him with everything he felt. "Let's go upstairs."

"So this is our last lunch," Iris said. "And I was hoping to see you this weekend, but I have to head to the city before rush hour. My editor wants a meeting. I could come back after, maybe Saturday night?"

Maji shook her head. "I'm on duty."

"Oh, right, the bodyguard thing. Lucky Rose. God, she's sparkly."

Maji didn't appreciate Iris using the term she herself had taught her, for a woman with a certain eye-catching, captivating something. Of course Iris saw it, too. "I suppose."

"Oh, like you don't see it. If she batted for our team, I might feel threatened."

Hmm. Apparently Iris hadn't bothered to double-check her assumptions with research. If she had, Rose being faculty sponsor of the LGBTQ student group on her campus might have tipped her off. "Look," Maji said, pushing her empty plate aside, "we've run out of bullshit questions for your exclusive, right?"

"I'd say we're back off the record, Ri," Iris said, looking hopeful. "Anything's fair game now. Whatcha got?"

"Just wanted to confirm you have enough on me to leave the whole camp angle out."

"Oh. Well, I was just going to say you're teaching girls self-defense. Is that oblique enough?"

"Yeah. Thanks."

"Look," Iris said, swiping a finger across her cell phone's large screen and handing it to Maji. "The only photo I've taken. If even that's too much, hit delete. Go ahead."

The photo showed Maji working with a student, both from a

side angle so their faces weren't identifiable. And both somewhat anonymous in their gis, Maji's braid the most distinguishing feature in the shot. "I'm good with it, if Hannah is."

"Don't worry. I'm not going to expose Hannah and her private army."

Maji sprayed her mouthful of water across the desk. She reached for a napkin to dry off the desktop, and Iris. "Sorry. That's just too ridiculous, even for you."

Iris patted herself dry, waving Maji off. "Is it? I liked the theory, until this morning's silly little scenarios."

Maji ran a quick mental review of the morning lesson. Letting a potential threat think they had the power they wanted. Naturally, Iris when confronted had immediately lashed out, and ended up pinned to the mat by Bubbles, who seemed to enjoy playing the bad guy. The girls had done a better job of submitting to a certain amount of intimidation and physical control by their role-playing adversaries. But then, they'd had four weeks learning tactical strategy, Hannah-style. The following debriefs had provided lively and instructive conversation, the girls the best advocates for minimal force against Iris's stubborn skepticism. "So you still think *strike hard, strike fast, and get away* is the best approach in all situations?"

"Works for me." Iris eyed her critically. "And come on, you could have told them a story or two from Iraq, right? You didn't just play helpless there."

Maji thought of numerous times she'd had to witness violence without stopping it, to stay safely undercover until an extraction could be properly executed. It was torture, but better than blowing the mission or even succeeding in getting the target out at the cost of all the collaterals. "We make tactical choices everywhere, every day. Mission objectives before personal relationships."

"Wow. You really are still a soldier girl, aren't you?" Iris leaned back in her chair, tipping it onto two feet. "But you wouldn't let someone you cared about get hurt, on a theory. You came after me."

"We did. But we wouldn't have sacrificed all those refugees to get you out. When I picked up that AK and starting firing, that wasn't my training kicking in. That was a fail on my part."

"Well, it worked. So thank God for failure. What did you think you were going to do, talk your way out?"

"That's what Civil Affairs does. Hearts and minds, remember?"

"Well, those goons don't have hearts or minds. They deserved what they got."

"Not from me."

"And why not you? Rules of engagement let you kill the enemy combatant, right? They would have killed you, after all."

Maji stood, leaving her plate. She needed to get out of that room, away from Iris before she said more than she was allowed to. "I'm nobody's judge, jury, and executioner. I don't decide who deserves to live."

Iris rose and leaned across the desk. "Well, if it came down to me or some jihadi, I hope you'd pick me."

"I wouldn't count on it." Maji let the door slam behind her.

After a full week of very intense role-playing in the dojo, Rose was happy to start the weekend with Sander gone. She could let down almost all her guard with just Dev and Tom in the house with them. And she'd stopped worrying about what she was allowed to say or not say around Frank, finally. The seven of them around the dining table felt like a large family.

Rose watched Maji finishing the kitchen cleanup. Angelo had returned to his work in the basement, and Jackie had disappeared as soon as the meal was over, Dev trailing dutifully behind her. Frank and Tom had tried to stay and help, but Maji had shooed them out. She had no trouble bossing the men around, Rose noticed. *But she only orders me around when there's danger. Is that respect?* As Nonna said, she shouldn't assume. She should ask. But Rose didn't want to intrude. When Maji gave herself hands-on tasks, Rose had come to realize, she was giving herself time to think.

Rose hoped it wasn't her selfishness causing Maji to fret. "If you really don't want to take me to the market, I can just send Frank."

Maji turned and removed the apron that looked so incongruous on her. She looked neither surprised by Rose's proximity, nor irritated by the reference to Angelo overruling her judgment. "You've been overexposed lately. Makes me uneasy."

Rose thought of how Maji had kissed her, here in the kitchen, after the sailboat incident. She acted no less protective now. "Well, I'm willing to take the risk. But it's your call. I go where you go, do what you say, don't ask questions, remember?"

Maji didn't smile at the reminder. "It's not for much longer."

"I wasn't complaining." Rose picked up a dish towel and started drying. Busy hands she could keep to herself. "Though I am sorry we'll miss the last week of camp."

"It's mostly the kids learning how to keep on training once they get home. You don't really need that."

"Yes, I do. I plan to keep up as much as I can, even with school." Rose hadn't realized how invested she had become, but it was true. "Where can I find someplace that teaches what Hannah does?"

Maji almost smiled and picked up a towel to help with the drying. "You can find martial arts clubs on campus, some dojos in town, depending on where you teach next year. The mind-set will be different, but at least you can keep up physical training."

Rose let the fact that Maji knew she was on the academic job market go without comment. "You mean hit first, then run? Or whatever the Krav thing is."

Maji glanced at her sideways. "Shop for a good sensei, a good dojo with the right spirit. Hannah can give you recommendations. No place Iris would go."

"I noticed she left early today." Rose took the opening. "Are your interviews done?"

"Well, she's gotten all she's getting."

Rose stopped her busy work and faced Maji, whose face remained tellingly blank. "Are you ever going to forgive her? For betraying you."

"For that, whatever. For getting Palmer killed, never."

Rose leaned a hip on the counter, intentionally giving Maji some breathing room. "Is that really fair? Journalists report on events, they don't cause them."

"She went in without us, against orders, knowing soldiers would go in after her and likely get killed doing it. The fact she thought it would be people she'd never met getting hurt doesn't make that better."

"No, I suppose not. What happened to Palmer?"

"Mashriki's men saw he had the highest rank, so they grabbed him, put a gun to his head, ordered us to lay down arms. Which we did. Then they separated us, and we expected to get interrogated, beaten— the usual. Instead, they filmed Palmer's beheading, hung up his dog tags, and put his body on the fire. Then they brought us back out to watch him burn." Maji's voice was flat, her eyes pinned to the wall beyond Rose.

Rose moved to embrace Maji, her instinct halted when Maji scooted abruptly backward. But she didn't leave the room at least. "I heard about that video," Rose said, stepping back again to put Maji at ease, as if that were possible. "Oh my God, his parents!"

"My last stop before New York. Real salt-of-the-earth folks. Like him."

What was there to say? "I'm so sorry."

Maji's face shifted, from miles away to back in the room, though still eerily blank. "Try to sleep early. We need to be at the market right when it opens."

Blinking at the dismissal, Rose dried her hands and took a step toward the living room. "Is the air on upstairs?"

"Yeah. Jackie was too hot last night."

So her own bedroom window was closed, and Maji would sleep in Carlo's room tonight. Relief and disappointment jumbled together. "Oh. See you in the morning then." She wanted to add some word of comfort, but *sweet dreams* seemed crass. "Maji? I don't blame you."

"That makes one of us."

What? Oh. "I meant, for staying mad at her. I'm sorry you have to deal with that, with all this going on, too."

"I'll be fine by morning," Maji said. "Good night."

CHAPTER TWENTY-FIVE

They rode along the water, bathed in sun as it began to burn off the fog over the Sound. Rose began to sing. Maji enjoyed Rose's voice behind her, the feel of her hands clasped lightly against her belly, her thighs pressing in to hold on as they leaned into the turns. Rose hadn't pretended their conversation last night hadn't happened, but she hadn't made a big deal of it. "How are you?" was all she had asked.

"Ready to roll," Maji had said—and she was. Getting away from the House that Death Built, and not to more scenarios at the dojo for a change, sounded great. The market meant a host of familiar faces, vendors for the local farmers, and sometimes even the farmers themselves. Maji wished she could allow Rose the luxury of chatting with each and every one, letting her inner anthropologist out. But quicker was safer.

Maji wove the bike slowly through the parking lot, scanning the few vehicles on-site this early. No obvious red flags. At the far side, she stopped and let Rose dismount, then parked in a lined-off corner in the shade.

"You won't get a ticket?"

"Never have before," Maji replied as they pulled off helmets and gloves. She took a minute to scan the grassy lawn covered in vendor tents. "Fastest way out is here." She pointed to a dirt footpath leading into the parking area near their corner.

Rose nodded, and slipped on her Jackie Os. She fluffed her hair back up, still listening.

"All the stalls run parallel, five rows, four aisles. There's grass on the far side." Maji pointed away from the parking area. "Then a fire lane. See where it curves out toward the water?"

Rose nodded again. "Turn right and head uphill to reach the bike. Anything else?"

"Yeah. Restrooms are at the far end."

"I know. I've been here dozens of time. And I've managed never to have to rely on that restroom."

Maji chuckled. "Smart." She thumbed a switch on her watch, confirmed the GPS was active and that she could both hear and transmit, and spoke. "Rios to Taylor."

"Go, go."

"We're at the market, Water Street and Main. What's your twenty?"

"Couch. Jackie's barely up and not nearly caffeinated enough for golf." He paused. "I have you on-screen. Both of you show."

Then Rose's tracking fob was sending clearly at this distance, also. "Let's shop," Maji said, opening the bike's seat compartment to stow their gloves. They clipped their helmets to the bike and headed for the produce stands.

Rose touched her arm, and they both paused. "Can't we leave the coats with the bike, too?" she asked. "It's starting to get warm."

Should she tell her it was either the jackets or bulletproof vests? No, that was uncalled for. "Please leave yours on. It's Kevlar air mesh, strong but porous. And we'll be quick."

Rose looked doubtful. "Seems like overkill." She moved her stiff, reinforced arms robotically, "All this Mad Max business."

Maji chuckled. "Your skin's worth protecting, trust me. Kevlar is a girl's best friend."

As they walked among the stalls, shoppers and vendors alike exclaimed over Maji. A bouncy redhead at the flower stand hopped off her stool to give Oyster Cove's prodigal daughter a squeeze. "How long you been back, girl?"

While they talked, Rose admired the lilies, calendula, delphinium, and bee balm. Maji paid the redhead for a bouquet and put them on hold for Frank.

Moments later, a man with a stroller caught Maji's arm. "Rios! Captain Andrews said you were home. Look who joined us while you were on tour." He held the baby out to Maji, who made admiring noises but didn't ask to hold it. "You gonna stick around? Join the force?"

The off-duty cop let Maji off easy, but a few stalls later, an avuncular gray-haired man in preppy shorts and polo shirt stopped them. Maji squinted at him, moving between Rose and the stranger.

"John Sanford, Nassau County Credit Union. We'd be proud to have you on our float, if someone else hasn't grabbed you up already." He shook her hand and backed up, seeing her confusion. "The Fourth of July parade, Ms. Rios. We like to honor our vets." He gave her his card, so she could call him to say yes.

Maji was polite to everyone who stopped her, but clearly antsy with the delays. Rose lingered on the periphery, keeping one ear open while she took her time examining the bounty of June on Long Island. The piles of greens—chard, kale, and broccoli rabe, in addition to the standard spinach and lettuce, pulled Rose into one stall, while the strawberries and sugar snap peas called to her from another. The root crops still hanging on from winter—scallions, leeks, carrots, potatoes, beets, and yellow onions—just sat quietly, hoping to be noticed. She gave them their due. Rose passed over the chives, dill, and cilantro, taking care of their large basil order before Maji got too fussed and rushed them home again.

"Sorry," Maji said when they were alone briefly. "I didn't expect this. Let's get the basil, and beat it."

"Done." Rose smiled. "Maybe we can slip out before someone asks you to run for mayor."

Maji blushed. "No chance."

As they wound through the shoppers toward the bike, Maji stopped and directed her attention ahead of them, thumbing her watch as she did so. "Two guys in suits, both carrying."

She fished the bike keys from her pocket and handed them to Rose. "If I'm not there when you reach the bike, take it, ditch it when you're able, and hide. Clear?"

Rose nodded, speechless. Run—alone? The men were coming toward them, never glancing at the stalls. Maji took her elbow and guided her forward, then turned them into a U-shaped stall. *Won't we be trapped here?* Panic welled up, despite Rose's trust in Maji's judgment.

"Maj!" the vendor exclaimed.

"Hey, Marty. Long time. Got some trouble on our tail. Run interference for me?"

"Sure, hon."

"Under and out," Maji said into Rose's ear. "Now!"

Rose didn't hesitate, just hit the ground and rolled under the nearest table, popping up on the far side.

As she glanced back, one pursuer was flailing backward toward his partner, who caught him as Maji turned her way. Rose picked up a melon and lobbed it at the encumbered thug, yelling, "9-1-1," as she let it fly. Then she turned and ran for the bike, not waiting for the satisfying thwonk it made, or the tangled pile of angry limbs to sort itself out.

❖

"Dial it in, Marty," Maji bit out as she planted one hand between two stacks of strawberry baskets and vaulted over the table, sprinting off after Rose. To the urgent voices in her ear, all she said was, "Stand by."

As Maji neared the bike, she saw a man approach from behind Rose, who was fastening on her helmet. "Six o'clock," she yelled, putting a last blast into her already pumping legs.

Rose spun and kicked her pursuer in the knee, a nice sharp side kick that drew a yelp and bent him over the wounded limb. He reached one hand out to the bike for support, shoving the other under his jacket for the pistol undoubtedly there.

Maji reached the injured man as Rose was mounting the bike, fumbling to put the key in and start it. She struck him once, hard, and he sprawled behind the bike. She moved to check his pulse, giving her update as she leaned down.

"Two tails lost, one down parking lot, and"—a black SUV honked and tried to jockey through the now-crowded lot—"driver stuck in lot," she finished.

Leaving the downed man be, she hopped on behind Rose. "Go, go, go." For the comm, she added, "Clearing out. Stand by."

"Hooah," Dev's voice replied.

Rose rolled on the throttle and the bike leaped forward. She braked, throwing Maji into her back. Her bare head hit the back of Rose's helmet with a sharp crack. Her vision blurred. "Ease it on, and point us down the path," Maji managed to spit out, blinking hard.

"Can't we just trade places?" Rose's voice climbed with each word.

"No time. Black SUV on our tail." And indeed, the big vehicle was trying to turn around and wend its way out of the tangle of cars, to get onto the access road the bike was headed toward. At least she could see it clearly again.

As Maji clung to her, Rose tried again, this time carrying them smoothly down the incline and onto the fire lane, headed toward the water. When the paved lane ran out, Maji tapped her to turn right, and they passed between the waist-high poles meant to keep cars off the bike trail. A few hundred feet down, as they started to gain on a group of unwitting bicyclists, Maji tapped her again. "Okay. Stop, but don't cut it."

Rose pulled over smoothly and stopped. Maji hopped off the back and gave her a hand scooting back. She unhooked her helmet from the bike and slipped it on, ignoring the sting where it pressed against her throbbing forehead. "Okay to just hang on?"

Rose nodded. "Sorry."

Maji slid on. "Sorry, hell. You rock."

They zipped past the bicyclists, leaving a muted protest behind them as the pack realized what had happened. As soon as the trail met road again, Maji slowed and threaded the bike out between the anti-car posts, onto the street.

"Now what?" Rose asked.

"Long way home." Maji turned them onto a two-lane highway, picking up speed on the long open stretch. From behind them, a siren sounded, growing louder.

"Thank God," Rose breathed.

"Don't thank her yet," Maji cautioned, pulling onto the shoulder with the bike pointed toward the median. "And don't let go."

The NYSP car pulled up behind them, and from each side an officer in a domed hat emerged. Maji waited as they approached the bike, speaking softly. "Delta Tango Charlie One Five One. Copy?"

"Copy. We show you on northbound parkway, County Road cross."

"Not for long. Stand by." To Rose, she added, "Hang on tight."

The officers within yards of them, Maji slammed on the throttle and hurtled the bike across the highway. The uniformed men dashed back to their vehicle. The bike bounced into the recessed median, and she throttled on again to pop them up and into the lanes going back the way they had come.

When the heavy police cruiser tried to follow in their path, its undercarriage made a grinding shriek on the incline down. It roared up the opposite side, leaving a trail of oil as it went. The driver pushed it hard, even as the rapidly drying pistons began to knock.

The bike zipped quietly down the two-lane road, the siren and its source receding in the mirrors. Maji eased off the throttle as they began passing neighborhoods again, and turned right, slowing to residential speed.

Rose relaxed with the decrease in speed, but kept her grip tight, in case. They seemed to be crawling along the little tree-lined street. Any second the cruiser could appear behind them. A few houses into the second block of modest single homes with neat yards, Maji turned the bike sharply left, and they bounced down a grass and dirt alley lined by fences and garages. The bike skidded to a stop by the gate in a tall wooden fence.

"Open the gate!"

Rose hopped off, thumbed the gate handle, and shoved it open. Maji drove silently into the yard, the gate closing behind them. As she set the kickstand, a brindle Doberman-boxer mix dashed from the side yard, barreling toward them. Maji lunged past Rose and met it as it rose up. Before Rose could suck in enough breath to scream, Maji had the big dog by the throat, pinned to the grass.

"Barkley! Hush!" Maji commanded. The dog whimpered, wagged its tail, and tried to lick the hand planted at its throat.

Rose slumped back against the closed gate. What would come at them next?

The door at the top of a short set of concrete steps opened, and a statuesque woman in her late thirties, yellow-blond hair falling in her eyes and bathrobe clutched to her chest, glared at them. *Amazons?* Rose nearly giggled, heady with relief and the surrealness of it all.

"Always an entrance," the Amazon said to Maji and grabbed her into a tight embrace. "Who you running from?" she asked with a smirk as she let Maji go, eyeing Rose knowingly.

Maji ignored the question and the innuendo. "Sorry about the wake-up."

"No sweat, Jailbait. I'm due at the station anyway."

"Can I use your landline?"

"Still in the same place."

Maji headed through an arched doorway into the dining room and began dialing. "Lost them. Yours secure?" Rose heard her say.

"I'm Karen," the Amazon said, pulling Rose's attention back into the kitchen, and to their host. "Sit down. Coffee?"

Rose shook her head. She needed to come down before she fell down. "Water, please."

Karen brought her a glass from the tap and tilted her head toward the next room. "Nice to see Maji with someone her own age."

"Hey!" Maji's voice piped in. "No stories."

Karen straightened her robe, lowering her voice. "When she was sixteen, she had this fake ID from Columbia…"

"*Seven*teen. And it was real."

While Karen went to dress for work, Rose closed her eyes and stroked Barkley's silky ears, taking comfort from the solid body leaning in to her thigh. A few minutes later, Karen returned, nicely pulled together and buttoning a white short-sleeved uniform shirt with *Fire Marshal* embroidered on it. An expletive from the other room turned both their heads. Maji appeared in the doorway, looking vexed.

Karen caught Rose's eye and shook her head, smiling. "Still not a morning person, huh?"

Maji didn't correct her, or explain. "Could you drop us off on your way in?"

Chapter Twenty-six

They rode slunk down in the Jeep like teenagers ashamed to be spotted with a parent, much to Karen's continued amusement. "Brenda's gonna love this."

"Still together?" Maji asked from the space between the front passenger seat and the console, bracing herself against the bumps in the springy suspension. A blooming headache reminded her that she should have asked Karen for an ice pack, earlier. But she'd been preoccupied.

"Don't sound so surprised."

"No, of course. But, you know. How is she?"

"Four years clean and sober," Karen answered with pride.

"Wow."

"Damn straight, wow. Doubting Thomas."

"I was pulling for her," Maji objected. "Well, say hi, okay?"

"Say hi yourself—you two come for dinner sometime, and we'll catch up," Karen suggested. "You can go out in public with her, can't you?"

"Not after today," Rose piped up, eliciting a true guffaw from their driver. Maji didn't laugh.

Without asking, Karen pointed the Jeep toward Hannah's house, as Maji knew she would. "Coast is clear," she announced, pulling up to the curb.

As instructed, Rose slipped out of the Jeep and rabbited for the back porch. Hannah caught her in a hug, and together they watched Karen and Maji muscle the bike out of the back of the Jeep, into the garage. As Maji gave her signature thanks and good-bye nod, Karen took hold of her wrist and spoke earnestly. Maji said something curt but polite and was released.

When Maji reached the back porch, Hannah asked, "What did Karen say?"

"Just that I'm too old to be messing around with married women,"

Maji answered, then looked Rose in the eye. "Which I never did. Knowingly."

Rose just turned and walked into the kitchen, and sat at the table there. Maji walked past her, talking to herself. No—talking on the comm again. "Package secured. Yours?" She listened a few seconds. "Will extract after debrief. Out." She opened the cabinet over the sink, then turned to Rose. "Water?"

"Please," Rose said.

Maji handed her a glass and washed four pills down with half of her own.

"Injuries?" Hannah asked.

"Just a bump." She peeled off her bike jacket and hung it on the back of a chair. "Let's do the talk. I need a shower."

"Sit," Hannah commanded. She fished in a drawer and pulled out a small flashlight. Pulling a chair to face Maji, she asked, "Any bumps besides the goose egg on your forehead?"

"My fault," Rose said.

"Nonsense," Hannah replied, while shining the light in each of Maji's eyes and closely watching the reaction.

"No, really," Rose tried again. She couldn't seem to put more words together. Had she hit her head, too?

"Really, she did great," Maji said. Then she described the two men, how they were dressed, how they behaved. "Might have been posing as Feds," she added. "Didn't wait to find out."

"What if they were?" Rose asked. "Feds, for real."

Maji shook her head, winced, and accepted an icepack from Hannah. "They would have identified themselves. Loudly, and with badges. These guys wanted to corral us before engaging."

Rose drank down the rest of her glass. "Good. I'm glad I didn't kick a federal agent."

"She got the knee, after a nice roll-under, and before driving like a pro," Maji told Hannah.

Hannah raised one brow. "And then?"

"Sirens picked us up on the parkway. I pulled over at County Road, and let two guys in state trooper uniforms approach."

"They really weren't cops?" Rose asked.

"This level of planning suggests they've been in the area, waiting for an opportunity," Hannah noted.

Rose looked into her empty glass. "Hungry," she said.

"Of course." Hannah stood and left them sitting, Rose feeling too dull to move and Maji with her head reclining on her chair back, and her feet on a second chair. Hannah set plates and silver before them, and brought Shabbos leftovers to the table. "Eat. It helps."

Rose started unwrapping the cucumber salad, the broiled salmon, and the cold potatoes. "Bubbles?"

Hannah smiled at her, and heaped large portions onto Maji's plate. "She and Rey came for supper, yes."

"Missed him again," Rose said and took a bite of salmon. Almost right away, her head felt clearer. She ate slowly, watching Maji clear her plate with uncharacteristic speed. Food must be a cure she was used to. Rose smiled for the first time since before they'd spotted the men in suits. It felt so long ago. "May I go lie down?"

"Take a bunk upstairs, middle bedroom," Hannah replied. "And you may take that shower now," she added, to Maji.

Maji stood. "C'mon. I'll give you the five-cent tour of the upstairs."

Rose woke and looked around, surprised the room was still bright. Surely she'd slept all day. No, the clock on the desk said 1:25. She rolled off the bottom bunk—Bubbles's bunk, according to Maji—and took a few minutes to search for signs of the two when they had shared the room, years ago. A yield sign on the back of the door suggested they had pillaged street signs as teens, like some of her high school friends had. An old poster from a 1995 Ani DiFranco concert tour hung on the wall. Rose leaned in close and read the inscription: *Missed you!—A.* She made a note to ask about that.

On the bookcase, a stack of textbooks looked as if they'd been pulled off the shelf and returned in a stack rather than a row. Rose remembered Hannah's promise to remove any identifiers from the dojo, and Bubbles's concern over the possibility of Iris staying in their room. But if Iris saw books on Farsi, Arabic, and general linguistics, what could she glean from that? Rose picked up the text on top and opened the front flap. Maji's real name, with a phone number and *Columbia University Department of Linguistics* were written inside, in neat print. The interior pages had highlighting, turned down pages, and not-so-neat notes in the margins. Definitely an item to pack away during Iris's visit.

She set the book aside and reached for the manila folder under it.

"If you can't sleep, that one will put you right out."

Rose turned and was relieved to see Maji smiling in the doorway. "Sorry. Hannah put these away to protect you from snoopers, didn't she?"

"You're allowed. Go ahead, open it."

Rose flipped the folder open, and read the title of what was clearly Maji's master's thesis. *Toward a Concordance Methodology for Farsi, Arabic, and Hebrew in the American Diaspora.* She skimmed down the page and understood very little. Not because it was written poorly—it read like a master's thesis should—but because the lingo was entirely out of her wheelhouse. Rose felt like she was witnessing another transformation of Maji, as believable as the Ri persona, but more relatable to her own academic world. "Did you really start at Columbia at only seventeen?"

Maji looked surprisingly shy at the question. "No, I was a sophomore by then. And dumb enough to think that an ID would convince Karen she could go to a club with me."

Rose laughed. "Didn't work?"

"She met me, but it didn't go like I'd hoped. I got drunk and stupid. Wound up in the ER. Papi had to come bring me home, and he blew my cover."

"And she's called you Jailbait ever since?"

"Yep. Can't blame her. She fought to become one of the first women in the New York City fire department. If anyone had found out she dated a juvenile, well. I'm lucky she still talks to me at all."

Rose offered her the gentlest smile she could. "People seem inclined to forgive you for all sorts of things."

"More than they should." Maji looked past Rose, her eyes sweeping the room and alighting on an unopened package on the desk. "What's that?"

"Don't know." Rose was glad she could answer that honestly, after snooping so boldly. She had seen it was addressed to M. Rios, c/o Paragon Security at an address in Madrid, and had left it alone. "Here." She handed it to Maji and watched her face, looking for answers to a question Iris had raised earlier in the week. She'd implied that Hannah had trained Maji, and perhaps others, to gain employees suitable for her private security business. Maji's face didn't betray anything as she ripped the packet open. A slow smile when she pulled out a music CD and read the back made Rose twice as curious.

"Fan mail?"

Maji's eyes flitted back and forth, her smile not entirely wiped away. "Just a gift from a friend." She left the package, but held on to the CD. "Meet me downstairs in five."

And then she was gone. Rose went down the hall to find the bathroom, wondering at the enigma that was Maji—soldier, scholar, juvenile delinquent, and child prodigy. Pretending to be a gangster's moll, street-smart and tough as nails. Now that Rose knew her better, only the last seemed unlikely.

Hannah pulled the runabout up to the swim platform twenty yards out from the estate next door to the Benedettis'. From there the boathouse was just visible. She surveyed the horizon with high-powered binoculars. Maji wished they could have waited to return until after dark, but she understood it would be best if they were back in the house when the Khodorovs arrived. She looked at Rose, also lying in the belly of the boat, and gave her a small smile. Rose flashed a grin back, her spirit of adventure apparently intact again.

"All right," Hannah said both for their benefit and for the guys covering them from inside the boathouse. "On our way."

In less than a minute, the boat bumped up against the end of the near dock protruding slightly from the edge of the boathouse. Dev gave them a quick hand out, and they scrambled for the rear of the building, in the depths of shadow. "Welcome home," he said.

Then he stood with binoculars up, scanning the Sound while Tom climbed down from the rafters, his rifle over his back.

"Home sweet home," Rose said dryly. So maybe it wasn't such a grand adventure for her, after all. The sight of guns always seemed to erase whatever fun she found in the sneaking around. Maji couldn't blame her.

"We're late to meet the caterer," Tom said, powering by them on his short, sturdy legs.

"Oh God, today?" Rose asked.

"Not you, just us," Maji answered.

"Oh, okay." Rose sounded both relieved and disappointed. "Which one did Angelo pick?"

"Cuba Libre."

"Good! Music, cleaning, and the best food of the lot."

Also, Maji thought, the FBI's way into the house. Time to start seeing Special Agent Martinez in action.

"Smooth trip home?" Angelo asked as Maji and the guys reached the basement.

"As silk. Did Frank make it to the market?"

"Yeah. Got a trunk load of produce, and leads on the guys who tagged you."

"I could have had a team on-site within an hour, if you'd called me," Rey said.

"Sorry," Angelo offered, though he wasn't. The last thing he needed was a bunch of Feds poking around, if Sirko's operatives had left anyone on watch to notice them.

"Goldberg," Dev said to Rey, not waiting to be introduced.

Rey took his hand, shook, and moved on to Tom. "You're Taylor?"

"Yes, sir. And what are we calling you?"

"Raul Machado. Here's my card. Direct line's on the back. I'll answer as Cuba Libre Catering, but it's secure. Call the number on the front only if you want food delivered."

"Got it," Angelo confirmed for them. "Oh, and this is Sergeant Rios. She goes by Ri."

"Hey," Maji said, not offering her hand. She did, however, take a card. Neither of them indicated that they had met before. The guys already knew now that Ri and Hannah were connected. A family tie to their FBI liaison was more than they needed to worry about.

They had run through almost all the initial logistics for the Fourth when Frank's voice said, via their comms, "Khodorov just pulled up. Here, not at the Big House."

"Time to see you out," Angelo said to Rey, as the team hit the stairs.

Angelo stepped out onto the front landing behind Rey, just in time to look surprised and give a friendly wave to Sander. He used his outside voice to send Rey off. "Email me your final quote tomorrow, Raul. I'll send a guy by with the deposit Monday."

"*Excelente*," Rey said, shaking his hand. He climbed into the Cuba Libre minivan with barely a glance at the notorious Russians.

"Well," Sander said, using his indoor voice as his father and their driver climbed out of the car, "I see why you picked that one."

"Hey, they had the best food, okay? All the girls agreed."

"And they all saw him, too, right?"

"Yeah, but Rose ain't swayed by any factors other than food."

"She's gay?"

"Queer as a three-dollar bill. I never mentioned that?"

"No. How's that for your straight-acting girlfriend?"

"Like dieting in a candy store," Angelo said.

Chapter Twenty-seven

Rose heard music as she approached the kitchen—horns and fiddle as well as an electric guitar and drums, with a woman singing throaty Spanish. Rock? Zydeco? Hard to classify, but definitely engaging. The urge to dance hit her, and she saw as she peeked into the kitchen that she wasn't alone in that. Tom and Maji were dancing, separately together like two friends at a party. When Maji caught her looking, she stopped cold. Tom crashed into her, and they both staggered sideways.

"Don't stop on my account," Rose said, when the pair had righted themselves.

Maji punched a finger into the CD player, and stillness reigned. "Sorry if we woke you."

"You didn't." Why Maji was embarrassed, Rose couldn't imagine. "Why haven't I heard this band before? They're so infectious." She picked up the CD case before Maji could stop her—surely the one Maji had received at Hannah's. The inscription on the back was similar to Spanish, but not Spanish.

"Erlea's more of a European sensation," Tom responded.

Rose handed the case to Maji. "You have a lot of friends in music." At Maji's uncomfortable look, she handed the CD case back. "Sorry. I noticed the inscription on the Ani poster, too."

Maji didn't provide any more information, just took the case and removed the CD from the player.

"Oh no, really. I'd love to hear the rest. Even if you're too shy to dance."

So the music filled the kitchen like sunlight, brightening the overcast morning. Rose even caught Maji singing along when she thought no one was paying attention.

Angelo stumbled into the kitchen as they were finishing breakfast, looking like he'd been up half the night. Rose worried about the hours he was keeping, the stress. "Loud," he said, as if he was hungover. "Too loud."

Tom hopped up and turned the volume down. He handed the case to Angelo, who squinted at it. "Friend of Ri's," he said with a touch of pride. "Made it big in the Eurozone."

Angelo squinted at the front and seemed to be struggling with the writing on the back. He waved it at Maji, frowning.

"It's a Basque slogan," Maji said, retrieving it from Angelo and slipping the CD in. She rose and headed for the living room. "Get some coffee, and come see me." She nearly collided with Frank as he entered, carrying the Sunday paper. She didn't greet him, just stepped aside to let him pass, then disappeared upstairs.

Rose watched her go, wondering at the mood change from apparently carefree dancing to near sullenness. What was she afraid of today?

Angelo's knock on her door—*shave and a haircut*—didn't lift Maji's spirits any. There was too much he wasn't telling her, and today it bugged the hell out of her. On a normal mission, each player knew only as much as they needed to. But this op hadn't been normal from day one. "*Al-bayt baytkum*," she called out. Literally, *The house is your house*; colloquially, but not this time, *Make yourself at home.*

Angelo slipped in and closed the door behind him, and pointedly took off his shoes, like a good guest. "So it's like that, is it?" He sipped his coffee, standing away from the desk where she sat. "What's eating you?"

She continued using Arabic. "Yesterday. Who knew we were going to the farmers' market besides Frank?"

"I see," he responded in Arabic. "I already told you, he's trustworthy. He said nothing to Gino until I instructed him to. After you and Rose were safe at Hannah's."

"So who else knew where we were?" Maji asked.

He winced. "Seems Sienna's been bugging Rose to go out and play together. Daddy's girl still wants to play with the big kids. So Rose told her she could tag along to the market, if she was willing to get up early enough. 'Course she wasn't, which is why Rose offered. But Sienna whined about it to Ricky."

"And you didn't warn us?" Maji hopped off the bed and put her face inches from his. He didn't flinch.

"I'm not getting audio on Ricky anymore," Angelo explained. "So I'm sorry. I'm doing my best."

"Do better."

Rose took her time reading the Sunday paper, rotating finished sections with Frank. When Jackie finally came down and settled in with coffee, Rose waited for her to speak first. Like Angelo, she was more lucid after coffee.

"Hey," Jackie said, tapping the paper shielding Rose's face from view.

Rose lowered the section. "Good morning."

"Sure," Jackie said, sounding unconvinced. More coffee would be needed. "Ang give you the safe house talk?"

"Yes," Rose said. "Complete with what to pack in a go bag."

"So you're ready, then."

Rose set the paper aside. Everyone in the house seemed to be on edge, or grumpy, or both. "Not yet. I'll go pack now." She rose to go.

Jackie reached out for her hand. "Hon. I'm sorry. This ain't the side of the family you should have to see."

"I'm all grown up, Aunt Jackie. No need to protect my delicate sensibilities." She patted her aunt's hand to take some of the sting out of her words and headed for her room, and solitude.

Upstairs, Rose passed the open door to Angelo's room, the closed one to Carlo's. What secret business were they up to now? If they were even in there. Maybe they'd gone down to the boathouse again, their favorite place to be alone.

Rose looked around her room, the room she had thought of as her own since her first summer visit at nine. It held none of the signs of her personality, unlike the little room with the bunk beds shared by Bubbles and Maji in their younger years. Clearly Maji had planned to spend her vacation on Long Island there.

Rose looked at the stack of books on the bedside table—all the nonfiction works relating to traditional foods, the movement against GMOs and the corporatization of farming, and ethnological field research methods. Today, none of them spoke to her. Neither did the paperbacks she'd brought, though they did bring to mind the discussion by the pool where Maji had revealed a surprising discernment in lesbian romance.

Rose sighed. If she couldn't get Maji off her mind, maybe she could find the answer to one of her many questions. She fished her laptop from the closet shelf and booted it up. She typed in a search for Erlea, the name of the band on the mysterious CD. A Wikipedia article in Spanish came up. She worked her way through it, discovered that Erlea was a woman, not a band. Rose was relieved that she could understand so much without using a translator—either mechanical, or in the next room over. At the bottom, there were links to news articles. One was in English and led to a story about the Spanish Guardia Civil and Interpol working together to foil a murder attempt on the singer and secure her father's safe entry into peace talks on behalf of the Basque separatists. The events fell between when Maji would have left the hospital in Germany and her return home—the missing months.

Rose closed the laptop, feeling as though she had trespassed. Now Iris's speculation about Maji working for Hannah's company didn't seem so far-fetched at all. Still, having an autographed CD didn't prove she had somehow helped to save the life of a Europop diva. Maybe she had just been on vacation.

Feeling oddly disloyal, Rose opened the laptop back up, and went to YouTube. She entered a search for Erlea and found a host of bootleg concert clips. Those didn't help, though the music was lively, even with poor sound quality. Finally, she stumbled onto the official Erlea channel, and a series of professionally produced music videos. The last she watched, over and over, used a mix of Spanish and Basque, like many of Erlea's songs. But it showed Erlea struggling with herself—literally. Two Erleas circled each other, sparring. When she watched on full screen and froze certain frames, Rose could tell that the twin Erleas weren't just a special effects trick—they were two very similar but not identical women. And she was ninety-nine percent sure who the Erlea body double was, in makeup and hair styling and even tattoos that matched the real Erlea's look so closely it would be hard to distinguish the two. "It's what I do," Rose heard Maji say again, so casually, in her memory. Some vacation.

Sunday dinner with the Benedettis was always a bit like watching three Ping-Pong matches going on at the table. Maji didn't even try to follow the conversations competing with each other. Normally the chaos didn't bother her, but yesterday's crack on the head was affecting her more than she'd admitted to Hannah. The headache itself was gone, but bright light bothered her and she just couldn't weed out all the voices. It was too much.

"'Scuse me," she said, heading for the kitchen. Conversation didn't stop. As the swinging door shushed closed behind her, the relative quiet immediately soothed her.

"Ri?" Rose's voice was soft against the tumble of voices that cut off again when the door closed, providing them a moment of privacy. "Are you all right?"

"I'll be fine. Anybody asks, tell them I'm PMSing."

Rose filled a glass with ice from the refrigerator door, the crunching sound unusually loud to Maji's ears. She added water, a mercifully quieter act.

"I'll tell them whatever you want, but I want the truth. Sit."

Maji sat, smiling weakly at how much Rose sounded like her grandmother when she got bossy. "Thanks." She drank the cold water slowly, wincing at the brain freeze that followed.

"Hannah says you spent months in neurological rehab. She asked me to keep an eye on you. I think you have her worried."

Neuro rehab. Crawling, walking, and eventually running obstacle drills, until the Army was satisfied she could perform in the field again. She'd been an asshole to every medic who tried to help her, the first couple months. Only the speech pathologist had seemed to understand how frustrated she felt, how furious it made her to find everything so damn difficult, and every little improvement so hard-won. Would it have been easier, she wondered now, if she hadn't been beating herself up during that time for the things she thought she'd done? The fight between wanting her mind and body back and believing she didn't deserve it had been the hardest part.

"Hey," Rose said, cradling her against her shoulder.

Maji let herself be held. She hadn't realized until then that the tears had started again. If the fugue was back, how would she make it through the next few weeks? Fuck it anyway, she didn't have time for this! She pulled back, out of Rose's gentle hold. "Let me get a good night's sleep, and if I'm an asshole again tomorrow, tell me. Deal?"

"Sure. Do you want to come back in?"

Maji shook her head. One conversation was hard enough. The thought of three or four at once made her slightly nauseous. "Maybe by dessert."

Rose slid the tray of cannoli out of Maji's reach and refilled her water glass. Then she set a half glass of red wine near Maji and dabbed a little on her collar. "There. Imbibing, Angelo style. That's a stress reliever my family can understand."

Maji tilted her head, looking up at Rose's twinkling eyes. "You're a saint like your mother, hon. A real saint." It was a poor impression of Jackie, but at least she'd had the will to try.

Rose's laugh gave her the first warm feeling of the day. Maji stared after the closing door and wished anew for a rewind.

"There's my girl," Angelo said, opening his hands wide. Gino, right behind him, grunted his greeting to Maji, who only nodded back at them, raising her wineglass.

"Sorry to be poor company, Mr. B," she said. "Is dinner over already?"

"Plenty left if you're hungry," he said. "But first, why don't you join us outside a minute."

Maji rose and followed them onto the veranda. Angelo hoped she wasn't too far off her game. Rose seemed worried, though she had played it off well when she rejoined the family in the dining room. The woman who married an operator had to be able to play-act with family, friends, and the whole world outside their insular unit. Angelo could see Rose doing that, to protect Maji and the unit. He hoped Maji could see that potential in her, too.

Gino leaned back on the patio rail, missing the view of the sunset. "I'm going to say this to you directly, because you don't seem to listen to Ang here so well."

Maji nodded, ignoring the sunset as she faced the capo. Angelo kept his hand protectively on the small of her back, like a good boyfriend.

"You go outside these walls on your own again, you're on your own. Nobody's coming to get you, and nobody's giving anything up to get you back. Are we clear?"

"Yes, sir. And Rose?"

"She won't go out again," Angelo said. "Not after today."

"But if she did? I mean, I tried to talk her out of our stupid trip this morning. Practically got killed, for what? Basil." Angelo felt Maji's back flex as she talked, her Ri attitude charging back up.

"You make it very clear to her," Gino said to Angelo, as if he'd raised the point, "same goes for her."

"But G—she's family. No offense, babe."

"Family lives here," Gino replied. "My sister wanted that girl to be raised right, she'd have stayed here and married the guy who knocked her up. You don't run away and change your name if you want your Family's protection. And look how the girl turned out, coming up in Califrootie."

"Ow," Angelo said. "That's harsh, even for you."

"Harsh? What do you know from harsh? We're talking about a guy who thinks you crossed him, he kills your whole Family, and you last of all."

"I've heard those stories about Khodorov all my life," Maji said. She gave Gino one of those little half shrugs. "Brooklyn. But he's on your team, right? I thought we were worried about this Sirko asshole, not him."

"He is. But if Sirko got what he wanted, who do you think Khodorov would blame? Sirko? No. He'd take it out on my people. My family first, then my guys' families, then my guys, then me. That's his thing."

"Shit," Maji exhaled, looking past Gino to the painted horizon. Angelo wondered if she noticed the beauty.

"Yeah, fucking right, shit. So don't take it personal if I don't prioritize a couple girls with attitudes over my whole Family. Capisce?"

"I'm sorry, Mr. B," Maji said, looking at him again. "I totally get it now."

Angelo kissed his mother good night at the Big House door and headed back into the living room. Uncle Lupo and Gino had the two armchairs, and Ricky sprawled on the couch as usual. Over by the picture window, Nonna snored in the last armchair. So he'd have to move her, or share with Ricky.

"You want me to take Nonna to her room before we get started here?" he asked.

"Nah. Let her sleep. She turns those damn ear bugs off, she's out," Gino responded.

Angelo motioned for Ricky to give him some space and got a percentage of the couch in return. "So, what's so important we get the pleasure of your company at Sunday dinner?" he asked Uncle Lupo. His grandfather's old friend and consigliere hadn't socialized with them much since Max, and then Gino, had inherited his services.

"I should come more often," Uncle Lupo conceded. "Not just when there are Family issues to discuss."

So Khodorov had brought up Vienna already. Excellent. Angelo put on a wary face. "Issues that concern me?"

"Relax," Gino said. "You'll be flattered." Ricky snorted, and Gino gave him a glare. Looking back to Angelo, he announced, "They want to buy you from me."

"And I should be flattered by this? That I can be traded, like a ball player? I'm not some schmuck wiseguy on one of your crews. I'm blood."

Lupo opened his hands, showing his palms in a placating gesture. "And so here you are, at the table. Think about the business side, for a moment. After this project, what do you have in the works?"

Angelo shrugged. "I'd come up with something."

"And your girlfriend?" Gino asked.

"Ri? What about her?"

"You stay under my roof, it's time you settled down," Gino said. "You could do better, but she'd do."

Angelo flushed. "Ri's just visiting. And no offense, G, but I know how you feel about spics. So what am I missing here?"

He looked at each of the three men, all of whom seemed reluctant to answer.

Finally, Uncle Lupo spoke up. "Khodorov offered to move you to Vienna, where he has a base. And he intimated that your continued *partnership* with Sander wouldn't cause a problem for you there. He used a word we didn't ask him to translate."

Angelo paled. Yuri had outed him? "He thinks I'm...sleeping with his son? Jesus."

"What'd you think people would think?" Ricky piped in.

"Fuck you," Angelo shot back at him. "People who know me know better, people who don't—don't count. Besides, practically anybody a Russian likes is a *partner*. And I am making them a pile of money. I rank."

"We know you," Gino said. "But the rest of my associates? They only know what they see."

"And the longer you work with that fag, the more they see...you know," Ricky added.

Angelo and Gino both glared at him. Lupo sat back, watching the three. Angelo broke the tension. "G, are you saying I'm not safe here? 'Cause of this...misunderstanding?"

"Vienna is a lovely place to live. Your mother might like to visit," Lupo said.

Angelo looked at Gino's mask of a face, Lupo's faked serenity, and Ricky's thinly suppressed glee. "So this is a done deal then?"

"We will let you know our decision tomorrow," Gino replied. "And you will abide by it."

Dismissed, Angelo stood. "Yes, sir."

CHAPTER TWENTY-EIGHT

With no one leaving the estate, Monday was designated Pesto Day. They took their stations around the kitchen, with cutting boards, large knives, and the food processor standing by to turn the piles of raw ingredients into green gold. Maji tapped her large knife restlessly against the board, anxious to get busy.

Angelo put on a demo CD of the Cuba Libre band, and Latin rhythms filled the room.

Sienna leaned in close to Maji and whispered in her ear. "Maybe now Nonna won't hear so good. When you don't want her to, then it's every word you say."

After a few minutes, Maji's feet and hips moved of their own accord to the music. She gave Sienna a little hip check. Sienna bumped her back.

"I wish I could move like you," Sienna said, back to the leaning in but no longer whispering.

"It's in the genes, maybe," Maji said. "But you can learn."

Ang pointed his knife at Rose. "Rose did. You took classes, right?"

Rose colored. "If you count Latin ballroom, I'm not bad. But nothing club style."

"Your dance card's gonna be full at the Hotel Nacional party, anyway," Angelo said to her. "Even Nonna's gonna have guys lined up to spin her around the floor. Right, Nonna?"

"What?"

Angelo took Maji by the hand, and they fell into step together like they had many times before. Whenever they prepped for an op in Central or South America, they practiced whatever was current in that arena. The dance floor was an excellent place to pass information without being overheard.

The floor here was a bit tight, however. Sienna and Jackie moved back to give them space, but Nonna just scowled. "If you're not going to help—"

"Get out of my kitchen!" Maji and Angelo said along with her, grinning at each other.

Angelo switched the stereo settings to pipe into the living room and took Maji by the hand again. "Oh, come on," he said in response to her look. "We'll be back to earn our share. You will not miss the world-famous, orgasmic Benedetti secret family recipe pesto."

Sienna followed them into the living room, looking envious. She plunked herself onto the couch. "Ricky never takes me dancing. How am I going to learn before the party?"

"Does he know how?" Angelo asked. When Sienna waved a hand to indicate her husband was only so-so, he added, "So go get him. He better brush up, too."

"He's out."

Angelo's face lit up. "I gotcha covered."

He disappeared into the kitchen and returned with Rose in tow, protesting as she wiped one hand on her apron.

"You lead, or follow?" Maji asked, looking at Rose skeptically.

"Ri!" Sienna said, clearly enjoying the scandal.

Rose gave her a rare patronizing look. "That's not an offensive question. Women still need one of each, when they partner dance." She turned to Maji. "And the answer depends on the dance. What have we got?"

"Salsa, rumba, Latin swing, merengue, and tango."

"Oh. Well, if we stick to ballroom, I can lead the salsa. And a waltz. I can follow tango. But I don't know the rest."

"You two are in luck," Angelo said. "Ri grew up with all of those. We can show them, right?"

Maji frowned at him, wondering what his agenda could be.

"Jeez, Ri," Sienna said. "I can't believe he has to talk you into dancing with him. I'll trade you Ricky, and throw in his Corvette."

Maji rolled her eyes and shook her head, smiling. "Whatever. At least it's exercise."

Angelo kept the music loud enough to feel the rhythm, but low enough to talk over. He and Maji demonstrated their version of the salsa, while Rose led for Sienna, showing her the more basic moves.

"You're so good," Sienna said to Rose. "How did you learn to lead?"

"Classes," Rose answered.

"Yeah, but…"

"She's from California," Maji offered. "They got same-sex classes, dance parties, even clubs. Just like New York."

"For guys, yeah. I been in a gay bar. I didn't see any women dancing."

"You just went to the wrong place," Maji insisted. "I been to places you'd love."

"You have?" Sienna asked. "Why?"

"No guys hitting on you," Rose said. "Just dancing."

Sienna stepped on Rose, and swore. She stopped and looked down at her feet, clearly embarrassed and frustrated. "I'm sorry. You're good, I'm just…"

"A beginner," Rose said. "You're doing fine."

Sienna looked uncertain. "Ricky don't like it when I dance with other guys." She looked to Rose, then Maji. "Can we go on a girls' night to the city? You know, after."

"I guess." Rose gave Maji an uncertain look. "You said you know places?"

"Yeah. But if you want to impress the ladies there, you're going to need to up your game." Maji grinned at Angelo. "Show her the good moves."

Angelo shook his head. "Sienna needs me more." He cut in on Rose, offering Sienna his hand. "C'mon, let's make you look good for the party."

Rose and Maji looked at each other. "Don't be shy," Angelo called over, never missing a step as he led Sienna through a basic set.

"Can you lead?" Rose asked.

Maji gave her a wicked grin. "This is my soundtrack since I could walk. On the dance floor, I can do anything you want me to."

"Ri, play nice." Ang gave them a wink, and Sienna giggled.

Rose blushed deeply, and held out her hand. "Fine. Be gentle."

Maji took the lead and was pleased with how easily Rose kept up. She was a relaxed follow, keeping her left hand light on Maji's shoulder and maintaining eye contact. Just a small tug on their joined hands or a gentle press of the hand on Rose's back was enough to communicate. Maji didn't smile—if she did it would morph into a stupid grin. Instead, she let the warmth radiating between them sink into her already sinuous hips. When Rose missed a beat, Maji glanced over her shoulder and saw Ricky standing in the doorway, enjoying the show. "Ignore him. Please," she said.

"With pleasure," Rose said and found the rhythm again.

Angelo, too, noticed Ricky taking in the little party. Sienna waved him off and just kept practicing her new moves with him. So Angelo danced Sienna over closer to the door. "Wanna cut in? Assuming you can handle a woman this hot."

"Ha-ha. Some of us got work to do."

Angelo stopped and gave Sienna an apologetic look. "You excuse us for a minute?"

Sienna looked disappointed, but Angelo knew she was used to being displaced for business.

He waited until she'd found a spot to watch her new buddy Ri and her cousin. "Seriously, Rickster. Where you been?"

"Out."

"You're going out when the rest of us are on lockdown?"

"Sure. Nobody's enough of an idiot to mess with me."

Angelo snorted. "Or Sirko knows nobody'd trade anything of value to get you back."

"Fuck you. Where's your boy genius at?"

"My house—working."

"Alone? Since when do you trust him?"

"My guys are in the house. Besides, what's he gonna do?"

Ricky's face fought to hold back his thoughts. "He won Nonna over. He'll steal your mother next. It's what they do."

Angelo's bark of a laugh caused a halt on the dance floor. "So what if he does? They'll have someone to dance with at the party. Like your wife."

As he spoke, Sienna danced by herself, imitating as best as she could on her own.

"Fuck me," Ricky whispered, his eyes glued to Maji and Rose. "You and Ri ever…you know. A three-way?"

"No." Angelo paused. "And if you have, I don't want to hear about it."

"Those two could put on a show for me, though. Come on, don't you see it?"

Angelo bumped him, hard. "She's my cousin!"

"She ain't mine. Hell, even Carlos wanted a piece of that. What a waste, huh?"

Angelo pushed him out the door. "Get. Just get out of here. Go."

"Fine. I gotta take care of something, anyway." Ricky grabbed his crotch as he spoke, then scooted through the door before Angelo could reach him.

"He's such an ass sometimes," Sienna said, taking Ricky's place beside Angelo. "Maybe I better go check on him."

Angelo thought she looked more hopeful than actually annoyed with Ricky. Not for the first time, Angelo wondered about the two of them. Straight couples would always be a mystery.

When Angelo returned from checking on Sander's progress, the whole pesto crew was just sitting down to plates at the Big House patio tables. The Sound looked smeary in the distance, the humidity hazing up the view. "You're going to be so glad you helped in the kitchen," he told Maji, with a wink.

Maji took her first bite of pesto on homemade pasta and said something unintelligible but nearly ecstatic before swallowing it. She mouthed "Wow," at him, her eyes wide.

"Told you," Angelo said. "Don't I always look out for you?"

"I take back everything I said about you before," she deadpanned. "For this, I would actually think about marrying you."

"Me? It's Nonna you should marry—you want the family recipes."

Maji extended a hand dramatically toward Nonna and spouted flowery Italian in her direction.

Nonna kept a straight face, but not without visible effort. "I'm too old for you, *bambina*. 'Sides, it's Rose been writing all my recipes down. Work on her."

Maji grinned and turned to Rose, reaching for her hand. But before she could unleash more Italian, Rose raised a hand. "I'm pretty sure the Army would object."

"For this pesto, I would go AWOL."

"If Rose wanted a ring on it, it'd be done already," Sienna piped in. "Right, Rose?"

Rose gave her cousin a look of appreciation. "Thank you."

"So why don't you?"

"Why don't I what?"

"Have some woman wearing your ring," Sienna said. "You're gorgeous and nice and smart. You got a good job. There must be a lineup, back home."

"Well…" Rose looked genuinely uncomfortable.

"I know, I know. You were really down last summer over that one. But you must have had dates since then."

"She doesn't need to date—she only needs to cook," Maji quipped. "Lesbians love potlucks, right?"

Rose gave her a cold smile. "You tell me. You seem to be the authority. Excuse me."

Sienna turned to Maji as the screen door banged shut. "Now you went too far, Ri."

"With what?"

"The flirting. Can't you tell she has a crush on you?"

"No." Maji looked toward the screen door. "She does not. Besides, we're just kidding around. Don't you and your girlfriends kid around?"

"Sure, but we're all of us straight. Nobody's feelings get hurt."

"Shit. You really think I—"

Conversation paused as the screen door swung back open. Rose came through, holding a baking pan in both hands. "As I recall, Ri, you like tiramisu almost as much as pesto." Rose began cutting pieces and scooping them onto dessert plates.

Maji looked wary. "It may be a tie."

Rose served all but Maji, as the others held their tongues in anticipation. She set her piece aside and scooped a large helping onto the last empty plate. "So," she said, "what would you bring to the table? You know, as a dowry."

Sienna and Jackie and Angelo looked at each other, sharing their amusement.

Angelo grinned. "You're the one started this, Rios. Put up or shut up."

"I have a great sense of humor..." Maji's voice rose as it trailed off.

"That sounded more like a question than a statement," Rose noted. "What else have you got?"

"Um..."

Sienna looked both delighted and sympathetic. "Help her out, Ang. She's your girlfriend!"

He looked Maji over, with a smile that said he was playing along. "Okay, well, she's good at doing dishes. A real trouper."

"I have a dishwasher. And it's very quiet." Rose looked thoughtful. "Will you teach me to merengue?"

Maji blinked. "Sure."

Rose offered a forkful of tiramisu to Maji, who leaned hesitantly forward and let Rose feed it to her.

Maji groaned, shutting her eyes in bliss, apparently oblivious to the chuckles of the others. She opened one eye and looked at Rose, as if gauging her mood.

Rose took another spoonful but held it back, one eyebrow arched. "Will you teach me the tango?"

Maji looked crestfallen. "I only know the follow." She perked up slightly. "How 'bout the rumba?"

"You're not selling it," Rose said, giving her another forkful anyway.

As Maji sighed through the next ecstatic mouthful, Angelo said, "Jeez, Ri, just learn how to cook, already."

Maji pulled herself up and called him an idiot with her face alone. "As if."

"Oh, here," Rose handed her the whole plate, "knock yourself out."

Maji took the plate without a word and disappeared into the kitchen, the sound of laughter behind her.

Angelo followed her in. She defended her plate with a raised fork and a steely look.

"You're finally having some fun, huh?"

She stopped playing and just looked at him. "What are you setting Rose up for?"

"I'm not. I'm letting her off the hook."

"By making her look like an unrequited fool? You been pushing us together all day. It's not fair to her."

"To her? Look, anybody catches her looking at you funny, word's already out she's got a crush. You hold your side together, they'll think that's all it is. And when you do get together later, it won't be such a shocker."

"Later? There's no later for Rose and me. And you know why."

He gave her a funny look. "Well, there's enough questions floating about me, as it is."

"What kind of questions?"

"Khodorov intimated that Sander and me are more than colleagues. To Gino, during negotiations for my move to Vienna."

She snorted. "What are you, afraid Gino will screw up your timing by jumping the gun?"

"No—and yes, plus I got more to finish before we get this baby all the way home. And if he's enough of an idiot to hurt me, there goes all my plans for protecting the Family. Speaking of which, you talked to Tom yet?"

The stone mask slid down over her features. "I haven't figured out what to say."

"You got eight languages. Find the words."

"What you want is unspeakable." She left the unfinished plate on the counter and walked away from him.

CHAPTER TWENTY-NINE

Rose and Sienna did the sidestroke together, close enough to talk while swimming. What felt like an easy warm-up seemed to be exercise for her cousin. Thunder rumbled in the distance, reminding Rose of the day Angelo had plucked her out of the pool while Maji ran after a drone. A woman with a handgun, against a flying machine with unknown weapons. She glanced over at Maji, who sat in the shade on a lounge chair, a cap and dark glasses hiding her face. And yet Rose was sure Maji was taking everything in, as well as listening on the comm to whatever was happening in the house.

"You think the light bothers her?" Sienna asked.

Rose flushed, caught looking. But Sienna's question was innocent enough. "Why should it?"

"Ang mentioned Ri's got some issues, you know, from the war. I just thought, maybe."

"What kind of issues?" Rose stopped moving forward and started treading water, her back toward Maji.

Sienna put her feet down, seeming happy to stand for a moment. "Well, besides the facelift, there's the moods and the headaches. And he's a little worried about fireworks. But how can we have a party on the Fourth, and no sparkles?"

Rose remembered the last time she went to town to see the *sparkles* with Sienna and the family. The bigger the bang, the more Sienna liked it. "I suppose a lot of vets have trouble with fireworks. Maybe we could do some kind of light show instead. More ooh and aah, less kaboom."

"You really do like her, don't you? I mean, *like her* like her."

Rose wondered how much to admit to. She smiled ruefully, feeling dishonest. "Well, you wondered why I'm still single. Apparently only the unattainable appeals to me." The look on Sienna's face startled her. "Plus, I would never get between Ang and a woman he cared about. Even if I could."

"Oh, come on. You could if you wanted."

Rose frowned. "Flattering, but no. People are what they are. I don't waste my time on straight women."

"Well, maybe Ri's bi. Or maybe she's gay, and she just don't know it. I hear that happens." Sienna shaded her eyes with her hand, the better to assess her cousin's girlfriend. Rose knew without turning exactly how Maji looked in her running shorts and crop top, her shoulders and abs showing. She didn't have to wait long to hear how Sienna saw her. "And she is, kind of...muscly. Not that she's butch exactly. But she is a badass. You can tell by how she walks and talks."

Yes, Rose thought. Much more here than in the dojo. There Maji had nothing to prove, no persona to project but her own. "Well, she's Ang's badass. So that's that."

Tom ambled out with a pitcher in his hand and an empty glass. "Iced tea?"

"Thanks." Maji wondered why he hadn't just asked over the comm. When he motioned to her to switch to listen only, she knew she would find out.

"You got the headaches again?"

"Nothing serious. Little light sensitive. A bump on the head will do that." She was dodging, and they both knew it. He'd seen her a few months ago, in the field when she wasn't a hundred percent yet.

"So will enough stress. Not the kind you do great under—the kind you don't."

Tom knew her too well, the price of living and training side by side. And yet she'd never told him her real name. That could wait, maybe forever. On this op, the part getting to her, the clock was ticking.

She sighed and took her shades off to look him in the eye. "I'm not okay. But I will be."

"Maybe Dev should check you out."

"No. All I need is some rest, a chance to let the neurons reset and calm down. Don't call the medic. But you can help."

"Anything you need. Neck rub?"

She had no idea how to get from the safe ground of her injuries to the big ask. "Nah. You've already given me two nights without a watch. Sleep's the best."

"Maybe Dev's got supplements or something. A B-12 shot. Let's ask."

"Maybe. It's more stress than anything, at this point. Couldn't hurt."

"Maybe it's time to rotate protectees, Ri. You got no shields around yours—that's stress you don't need."

Stop dancing, Rios. Tell him. "I got enough. No, it's the endgame that's bothering me. You know it's gotta be bigger than our brief, right?"

"'Course. Two biggest targets we could go after, and our key player operating without a cover. Feds can't be fully briefed, or we'd have been shut down by now. At this point, I'm not asking any questions, on a strictly CYA basis."

"Amen, brother. Glad you caught up. And Dev?"

"He sizes it up about the same. Only he asked the question I was afraid to say out loud."

"You want me to say it for you?"

"No. I don't hear it, I can pretend it isn't true."

There was no way to soften this truth. One of their own was going down, and they couldn't stop him without sacrificing the mission and a slew of civilians. "Well, it's too late for me. I asked, and he told."

"Jesus, Ri. No wonder you're in knots." He looked away, then back at her. "He can't think we're going to help him."

And yet, Angelo expected it of them—the only sacrifice larger than risking your own life. Back when Tom was on a normal all-male team, she knew he'd taken point on disarming a homemade nuclear bomb hidden in a high-rise. "You got called to work a dirty bomb once, right?"

"It's not the same. Even with everyone else evacuated, they weren't safe. The chance it was a normal explosive dressed up was negligible. Wasn't a true me-versus-them call."

"Then why did you make them evacuate?"

"Just in case. Just to give them a chance."

"Well, this one's real. And there's only one way to keep his hands steady. He needs us."

"I'd rather take on a nuke, Ri."

"Me too, brother. Me, too."

As she ran to the shelter of the kitchen, Rose noted Maji standing under the shallow overhang, waiting to make sure everyone else was safely out of the storm before following them in. Sienna had made Frank walk her up to the house at the first sprinkles, holding an umbrella over her like a valet. Jackie and Tom had dashed in as the rain began in earnest. Rose felt a little guilty, coming in last, savoring the downpour.

Lighting flashed, and the smell of ozone filled the air. When the boom came a few seconds later, the kitchen windows rattled. Rose watched Maji close her eyes and sway slightly. She recalled Sienna's gossip about Ri's trauma and knew some of that was just part of the Ri cover, ways to explain behavior that might otherwise raise questions. But some part of it must be grounded in truth. Hannah was worried, after all.

Rose took Maji by the elbow and guided her inside. "Sit down."

"I'm fine. Probably low blood sugar." But she didn't look fine—she looked pale.

"Tom! Get Dev," Rose barked into Maji's ear, hoping it was the one with the comm in it. At Maji's wince, she said, "I'm sorry. Is he coming?"

Maji nodded, her eyes half closed against the overhead lights. Rose moved to the wall and flicked the lights off.

"Thanks." As Rose saw Dev in the doorway and moved to fill him in, Maji caught her wrist. "Hey, will you keep everybody out of here for a little while?"

Rose saw pain and vulnerability in Maji's eyes. She nodded, wishing she could do more. "Sure. Wait. You're shivering." She grabbed a beach towel left behind by a dry Jackie and wrapped it around Maji's shoulders. "I'll go turn the damned AC off."

"You wanted to see me, you could just ask," Dev said, checking Maji's pupils. The penlight sent knives through her eye sockets, but she managed not to squirm, breathing through it. "Besides the photophobia, what else?"

She thought about downplaying her symptoms, but decided against it. He was the team medic, and if she couldn't perform under stress, she would need him even more. "A little trouble with multiple conversations, finding words in a pinch. And some headaches. Distracting, not disabling." But in a crisis, bad enough.

"And you thought a woman's TLC would do the trick? Typical." He tested her peripheral vision with a sneak attack, and she batted his hand away. "Not bad. More rest might do. If you sleep alone."

"Dude, why do you give me twice the shit you give the guys?"

He snorted. "Just keeping you grounded. You already have a fan club. You don't need me piling on."

"Having your team's support is not having a fan club. You know I don't expect any more or less than any other operator."

He ignored her briefly, putting the electric kettle on to boil and fussing with a teacup. He returned shortly with a steaming mug and sat across from her. "Tom's in love with you, and Ang thinks you can do anything. First one's trouble, second's dangerous. 'Cause you may be hot shit, but nobody can do anything. And he should know better than to ask."

The thing about Tom slid into her brain and skated right by. She focused instead on Ang knowing better. Had Dev figured out what Ang wanted of her, as well as his endgame? Her head hurt too much to read the nuances. She needed blunt, like a blunt object.

She reached for the transmitter, to key the radio silent.

But Dev said, "Shh," and pulled the towel closer around her. "Frank's got no comm, and we blocked Ang. It's just us three. And you look like you might puke. Just shut up and breathe for a minute."

With a bedside manner like that, no wonder he was selling cars. She almost smiled. Dev motioned for her to drink, and she blew on the mug, then sipped. Some kind of ginger tea, with extra herbs. Ayurvedic treatment.

He reached over and took her left hand, squeezing a spot that made her gasp, then relax.

"Tea and accupressure. Which week in combat medic training did they teach you that?"

Dev just gave her the little smile he reserved for old ladies and colonels with ridiculous expectations. "The week we learned how to use what's on hand. And self-care—which you clearly aren't practicing. No wonder you're a mess."

"Thanks." She sipped some more. "Camp's been helpful. And I was doing fine under stress until…"

"Till our fearless leader dumped the dirty work on you."

So he really did know. Maji guessed Angelo had picked all three of them for their ability to suss out the truth in the absence of any real information and still talk to him. Maybe even help. "I could talk to Hannah. Firewall's down, for once. But I should do it face-to-face."

"Cohen? No. She's in JSOC's pocket. This part of the op has to stay completely off book."

Maji looked at him squarely, feeling the tea and acupressure, along with sharing the weight of her burden, centering her again. "It is. But she's on board, and we're going to need her skill set to pull this off. Not to mention connections, since we can't use our own."

"You can say that again. I got a wife and kids to think about. Twenty years at Hotel Gitmo's not in my plans."

Maji blinked. She had assumed Dev was assigned here, like her. "Does JSOC even know you're here?"

"Why should they? I can spend my hundred and twenty however I want."

Wow. He wasn't on assignment, like her or Tom. "Tom said he'd rather face a nuke." Neither of them smiled, and Maji felt the urge to change the subject. "Mira and the girls will have you back soon. I miss them."

"They miss you too, Ri. When we're done here, come see lovely Jersey."

"Thanks." It was hard to picture him in a real neighborhood, though. "You really went with regular Reserves? After all this." She sucked down the cooling tea, watching his face form an answer.

"When you settle down and have kids, you'll understand. The whole world shifts. They put up with my bullshit lifestyle too long, as it was. Now I only have to go up to Conneticut for my Reserve time, and I still get to be a combat medic. Good thing, since I can't put Delta on my resume."

Maji stared down into her nearly empty mug. "I shouldn't ask you two to help. Not with this part. Hell, you both outrank me."

"Yes, Sergeant, we do. Plus, we have more field experience. And we'll follow you to hell and back, whether you ask us to or not. Question is, how do you want to accomplish this extraction?"

She felt fuzzy-headed. Extraction? That was a nice way to put it. "Obvious, dude. We just make sure nobody knows any of us were involved. Oh, and nobody comes after the Benedettis for it." Why did she want to giggle? It wasn't funny.

Dev peeled her right hand off the mug and gently pressed the spot that had made her want to yelp earlier. "You've got a sniper, a medic, and the best-connected PMC in the world on your team. Together, we should be able to manage one perfect op."

For the first time, the answer seemed obvious. Maji hoped she'd remember it when she woke up. "Dev. What'd you put in that tea?"

"Herbs, dude. And now you're going to sleep."

"Is that a prescription?" The words felt too big for her mouth. Was she slurring?

"It's an order. Your brain needs to reset itself. Before you go back on watch tonight." He glanced away. "Tom? You got Rose handy? Sweetie pie needs to be tucked in."

Tom laid a mumbling Maji on the bed in Rose's room, rather than Carlo's. He offered to give Rose a hand, but she refused. Maji appeared to be sedated, but not belligerent. She didn't protest when Rose slipped off her shoes and giggled when her socks slid off.

When Rose tugged on her shirt, however, Maji managed to pull herself upright. She looked a little disoriented.

"You're in my room," Rose said. "I'll close the window if you want."

Maji shook her head. "You like fresh air. Am I on watch?"

"No. You're just taking a nap." And Rose decided Maji could do that just as well in her top and shorts. "But tonight you can sleep in Carlo's room."

Maji shook her head, apparently trying to focus on Rose's face. "Back on watch tonight."

"There's an alarm on the window. Surely I'm safe enough with you in the next room." Rose pressed Maji back until her head rested on the pillow and pulled the sheet over her.

Maji squinted up at her. "*Junta* don't care about windows. I keep you safe, *chica*."

"Maji? What are you talking about?" They were many miles and years aways from Central America's bloody conflicts. "There's no *junta* here."

Maji blinked and frowned. "Sorry. Someplace else. Brooklyn."

The brownstone. Where Sal played his part in the New Underground Railroad. "How many kids stayed with you?"

"Lots. Always scared. Saw stuff no kid should see. Too late to save them. But I could still help."

"By sleeping on the floor, by the door?"

"Nobody gets by me. You can sleep in my bed. Safe now."

Rose stroked her forehead. "Okay. *Shhh.*" She wondered just what Dev had given her. As she watched, Maji turned onto her side, snugging into her pillow and pulling her knees up. Safe in Rose's bed, but mentally back on the floor in her childhood home. On watch for some poor child she'd befriended and given up her own bed for—many times, Rose gathered.

Rose wished she could soothe away the terrible images that must haunt Maji's mind, having heard those stories. She remembered the camp sessions where they practiced witnessing—listening to each other's stories without judging or even commenting. She could imagine Sal Rios doing that for undocumented fugitives of violence taking refuge for a night or two in his home. Witnessing for them at his kitchen table, over comfort foods from their homelands, while Maji played nearby with their traumatized children.

In camp, Maji had said things that seemed now like pieces of a jigsaw puzzle beginning to form a picture. That it was easy to hurt a person, but hard to learn how not to. That listening was harder than fighting. That not being able to help was hard, but stopping yourself from helping was the hardest. Rose could always tell when Maji said these things that there was a story behind them. But each time, Maji let the girls tell their own stories instead of her own. It was a great way to teach. And to protect yourself.

CHAPTER THIRTY

Rose stretched the length of the sofa and yawned. "Tom. I've got to go lie down. But Ri's still sleeping. Do you think I should—"

"No worries," Maji said from behind her.

Rose jumped, then pulled her legs in and set them on the floor, turning to look at Maji. "I really am going to put a bell on you." Maji didn't smile, but she was clear-eyed and dressed in new shorts and a full-length T-shirt. Her hair was still damp, and freshly braided. So she'd been up long enough for a shower. "You must be hungry."

Maji stopped her before she could rise. "I got it. You should sleep." She gave Tom the tiny nod. "You, too. I got watch."

She was off to the kitchen before either of them could argue. Rose looked at Tom, puzzled by Maji's brusqueness. "She looks much better."

Tom rose and offered her a hand. When she stood, he said quietly, "She had a hard day. Now she's embarrassed."

"Everybody has a bad day sometimes." Rose could think of several that involved men with guns.

"Not our Ri. Catch her in the morning. She'll be back on her game."

Rose found her room disappointingly empty, the window open. And the sheets changed to a crisp, fresh set that didn't smell like anyone. She didn't look forward to Maji back on her game. Back behind the shell of perfect Ri.

A surge crested through Rose, and she sat upright, gasping in the dark. She had been dancing with Maji—a hot salsa, turning nearly into sex right on the dance floor. At the recollection, another wave washed through her, bending her upright. Rose leaned back on her elbows and let the sensations slowly ebb, wiggling the last tingle out of her toes.

A dream hadn't woken her like that since she was an adolescent, her subconscious speaking loudly to her in her single bed. All these years later, the message didn't surprise her, only the intensity.

Had she made any telltale noises? Rose had heard Maji slip into the room earlier and bed down by the door almost silently. She worried less now about having embarrassed herself than the possibility of disturbing her personal ninja's rest. The floor still wasn't where she wanted Maji, but at least now she understood.

Rose listened into the velvety darkness. In the cool stillness, the cicadas sounded out of proportion, like traffic thrumming by in the night. She rolled quietly off the side of the bed and stepped toward the bathroom. A snuffling from the doorway caught Rose's ear, and she turned instead to the spot where she knew Maji would be, hopefully sleeping soundly.

Rose tiptoed closer and realized that Maji was crying in her sleep. What kind of bad day caused that? Between little gulps of air, Maji mumbled something indistinct but plaintive. Should she wake her? Remembering the last time she'd tried that, Rose stood out of reach and called to her instead. "Maji! Wake up." No response. She clapped sharply, like Hannah in the dojo. "Wake up."

Maji made a choking noise and rolled to look up at Rose. "*Qué? Qué pasa?*"

Was she here, or on her floor in Brooklyn again, Rose wondered. She crouched down and wiped Maji's damp cheek. Either way, she didn't need to be alone with her grief. "You were crying. Are you okay?"

"Sorry," Maji answered, sitting up and bending her head to mop her face with her T-shirt.

Rose slid down to the floor before Maji could collect herself completely and gently wrapped her, one arm and leg behind her like a backrest, the other hand stroking the loose hair off her forehead. Instead of pulling away, Maji tucked her head into the space between Rose's ear and collarbone and let herself be held. Her breath tickled Rose's skin in a soft, steady rhythm, but Rose could swear her pulse increased.

When Rose finally had to shift for her own comfort, flexing the backrest leg out and bending it to curl in around them, Maji straightened up, pulling Rose's other leg over hers. She ran one palm up to Rose's knee, then to her hip, and up the arch of her back, under Rose's long, loose T-shirt. Rose closed her eyes, soaking in the slow, thoughtful caress. When she opened them, Maji's eyes were level with her own, the wounded look in them mixed with a questioning. Rose leaned in a fraction, and the hunger of Maji's kiss rocked her. They entwined,

Rose's legs circling Maji, both their arms pressing their torsos together, mouths melded. As Maji's tongue touched the roof of her mouth, Rose felt another wave roll up through her body, pitching her within Maji's arms.

"I'm sorry," Maji panted, pulling back and looking into Rose's eyes.

"I'm not," Rose replied, hugging Maji to her, speaking with her lips nearly brushing Maji's ear. "I'll play whatever game of pretend you need, out there. But you know how I really feel. And I don't owe you an apology for that." She kissed the sweet spot just below Maji's ear, tasting salt.

With a quick twist, Maji was up on her knees and starting to stand. Rose reached out for her, clasped her wrist. Maji reached down and took Rose's other hand, pulling her to her feet.

Maji let her go, rocking back. "I'm sorry," she repeated. The pain in her eyes said she wasn't playing, but she was moving away, inside, to some place Rose couldn't follow.

Rose tried to close the physical gap between them, but Maji laid one hand gently on her sternum, her arm a bar. "I can't," she whispered, her eyes pleading for understanding.

"You already are," Rose replied, covering Maji's hand with her own, pressing it into the beating of her chest. "Either get into my bed, or get out of my room," she added. "Please."

Maji stared at her a brief moment, as if frozen in place. Then she dropped her head, pivoted, and slipped out the door.

When Rose went downstairs late the next morning, Maji was gone. At some point, she'd come back in and removed her bedroll without making a sound. The door to Carlo's room was open, and Rose walked in. The bathroom was empty, too. She peeked into the closet, her sheepishness replaced by relief at the sight of Maji's few pieces of clothing hanging there.

In the kitchen, Frank loaded dishes into the machine, alone. He smiled at her as she entered. "Sleeping in, huh? Like a real vacation. You want some breakfast? We got eggs and bacon leftover."

"No. Thanks. Just coffee. I'm not trying to put weight on, like some people."

Frank walked her to the Big House, not leaving her at the base of the curving steps up to the patio as usual but accompanying her up. At the top, they found Dev standing watch with his back to the kitchen door, his eyes hidden behind mirrored sunglasses. In his khaki cargo pants and button-down denim shirt, he looked like a hired gun. Especially with the gun in full sight at his hip.

"Dude," Frank said, giving him the up-nod.

"Dude," Dev replied.

"Have you been out here all morning?" Rose asked. It was heating back up again, and he had no water bottle in sight. Not even a glass.

"Couple hours." He flexed his long legs, putting a little bend in his knees. But his posture remained like a cop on crowd duty—tall and erect, with his hands clasped lightly in front of him. There was no complaint in his voice.

"Well, come have some lunch," Rose suggested, "and cool off."

"Thanks, no," he said, stepping away from the door to open it for them.

Frank took the door from him and waited for Rose to go through. She hesitated. "At least let me get you a drink."

He gave her a polite nod. "Thanks."

Inside, Rose and Frank found Sienna and Aunt Paola and Aunt Jackie at the dining table, with Nonna. Nonna appeared to have nodded off and startled at their entrance. "You wanted to see me?"

"We're all done," Aunt Paola said. Something in her tone made Rose feel she'd missed an appointment.

"I'll run you through what we picked out," Jackie said. "And Frank, Ricky wants you."

"Sure. Where's he at?"

Sienna's face lit up, and she directed the answer to Rose. "Down at the rec room, setting up the stuff Ang ordered for us."

"Oh, good," Rose replied. The last thing she wanted today was a workout with Sienna. Even if it meant she got to hit something.

Frank left them, and Paola excused herself. Sienna helped Nonna walk unsteadily out to her favorite spot in the living room, while Jackie quickly ran Rose through the plans for dressing up the house as the Hotel Nacional.

"No one's actually staying here, are they?" Rose asked, hoping they weren't pushing the legendary Cuban meeting analogy that far. One afternoon and evening being nice to a crowd of Family associates might be more than she could stomach, as it was.

"Hell, no. They got drivers. Nobody has to stay over," Jackie replied. "Maybe Uncle Lupo. He likes to drive his boat over. And he never sleeps on it. He gets too tanked up, Paola will find him a room."

"Well, that's a relief. And your house?"

"Strictly off-limits. Not even a friendly tour of the place. One thing the Big House is good for, it's keeping nosy wives out of mine."

And away from Angelo and Sander's work space, Rose noted. Although by next week, maybe they would have closed up shop. "Aunt Jackie? After the party, I'll be free to leave, right?"

"Sure, hon. But Ang would love it if you stayed a few days more, waved him bon voyage."

"Bon voyage?"

Jackie looked at her sideways. "He's moving to Vienna, end of next week. He didn't tell you?"

"No." So that was Ang's cover for getting into Witness Protection. Maybe he'd disappear between Long Island and his flight to Austria. "How do you feel about that?"

Jackie shrugged. "I can visit. I hear the food's good. You should make a trip with me, maybe winter break. You get those in college, right?"

"Most schools, yes. I'd like that. Thank you."

"Don't thank me. I need a girlfriend along, keep me out of trouble."

Rose gave her a smile she didn't feel inside. "It'll be fun."

Sienna came back in. "Ready?"

"Not quite," Rose replied, looking to Jackie. "I offered Dev a drink."

"Good thinking. Call him in."

"Aunt Jackie," Sienna protested. "You know Daddy wouldn't like that."

"So? He's not here, is he. Besides, this isn't even his house."

Rose stared at them. Dev was relegated to the porch due to one of Uncle Gino's many and varied prejudices? "Dev is a decorated veteran. What could your father possibly hold against him?"

Sienna squirmed. "He's too dark. You know how Daddy feels about the blacks. And the spics, of course. Well, just the Mexicans and Puerto Ricans really, but he lumps them all together. You know."

Rose took a step back. "No, I don't know."

"And you shouldn't, either," Jackie agreed. "It's stupid."

Sienna bristled. "Hey. These days, you got the Mexican cartels and the gangs to deal with. Daddy's not some redneck. He just gets worked up about people that threaten the Family. You know."

"That's so reassuring."

Sienna missed Rose's sarcasm and smiled, seeming relieved.

"Dev?" Jackie called through the kitchen. "Come in a minute."

Seeing Dev politely down a glass of water under Sienna's watchful eye, Rose marveled. How could she even call these people family? They all profited from crime, no matter how you dressed it up. She needed to hang on to the fact that Angelo was working, right now, to take down Gino. And that she was on his team, like Dev and Maji and Tom.

Maji bid Rey good-bye and left the Cuba Libre catering office via the back door. A waiting landscaper's truck had its side panel open. She hopped in, shut the door behind her, and tapped twice on the screen behind the driver.

Arriving back at the estate with the last delivery of plantings for the driveway, Maji hopped out through the side panel doorway. She narrowly missed the aromatic pile of mixed compost and topsoil the landscapers were spreading in the newly created swaths of flower beds. Down toward Angelo's house, she saw Jackie pointing and gesturing in an attempt to communicate with one of the day laborers. Maji jogged down to them. *"Buenos días."* She looked to Jackie. "All good?"

"Ri!" Jackie looked around. "Where the hell have you—never mind. Can you tell him I don't want anybody digging up this area here? We're gonna rope it off for the party."

Maji turned to the worker and explained, in Spanish. They went back and forth a moment, getting clear.

Jackie gave them both an awkward, *"Gracias,"* and walked with Maji toward her house. "Thought you were at the doctor's."

Maji looked down at her running clothes. "I've made a full recovery. So good that I went for a jog. Tom will be back soon, too."

"Well, whatever Ang has you up to, I hope it was worth it. I know you can take care of yourself, but nobody's bulletproof."

Getting shot was the least of her worries, Maji thought. But that wouldn't reassure Ang's mother any. "Yes, ma'am."

"And you're done with this foolishness now." It was a statement, not a question.

Maji let Jackie think what she wanted to. And also Rose, who seemed relieved to see her. Neither of them said anything about her outing as they prepped dinner, with a hand from Frank and then Tom, when he arrived. Maji didn't think Rose would have brought it up, even if they'd been alone. Or what had happened last night, either. Rose was operating in what Maji thought of as her friendly reserved mode, the one she used with people like Iris. She wondered if Rose was mad at her, or just tired of the charade. Couldn't blame her, either way.

Angelo asked to see them after supper, so she and Rose tromped down to the basement, along with Dev. Maji ignored his offer of a seat, and the other two took their cues from her. So he delivered his orders to Maji, standing. "Dev will get you out of here in the morning—early, like today. We're running a test, might take all day."

"What kind of test?" Rose asked.

Well, if he didn't want questions, he shouldn't have invited the civilian. Maji waited to hear the answer.

"Testing for a leak. Sirko knows too much, and we've ruled out bugs and tracking on the cars, even more drone surviellence. So it's got to be a person. I have a theory, but I need to confirm."

Maji crossed her arms. If Ang had just left the damned bugs in place, he'd know what Ricky was or wasn't up to. Unless, she realized, he wasn't talking about Ricky. Or really wasn't sure. *Shit.*

"Someone here?" Rose said, her voice rising. "And you're sending Ri out as bait?"

Angelo frowned. "'Course not. She's going the safest place possible, while we check whether Sirko sends somebody to the places she might be."

Back to the dojo, Maji thought. A last day of camp. So that's why Rose was here. "Is it really safe enough to give Rose the option?" she asked him, in Arabic. She ignored the look she could feel Rose giving her, the frustration at being left out.

"We can cover for her, if you're both out. And she'll be as safe as you at the dojo, right?"

"It's the getting there and back that makes me sweat," Maji replied.

"Leave that to your team," Angelo answered in English. "So, Rose, one last day at the dojo. Yes or no?"

Rose looked from him to Maji, and back. "I'd love the chance to say good-bye to the girls. But I can forgo that, if it will put Ri in any extra danger."

Angelo smiled broadly. "Go up with Dev, check out the clothes you'll need in the morning. And you…" He turned his gaze back to Maji. "Next time you joke about marrying her, you better be prepared to make good on it." No one laughed. "Stay behind a minute."

Maji waited until the door at the top of the stairs closed. If another shoe was about to drop, at least only Tom and Dev would hear it with her. "What?"

He touched his transmitter and motioned her to do the same. She switched hers to listen-only. "Tom met with Hannah today?" he asked.

"Yep."

"Were you with them?"

"Nope."

"I don't suppose I should ask how the plan's shaping up."

"You asked me to handle it, I'm handling it. Tomorrow she'll bring Dev up to speed. That's all you need to know."

"Dev? You brought him in, too?"

Fewer questions would suit Maji better. "You want this done right?" She gave him a second to acknowledge. "I need enough hands on deck, then. Hannah's behind her screen, where she needs to stay. I'll be out in the open. So I need both of them in the shadows."

"Okay, I get the picture. Stop talking. When the plan's set, tell me what I need to know."

Maji was happy to stop. The less he knew, the more realistic his reactions would be, even improvised. "We're on the same page."

He switched his transmitter back on, and she did the same. "The AC's back on. Tomorrow's an early day, even for you. So get some decent rack time. Clear?"

Sure it was clear. Somehow they knew she'd started her night last night on watch in Rose's room, and ended it in Carlo's, alone. Even though her comm had been on alarm-only mode, no voices to disturb her sleep, and no transmitting except in case of emergency. She should be used to it by now. When you worked with operators, privacy was an illusion. Only your thoughts were really your own, if you were careful to keep them to yourself. "Who's got my watch?"

"I do," Tom's voice said. "Me and Ang, until oh four hundred. Dev will roust you at four thirty, get you out of here before five."

"Tomorrow's not garbage day, is it?" She really didn't want to be smuggled anywhere in a garbage truck ever again. Especially crammed in with Rose.

Angelo's bark filled the basement and echoed in her comm. "Recycling. And don't worry. We got you uniforms."

"What about you?" she asked him. "Even a ghoul like you needs sleep."

He squinted at her. "Now who's in whose lane, babe? For your information, I'm ninety-nine percent done. And I can't finish up until I've got some privacy, anyhow."

So he'd sleep when he could, and complete the program when Sander was back in the city. "All clear. I'll be in my room."

CHAPTER THIRTY-ONE

When Hannah tapped her, Maji immediately bowed out and followed her into the hallway.

"Angelo's test is working. I've called around to the other dojos and self-defense classes in the area, and three have reported back so far. Two men dressed as military police are looking for you. They have photos of both you and Rose."

Maji spent all of ten seconds weighing the choices—try to get home, knowing the estate would be watched and they might be intercepted on the way, or wait and see if these guys showed up. The first was risky, but the second put the kids in danger, as well as themselves. And Bubbles. And Hannah. "We should go."

"I think not. We have your transport home arranged. Dashing out is unwarranted."

"And Sirko's agents are good. They could actually end up here."

"It's a possibility. So let's prepare the others. Tap Rose first."

Rose turned pale at the news, but took her instructions calmly. "Why not just hide now?" was her only question.

"Waste of our last day, if they don't show. This place isn't advertised. And it looks like a normal house for a reason."

"But still, people in town must know. Oyster Cove is a small place, and lots of families act as hosts."

And Sirko's guys might ask good questions, not just knock on doors. "We'll be all right. So will the kids."

"Of course," Rose agreed, looking as uncertain as Maji felt.

Lunch was held entirely indoors, for the first time during this year's camp. The whole group sat on the mats, except for two in the kitchen to act as sentries for the rear door.

"Goldberg to Rios."

"Go go."

"Eyes on the rear door. Mrs. Altadonna says hi."

Maji smiled and whispered to Rose, who leaned over to Hannah and relayed the message. Hannah sent a nod back to Maji.

Of the rest of the group, only Iris seemed to notice any communication had occurred. She gestured impatiently toward Maji, then hissed, "Ri."

"What?" Maji said in a mock whisper. A few sets of eyes followed the interchange. "It's all cool. Relax."

As the students began standing up and clearing their plates off to the kitchen, Bubbles clapped twice and gave one of the orders the girls were prepared for. "Mill about!"

Hannah walked calmly toward the front door and looked at the two men in Army fatigues quizzically. Then she pointed to the sign on the door telling visitors to go around back. As they turned and started walking down the steps, she barked, "Now!"

Maji pulled Rose out of the milling throng and opened the side door to the parkour climbing tower. "Back to the wall," she said, and followed Rose in, stepping backward so that they would both be facing the door. Then she secured the door from inside, and waited.

She couldn't make out the knock on the back door through the clatter of dishes in the kitchen and the tumultuous voices of the students. Then a double clap broke through the noise, and Hannah's voice rang out. "Girls! Quiet please. We have visitors, and I can't make out a word they're saying. Gentlemen, what can I do for you?"

"Ma'am, we're looking for this woman." There was a pause. "Is she here?"

"May I ask why?"

"Sergeant Rios is absent without leave. If she comes in voluntarily, discipline will be light. We're here to give her that opportunity." The man pitched his voice as if trying to reach someone in another room, someone hiding.

"Well, I haven't any soldiers for students, I'm afraid. Why would you think she was here?"

"She might not have told you she was a soldier, ma'am," he replied without actually answering. "We've heard she's in the area with another woman. Do you know this woman?"

"No. Tanya—this is my lead instructor, Tanya. She's here some days that I'm not. Tanya, do you recognize either of these women?"

"Nuh-uh, Sensei. Sorry."

"Are they dangerous?" Iris's voice piped in.

Maji closed her eyes. Iris would go off script.

"We're not at liberty to say, ma'am."

"Then why would we help you? I'm a reporter, you know. For the *Herald*. And if you don't want to see your faces in tomorrow's headlines—"

Hannah clapped twice. "That's quite enough," she interrupted. "I'm sorry we couldn't be of more help, gentlemen."

"Could we take a look around the premises, ma'am?" the second man asked. "I'm sure we won't find anything, but your compliance would let us complete some Patriot Act forms in your favor."

"Are you threatening her?" Iris sounded believably irate. Hell, she probably was. "I can't believe this. I'm going to call my editor."

The locker room door slapped as it opened and closed. "I'm so sorry," Hannah said. "Go get her and send her outside."

"Gladly," Bubbles responded. The locker room door made less noise that time and muted the voices behind it. Shortly after, though, footsteps stomped across the hallway and the exterior door slammed.

"We don't usually allow adults in class," Hannah said in the silence following Iris's departure, sounding apologetic. "Why don't I give you a tour? It won't take long."

Maji listened to Hannah narrate the nickel version of the dojo tour. She felt Rose's hands slide onto her hips, and she put her own over them. Rose's breathing was a little shallow, but sounded otherwise normal.

"I see you have a Rios," the first man's voice reached them, slightly echoey from the locker room. *Door must be propped open*, Maji thought. And the girls were keeping beautifully quiet. Acing the scenario, so far.

"I'm a Rios," came Soledad's voice. The only Hispanic-looking student. *Way to step up, hermana.* "So? Can I see the picture?" After a brief pause, she commented, "I got three sisters and eight girl cousins. She's not one of them."

"Thank you, Ms. Rios," the second man said.

"All right, girls, it's time to get back to lessons," Hannah said. "If you need to wash up, please do so now." The sound of movement and teenage chatter started immediately. "I'll show you out," she added over the noise.

No more men's voices reached them. Class resumed with mat drills, and moments later, there was a brief rhythmic tapping on the tower door. All clear. "They're gone," Maji said.

Rose exhaled, her breath tickling the back of Maji's neck. "Can we get out then?"

"Sorry," Maji answered. "Not yet. Rios to perimeter."

"They didn't touch or drop anything at the back side of the building," Dev reported.

Tom's voice came next. "Nobody watching the front from the street. I borrowed a dog, gonna take a leisurely stroll and look closer."

Maji wanted to ask where he'd gotten a dog, but held the question. Time to debrief later.

Rose's eyes adjusted to the tiny bit of light inside the big wooden box that held them. She hadn't even known the hiding place was there; but since it locked from the inside, that must be what it was there for—to keep unwelcome visitors out. And now it felt like it was keeping them locked in. The stuffiness had increased since she and Maji had stepped in and starting breathing all the air. She took her hands off Maji's hips and started feeling out the interior dimensions.

"You okay?" Maji asked.

"Mostly. When do we get out of here?"

"When class breaks, we blend in and head for the locker room."

"How soon?"

Maji's hand brushed down the back of her shoulder, along her arm, and finally found her hand. "Ten, fifteen minutes. Piece of cake." Her hand lifted Rose's. "Close your eyes and stretch. Up, up, tall as you can."

Rose reached high, straining for the ceiling. Nothing. She followed Maji's soothing commands and was able to just press out on both sides of the box. Then she found the inside of the lower landing, about shoulder height, and the slight slope of the front wall they usually leaped at to scramble up. "Bigger than it seems."

"Plenty of room. You could do a whole yoga class in here. Okay?"

The memory of Maji asking *Okay?* several times over the course of their first night together startled Rose. Every touch had been more than okay then, the question only serving to remind Rose that she was in control, no matter how wild the wonderful stranger's bold physicality made her feel. No wonder they weren't supposed to do that again. Rose had worked hard to stuff those memories into a safe corner of her mind, to behave so that no one could tell how much more she wanted. And not just really delicious, searing intimacy in bed. She wanted more of Maji the sly wit, the encourager, the quiet prep chef, the sexy dance partner, the easy company. Hell, she wanted to cook that woman something delicious and feed it to her by hand.

"Rose." A hand closed on her arm, small and strong and very warm. "Rose!"

Rose opened her eyes in the near dark and put her hand out, finding Maji's shoulder. She slid her fingertips along Maji's collarbone, up her throat, and onto her cheek. "Yes," she said, and closed the small distance between them.

Four fast knocks on the door brought Maji to her senses. She pulled her hands out from inside Rose's T-shirt, gasping. "Jesus! Come on."

Taking Rose by one hand and flipping the toggle lock with the other, Maji led them into the relative brightness of the mat room. The interior of the room was shadowed, the overhead lights off. The tactical part of her brain kept her focused on reaching the locker room through the milling screen of students.

"You guys okay? You're pinker than Amber after burpees." Bubbles didn't wait for an answer, just popped into the sink area and ran them two cups of water.

Maji drank hers down gratefully, willing her pulse to slow down while peeking over the cup's edge at Rose. She'd lost control again, hadn't even tried to stop Rose. Being alone was too dangerous. She was going to need to rotate duties with Dev and Tom if she couldn't keep her head anymore.

They hugged all the students who buzzed in and out of the locker room, checking on them and reliving the excitement while they changed to go home. When the room was empty of all but Rose and Bubbles and Maji, Hannah entered. "Whose car did you borrow today?"

"Suarez family." The recycling truck had paused long enough to let them out by the driveway.

Hannah raised an eyebrow but didn't comment. "Address? Parking instructions? Dogs or other hazards?"

"1024 Maple, three-quarters into driveway, facing out, hand brake on. No hazards but friendly neighbors." Maji looked at Bubbles hopefully. "You gonna drive us?" The sedan had a small trunk, but they could manage for a short ride.

"No," Hannah answered. "I'll get the car back. You two will stay put."

Maji had missed the change of plans, despite having her comm on. She frowned. "If we're missed at the estate, there'll be other trouble to deal with."

"Angelo is handling that," Hannah assured her. "Now, you two will leave tomorrow with the students, if we have confirmed there is no ongoing surveillance. I've already unscrewed the refrigerator light and turned on the IR blocker. Brief Rose on the protocols, please." She turned to go.

"But…"

Hannah turned back and surprised Maji with a hug. "Love is nothing to be ashamed of. Just protect Rose's privacy, eh?" she whispered before pulling back.

Maji could only gape at her.

Bubbles gave Rose a quick squeeze and followed Hannah out. She caught the door just before it swung closed. "There's stuff in the fridge. And, um"—she winked—"don't do anything I wouldn't do."

Maji looked at Rose, still slightly flushed and a bit disheveled, and stepped over one of the benches to give herself some distance. "Protocols. Right."

CHAPTER THIRTY-TWO

So now what?" Rose asked.

"We stay away from the windows, don't turn on any lights. Is your phone off?"

"Yes. For how long?"

"Right now, it looks like tomorrow afternoon."

"Oh. So we...sleep here?" Fear clouded her expression. "Not knowing when those men might come back?"

Maji shook her head. "I'm sorry. I should have said. There's a team watching the building, perimeter sensors in the lawn and on the roof. Nobody's coming in."

"Well, then. Anything else I should know?"

"Yeah. It's going to get pretty warm around sunset." Seeing that Rose was waiting for her to explain, Maji did. "In case somebody's out there using thermal imaging to see if we're in here, the building has infrared blocking. Basically, the walls warm up to mask our heat signatures. So we don't have to spend the night hiding out in the shower stalls."

A wicked glint appeared in Rose's eyes. "Are we allowed to run the water?"

Maji stone-faced her. "You can use the locker room if you need to."

"Wow," Rose said. "You really lose your sense of humor when you're scared."

"I'm not scared," Maji snapped. "I'm on duty." A cough that sounded suspiciously like *bullshit* sounded in her ear. "Dev," she said, "shut it or lose it."

"May I use Hannah's computer?" Rose asked.

"No. No electronics, including the microwave. I can find a pack of cards."

Rose did not look amused. "Really. We have fourteen hours alone, and you want to play cards?"

Maji ignored the comments coming through her earpiece, not wanting to tip Rose to their encouragement. What did they know? "Yes. Let's sit in Hannah's office."

Rose indulged her in a game of gin rummy. Maji asked her about life in an Ohio college town and smiled and laughed in the appropriate places, while monitoring the comm and trying not to think about how she'd manage to keep her distance the entire rest of the night. Maji wasn't sure Rose understood that if she made a serious move, her resolve would shatter.

"What about you?" Rose asked after about an hour. "Can you work for Hannah while you're a Reservist?"

Maji raised a finger to her lips and switched her transmitter over to listen only. "What do you mean, work for Hannah?"

Rose looked taken aback, by her tone if not the question. "Well, you clearly work for Paragon sometimes. Don't you?"

Maji closed her eyes. The CD—dammit. "Just the once. And I'd rather not discuss it with the guys. Actually, I plan to finish my master's. That's as far ahead as I can handle, right now. And I'd like you not to talk about that when they can hear, either. School is under my real name."

"God, it's complicated to be you." Rose sounded sympathetic, not snarky.

Maji sighed, accepting the unpleasant truth stated with such diplomacy. "Not usually. Work and home never bumped into each other like this before."

"Right," Rose said. "You can turn that thing back on if you like. We can talk about me all night—I'm an open book."

Maji nodded and made a show of turning the transmitter back on. "There might be a paperback in one of the lockers if you're sick of talking."

"I don't get tired of talking with you," Rose said. "But I am thirsty. Is it getting warm already?"

Maji checked her watch. "Starting to. Follow me." She got up and led them across the hall in a quick, low crouch. Until it got a bit warmer, they should probably stay in just the office and the locker room.

They gulped down a series of little paper cups of water. "Just how warm will it get?" Rose asked.

"Perfect for hot yoga. Not so much for sleeping."

Rose stripped off her gi top and hung it in her locker. She handed the tracking fob to Maji. "Here. I'm going to wet down."

While the water was running, Angelo came onto the comm. "Rios. Just FYI—I came out to Ricky. So you're off the hook. Knock yourself out."

"What the fuck, Ang?" Was he trying to get himself killed *before* the Fourth?

"I needed to get Sander out of here. If Papa Bear gets wind of today's attempt, he might do something rash. So I'm on a mission, but you—you just take a night off."

"Ang—"

"We're putting you on alarm-only, Rios. See you tomorrow. Out."

"Wait!" But it was too late. Dead air.

"Everything okay?"

Maji turned and saw Rose, wrapped in a towel but glistening all over with droplets. "Um, yeah." She swallowed. "Fine. Here," she handed Rose her T-shirt and gi pants. The bikini underwear fell to the floor, and she blushed.

"I'm not putting those back on," Rose said, holding out one arm as if to catch a breeze. "Evaporative cooling. Do you think it's dark enough yet to chance the kitchen?"

To hell with staying in the locker room. "Yes. If we stay toward the wall."

Rose stopped in the kitchen doorway. "Should we close the blinds?"

"No. No changes to how the dojo looks every night. We don't know if they had it under surveillance before today."

"Oh. But what about the windows? Surely they aren't heated."

"Nope. An IR device can't get a good reading through glass. Just don't turn on any lights."

They gathered a picnic-worth of food by the glow of the streetlights and carried it into Hannah's office. There they could eat without concern for anyone registering their movements through a window. Rose retucked her towel several times before the desk was set for supper. "You should try this," Rose said. "It really helps."

Maji nodded mutely. Rose in just a towel was interfering with her speech center. "Stay here," she managed.

The tepid water washed away the day's sweat. Despite Rose's advice, Maji pulled on a clean T-shirt and workout shorts. She felt too exposed as it was.

Rose gave her a smile and popped a cold grape into her own mouth. "Try these," she said. "No, wait." She plucked one from the bunch and stepped close to Maji. "Close your eyes."

Maji didn't.

"I promise not to grope you. Come on."

Maji closed her eyes and felt the chilled grape brush her lips. She opened them and sucked the grape in, catching just the tip of Rose's finger with it. She waited until Rose had all her digits safely back in her own control and crunched down. The sweetness filled her mouth as she watched Rose watching her.

"Another?" Rose said with a wicked smile.

Maji shook her head. Her legs trembled from adrenaline, taking the cue from her brain to run. If Rose touched her again, she was done for.

"Are you okay?" Rose's eyes shifted from teasing to concern. "Oh," she added, touching her ear with a questioning look.

Maji fought the urge to lie, to let Rose believe they had an audience, to play to her sense of propriety. Instead, she took a deep breath and slid behind the desk, safely out of reach. "Alarm-only," she replied.

"No voices in your head?" Rose asked. "And they can't hear us." She took in Maji's discomfort and distancing behavior. "You don't want a night alone with me. I get it." She pulled her towel tighter and headed for the door.

Maji watched her go. *Rios, you* pendejo. She crossed the hall to the locker room and reached to push through the door. A memory of rushing through the back door of the diner to confront Rose's kidnappers flashed through her mind. Maji froze. She hadn't been scared then. Why now?

The door opened and Rose stood there, in gi pants and a T-shirt. Looking cross. "Excuse me."

Maji leaned her outstretched hand onto the doorjamb, not blocking but not retreating either. "I'm not playing you. I just can't do this to you."

"What is it you think you're doing? If you don't want to spend another night with me, that's between you and you." Rose crossed her arms, letting the door swing back toward Maji, toward closing her out.

Maji stepped forward enough to catch the door, but still not crowd Rose. "I'm in no position to offer more than a couple of nights. I know I would want more than that, and I'm guessing you would, too."

"Well, as my grandmother says, never guess—always ask."

But asking would yield an honest answer, and Maji could not bring herself to find out what it would be. "It's just, settling for a hookup doesn't seem like you."

"Before this summer, I would have agreed with you." Rose paused, still frowning. "But then, before I met you, I'd never invited a stranger home. That wasn't like me. Between playing make-believe at home, fighting men with guns, training to…well, I don't know what I'm like anymore. I played my whole life safe up until now, and where did it get me? It turned me into an ivory-tower mouse. And *that* is not who I am. I could be another Vandana Shiva, for all I know. If Hannah sees it, maybe I should, too."

Finally some safe ground. "You could do anything, be anything you want to be."

"Except be in love with you."

The words felt like a punch in the gut. "I can't. You'll…" *What, Rios? Get hurt? Hate me?*

"Tip my hand? Do something reckless, and get your friends killed? I'm not Iris, Maji."

To hear Rose speak her name felt achingly bittersweet. Maji closed her eyes. "No. It's not that."

Rose grasped her hand and leaned a shoulder on the open door, propping it so Maji could let her arm go and just hold on, hand in hand. "So tell me what it is."

"I can't." Not tonight, not next week, not even after Angelo was gone.

Rose gave her hand a squeeze and held her gaze. "You have five languages I don't understand a word of. Try one of those."

"If I could tell you everything, I would," Maji began, in Farsi. "I would tell you about my work, about my fears, about how badly I wish I'd met you before I gave my life to the Army. But I can't. I can't even tell you why I can't tell you. All I own anymore is my thoughts—and I'd give them all to you, if I could."

Rose gave a soft tug, no harder than a dance lead, and Maji stepped into her arms, clinging fiercely with her face buried in Rose's neck. She wanted to cry, or scream, but all she could do was vibrate silently, inhaling Rose's warmth.

"Sh, it's okay," Rose murmured, stroking the back of Maji's head. "No one's making you do anything you don't want to. Let's just try one night without fear."

Without letting Rose go, Maji pulled herself to her full height, nearly as tall as Rose, and lost herself in those deep brown eyes sparkling with golden flecks. Still in Farsi, she said what she'd been afraid to admit, even to herself. "I love you."

Rose might not have understood the words, but the intensity of them took her breath away. She cradled Maji's face in both her palms and kissed her deeply. When they came up for air, Maji murmured more indecipherable words and peeled Rose's shirt off, running her hands over her bare back as they kissed again.

Before Rose even realized that she had walked backward toward the sinks, her backside pressed into the counter. The memory of what she had wanted to do that first night in the kitchen hit Rose, and she slid her hand up under Maji's shirt, pulling it over her head. She ran her hands over Maji's hard shoulders and corded back muscles, and reached the waistband of those infuriating little shorts. Rose slipped her hands inside them, finding no barrier to Maji's hot skin, and cupped her butt, pulling Maji tight against her. Feeling increasingly feral, she broke their kiss and nipped Maji's neck. "Naked. Now."

Maji took a half step back and shimmied her shorts off, then reached for the drawstring to Rose's pants. As they whispered to the cool tile floor, Rose reached again for Maji, looking her in the eye. Maji growled out an untranslated phrase, some kind of demand.

"Yes," Rose said. Whatever Maji wanted from her—yes.

Maji crouched slightly and grabbed Rose by the hips, boosting her up onto the counter. She ducked one shoulder under Rose's knee and lifted her other foot up, letting it rest by the sink basin. Then she slid one arm around Rose's hips and leaned in. Rose gasped at the first touch of Maji's mouth, and the second, and…the feel of her fingers, teasing. Rose braced her foot against the sink and hung on to the towel dispenser, her naked back against the mirror. "More," she managed.

Within seconds, Rose stopped making words altogether. What she shouted, even she couldn't decipher. And then she laughed, overwhelmed by the rush of pleasure and the absurdity of writhing on a restroom counter. As Maji started to kiss her belly, Rose grasped her shoulders and levered herself up, wrapping both legs around Maji's waist.

Maji gave a deep-throated groan of satisfaction and buried her face between Rose's breasts. She sucked one into her mouth and caressed the other, then rolled the nipple hard.

"Maji!" Rose arched and reached for her fierce lover's face, finding her eyes.

The alarm in the green depths surprised her. "Hurt you?"

"No," Rose answered. She took two calming breaths while Maji waited, concern and desire warring in her eyes. "No more countertops. I want you in the shower."

They tumbled into the nearest shower stall, leaving the curtain open. Rose backed Maji up against the wall, pinioning her arms over her head while she explored her neck, her clavicles, her breasts and ribs. The warm water sluiced over them both. Rose sought Maji's mouth again, but set her arms free, their fingers entwined. "Open," Rose breathed into Maji's ear.

Maji pressed one foot against the far wall of the shower enclosure and nodded, seeking her mouth again. Rose sucked Maji's tongue into her mouth and slid inside her incredibly sweet, hot wetness at the same time. They cried out against each other, the kiss breaking and reforming while Maji thrust her hips to meet Rose's hand, undulating slow and steady. Rose could feel Maji holding back, savoring the connection while the tension in all her muscles rose. She wrapped her free arm tightly around Maji's waist and whispered her thumb over her lover's clit. "Reach for it, baby," she whispered in her ear.

Nearly nose to nose, they breathed each other in, dancing in place. Maji's eyes held Rose's, yielding and slightly glazed. Rose pressed a little harder. "Reach for it."

Rose felt herself coiling up inside as Maji tensed all over and finally cried out, "Rose! Oh God, Rose." She looked a bit shocked as she pitched forward. Rose caught her, holding her fast.

Rose kissed her tenderly. Her own legs started to tremble. Maji's arms on her back moved in slow circles, and the kiss grew deeper. Rose reached blindly for the knob and shut the water off.

"Out?" Maji asked, still seeming almost disoriented.

Rose nodded, smiling. Every nerve ending from her scalp to her toes tingled. But it was the effect she had on Maji that gave her the euphoria. That, and maybe a few endorphins, too.

"Hungry?" Rose asked, handing Maji a towel.

"Ravenous." Maji felt her lips twitch.

Rose raised one eyebrow, failing to hide her satisfaction. "For food."

"That, too."

They patted each other dry, on track for supper until Maji began licking moisture from her neck. The hunger returning to Rose's eyes inspired Maji to pull her close. Maji stepped back as Rose leaned in to kiss her, and the changing bench touched one calf. Maji sank onto the long, narrow wooden bench, pulling Rose onto her lap, across her legs. Rose shook her head and stood.

Maji looked up, letting her disappointment show. But then Rose looked down and smiled, putting a hand on Maji's shoulder to steady herself. She stepped across the bench with one foot, leaving the other between Maji's legs, and lowered herself back down to face her properly. "I like to be able to see you," Rose said.

As Rose slid her gaze down Maji's body, through the space between them, Maji fought the impulse to pull Rose's hips tight against her own. Instead, she brushed her fingers along Rose's cheek, her neck, her shoulders. She lifted one of Rose's breasts to her mouth, sliding her other hand to Rose's back for support as Rose arched in response, with a small sound of pleasure.

Rose didn't speak, just reached both hands behind Maji's head and slid her fingers into the thick strands of hair, working the braid loose. Rose pulled Maji's head back and gave her hungry mouth an exquisite teasing with her tongue. Maji heard herself whimper, an admission of wanting so keen Rose responded by delivering her whole mouth. Rose's hips rolled against Maji's thigh, moving of their own accord.

Maji slid her free hand behind Rose, bringing the other around to the gap between them. At the touch of her hand, Rose's pelvis tilted forward, seeking. Maji broke the kiss, looking Rose in the eye. The need there shook her, not because she couldn't meet it, but because she didn't trust herself to hold back when she did.

Trembling with the effort of restraint, Maji slid three fingers slowly inside the lush wet silk, glorying in every sensation until the base of her palm met Rose's labia. Rose pressed hard against her hand, and Maji curled the fingers inside her. Rose moaned loudly in response, and Maji nearly came just from the sound and sight of her pleasure. As the nearly unbearable sweetness swelled inside her chest, Maji thrummed her fingers against the tender spot deep inside Rose.

Maji kept her eyes glued to Rose's, the most beautiful sight she'd ever beheld, until Rose's head rolled back, and she crushed Maji's face to her chest. Although nestling between Rose's breasts was delicious in and of itself, air was in short supply. Maji made a sound against Rose's sternum, and Rose loosened her hold. Maji sucked in a lungful of warm oxygen and smiled up at her.

Rose placed little kisses all over Maji's face, laughing softly. A thought about six weeks of foreplay occurred to her, but they were bathed in sweat, and "You are so salty," came out instead. She licked the base of Maji's neck, heard a deep moan rising up, and felt Maji's hand flex, still inside her. The immediate wave of pleasure rocked her sideways, and she felt dizzy.

Maji moved slowly, holding Rose steady while she drew her hand out, sending aftershocks all the way to Rose's toes. The sweetness of Maji's touch and the tenderness in her eyes made Rose tear up.

"Okay?" Maji asked, her voice matching her eyes and touch.

"Perfect," Rose said. "And hungry."

They helped each other stand on trembling legs, sliding against each other as they kissed some more. Rose started to press into her, forgetting all of her body's other needs. Maji wobbled, the backs of her legs hitting the bench, and every muscle in her glorious physique hardened, bracing to keep them both from falling.

Rose stepped back, pulling Maji with her. Maji followed her to the sink, where they stuck their mouths under the taps and drank deeply. Maji took her hand, and they walked to the showers in silent agreement. Rose turned on a tap and stepped in, pushing Maji toward the shower next door.

When she stepped out, rinsed and refreshed, Maji handed her a towel, holding it at a safe distance. "Food next," she said.

Rose wrapped her towel around her chest, matching Maji. If that was all the English she got from Maji tonight, it would do. They headed back to the picnic in the office, beaded with cool clean water and leaving a trail of damp footprints on the hallway's warm linoleum.

The grapes weren't chilly anymore, warmed with the room's artificial heat. But the juicy flesh felt just as succulent, and they silently fed each other, smiling at the shared recognition of holding back—for now. They managed to consume some nuts and a few hard-boiled eggs, plus a whole pitcher of iced tea Maji fetched from the fridge. And then Rose gave Maji the look, and let her towel drop.

CHAPTER THIRTY-THREE

Maji woke up, one hand touching Rose, mostly still on top of the sheet and pillows she'd found in the laundry room and turned into a makeshift bed on the mats farthest from the windows. They had moved apart in their sleep, seeking coolness without letting the contact go completely. She smiled and stretched. The tiniest hint of predawn showed through the front windows. It would be an hour or two until enough morning light reached them to worry about modesty. She checked her left ear to make sure the comm was still in. Her watch was secure, so she hadn't lost herself so much she'd torn it off. And no alarm had sounded all night. Hallelujah.

Rose reached out in her sleep and found Maji's hip. The way she ran her hand inside the dip from hipbone to thigh, Maji knew she must be awake now, too. But she didn't speak, not wanting to break the spell just yet. Her body moved in response to Rose's touch, acting on its own accord, as it always did around Rose if she couldn't manage to stop it. Today that didn't feel like failure, and she tried not to think about what this gift of time and privacy meant. As her thoughts started to stray to the team and the mission, Rose's nails running lightly over her ribs brought her back to the mat, to their world of two. She let out a purr and covered Rose's hand with her own.

Rose slid up against her back, spooning snugly with her mouth by Maji's ear. "Have I mentioned how much I adore your body?"

"And I thought it was my sense of humor that won you over."

"Welcome back to the English-speaking world."

Maji tensed at the reminder of her inability to speak the truth last night. Or had she? Rose seemed to get the message.

She did now, too. "Use any language you want," Rose said, pressing closer and nibbling the rim of Maji's ear. "But be warned the...Farsi?...sets my blood on fire. Maybe it's the delivery, not the words." She slid her hand down the inside of Maji's hip again, across her belly, and brushed it across her breasts.

Maji arched, following the caress. "I don't know nearly enough dirty words in my mother's language," she said in Farsi. Rose squeezed her nipple in response, rolling it lightly as she dipped her tongue into Maji's ear.

"Touch me, Rose," Maji said in Spanish. "*Comprendes? Tócame. Cógeme. Poseéme.*" She tried to roll toward Rose, but Rose only let her get as far as flat on her back.

Rose moved over her, stretching her arms over her head and nudging her legs apart with a knee. "*Te comprendo, querida.*"

They had just dozed off again when Maji tensed, waking Rose. "What?"

"We have twenty minutes to get decent," Maji said. "Hannah's on her way over."

"Damn. Your comm's back on, then?"

"Yeah." Maji kissed her scalp line, inhaling deeply.

She's missing me—us, or this, anyway, Rose thought. Well, that made two of them. "Tell them thank you," she said, raising her voice a bit.

"Ang..." Maji growled. She sighed. "Message received."

"What did he say?" Rose propped herself on an elbow and looked Maji in the eye.

"Nothing that bears repeating." Before Rose could prod her, Maji stopped and listened again, frowning. "Yeah, that I'll tell her."

Maji was up in a flash, offering Rose a hand up off their makeshift bed. Rose took it and wrapped the sheet around her nakedness. "Break it to me gently."

Maji gave her a brief, tender kiss. "It's time to pretend again. I'm sorry."

"Well," Rose began. "Oh, fuck it. I suppose there's no point in being pissed. We both knew it was a time-out, not a honeymoon."

The look on Maji's face made Rose regret her choice of words, even as it shifted into a wry smile. "*Je ne regrette rien.*"

I regret nothing, Rose translated mentally. "Good. After last night, if I catch you brooding, I may take it personally."

Maji gave her a soft smile and the barest whisper of a kiss before walking toward the locker room, naked. She paused and looked over her shoulder. "Let's get dressed. I'm hungry again."

❖

Despite the debriefing Hannah held for the girls and instructors first thing on Friday, they still wanted to relive the excitement over the lunch break.

Maji enlisted them to help instead. "We're still hiding out," she said. "You go on out on the porch, look normal for us. Okay?"

Being good kids, they looked disappointed but took the task as a consolation prize.

"Do you think Hannah would mind if I took a nap in her office?" Rose asked.

"Not at all," Hannah replied from behind them.

Rose jumped. Now she knew where Maji got her sneaking-up skills. "Thanks."

If Hannah noted Rose's embarrassment, she didn't show it. "Getting home should be uneventful, but you'll want to be as sharp as possible, just in case."

Watching the back door close behind their sensei, Rose said, "She must know."

"Hannah knows pretty much everything. About everyone."

"Well, she's very gracious about it."

Maji gave her little half shrug, and an almost smile. "She likes you." She popped into the laundry room, then handed a pillow and a crumpled sheet to Rose.

Rose inhaled the sheet and handed it back, keeping the pillow. "No reminders, or I may just drag you in with me." The realization that she probably could do that warmed her, and she couldn't stop the smug smile that tugged at the edges of her mouth. "Talk about leaving it all on the mat."

"Say good night, Rose," Maji said as she pushed the door to Hannah's office open.

Rose gave her a featherlight kiss on the cheek as she passed through the doorway, the pillow clutched to her front. "Good night, Rose."

Maji was just pushing the door to Hannah's office open again, sorry to have to wake Rose after less than an hour, when a hand settled on her shoulder. She spun around and nearly cracked skulls with Iris.

"What are you doing back here? Are you crazy?" Iris demanded.

"We didn't leave."

Iris's expression shifted from righteous concern to flirtation. "Damn. Now I wish I hadn't run off."

But playing was not on Maji's agenda. "And what the fuck was all that going-to-call-my-editor bullshit?"

"I was trying to help." Iris continued standing too close. "Hey, I made them squirm, didn't I? And I got their license plate number."

Maji took a step back, propping the door open with her backside. "You drew attention to yourself, to this place, to the kids. You raised the risk level for everyone."

"Why do you blame me whenever I try to protect you?"

Maji shouldn't tangle with Iris when she was this tired. But if Iris demanded answers, she could take what Maji had to dish out. "Because your tactical judgment sucks almost as much as your ethics. And because I don't want your protection. I don't need it."

"If you think that, you don't know the danger you're in."

"I know as much as I need to."

Iris laughed bitterly. "Is that what he tells you, your so-called friend? I don't even have the full story yet, but I can tell already he's stirring up a hornet's nest."

"So walk away from your Pulitzer."

Iris looked uncharacteristically earnest. "I will, if you go with me. Right now, before you get hurt."

"That's not on the table."

"Don't write me off like that. Ri, if you want me to take a knee, I will. I want you on the road with me. Think of the difference we could make, together."

"Not interested."

"I'm not talking about being a hired gun, just keeping me safe. I'm not even going to play the sex card, though God knows, we're hot together. You can't deny that."

"Look, I—"

"Wait." Iris put her hand to Maji's lips. "I want you as a real partner, Ri." She dropped to one knee and smiled imploringly up. "Marry me."

Maji stared down at her, then sighed. "Here. Get up, Iris."

Iris took her hand, and straightened up. "There's nothing the Army can give you that I can't. Come out, and walk away. You'll have a job, health care, incredible travel—and me. We'd be unstoppable."

"And when I lose my legs to an IED? Or a bullet severs my spine? Will you drop your forty weeks a year and the Pulitzer chase, and make a new life with me?"

Iris gave her that all-too-familiar look of dismissal. "You can't scare me off that easily. I've seen you out there, and I've seen you in here. You're not standard issue."

"You don't know who or what I am." *And you never will.*

Iris grinned as if she'd won the argument. "Oh, whatever you really are, I'm sure it's classified. In fact, if I didn't know better, I'd think you were Delta."

"But you do know better."

Iris gave a snort. "Who's to say? For years the Army claimed not to have a Delta Unit. Now it swears there's no such thing as a female Delta operator."

"Not much point speculating on that, unless you're pitching to the *National Enquirer*. And now we're done talking."

"You want to shut me up, you know how to make me." Iris pressed into Maji, breathing into her ear.

Maji put a hand between them, to push her back. When Iris misinterpreted the move, sliding a hand to Maji's belly and sucking on her earlobe, Maji put the offending hand in a wrist lock.

Iris flinched away. "Ow!" Her eyes flared. "Let me go."

"After you back up. Back, back…" Maji walked Iris out the door, and it closed between them. Maji exhaled loudly, mad at herself for losing control so easily.

She heard Bubbles's voice in the hallway, along with the sounds of students banging their way into the locker room. The top of Rose's head peeked over the desk.

Maji looked back at her. "Sorry about your nap."

After the hugs and good-byes, they slipped out the back door into the parking lot full of host-family cars waiting to take students away for a long weekend. Maji and Rose wove between the cars and slid through the little door in the fence and into the waiting Humvee.

Dev didn't say a word on the short drive. Whatever choice words he had in store for her, at least he was nice enough to keep quiet while Rose dozed again. Of course, he probably hadn't slept last night, either, on watch. Maybe he was just too tired to give her any shit.

As they pulled up to Angelo's front door, Maji shook Rose gently. "Home sweet home."

Rose stirred, groaning. She sat up, getting her bearings. Sleepy looked adorable on her.

Maji gave a fleeting thought to carrying Rose indoors, up the stairs…No—she needed to get her head back in the game, to stop thinking like that. She sighed.

Rose leaned back, stretching, then gave Maji's hand a squeeze. "Yeah. Damn."

"Grab another slice, hon, or you won't get more," Jackie said to Rose.

Rose really didn't want more pizza. She worried from the way the guys dove in, nearly wrestling over the pizza, that they hadn't eaten at all while watching over the dojo.

Maji, too, had inhaled three slices and a heaping pile of salad. Rose marveled at her appetite. The comparison made her blush. "No more for me, thanks."

Frank passed her the big wooden salad bowl with a quiet smile. Did he know, too? Well, it couldn't possibly surprise him. And her taking Maji to bed hadn't fazed him, before. He really was a sweetheart. She returned the smile and accepted the salad.

"I was worried sick," Aunt Jackie said for the fourth time in the two hours since their return.

"I told you they were fine, Ma," Angelo replied for the fourth time. "Hey, Ma—if you won five million, what would you do with it?"

"I don't need five mil, Ang. Nice try."

Rose smiled at him across the table. For years, she'd seen him use that distraction on his mother. Her answers were usually inventive, related to whatever had disturbed her. Like the time Carlo had scraped the side of his car up, and her idea of just punishment was "If I had a million bucks, I'd pay a cop to follow you around and give you tickets every time you got behind the wheel."

Rose looked to Frank. "What about you? Where would five million take you?"

Frank looked thoughtful. "I'd get a sporty car—not a Vette, something with class. A Jag, maybe. The rest…I guess, women's shelters. You know, for women and kids getting out of bad situations."

"And what about places like Rose and Ri's self-defense school? Teach them how to stand up, not get hurt in the first place." Jackie seemed fully engaged, back in the present.

"And programs that teach men to deal with their own shit, rather than taking it out on the women who love them," Maji pitched in. "Can we cover that, too, Frank?"

"Sure, yeah, all of that."

Rose gave his hand a squeeze. "In that case, send a little to the women who abuse, too. Gay or straight, they do exist."

He nodded seriously. "Okay, Ang, here's the rundown: three mil to the shelters and whatnot, one mil to help guys tackle their own shit, one mil to help women who hurt women, or kids, or whoever."

Angelo extended his hand across the table and shook Frank's. "Done." He looked around the table. "Who's next?"

"But be careful what you wish for," Jackie warned. "This kid has a funny way of making things happen. And now he's gonna be rich, you never know."

"Too late for us," Tom replied. "We've played this game a lot, the last few years. No updates, Ang."

Angelo looked to Maji. "What about you, Ri? Any updates?"

Rose wondered what Dev and Tom had wished for. Something for themselves? Or as she guessed for Maji, only help for others?

"Ri already won the jackpot," Dev interjected, his eyes flicking to Rose and then settling on Maji. "Asking for anything more would just be greedy."

Maji flushed deeply, but held her tongue.

"He's just jealous," Tom assured the table as a whole. "Face it, dude, you miss your wife. We should all be so lucky as you."

Angelo raised his hands. "You'll all be home soon, I promise."

Maji excused herself from the table. "I gotta fall into bed before I fall down."

"How's your head?" Dev waved his fingers by his eyes, suggesting visual disturbance or other symptoms. Done with brotherly harrassment and back in field medic mode.

"Three-ish," she answered honestly. Mild symptoms. She inclined her head toward Rose. "Keep her safe."

The guys all nodded, and Rose raised one ironic eyebrow, then smiled in resignation. "Sleep well."

In the doorway, Maji turned back. "What time's my watch?"

"We got you," Angelo replied.

The whole team had probably been up all night, too. At least she'd worked in a nap. But her muscles ached and a dull throb was starting behind her eyes, so she didn't argue. Tomorrow she'd be back to top form, and she'd make sure to stay that way until the mission was complete.

Lying in Carlo's old bed, staring up at his ceiling by the light of the alarm clock, Maji thought not of the night before but of the next few to come. As soon as the Hotel Nacional party was over, they needed to be ready. She wasn't there yet, but for the first time since Angelo had dropped his bomb on her, a plan was gelling in her brain. And though she'd need to talk to Tom and Dev to smooth out the logistics, just knowing she could do what she had to was a relief. And she wondered what role last night had played in getting her to that mind space. Later, maybe, she'd look back and feel bitter at Angelo for his puppeteering. But tonight she wouldn't fight the rare peace she felt.

Rose woke alone, half expecting to find Maji in her bed. She closed her eyes against the bright morning light and let herself replay bits and pieces of their night in the dojo. Now that was a place of enlightenment. No one Rose had dated, or slept with, had ever been so honest about the effect she had on them. No wonder Maji had insisted they keep their distance, an artificial wall of dispassionate civility. How would they manage that, the next few days?

Rose looked at the clock. After ten. She rolled off the bed and stumbled to the shower. As she toweled off, Rose thought for the first time beyond the summer. What would Maji be like on an everyday basis? And how much longer was she indentured to the Army, anyway? Rose resolved to hold her questions, her doubts, for a few more days. Maji and Angelo—the whole team—had bigger issues to deal with than her domestic tranquility. She chuckled, pulling on her swimsuit. A private home life with Maji did not sound tranquil.

Maji sat backward on the dining room chair, trying not to move when the tattoo pen tickled. Dev had inked the band of thorns and roses around her right bicep already. The heart with *A + R 4ever* on the back of her left shoulder was setting nicely. She kept her palms on the dining table, her head bowed toward the floor, willing her muscles to stay relaxed. Dev hated to erase the squiggles, and it was no fun on her end, either. Even with a good night's rest under her belt, she'd pass on that.

"Morning." Rose's voice sounded relaxed.

"Still?" Dev replied. "Feels like lunchtime."

"What would you like me to make?" Rose's feet appeared in Maji's field of vision in flip-flops.

"Didn't mean it like that, ma'am." The pen cap snicked shut. "Were you headed for the pool?"

"Yes, but I could use breakfast, myself."

"Good. Please don't go out just yet," Maji added, daring to move enough to speak. "Tom will be up again soon, and Frank should be back in a bit. We're going to be at this a little longer."

Rose let out a little hum. "May I watch?"

"You can look, but don't touch." Dev uncapped the pen again.

Maji turned her head slightly toward him. "Dude."

"Meant with all due respect, ma'am."

"Dev," Rose replied, sounding testy, "if you call me that again, I will start saluting whenever I see you."

Maji snorted. "Sniper check, dude." Of course, Rose didn't even know Dev's rank. But in their circles, getting treated as if you were an officer didn't go over well, even if no snipers noticed.

"Not from a civilian, dude," Dev countered. "Let's try and remember she is one."

"Ignore him, Rose," Maji said. "The ink fumes go to his head."

"Well, they are beautiful designs. How long will they last?"

"Five to ten days, depending," he answered.

Rose didn't ask what it depended on. Smart move. Maji couldn't see her feet anymore, but she smelled close by. That didn't make staying still any easier. She consciously slowed her breathing.

"How about a bee?" Rose suggested. "You know, like the one Erlea has."

Maji wondered just how much Rose had figured out about that trip to Spain. If she'd read the news coverage, there were connections she could make, even without any classified information. "No," she snapped.

Dev didn't ask. "I'm just going to finish this one, and then she has to sit very still some more," he said to Rose. To Maji he added, "We'll get that last one later."

She'd be topless to let him caligraph the middle of her back for that one. No audience. Dev worked in silence another few minutes, then capped the last pen. "Done. Give it five, at least."

"Mm-hmm."

"Thank you for all your help, Dev," Rose said. "I know you're giving up time with your family to help mine."

"I'll have plenty of time with them soon. And any one of us would do the same."

"Still, I'm sure they miss you. They finally have you at home almost full-time again."

He chuckled. "Not again. First time. They won't know what to do when I'm not disappearing every few days, or weeks, when I—"

Maji cleared her throat loudly. "Stop talking," she hissed in Arabic.

"You haven't told her yet?" he replied in kind.

"No, and I'm not going to," Maji spat back, trying not to tense all her back and shoulder muscles. "It's not like we're engaged."

"Oh, for pity's sake, just ask me to leave the room," Rose said. Her flip-flops slapped on the kitchen linoleum, and Maji heard her banging cupboard doors next.

"Mind your own fucking lane," Maji said softly but clearly, knowing Dev could hear.

"Hooah." He gathered his ink set with a tumbling clatter of pens falling into the plastic case. "I'll go roust Tom."

Rose noticed that everywhere she went on Saturday, if Maji was nearby, someone else was always present. When she tried to speak with Maji semiprivately by the pool, Maji gave a little tap to her ear. To remind her that even there, they weren't alone. By bedtime Rose had had enough. She set her book down by the living room couch and found Frank and Maji in the kitchen, cleaning up the last of the night's detritus from dinner for seven. Nobody in this house let her clean when she cooked.

There was no way to approach Maji without going through Frank. "Frank, would you give us a minute?"

"Sure, hon." He dropped the dish towel on the countertop.

"No," Maji countermanded.

Rose looked around Frank at her. "Shall we talk with him standing between us?"

"Take a seat, Frank." The expression on Maji's face was hard to read.

If Rose didn't know better, she'd think Maji was angry. But now that she did, scared seemed like a better guess. She stepped aside and let Frank pass, then leaned one hip against the counter, careful not to get too close. "Will you join me tonight?" She hoped that sounded like a question, not a request or a plea.

"No." Maji didn't quite meet her eye.

Rose crossed her arms. "Last night, I assumed we were both catching up on rest. Will you not be coming back to my room at all?"

"I don't trust myself to stay on the floor." Maji tapped her ear.

Well, if she didn't want her friends to hear, she could turn the damn bug off. "So you didn't get me out of your system, then."

"I don't think I could, even if I wanted to." The look in Maji's eyes was pain.

Rose resisted reaching out to her physically. "Do you want to?"

Maji sighed, drew herself to attention, and looked Rose in the eye, her feelings shielded now. "The next three days are critical. I need to keep Angelo alive and then get him out of here safely. To do that, I need to be a hundred and ten percent on my game. You can help by keeping your distance."

"Three more days," Rose agreed. Of course Angelo's safety came first—and Maji's, too. "But once Ang is safe, I make no promises."

Maji relaxed visibly. And a hint of sadness crept into her eyes. "Thank you."

"No," Rose said. "I let myself forget what you're really here for." She brushed a lock of Maji's hair, escaped from her tight braid, back behind her ear, not letting her touch linger unfairly. "Thank you."

CHAPTER THIRTY-FOUR

Sunday morning, Angelo had to stop his coding to answer a summons to the Big House. All Ricky said on the phone was, "You got a delivery."

Sienna opened the door as he reached it, looking excited to see him and anxious at the same time. "I heard your news," she said. "C'mon, they're downstairs."

"What are?"

"The tables. Didn't Ricky tell you?"

"No, Sienna. Apparently you can catch gay over the phone. What tables?"

She shushed him, looking around as if someone might overhear. "The blackjack and such. A bunch of guys showed up with a truck and left them here."

Down in the large rec room, six gaming tables huddled by one wall. In the far corner, the heavy bag and mats waited for someone to remember them. "Just tables?" he asked. "No cards, chips, dice?"

"Oh, yeah. Over there." Her cell phone rang, and she turned away.

Angelo started opening the boxes, looking for the tokens. Behind him, he heard Sienna's half of the conversation. "How should I know where you put it? Am I your mother?...Very funny." A long pause. "Pick your own shit up for a change, Rick. It's probably under your pants again." Another pause. "Jesus. Just hold on, I'm coming."

He turned and looked at her sympathetically. "I'll let myself out down here."

"Good. And if I was you, I'd go back to girls—men are dogs." She turned to leave before he could even summon a laugh.

When she was halfway up the stairs, Angelo found the right box. Enough tokens for all of Khodorov's circle, and plenty to spare for Sirko. He let himself out the door under the patio stairs and walked home, barely noticing the weight of the box. What he brought to the party would be considerably lighter.

Angelo raised his glass in a toast. Rose and Jackie and Sienna stopped talking, but Paola was too caught up needling Gino about something to notice, and Ricky was droning on to Maji about motorcycles. Angelo clinked his glass with a knife, and the hush he sought finally fell. Even Nonna looked expectant.

"I know we got the party in a couple days, but as far as I'm concerned, this my real last supper with all of you. Nonna, Rose—I will miss the magic you work in that kitchen. The finest chefs in Vienna got nothing on you."

"How do you know?" Ricky challenged. "You never been."

Gino shot his son-in-law a look that made him glance away.

"Fair enough. But I'll bet you a thousand bucks—no, euros—that I'm right. Sienna can be the judge."

"She ain't visiting you."

Sienna looked aggrieved. "The hell I'm not. You don't want to go, I'll go with Rose and Jackie."

Angelo saw his mother and Rose exchange a look and jumped back in. "Deal. But for today, can we agree that this is the best Italian meal in all of New York?"

They all raised their glasses, clinking and starting up conversation again.

"No marriage proposals tonight, Ri?" Sienna said, leaning across toward Maji. She looked to Rose, at her side. "You must be slipping."

Maji reached for the serving plate for seconds. "No complaints." She caught Rose's eye. "I just have a thing for pesto."

"And tiramisu," Angelo added.

"And"—she paused, pointing her fork at Angelo—"I was told to play nice." She looked at Rose again. "I'm sorry."

"No offense taken. Angelo helped me see the compliment was sincere, even if the delivery lacked grace."

"Ouch," Sienna whispered loudly.

Ricky snorted. "You would take relationship advice from him."

Gino shoved Ricky's plate roughly away from him, into the center of the table. "You're excused."

Ricky blanched. "Um…"

"Now."

Everyone watched Ricky silently leave the table, except Angelo.

He watched his mother, who was looking from Gino to him and back again, worry etching her brow.

It was dark by the time they walked down to Jackie's house, Dev out front, Tom at the rear. Angelo and his mother walked close together, behind Dev. Maji could pick up most of what Jackie was saying, grilling Angelo about who knew what, and how safe he really was. She didn't envy him.

Maji slowed her pace, expanding the distance between Angelo and Jackie, and her and Rose. Rose brushed her arm lightly. The ripples that simple touch set off made her glad they weren't alone.

"Could you turn your comm off a moment?" Rose asked.

Maji thought to tell her that she and Ang weren't wearing them up at the Big House anymore, in case Gino got paranoid as the big meeting approached. Instead, she just nodded and touched her watch. *Coward.* She motioned Tom to fall back, to give them a bit of privacy.

"You're missing Ang in advance, aren't you," Rose guessed. "Asking Nonna about him."

Maji shook her head. "No. I just like the stories grandparents tell. Even if they're not mine."

"Your mother's parents didn't survive the revolution, did they?"

Of course Rose would do her research, like a good academic.

"You been reading up?"

"Just her first book. And not to spy on you. I just got curious about the woman behind the legends."

Maji walked on silently. She couldn't blame Rose. There was plenty she'd love to tell her, things that would never make print. But that wasn't going to happen.

"What about your father's parents? Do you know them at all?"

Hell, it wasn't classified. "Only from Papi's stories. They were Pinochet supporters, unlike him. But then, he was a young man, a med student full of bold ideas. When Allende fell, they couldn't save him from prison."

"Oh God. Was he there long?"

Long enough to be tortured, Maji thought. Not long enough to break. "Just until Hannah got him out." She briefly weighed how much more to explain. "Mossad went in to extract a Jewish woman, a British doctor arrested for treating injured rebels. Papi was her assistant, and she insisted they take him, too." Rose would have to ask Hannah or her father, to learn more. It was their story. "His parents never knew what happened to him."

"Never?"

"Nope. Pinochet stayed in power until '91, and Papi didn't want to endanger his folks by contacting them. His mother became one of those women who demonstrated in the squares, demanding to know what happened to the disappeared. They died not knowing." Heart attack and stroke, Maji knew. Or broken hearts, depending on how you looked at it.

Rose took her hand. "I'm so sorry."

"S'okay."

"No, it's not. It's terrible. You don't have to be tough about it."

Maji sighed and tried to slip her hand out of Rose's. Rose held tighter. Maji stopped and looked her in the eye. "I'm not being tough. It's just—where I grew up, in my house, in my parents' world, people were always coming through with stories like that. Refugees from Guatemala, El Salvador, Nicaragua. And then the Iranians—more affluent, but same kind of hurt." She smiled sadly, tilted her head. "It's not about tough—it's just a different normal."

Rose's eyes, even in the dark, glistened. "Well, it's not normal to me, this losing family to senseless violence. I think of Max and Carlo murdered, and Angelo having to leave, and I get so angry I don't know what to do with it all. What am I supposed to do with it?"

"Keep hitting things. Bob, the heavy bag, Ricky if he gets in your way."

Rose laughed. "Smart-ass. That's the best you've got?"

Maji shrugged and started walking again, giving in to the small pleasure of Rose's fingers intertwined with hers. "Well, if you were a juvie, I'd say steal cars, get in fights, deface public property, get in fights, shoplift, get in fights, get expelled, and finally learn to hit Bob instead."

"Were you really that bad?"

Maji chuckled. "You'll never know from Mom's books. Editing protects us all."

"Do I have to ask Bubbles if I want the unedited version of you as a little hell-raiser?"

"Be my guest." She reconsidered. "But tread carefully. Those were hard days for her, too."

"Hmm. Maybe I'll just hit Bob."

The day before the meeting and Hotel Nacional party, the Big House was a hive of activity. Angelo breezed into the kitchen from the veranda, followed closely by Rey. Maji looked up and barely recognized him, transformed by a stylish scant mustache and thin beard line, with a tight T-shirt outlining his muscled torso. She raised one eyebrow, went back to chopping vegetables.

"Nonna? You need kitchen helpers?" Angelo asked loudly, leaning toward his grandmother's perch by the central island.

She shook her head. "Not yet. Do the cleaning first."

"Sure," Angelo replied. "Fetch Raul here when it's time." He pointed to Rey, who ushered in a string of small dark-haired women in maid's uniforms, speaking to them softly in Spanish. They followed their stylish leader silently across the kitchen and through the swinging doors into the house beyond.

A moment later, Gino stormed in. "Where's Angelo?"

Nonna looked up, squinted. "What?"

"*An-gel-o*," he repeated, raising his voice. "*Dov'è?*"

"Outside with the band, I think," Rose replied, gesturing with her knife.

Gino shoved open the door to the veranda, hollering, "Angelo! *Subito.*" He continued to stand in the doorway until Angelo appeared.

"Why is my house crawling with spics?" Gino demanded, his voice carrying indoors as well as out.

Angelo shrugged. "Cuba, Big G. Salsa band, Cuban food, you know. Am I on the wrong page here?"

"Not them, for Chrissakes. The bunch inside. I walk in my office, there's two going over it."

"Going over it? How?"

"Well—vaccuuming, brushing down the curtains. That ain't the point. It's my office."

Angelo raised both hands. "'Course. I'm sorry. I shoulda showed them which rooms to prep, which are off-limits. I thought my guy took notes when he was here the other day. I'll fix it." He hurried off through the swinging doors, into the house.

Gino shrugged. He walked to the stove, lifted a pot lid. "How's it coming, Ma?"

"It's coming fine without you. Get outta my kitchen."

Gino kissed the top of her head, winked at Rose, and went back out on the veranda. His footfalls receded down the stone steps.

"Nonna?" Rose ventured.

"What, hon?"

"Is my father Latino?"

Nonna squinted at her. "Your father? Your father is the man who raised you. You want to turn Gerald in now?"

"No, I just…" She sighed. "You just seemed so perturbed by Uncle Gino."

"Perturbed don't begin to cover it. I raised him better than that. He forgets that in my day, the Italians were dagos, or wops, or worse. We were the spics then." She glanced at Maji. "No offense, hon."

Maji looked at the old woman with new respect. "None taken, ma'am."

Jackie looked around the dining table at the gang—Frank, Dev, Tom, Rose, Ri. Then she zeroed in on Angelo. "So, what fun you got planned for your last night with just your friends and your poor old mother?"

"Just hang out, I guess. Feels like I've hardly got to see any of you."

"You had a lot on your shoulders," Frank said.

Jackie scowled. "You been doing everybody's work. I can't believe you had to oversee the caterers and everything. Like you don't have enough to do." She pointed her finger at him. "But don't take credit tomorrow. Let the light shine on Gino and that Khodorov. Try and keep your head down, for once."

"You're right, Ma—always are. But the Big House looks fabulous, don't it?" From the driveway lined with fresh flower beds to the bandstand and dance floor on the lawn below the veranda, the place could pass for a stately hotel. Inside, it still looked like just a large house, except for the rec room downstairs with its gaming tables. "Maybe we should practice blackjack tonight. How's your game, Ri?"

Maji raised an eyebrow at him, looking unhappy that he called her out. "Perfect. But I'm not playing tomorrow."

"Not even if I stake you?" he teased, trying to elicit a smile. "Ri can take the house, even against a double shoe," he added to his mother and Rose. His mother looked impressed.

Rose looked nettled. "I have no idea what you just said."

Angelo looked to Maji to explain, but she kept her face blank. Everybody was edgy in their own way tonight.

His mother stepped in. "Double shoe is two packs of cards. So Ri must be a good card counter. Very entertaining for the wiseguys, I'm sure. But who's funding the house?"

"Nonna. She and I worked out a deal. Whatever the house loses, our guests get to keep if they want. But they should be feeling pretty generous, given the outlook on their new investment."

"What if the guests lose? They'll be playing with real money, right?" Rose asked.

"Exactly, hon—wiseguys are terrible losers. It's a bad idea, Ang," his mother protested.

Angelo shrugged. "It's for charity. Anything they lose, or don't choose to cash in, goes to St. Maggie's Relief Fund. Makes them look generous—and you know they love that."

His mother looked skeptical. "Give those *babbos* a few drinks, all they'll know is they're losing money. You know what they say about wiseguys."

Angelo answered Rose's look before she could ask. "How much money does the average wiseguy need? Ma—punchline, please."

"More, hon. No matter how much they got, the answer is always *more*." She looked from an unamused Rose back to Angelo. "You better put somebody down there, make sure they don't punch out your dealers."

Angelo thought of the trained field agents who would be undercover as casino staff. "The Cuba Libre crew are pros, Ma. But if it makes you feel better, I'll ask Khodorov to put a couple of his guys in the room, just to keep an eye out."

"Maybe you two should be there, too," Jackie said to Tom and Dev.

Angelo shook his head. "I'm putting them down by the shoreline."

"Now they're lifeguards, too?"

"No, Ma. Somebody has to make sure Sirko don't sneak anybody in off the water."

"Also," Frank pitched in, "they can't really come to the party. It's Family only."

"I suppose. So tonight, what then—Scrabble? Parcheesi? Strip poker?"

"Jackie," Rose admonished, then blushed as the whole table chuckled. "Scrabble sounds good."

"Yay," Maji said with false enthusiasm, raising her glass of water to clink with Frank. "Sober fun."

Frank came into the kitchen carrying a tray of snacks for the group—popcorn, chips, and mixed nuts. "Rose is gonna make virgin daiquiris. Sent me to take orders—strawberry, mango, or lime. Anybody?"

"Mango," Dev said without hesitation.

"Mango," Angelo echoed.

Tom looked ambivalent. "Strawberry. Unless it's mango all the way. No point making her do extra work."

"Likewise," Jackie agreed. "Whatever the kids want, so long as mine has rum in it."

Angelo winked at her. "Then it's not a virgin, Ma."

"Nobody here is, funny boy."

Maji unfolded herself from the floor beside the coffee table and stood. "I'll go give her a hand."

"Make sure Rose gets some rum, too," Jackie instructed. "She won't take my Ambien."

Maji saw Rose setting up the blender, her back to the door. She resisted the urge to sneak up and slide her arms around Rose's waist. She knocked on the door frame.

Rose turned partway, and her face lit up when she spotted Maji. "Hi. Lend me a hand?"

"Just one," Maji replied, sliding her left behind her back and offering the right, palm up.

"I'll take what I get." She set Maji to retrieving frozen fruit from the chest freezer in the pantry and didn't comment when Maji came back with both arms full.

When they had one pitcher of each flavor ready, Rose started setting glasses on a tray. As she looked up from the task and caught Maji's eye across the island, her face betrayed an inner struggle.

"What?" Maji asked.

"I have a favor to ask, and I don't want you to take it the wrong way. I would have asked you even if we hadn't…Well, I would have asked because you see things other people don't."

"Okay. And?"

"At the party tomorrow, keep your eyes open for my father. Please."

Maji stifled her initial reaction. "I'd be happy to, but I think you overestimate my powers of observation. If you've met all the guys around the right age before and haven't formed your own theories…"

"Oh, I've had plenty of those. All as dumb as yesterday's. Maybe Nonna was right."

"Maybe. And maybe getting outed would be dangerous for this guy you keep calling your father."

Rose put her hands flat on the counter and pushed, a move Maji remembered from the first night she ever saw her, arguing with Frank. "How? It's been thirty years!"

"Maybe the Mafia has no statute of limitations on betraying a mob boss by sleeping with his underage daughter. Maybe your mother and Nonna know things you don't. You might consider respecting their decision."

"You mean maybe it's not all about me?" Rose sounded bitter. Then she laughed and shook her head. "Thank you."

"For what?"

"Reminding me what matters. I guess I'm not as well trained as you, to put the well-being of others before my own needs and desires." She paused to reflect. "Before this summer, I never even thought about that."

"Sure you did. You're kind to everybody, even when they're an asshole. You should never have to do it in a life-or-death context, that's all."

"Well, it's not going to come to that."

Maji knew she should have a reply, but she was worn out trying to say the right thing without saying too much. She rolled her neck, which gave a series of satisfying pops, and reached for the tray.

"You look so tired." Rose reached across and lightly touched Maji's hand. "Are you sleeping?"

"Some." She shrugged and opted for honesty. "Not well." In truth, the only time she had slept without dreams or hypervigilance was when Rose was wrapped around her. But that was too much honesty for tonight.

"Well, tomorrow's going to be a long day, if we have to stay up until the party's over. I've seen this crowd celebrate—they could go all night." She took her hand back and reached for two of the three pitchers. "Can you take something? Ambien or the like?"

Maji shook her head. "They gave me something at the hospital, but I tossed the rest. Drugs and I just don't get along."

"Well, I wish I could help."

Maji felt her face heat, thinking how welcome some presleep help would be. Rose noticed, and flushed as well. "Me, too," Maji conceded. "Thanks anyway."

When everyone but Dev, who had first watch, was sleeping, Angelo went for a walk. He had only meant to go out by the pool and look at the night sky, but before he knew it, his feet had carried him down to the boathouse. The scene of the crime, as it were. He tried to smile at his own humor, but it didn't feel funny. It was a good spot, away from the civilians, away from his mother, and Rose, and Nonna. They shouldn't see. And down here, if the team was careful about their placement, their roles would go undetected.

Angelo looked out across the smooth black water, glassy in the still night. If it was like this at go time, sound would carry. They'd need to be extra careful, or the FBI or JSOC might pick something up. Last thing he wanted was one of them to burn for this. He shook the thought off. He shouldn't worry—those three together could pull off anything, especially with Hannah's help.

Dev and Tom had put on a great front all evening, acting like they did at crunch time in any mission, full of bad jokes and dark humor. Maji had been quiet, somewhat removed. But then, it was normal for her to pull inward at this point, too. In fact, he was the only one who'd been out of normal form, trying to stay present for his mother and Rose.

As the back of the house came back into view, Angelo stopped on the dew-damp grass and looked up at the windows of the three women he loved most in this world. He hoped they were all sleeping. God knew, Maji needed to be on her game from here on out. He was counting on her for so many things now.

As for him, it was time to lie down and run through every moment of the next thirty-six hours. To see it all, step by step, to feel himself there and visualize everything going according to plan. After that, he'd have to make himself get some rest. One last time.

CHAPTER THIRTY-FIVE

Maji looked up from the lounge chair by the pool as Dev and Tom stalked out of the house. They wore black caps and bulletproof vests, black pants and boots. Each of them had a sidearm showing, in addition to a rifle. They stopped at attention across from Maji and waited for her to move the pool party indoors.

Maji leaned over to Jackie, whose eyes were closed as she basked in her bikini on the next lounge chair over. "It's time to go in. The guys need to leave."

Jackie sat up and startled at the sight of them. "Jesus! You'll melt down there." Her voice carried easily across the water to them.

Rose stopped swimming midstroke and righted herself in the water, checking to see what was happening. She stood and pulled her goggles off. "I hope you're taking water down there," she said. "I can bring you food, too, if you can't come up."

"Frank will be their runner," Maji said. Interesting that guns fazed Benedetti women so little, while the prospect of dehydration concerned them so much. "We need to go in now."

Rose nodded and pulled herself up the side ladder, leaving wet footprints on the cement as she claimed her towel and wrap. Catching Maji watching, she smiled before covering up.

Maji felt herself blush. "Have a nice time at the party," Dev said.

"I'll try," she replied. "Don't shoot any wiseguys."

"What?" Rose asked as she passed by.

"I'll be right in," Maji told her and headed over for a direct word with the guys.

Rose found Maji applying makeup in the large bathroom with two sinks that connected Angelo's and Carlo's rooms. "Mind if I join you? The lighting's better in here."

"Be my guest. In fact, you can help me hit the right note. Style-wise."

Rose studied her, fascinated by the transformation under way. "What are you going for? Your original tasteless look, or something more moderate?"

"Ouch," Maji responded, her smile belying the hurt tone. "More moderate—like Sienna gave me a makeover."

Rose smiled but didn't laugh. "Poor Sienna. Her tan is sprayed on, and she still thinks you got the natural look from time in the sun."

"Hey, now. She's smarter than that. She knows I fit in with the caterers better than with your family."

Rose nodded. "And how her father feels about that. Well, your dress is in good taste, at least."

"Thanks. I'm giving you credit for that. Remember our great shopping trip? The one Frank brought all the boxes home from."

Rose set her makeup box on the counter, opened it. "Oh, right. Good thing you mentioned it. Where'd we go again?"

Maji shrugged. "Doesn't matter. Wherever you shop when you're on vacation here."

"Honestly, I don't. Most of my clothes are from my mother. We're the same size, and she goes through outfits in a blink, writes them off as business. Which, in Southern California real estate, may be legit. I cherry-pick to make a lowly professor's paycheck stretch."

"Well, that explains the California casual elegance vibe. It suits you."

Rose smiled and took out her foundation lotion. "What about you? You do actually buy yourself clothing, I assume. What do you do when Angelo isn't dressing you?"

"When I was on base, I wore fatigues or jeans. That's about all I own anymore. Bubbles is waiting to take me thrifting. She's the queen of secondhand fashion."

Rose could picture Bubbles clowning around the racks of outfits, showing off unlikely finds. "That sounds like fun."

"Soon," Maji agreed.

Rose noticed she didn't say, *Why don't you join us?* Bubbles would surely invite her if she asked. But she resolved not to.

"When did your mother marry this Gerald guy?" Maji asked, looking at herself in the mirror, carefully outlining her lips, rather than Rose.

Rose blinked at the shift. "When I was ten. They started dating when I was eight. They met through work, of course. Why?"

"Nonna calls him your father. I just wondered what he's like."

Rose thought briefly. "You know, I believe he's the only man who has never spoken down to me. Even when I was eight."

Maji caught her eye in the mirror. "Sounds like good dad material. Has he been out here?"

"No. My mother's never returned. Not even for Grandpa's funeral." Which Rose could understand. "Not for Max's and Carlo's burials, either."

"And that makes you mad?" Maji's eyes caught Rose's in the mirror.

"Yes. Whatever happened, it was a long time ago. Nonna needed her. Jackie needed her." She sighed. "There I go again. I guess I should respect her decisions, even if I don't like them."

Rose went out and got her dress on, zipping it nearly to the top in back. It caught an inch from the clasp. She swore and went back to the shared bath. Maji was nearly done. The total effect was dramatic. To Rose she looked like a different person. Not Ri the soldier she'd almost gotten used to, but Ri the streetwise moll. Dangerous and, in that dress, attractive in a brassy kind of way. Potent. "Wow."

"What?" Maji asked, pulling the thick hair swept to one side into a large rhinestone-studded clasp. "You got an eye problem?"

Rose laughed at the tone, Maji's stance. "Now I could see you in Vegas, taking the house to the cleaners."

"Never played there," Maji said, her speech normal again. The hair slipped out, and she swore, trying to pull the clasp out of her hair. "Ow."

Rose came over to help her, started to delicately extract strands of hair from the metal prongs. This close, she could smell Maji's natural musk. "You should put on a tacky perfume. Otherwise, I may mess up your makeup."

"Is that a threat, or a promise?" Maji's eyes shifted from green to brown, and a hint of Brooklyn came through in the challenge.

Rose swallowed, and she had a vision of Maji in fatigues, verbally sparring with Iris. No wonder they'd slept together, in the middle of a war zone. Rose was certain she would have, too. She took a step back, releasing her hold on Maji's hair.

"You okay? Rose?"

Rose took a deep breath. "I'm sorry. I shouldn't have flirted. I thought I could afford to play a little, with you in Ri mode, but…"

"But it's still me." Maji looked resigned. "I've been wearing Ri over my own skin for years. It's been nice to remember what it feels like to just be me."

"Hold still," Rose said. She worked the clasp out of Maji's hair and handed it to her. They each held one half, their fingers touching. "You aren't standard issue Army. I know you can't tell me, and I don't need the details. But Iris was right about that much."

Maji pulled back, leaving the clasp in Rose's hand. "She doesn't even know my name. And if I can help it, she never will."

Rose set the clasp down by the sink. "That's a lot of heat, for someone you really don't care about anymore." Maji remained frozen in place, her face a familiar mask of studied blankness, and Rose fought the urge to shake her. "Maji Rios, don't get me wrong. I love the woman you've shown me. And I know there's much more to you. But if you should want some kind of future with me, get your house in order. Because there will never be room in mine for three."

Having finished her pronouncement, Rose kissed Maji lightly on the cheek and left.

Like shooting fish in a barrel, Angelo thought, looking around the formal dining room. It doubled well as a boardroom, or a conference room at the Hotel Nacional if he wanted to extend the party metaphor that far. Rey's cleaning crew had pulled back the heavy drapes and put every last leaf into the long, polished table now bouncing sunshine into half the made men's eyes. Each Family's capo, consigliere, and head tech guy or accountant filled the table's extended sides, squinting against the reflected light. Gina Luchetti and Nonna sat at one end, the only women in the room, invited out of respect for their dead husbands.

"Drop the damn blinds already," Nonna barked in Ricky's direction. He looked to Gino for consent before getting up from his seat in the ring of chairs lining both long sides of the room. Angelo knew he aspired to be at the table, not relegated to the outer circle. But he played errand boy without complaint today, and a collective sigh followed the dimming of the room.

From his spot with Sander at the far end of the room from the old ladies, Angelo could see everyone's faces except for Yuri's and Gino's. As expected, Gino acted solemn, trying to project some gravitas as the meeting's host and the co-owner of the big product launch. Like he wasn't the prodigal son, brought back into the fold by Khodorov's largesse. God knew, Gino believed it enough to sell it, and the others weren't about to challenge the charade if it would piss Yuri K. off.

"That's a lot of Cuban shirts," Sander whispered to him.

True, it looked as though a memo had gone out, specifying

required party wear. Angelo chuckled softly. "They all shop at the same place, huh?"

"No—their wives do."

Uncle Lupo stood out only for breaking the fashion trend, dressed in a white linen suit. Yuri hadn't bothered to play dress-up, but why should he? He could have shown up naked, and every guy in the room would have pretended they didn't see his pale skin covered in prison tattoos. But Angelo thought the capos should have worn suits, like Lupo.

He whispered his fashion critique to Sander, who replied, "Be happy they didn't turn up in Bermuda shorts and black ankle socks. The new business casual."

They both laughed, and heads turned their way. Well, so what if the guys eyeing them wondered just how close a partnership he'd forged with Sander? Yuri's fierce protectiveness of his son meant nobody would say anything out of line. At least not today, not here. And after tonight, fuck 'em all. Most of them were no better than Gino, just better trained.

Yuri looked over his shoulder at them. "Shall we begin?"

Angelo was pleased to see Gino hold his peace, smart enough to defer to Yuri, who ran the meeting like a board chairman. Later Gino would shine as the party host—man of the house, the lord of the manor.

Angelo and Sander gave a nice little dog-and-pony show that he could see bored the handful of tech guys in the room. For the others, it spelled out in simple terms what they were buying: a program that would make all of their transactions untraceable, and the ability to license the program to their own clients. Sander's patience with the Digital Banking 101 questions from the consiglieres started to fray. "Look," he said, "You just buy in, let your tech guys set things up, and then the computers will do the rest."

Angelo could see the older men's reservations, masked politely. "If it all sounds like voodoo to you," he said, pausing dramatically to look the capos and their consiglieres in the eye, "try and remember who it is you're dealing with here."

Yuri blinked at being put on the spot, but made a gesture of gracious acknowledgment. "A few weeks ago, I would have believed what we are offering today to be impossible, myself. But my son has tested, even enhanced, the program that our young Benedetti created. I now share with you my complete faith."

"As with any partnership my father enters into," Sander added, "if you are not satisfied, he is not satisfied."

"And I am never unhappy alone," Yuri concurred, managing to make his usual threat sound more like a promise today.

Gina Lucchetti's son Arthur, now the head of his family, stood. "If you say it works, I'll take that to the bank." He looked to the other capos for agreement.

They all nodded, faces serious. Bordering on earnest, Angelo thought. Good—they were sold. If Yuri said he was going to melt the polar ice caps with a satellite laser from space, they'd all buy stock in the water.

Yuri dismissed Angelo and Sander back to their ringside seats and moved on to distribution rights, profit shares, and details well within the comfort zone of all the men at the table. He opened the metal hardcase full of tokens and joked, "Do not give these to your children to play with. Do not take these downstairs to the game room, either. Each one costs you one million dollars and will deliver a hundredfold on your investment, over time."

Sander stood and briefly explained how the tokens were controlled via remote server access, and limited to use by one client each. "So think carefully about how many you need, given the distribution agreement we have outlined so far."

"And be aware," Yuri added, "that each transaction, no matter who makes it, will deliver to the program's creators"—he gestured toward Angelo and Sander—"a very small portion of the transaction fee it generates for you, the distributors."

"How small?" Arthur Lucchetti asked. Angelo remembered why he'd always liked Uncle Art. Balls of steel, that guy.

"One percent of your automatic deduction. As explained earlier, all this is automated. Should you find any variance when you check your accounts, you may see me personally for recourse. Any objections?"

Angelo would have keeled over if anyone there had raised one.

The capos dismissed the outer ring, and half the room filed out, led by Ricky and promises of mojitos on the veranda. On determining that only the techs and accountants really needed to stay and collect the tokens, make payment via their offshore accounts, and go over the deployment instructions, the capos and consiglieres began to rise as well, already shifting into a party mood.

Nonna stopped them with one raised hand. "Before you go and celebrate, I got a few words. After that, nothing more except, *Why is your plate empty?* I promise."

The men chuckled politely and sat back down.

Nonna stood by her chair, leaning on it. "Gina and I, we're the last of the women who helped their husbands run the business. When we were young, the Family's job was to take care of our own. If some people got hurt in the process, that was a price to pay, not a bonus. Stephano could talk to me, because he was never ashamed of the work we did. Some rackets you looked at, you said, let somebody else take that one. How many of you remember him saying, *If I wanted to be in the Cosa Nostra, I'd go back to Sicily?*"

Only one of the men, Uncle Lupo's age, raised his hand. Lupo caught his eye and nodded, his mouth turned up at one corner.

"These days, your wives don't want to know what you do. And you don't tell your kids either. I never made a secret what I think about choosing to do business you can't explain to your kids—especially your daughters."

To their credit, they were a tough audience. Angelo caught not a blink from any of them.

"So this thing my boy has made for you, it's sure to make you rich. So rich, even a wiseguy can see it's enough."

They smiled politely at the inside joke. *Where is the old lady going with this?* Angelo could see them thinking behind their carefully neutral expressions.

"Tonight you party, and soon you rake in the cash. But take this moment in time to consider why you're in this business, and whether it's a way of life you want for your grandkids. Anybody can run the rackets. Now you, with this thing, you could retire and set your kids up to do something different. Something better."

They waited politely.

"That's it. Have a good time tonight. It's been a long time since the Benedettis had a celebration in this house. *A nostra felicita.*"

Whose happiness? Angelo wondered at Nonna's blessing. Not theirs. Not for long, anyway.

CHAPTER THIRTY-SIX

It took Angelo a half hour to find Maji at the party, what with having to shake hands and take congratulations every second step. After the obligatory mingling, they took a breather by the parapet on the veranda, looking out at the late afternoon haze over the Sound. Behind them, Gino and Lupo talked with Arthur Lucchetti and Big Mike Garafalo, another capo.

"Where's that northside breeze you promised?" Arthur asked Gino. "It's muggy as the city out here."

"I ordered Cuban weather," Gino joked. "Gets the blood up. Have a mojito, try some roast pork, dance with your wife—you'll thank me later."

"I thank you already," Arthur assured him. "It's good to be in business with you again."

"Thanks, Art," Gino replied. "That means a lot, coming from you."

"But that speech your mother made at the end?" Big Mike added. "As if we could retire, just like that."

Gino cleared his throat. "Ma's got notions. You know how they get at that age."

"No disrespect meant," Big Mike backpedaled. "It's not the worst idea I've heard."

Lupo laughed. "Believe me, the older you get, the better it sounds. Aren't you sixty yet, Art?"

"Sixty-two. Three grandkids already. But my daughter don't bring them around. Mrs. B's got a point about the rackets."

"That ain't your rackets," Big Mike ribbed him. "That's your cooking. Learn to make a decent gravy, they'll come around."

Lupo left the men talking Italian cooking and joined Maji and Angelo. "I think they're ready for supper, Ang. Why don't you give them the food tour?"

Ang cocked his head at the dismissal and looked at Maji. "'Scuse me, babe. Duty calls."

"Enjoying the party?" Lupo asked when he and Maji were alone, the men having moved off to try the pork and other enticements.

"What's not to love," she answered, leaning one hip against the low wall. "I get to meet dozens of people I'll never see again."

"Now that sounds like a jilted girlfriend talking, and we both know better. You never expected Angelo to keep you here. And I trust he didn't promise to take you to Austria."

She shook her head and turned so he could see the heart tattoo on the back of her left shoulder. "But I really will miss him. We've been through a lot together."

"I didn't know the Army allowed tattoos on women." He didn't touch the ink.

Maji turned back to meet his eyes. "They let their standards down, all kinds of ways."

"I didn't mean any offense, young lady. You've been of real service to the Family. More than we realized, of course."

So, Maji thought, *either Ricky told you or you just put the pieces together. And Gino?* She shrugged. "Where I come from, friends look out for each other. He's had my back, too, when I needed him."

"And after Angelo flies away to a new life?" Lupo paused. "Perhaps you might need a new friend to exchange favors with."

She gave him an incredulous look. "I got friends my own age, thanks. No offense."

He laughed, fortunately. "Not that kind of favors. I meant the Family business. Believe it or not, we could use a woman now and then. Someone with street smarts, and good aim. And your kind of moxie."

"Oh—sorry. That's flattering, really. But my ass already belongs to the Army. Even at part-time, I'm done being owned."

Lupo smiled graciously. "Well, I hear re-employment for veterans isn't all we hope it might be. If you find yourself in need of pocket money, don't forget us." He drew a business card from the breast pocket of his still-crisp suit. As she looked it over, he took a Cuban cigar and a glass of champagne off the passing server's tray.

She accepted the glass and made a show of tasting the bubbly. "The less I know about your business, I figure, the better for me."

He smiled, clipping the end of the cigar. "Wise. Still, your discretion is what impressed Gino and me. That, and you know how to keep your cool in a crisis."

Maji shrugged. "Guns don't scare me as much as maybe they should. But I really don't like using them. Oh—please don't light that thing just yet."

He clicked the lighter closed and slid the cigar into his breast pocket. "Of course. Now, what services you might provide would be negotiable. All we insist on is loyalty—and discretion."

Maji raised one eyebrow. "Ang's secret didn't hurt anybody but him. And this thing you're celebrating tonight, I'm happy being out of the loop on that." She handed his card back. "Whatever kind of favors you have in mind, I'm not the woman you're hoping for."

Hours later, Angelo headed toward the girls' table to check in with all the women he loved. On the way, he overhead Big Mike say to his consigliere, "One percent? Hell, I'd have gone to ten, never thought to bitch about it."

His mother waved him to a seat at the table as he approached. Rose and Sienna smiled to see him, and Maji gave a little nod. Nonna didn't even look up, her head close to Gina Lucchetti's so the two could hear each other. Latin horns and guitar wafted up from the lawn along with the smell of roasting pork. It was a perfect night.

"How's the food? They do okay?" he asked the whole table.

"I got you a plate, but Ri ate it for you," his mother said. "It's good if you like garlic."

"I'll get you another," Rose said, standing before he could protest. She laid a hand on his shoulder. "Relax awhile."

Sienna reached behind Maji and put her hand on her upper back. "Ri keeps making up new things whenever we ask her what this means. What is it, really?"

"I told you," Maji said. *"For long life, laugh daily."*

"Or was it, *For stupid tourist, stupid slogan?*" Angelo said, then flinched. "Ow! Pinching is juvenile, Ri."

"So are your jokes."

Sienna laughed. "God, you two fight like a real couple."

They all looked at each other, as what Sienna had meant registered. His mother scowled at Sienna. "Watch your mouth."

Sienna blushed. "Sorry. I didn't mean anything."

"Well, don't mean it to yourself—for a couple more days, anyway," Angelo said in a low tone. "Can you manage that?"

"I said, I'm sorry."

Rose saved her cousins any more discussion by setting a heaping plate in front of Angelo with a flourish. "*Ropa vieja*, cooked off-site and finished on the grills," she said. "*Moros y christianos*, also known as white rice with Cuban-style black beans."

"If you don't love those, I'll take them," Maji offered. It was good to see her appetite back.

"*Plátanos maduros*," Rose continued, ignoring the interruption. "They're almost out already. And of course the yucca."

"That's where the garlic is," his mother added. "Chunks of it."

"Yeah, well, I don't think I'm kissing anybody tonight," Angelo replied. He popped a caramelized disk of fried plantain into his mouth and groaned. "If this was my last meal, I wouldn't complain."

Maji stood abruptly. "Lemme get you a drink. The usual?"

Maji left the table, nodding to Paola as she came to take a seat with the Benedetti women, and crossed the veranda to the bar. She let two middle-aged women with matching blond highlights in their dark hair go ahead of her. A man, one of so many in Cuban shirts and pressed slacks that she had stopped trying to tell them apart, insisted on letting her go ahead of him. So she got a glass of red wine for Rose and stood aside with it. When the wiseguy took his beer and headed back to his own table, she approached the bar again.

"The usual for Angelo," she said in Spanish. "And a Coke for me, hold the rum."

Rey poured the two tall glasses for her. He scanned for other guests nearby before speaking. Apparently he didn't trust that no one else spoke their language. "You want to dab some on you, like he does?"

Maji shook her head. "Not part of my cover. And I've had too much champagne already. Fortunately, rice and beans really soaks it up."

"Yeah. When we're all done here, come hang with my family sometime. Without the motorcycle, of course."

Maji realized that Bubbles hadn't told him that she almost never drank, even when she wasn't driving the zero-tolerance machine. She wondered just how much of their teen years he knew about. "Sure. Thanks."

"You holding up okay, Rios?"

Maji nodded and sipped on her Coke. She should get back to the table. "Glad to be done soon. You, too, I'm sure."

"Hell yeah. La B—" he stopped himself from saying Bubbles's distinctive name. "The wife misses both of us."

"Has she seen this?" Maji ran her hand over her jaw, in reference to the neat line of facial hair he wore.

"Nah. I gotta shave before I get home tomorrow. She'd go crazy if I showed up in this drag."

Maji was about to give him some encouragement in that direction, when Ricky's voice rang out behind her. "You better take your boyfriend that G and T before he gets jealous."

She turned her head only. "Hi, Ricky."

"Nice ink," he said, pressing one finger onto the brush strokes on her back while running his eyes over her bare arms and shoulders. "What else you got?"

"Nothing you'll ever get to see."

He swayed slightly and grinned lopsidedly. "That makes two of us, then."

"Watch it." They both turned at the sound of Gino's voice. "Ricky, go ask my daughter to dance. She looks neglected."

Ricky bobbed his head and walked away. Gino turned back to Rey. "He's cut off. Understood?"

"Yes, sir. What can I get you?"

"Gimme a red." He spared a glance for Maji. "And you. Wait for me."

When he had his glass, Maji handed him Rose's. "Would you? Thanks. I didn't know how I was going to juggle."

As they walked back to the family table together, she felt Gino's sideways glances. Finally he asked, "Lupo have a chat with you?"

"Yeah. But I think I disappointed him."

"Just as well. You done plenty already. 'Course, you do understand—"

She took a chance, cutting him off. "Discretion, yeah. I may not be in your business, but where I came up, we had our own *omertà*."

"Good. Then we understand each other."

By nine p.m., the children at the party were getting whiny or falling asleep in their mothers' laps. Maji felt all the Coke she'd consumed gnawing at her stomach. It was too full of the food she'd shoveled in to try to kill the buzz from the champagne. And now there was a queasy feeling creeping in. "I need some air," she said, pushing back from the table.

"Sure you don't want to lie down?" Rose asked.

"No," Sienna objected. "You'll miss the fireworks."

Maji swallowed. Something was definitely not sitting right. "Just a walk."

"I'll go with you," Rose offered.

They descended the long stairs on the bandstand side of the veranda in silence. At the bottom, Rose said, "Let's get farther upwind of the grill."

Of course. She'd been inhaling the scent of cooked meat for hours. *You idiot, Rios.*

They skirted the few couples dancing on the temporary parquet floor. A café table at the far side offered some semblance of privacy. Nobody could hear them, at least. "How are the guys doing down there?" Rose asked, her eyes toward the waterline.

"Dunno. No comms tonight. Have you seen Frank?"

"No. He's probably down there with them. He's not much of a party person." Rose paused. "You mean I could have been whispering in your ear all evening, in private?"

Maji looked across the little table at her. "Yes, but then people really would have stared. More than usual, I mean."

"I hadn't noticed anyone staring at you."

Maji shook her head. "Not at me. You turn heads everywhere you go. And not just tonight, all dressed up." Although she did look gorgeous, in that dress that hugged all the right spots and the makeup that made her eyes impossible to miss, even from a distance. "You could never work undercover."

"Why, Sergeant Rios," Rose said, batting her eyelashes, "are you flirting with me?"

"Just being honest."

A small burst of light broke the skyline, followed by a modest pop. Then a squee sounded, followed by a smiley face overhead, and a bang. The dancers cleared the floor, the music petering out. Maji looked up at the veranda and saw the throng of guests, some with children in their arms or on their shoulders. "Guess it's showtime."

The band started up a little Sousa, which corresponded fairly well with the brilliant streaks and bursts overhead. Within moments, Frank emerged from the darkness beyond the dance floor, smiling when he spotted them. Rose stood and greeted him with a hug, and they stayed standing, looking up together. Maji watched them sharing the moment. What would she tell Rose later, if asked for her impressions of the men at the party? Frank's story, even if she knew it, wasn't hers to tell.

At the first lull in the action, Rose peeked around Frank's torso and motioned to Maji to join them. Maji stood and slid a hand around

Frank's waist on the opposite side of him from Rose. He draped his free arm over her shoulder, his warmth welcome against the cooling night. "All good at the shoreline," he whispered to her.

Rose's fingertips traced the lines on Maji's uncovered back, from the space between her shoulder blades to just above her waist, where the snug bodice tied the dress front and the skirt together. Maji moved her palm from Frank's hip to the small of Rose's back and pressed lightly. It was as close to a dance as they could ask for tonight.

When the finale was over, the sky hazed with smoke from the fireworks, the band returned to salsa. The three of them broke apart, Maji slipping away first.

"You won't dance with me, will you?" Rose asked her.

Maji shook her head. "Not tonight. Frank?"

"Sure." He took Rose's hand and led her onto the floor.

Maji sat and watched them, realizing shortly that she needed to move again. Too much acrid residue in the breeze coming off the water. She rose and made her way to the far edge of the floor, near the base of the stairs.

"No show for us tonight?" Ricky said as he reached the bottom stair. His breath carried a mix of liquor and cigar smoke.

"No show for you ever, Little Dick." The snide nickname just slipped out.

Ricky seemed too drunk to notice. "Then I'll just go cut in," he said, weaving across the floor toward Rose and Frank.

Maji followed, keeping some distance. She watched Rose shake her head and saw Frank's mouth move. And then Ricky put his arm between them, as if he could step into the space and displace Frank as lead. Maji stood still, watching Rose react calmly but decisively.

Before he knew that she'd done anything at all, Ricky was on the ground, seated, looking up at them. "Hey." He sounded confused, torn between anger and hurt.

"You tripped," Maji said. She put her hands under his armpits and helped him stand. "Let's find you a seat." *Near your wife, preferably.*

Ricky threw an arm around her shoulder, the hand landing on her breast. She moved it aside and leaned up into him, starting to walk him before he could get his bearings. At the foot of the stairs, she turned him and set him down. He landed heavily on the second step, then leaned back against the third and fourth, looking up at her. "Why you nice to me?"

Frank appeared at Maji's elbow. "Go get him some water," she instructed.

Ricky turned his head as Frank went up the stairs, his eyes following him. "He said you don't like me. 'Cause Ang don't. Why don't Ang like me?"

"You call him bad names, for one." She perched near him.

He shook his head. "No. Before he was a fag, he didn't like me then, too. Either."

"You can't be Carlo, Ricky," she said. "No matter what you do."

He nodded his head slowly. "Yeah." He sat quietly, digesting the deep news slowly.

A flash went off over by the grills, then another. "Hey!" Ricky roared, standing abruptly. Maji tried to steady him, but he batted her away and headed toward the source of the light.

"What on earth?" Rose said from beside Maji.

"Stay back," Maji said, as they watched Ricky grab a cell phone from one of the servers. "*Retrocédan!*" she ordered, striding toward Ricky. The server and her two alarmed-looking friends moved back as instructed.

"Spies," Ricky said, waving the phone at the frightened women. He raised the phone up, preparing to throw it on the ground. "Spics," he spat, as Maji's arm caught his. She twisted it behind him with one hand as she removed the phone from his grip with the other.

"Here," Rose said, taking the phone from Maji.

Ricky twisted in Maji's grip, his face purpling with rage. "Fucking cunt! Get your hands off me."

"Breathe, Ricky," Maji replied. *But not on my face.* "Take a deep breath."

He paused his struggle. "Stupid spics. Didn't you tell them no photos? Even the wives and kids know better."

Maji repeated the main message loudly, in Spanish. In English, she said, "Rose, show us what's on the phone."

Rose clicked through the photos for them. Nothing but the server's friends. "See? No harm done."

"Wipe them all," Maji said. Rose hesitated. "Now." Rose played with the buttons, and displayed the phone again.

"Thank you," Maji told her. "See? You did your job, Rick. Can I let you go now?"

"Yeah," Ricky mumbled.

Maji let her grip go and started to step away. "Hey!" she heard. *Just in time, Frank.*

Maji's head jerked back as Ricky grabbed a fistful of her hair, leaning into her face as she arched backward. "I was Carlo, I woulda fucked you both in front of that faggot, and then whacked all three of you."

Maji felt her dinner rise up into her throat. Then her head was free, and Ricky was puking near her feet, holding his crotch.

Frank was wrapping both arms around Rose, pulling her backward. "Ri!" she called, struggling forward against Frank's protective hold.

Maji shook her head, to warn her off. And then she threw a full meal onto Ricky's feet. The air smelled terrible, but at least less like smoke now.

"My shoes!" Ricky said, trying to straighten up. The way he winced, Maji guessed that Rose had landed a front rising kick solidly between his legs to set off the puking chain reaction.

Frank let Rose go and threw a cooking towel at him. "Screw the shoes. Go around the side and dump 'em. Mrs. B will kill you, you track puke in her house."

"They're four hundred dollars kicks, you moron!" Ricky gagged, and spat to the side. "She owes me four hundred."

Frank stepped up into his face, not even showing how disgusting Maji knew that must be. "You just threatened to rape and kill her, you asshole. Call it even."

"Fuck you."

Frank didn't flinch when Ricky's spittle hit him. "You want me to report this to Gino, give him the blow by blow?"

"Fuck you," Ricky repeated, but weakly this time. He stepped on the back of one shoe, and kicked it off. He stepped on the other with his sock-covered foot and wobbled. Frank steadied him. "Thanks," he mumbled.

"C'mon," Frank said. "I'll take you inside." He turned to Rose and Maji. "You two okay?"

Maji looked to Rose, who nodded. "All good, Frank. Thanks."

Rose examined Maji from a few feet away. There was vomit on her skirt hem and shins. And feet, no doubt. She held out her hand, and Maji took it. "This way," Rose said.

They stepped into the rec room-turned-casino, away from the grill's odors and the noise of music and voices. A pair of dealers stopped talking to each other and headed for separate tables. "No, no," Rose said. "*Continúan. Estamos cansadas.*"

The male dealer smiled at them and reached back for a chair by the wall. "Here. Rest." He eyed Maji. "Perhaps some water, *también?*"

"*Mil gracias,*" Maji said, sinking onto the chair.

The female dealer returned promptly with a paper cup and a damp towel. Rose wiped Maji's legs down while Maji drained the cup.

"You gave him the handshake, didn't you?" Maji asked.

Rose looked up at her and saw amusement. Rose felt herself color. "I did. Maybe a poor tactical choice, but…"

"No. You did fine. Thank you."

"You could have handled it, probably better. I just—those words, and he had you like that—I just…"

Maji took her hand. "I know. It's okay." She pulled her skirt edge up and wrinkled her nose. "I better go change, though."

"I'll go with you." She read hesitation on Maji's face. "Don't you argue with me, Rios."

"Hooah."

They jogged barefoot through the damp grass down to the blissfully quiet empty house. Rose waited while Maji stepped into the shower, her dress an empty shell on the floor outside the bathroom. The smell of smoke on her own dress made her want to change, too. She could join Maji in there…No, that wasn't fair. Maji was still on duty, and a little shaken up, besides. Sometime in the last few weeks, Rose had stopped thinking of her as invincible. The water stopped, and Rose tapped on the door.

"Yeah?"

"I'm going to go change."

"Okay."

When Rose stepped out of her own bathroom, wrapped in a towel, she expected to find Maji standing in the doorway waiting, in a fresh Ri getup with redone makeup. Instead, there she was on Rose's bed, curled up in tight jeans and a leopard-spotted top, snoring. Rose quietly pulled on her nightshirt, turned off the light, and lay down beside her.

Three hours later, the blare of the fire alarm bolted them both upright.

Chapter Thirty-seven

I t's only one fifteen, Ma," Angelo protested. "Dance with me."
      "And I'm old. I want to be up to see you off tomorrow." Jackie
looked at Yuri and Sander Khodorov. "When are you putting that bird
down on our lawn?"
      "Eight a.m. We must leave by nine."
      She nodded. "If you gotta. I'll set an alarm." She leaned in toward
Yuri. "Thanks for staying over. Don't let anybody trash this place."
      "Not on my watch, as they say." When Jackie had gone into the
house, Yuri tilted his head in that direction. "Nice woman. She will visit
us, yes?"
      Angelo smiled. *She'll get nowhere near you.* "She's looking
forward to it. Wants to bring Rose over, on her winter school break."
      As the plan stood, he and Yuri and Sander would take a helicopter
across the Sound to a private airstrip in Connecticut. From there, off to
Vienna in the Khodorov jet. It was a nice plan.
      Ricky started to pass their table, looking considerably more sober,
but very rumpled. Angelo reached out and touched his arm. "You seen
Ri lately? Or Rose?"
      Ricky shook his head. "Maybe they're off, um, together. I could
go look…"
      "You wish." Angelo looked around, scanning the thinned-out
crowd. "Well, where's Frank?"
      Ricky put his hands out. "How should I know?"
      Angelo rose and pushed his chair back. "'Scuse me." If Rose and
Ri weren't up here, on the dance floor, or down in the rec room, chances
were they were in one of Nonna's rooms, like his mother. With Frank
snoring nearby. But he'd feel better knowing for sure.
      "I'll come with you," Sander said, rising. He stopped midrise as
Dev came bounding up the stairs, his rifle over his back. Conversations
all over the veranda died, and a few hands went into jackets.

"He's mine," Angelo yelled toward the guests. Then he gave all his attention to Dev.

"Your house is on fire." Dev sucked in a lungful of air. "We called it in. Who's accounted for?"

"Just me," Angelo said. He turned to Yuri. "Send some guys to cover the waterfront. I want mine up here."

Dev met him by the base of the outdoor stairs two minutes later. He'd scared the hell out of Lupo, Nonna, and Jackie—but no Rose or Ri. Frank was with Jackie and now tasked to keep her at the Big House. Tom came pounding up the hill as Dev and Angelo took off toward the fire, Sander trailing behind them.

Lights and sirens richocheted off the trees as they approached the pool behind the house. Nobody back there. They jogged around the side of the house, close enough to feel the heat but not get hit by sparks and debris. Angelo waved Sander to keep more distance, and Tom to sweep the far side of the building.

Around front, a crew of firefighters was laying out hose, preparing to contain what damage it could. The garage, Angelo noticed, wasn't burning yet. Thank God he'd moved the tokens to Frank's apartment. The drive was empty of vehicles.

Angelo spun around, caught sight of a Hummer, and sprinted toward it. Nobody inside, and its back wheels were mired in the new flower bed. Beyond it, Ricky's Corvette rested on its side, on the grass. *See, Ri? Hummers can be useful, after all.*

"They're with the medics," came Tom's voice from behind him.

Angelo grabbed Tom and squeezed him hard, then let him go. "They okay?"

Tom nodded. "A few cuts, small burns, nothing critical. C'mon."

"Go see them," Angelo told Dev and Tom. He pulled out his cell phone as they jogged off and took Sander's hand in his free one. "Frank? Yeah. Everybody's okay. Listen, can you get Mom out without Gino noticing? Good. Take any car out there, drive her down to where the Humvees are."

"Safe house?" Sander asked. Such a bright kid.

Angelo nodded. "I'm not trusting anybody now. Except your dad, of course."

Sander watched the fire crew work, scanning the house. "Sirko. What he can't take, he destroys."

Angelo caught his mother as she spilled out of the back of the limo. "Time to go, Ma." He turned to Sander. "You give us a minute?"

Sander nodded and backed away. Sweet guy, really.

Frank waited in the limo until Angelo had said his good-byes, and been released from his mother's embrace. "What if Gino calls?" He held his cell phone out.

Angelo took it from him, dropped it, and stomped. "He asks later, it got broke in the circus down here. Follow me."

They met up with Tom, Dev, Maji, and Rose at the ambulance and formed a quick evacuation plan. Angelo was careful not to say in front of Sander which safe house to head for. The team knew, and Frank could just ride along. A few minutes later, a train of vehicles left the property—two Humvees, one limo, an ambulance, and the fire marshal's Jeep.

Angelo and Sander, the only ones left, spoke with the fire crew's lead and walked back up to the Big House. Even coming under control, the flames were warm on their backs.

In under twenty minutes, the Big House was clear of guests. Next the band left, and then the caterers. "Leave it all," Angelo assured the head guy, Raul. "Come back tomorrow for cleanup."

In the living room, he found Gino, Lupo, Yuri, Sander, Sergei, and Ricky waiting. He walked at Ricky, gaining speed as he went, and shoved him back into the wall. "You nearly killed them!"

Ricky spluttered.

"You wanted me, you should have come after me. Like a fucking man, you little shit."

"Stop." Yuri's voice was cool, clipped. The gun in Angelo's ribs felt chilly and hard.

Angelo released his hold, and Ricky got his footing back, wheezing. The pressure of the gun disappeared, so Angelo stepped back, holding his hands where Yuri could see them. But he kept his furious eyes on Ricky. "You never stopped giving Sirko intel, did you?"

"I did! I swear. Only what we agreed, nothing more." Ricky was pale, with a sheen of sweat on his upper lip.

Angelo winced. "Wish that was true. Frank was here, we'd know for sure."

"Where the hell is Frank?" Gino said.

"I had him get Ma and Rose out of here. Ri, too."

Sander waved the domestic discussion away. "Go back to Sirko. You gave him intel?"

Ricky looked too scared to speak, so Angelo did the honors. "After that guy in the club, there were a couple more run-ins. And since we couldn't risk giving Sirko anything real, we used Ricky to feed him misinformation. Or so I thought."

Yuri reached a hand back toward Sergei and took the silencer his body man had ready for him. He started twisting it onto the gun barrel, his eyes on Ricky.

"Musta been Frank!" Ricky blurted. "'Cause of the drugs, or—"

Gino stepped forward and smacked him hard. "*Basta.*"

"What drugs?" Yuri asked.

Angelo jumped in. "Frank used heroin, way back when. But when he got sick a little while back, we were worried. Turned out to be a false alarm, thank God."

Gino glared at him but didn't contradict him.

"Nice try, Rickster," Angelo continued. "But see, I used Frank to feed you some info myself. Then I sent Ri and the guys out to test whether it got used. First time, I wasn't sure. Second time, no mistake."

"No," Ricky protested. "The caterer! That guy was in your house, and all over this one."

"That's lame, even for you." Angelo looked to Yuri for a verdict.

Yuri stepped toward Ricky.

"Wait," Ricky pleaded, his eyes darting about. "I didn't sweep the house but the one time, before they came."

"How convenient." Also true, Angelo knew. He'd counted on it.

"No," Gino said. "He really is that lazy. You go sweep right now, Ang."

Yuri nodded. "We'll wait." He took a seat in an armchair, and the rest followed suit while Angelo went to search.

When he came back, nine of the fifteen bugs he'd found were in his hand. *Sorry, Rey.* Angelo poured them onto the coffee table. Ricky slumped down in his chair with a sigh. Gino looked relieved as well.

"We'd better revise our exit plan," Sander said, looking at his father.

Yuri nodded and thumbed his phone awake. "Bring the copter in now. We'll have the landing area lit." He looked at Angelo. "You need a separate way out of here. I'm not taking you up in the air with us now."

Angelo nodded. "Understood. I should get down to the house, see if I can salvage a couple things."

The front door opened, and they all paused to turn and look. Frank and Maji walked into the living room. "Hey," Frank said.

Angelo grinned. "Hey!" He gave Maji a hug and looked her over. "Everybody on the road?"

She nodded. "In the city soon. I'll tell you when they call to say they're tucked in."

Frank looked at the assembled group, and the pile of bugs on the table, and waited silently.

"I'm going to need a couple things from the house. See if they'll let you in. Be persuasive, but not stupid."

Maji nodded, looking exhausted but on task. Frank followed her out.

"So here's what I'm thinking," Angelo resumed. "I take half the code, Sander takes half and a case of tokens. I get the rest of the tokens from the house and meet you at the airstrip. You can secure the airstrip, right?"

Sergei nodded, and Sander said, "Yes, but how will you—"

"He'll take my boat," Lupo offered.

Angelo looked at him. "Thanks. But isn't it kind of slow?"

"Not since I put a new engine in. It'll do twenty knots, and the tank is full. Just have Frank bring it back, please."

"Okay, then. What time's the flight plan have us leaving Connecticut?"

"Ten a.m.," Yuri said. "Can you make it?"

Angelo grinned. "Vienna awaits. I'll be there by nine thirty."

"I don't like," Sander said. "You'll be exposed for hours, out on the water. At least take Sergei."

Yuri shook his head, and Angelo agreed. "I'll have Frank and Ri. They'll go down before they let anything happen to me. But there is one loose end I didn't want them here to see."

Yuri met Angelo's eye and handed him the pistol. Everyone else in the room sat up, tense.

Angelo handed the gun to Gino. "The caterer wasn't here before that day Sirko's guys chased Ri and Rose at the market." He nodded toward Ricky, whose color drained from his face again. "He was more worried for his own family than yours."

Ricky stood and stepped sideways, toward the hall, as Gino approached him. Sergei stepped behind him, a human wall to block his retreat. Ricky looked at Gino, pleading in his eyes. "Think of Sienna. They would have hurt her. Don't make her a widow, G."

Gino's voice was as flat as his eyes. "She can do better." He looked to Sergei. "Garage. There's sheet plastic you can use."

Sergei nodded and shoved Ricky toward the door. When Ricky yelled, "No!" and tried to fight his way back, Sergei spun him around, pinning his arm behind him. He clamped his free hand over Ricky's mouth, but Ricky struggled harder the closer they got to the door. Angelo ran and opened it for them, looking back in time to see Sergei get frustrated at last and give Ricky's head a brutal twist.

"Shit," Gino hissed. "Get him outside before his guts let go."

Angelo grabbed Ricky's feet, while Sergei and Lupo took Ricky's upper body. As they cleared the front landing, he heard Sienna call down. "Rick?"

Gino called back up. "He's outside, hon."

Angelo waved Lupo and Sergei to continue removing the body and stepped inside, shutting the door behind him. "He had to puke some more, Si."

"Jesus," she said. "Well, when he comes in, make him sleep on the couch. I had enough excitement for one night already."

Chapter Thirty-eight

Rose sat on the edge of the sofa bed in the office upstairs at Hannah's. She smoothed Jackie's hair back.

"Who is she?" Jackie asked again, her words slurring a little this time.

So Rose told her again. "Hannah is a friend of Ang's and Ri's. If it's safe in the morning, we'll go over and see him off. Try to get some rest."

"Can't help it," Jackie replied, her eyes closing.

Rose stood and left quietly, taking a last look around before shutting off the light. The cream-colored walls and tasteful art felt right for Hannah, but something about the layout, the desk with a couch and an armchair nearby, said *therapist*. She tiptoed over to the desk and stood behind the rolling chair to examine the framed photos on the desktop. One of Maji and Bubbles, looking a few years younger. One of Hannah, fairly recent. And one of a lovely blonde with sparkling eyes, holding a much younger Hannah. Or was it? The hair was dark and fell below her collar in a simple braid. Definitely Hannah, and the glowing woman with her must be Ava.

Rose passed Maji's room and saw both bunks were empty. The bathroom was empty, as was a small study, which must be Hannah's. The last door was closed, so she knocked lightly. No answer. Rose continued down the stairs and saw light coming from under the kitchen door. She pushed through and found only Hannah, sitting alone with a cup of tea.

"Where's Maji?"

"Working," Hannah answered. "You can use either bunk tonight. Would you like a sedative?"

Rose thought of Jackie, blissfully unconscious. And of Maji, who must be exhausted. "What do you mean, working? She's in no condition to be on her feet. Even before the fire, she was...she got ill."

"Ill, how?" Hannah poured a mug of tea from the pot on the table and pushed it toward her.

Lemony, Rose noted. She put her hands around the mug, comforted by the warmth. "There was an incident with Ricky, by the grills the caterer was using. Ricky threw up, and then Maji did, too."

"And then?"

"And then we went back to Jackie's house to clean up, and she fell asleep."

"How long before the fire started?"

Hannah's clinical tone made Rose want to throw the tea at her. "I don't know. I was asleep. Maybe three hours. What does it matter?"

"Every bit helps," Hannah replied calmly, as if Rose hadn't raised her voice at all. "How did she perform during the fire?"

How did she *perform?* Rose blinked. Did this woman love her goddaughter at all? "Like a trouper, of course. You trained her, after all."

"Rose. The next few hours are critical. If you are concerned about her fitness, I need to know specifics. How did you know about the fire? How did she respond?"

Oh, of course she cared. And she could help. Rose sipped the tea, recalling the details while Hannah waited quietly. "The alarm went off, and we both jolted awake. At least, I'm pretty sure she was asleep, too. At first I thought it was a drill like the one a few weeks ago. But then I smelled the smoke. Before I was even off the bed, Maji was calling 9-1-1 and checking the door handle, at the same time."

"Very good," Hannah said, touching Rose's hand lightly. "Breathe."

Rose took a second to come back into the kitchen, safe. "Then… she sent me into the bathroom to soak a towel and put it under the door. While she got the window open and checked the outside." She closed her eyes, picturing the events. "She made me climb down first, talking me through the holds. By then there was…the roof was on fire, I think. And then she was next to me, pushing me away from the house as we ran."

"And who thought to bring your go bag?"

"Maji."

"So she was all right, despite the smoke and heat and noise?"

Rose nodded. "Focused. Maybe angry, but not scared. We moved the Humvees for the fire trucks that were coming, and she used one to push Ricky's Corvette off the drive." Rose smiled faintly at the memory.

"Then she talked to the fire chief while the medics checked me out. I think I met Brenda. Karen's Brenda. She's nice. I wanted to follow Maji—I could see her over by the trucks—but Brenda wouldn't let me. Said Maji would be back for me. She knew her name. Maji's name."

"It's all right," Hannah said, gently squeezing Rose's hand. "You're safe. And Maji will be fine. Get some rest. I'll be right here."

Rose wanted to wait up, too, to keep hearing Hannah's calm voice until Maji walked in the door, whole. She yawned, not able to stifle it. "What about Angelo? Seeing him off?"

"Not safe enough for you. I'm sorry."

Rose nodded, and stood. She made it as far as the living room couch. Hannah spread an afghan over her, and crouched down to look at her, eye to eye. "Is it always like this, to love one of you?" Rose asked.

Hannah seemed to know what she meant. "If you choose Maji, you will have to let her go over and over and over. And it will never be easy. I can't tell you whether that's worth it, or not."

"Ava thought so." The pain in Hannah's eyes made Rose want to take the words back.

"Ava knew me from the beginning, and she knew what I did, and why. She was a clinical psychologist in Israel before we moved here. We lived and loved in the shadow of death, and we never took each other for granted."

"But then you lost her." Why were the tears running down her face, when she'd never even met the woman?

Hannah brushed Rose's cheeks with her thumb, a faint smile in her eyes. "Death will take everyone you love, whether you are ready or not. When she was first diagnosed, we actually joked about that, the irony of cancer threatening us more than bullets and bombs."

"I'm sorry," Rose said, struggling to keep her eyes open. Hannah's face blurred.

"Shh," Hannah soothed. "Sleep now. Just rest."

Angelo laid three bulletproof vests on the kitchen counter in the Big House, while Gino watched. "Ma's going to need a place to stay."

"Of course she'll be here," Gino answered the unspoken question. "We'll look after her. And you—try to be discreet for a while, over there. Word travels."

Angelo suppressed a smile. That was as close as Gino would ever get to saying *gay* out loud. The door to the veranda opened, and Frank and Maji walked in.

"All quiet by the boat," Maji said, wiping her hands on her jeans. Her forearm was bandaged, and there were a bunch of Band-Aids on her hands, but she looked ready to roll. Tired, a little sooty here and there, but ready.

Angelo gave her the nod and reached for the metal case of tokens. He stopped himself—first things first—and handed a vest to Frank.

"Where's Ricky?" Frank asked, removing his jacket and shoulder holster in preparation for putting the vest on.

"Out cold," Angelo answered.

"Now, you two, you make sure he gets there safe," Gino said. "They are riding over with you, right?"

"All the way to the airstrip. In full battle rattle."

"Come again?"

Maji finished strapping on her vest, right over her leopard-print shirt. "Vests and shit. Just in case." She frowned at Angelo. "I still don't like how long we'll be on the open water."

"Coast Guard's thick on the Sound, on our route." He took the last vest off the counter and slipped it on. "We'll come in close to the Navy base, where they keep the subs. Even Sirko wouldn't try anything. I told you, it's as safe as we're going to get."

Maji sighed. "It is what it is." She turned to Gino. "Thank you for your hospitality, Mr. B. I won't be coming back."

"I hear you. Things change, get in touch." To Angelo's surprise, he offered her his hand, and they shook.

As the three of them walked down the lawn toward the water, Angelo nudged Maji. "Very chummy."

"Yeah. Lupo offered me a job, too. Please tell me I was allowed to turn him down."

In her peripheral vision, she saw him nod. "After today, just the loose ends we discussed. And, Maji—"

"Don't." Whatever he would say that started with her real name, she didn't want to hear. "Let me focus."

"Hooah."

Frank entered the boathouse first, and on his clear they followed.

Angelo walked down the dock and placed his laptop case and the locked metal case on the stern of the Grand Banks. "Cast off the bow," he said.

Maji looked at Frank, shrugged, and walked to the bow cleat near the end of the dock. A hint of light warmed the sky over the Sound. She crouched and started unwinding the line from the cleat.

A hand grabbed her from behind, and a pair of booted feet landed on the dock. Over her shoulder she saw that the hand belonged to a wet-suited figure in an inflatable, the boat his buddy had undoubtedly just disembarked. She spun in her crouch, twisting the man's arm as the boat scooted under the dock. She let him fall backward into it and rolled herself down the dock, toward land.

Coming to her feet facing him, several feet between them, she registered first the gun trained on her. And then the red dot on his chest. She slowed her breathing, ready to move.

"Looks like a standoff," Angelo said. When the man didn't blink, he said, "Repeat that, Ri."

Maji repeated the message in Russian, and added, "What do you want?"

"The two cases," he said in a calm voice.

Maji spared a glance out to the water and noticed for the first time a small sub partially surfaced about a hundred yards out. "He wants the cases," she said in English. "For the sub Sirko sent."

The man's face twitched at the sound of Sirko's name. He said something curt in Russian, and Maji realized it was a name. The second man popped up by the dock across the empty slip, and Maji guessed he'd dropped off the inflatable into the water while she skirmished with the other one. Now his torso stood above the shallow water near the boathouse's far wall, his rifle pointing somewhere behind Frank.

"Frank," Angelo said slowly, "don't."

"Sorry, Ang," Frank said, and Maji turned just far enough to see him lift the two cases off the boat's stern. "I can't let them kill you. Or her."

"Frank," Angelo said, "you give them those, I'm as good as dead. And look—our friends got sights on them both. See?"

Frank looked at the red dot on each diver's chest. Surprised, as if he'd had no idea Dev and Tom were in the rafters with rifles.

"Ang," Maji said, "let him come as far as me." To the gunman on her dock she said in Russian, "He'll hand them to me, and I'll hand them to you. Nice and easy."

The two men in scuba suits looked at each other, noted again the red dots, and scanned the rafters. "Slowly," the one in the water said.

Maji took the first handle in her left hand and reached the other hand behind her for the second. *Make them work for it.* As the case touched her leg, instead of grasping for the handle she pulled her gun.

She flung the hard case at the man on the dock, rolled toward him, and came up shooting in the spot where he had been a second before. The other man was gone as well, and as she turned to run back down the dock toward Angelo, she saw the laptop case being pulled underwater between the docks.

The guys swung down out of the rafters, still holding their rifles, while the divers tossed the two cases into the inflatable and roared off toward the waiting sub. Dev sprayed bullets into the water after them, then turned with a smile to join the team again.

Curtains on performance number one, Maji thought. She was confident they had been convincing enough that Sirko would not hesitate to use the stolen chips and software. *Now for the hard part.*

Chapter Thirty-nine

At the sound of gunfire, the three FBI vehicles waiting outside the Benedetti estate roared in. The first stopped to cuff the two guys at the guard station, while the other two barreled up the long drive to the Big House. Guns drawn, six agents knocked, announced themselves, and entered the quiet house. They nearly ran into Nonna, in her robe.

"Not here! By the water." She pointed the way through the house to the back stairs.

Lead agent SA Seacrest motioned a team to search the house and led the others at a run toward the kitchen and the back lawn beyond it. "Land the bird," she said into her comm as they went.

The sound of distant rotors cut discussion in the boathouse short.

"Go time," Angelo said.

Maji gave Dev, Tom, and Frank each a quick glance. They were ready to move the show to where a new audience—one with access to the house's security cameras—could see. She gave Angelo the nod and took a deep breath, willing herself to relax. "Do it."

When Angelo's fist connected with her nose and cheekbone, the crack sounded more inside her head than out. She pinched the throbbing bridge of her nose with one hand and wiped blood away from her mouth with the other. Swallowing blood would make her puke again, and there was no time for that.

"Shit," Angelo said. "Did I mess up your vision?"

The eye might swell shut, but not right away. Maji shook her head and grabbed Frank by his jacket collar. "Roll, and then stand up. When you get hit, stay down."

He nodded, and she jammed one foot by his hip, rolling herself backward and him out the door of the boathouse. She let him fly, rolling herself into a low crouch that Tom could clear easily. At the crack of the rifle, she stood and ran out the door after Frank.

As Maji checked Frank's pulse—which was strong, but dangerously high—Angelo came backing out of the door, his hands raised. A bullet to the vest knocked him backward, and she sprang toward him, leaping over Frank's prone form.

As Maji tackled Angelo, more pops sounded from inside the boathouse. She felt a sting on her shoulder, one of Tom's precise shots just grazing her. Then the ground rose up to smack Angelo, and her ribs crunched into his shoulder. Maji stayed on top of him, a human shield, while pulling her gun back out of the waistband holster. As she fired blindly through the door, the engine of the big boat roared to life. She hoped Dev and Tom made it to their Coast Guard *capture* without any interference. Sirko's crew had provided enough surprises already.

Overhead, the rotor noise grew quickly louder.

"Why am I still here, Rios?" Angelo asked as Maji rolled him onto his back and made a show of checking his vitals.

"Don't worry—a good soldier always has a Plan B." She found his jugular and took a slow breath to steady her hand before inserting the tiny needle.

"Ow," he said, his beautiful brown eyes widening. Then he smiled crookedly. "Tell Ma and Rose I love them."

Maji nodded, too choked up to reply.

"Now, you gotta sell it." His voice weakened, even as he clung to consciousness.

"Stick to your own lane," she replied.

"You are my lane."

"Not anymore."

His face struggled to smile, as he slid into oblivion. "Fuck you."

"I love you, too," she told him, fighting against the tears. Maji left her gun on the ground, covered in her fingerprints, and stood. She faced into the churning air and the grit stirred up by the helicopter with *FBI* on its side. Waving her arms, she yelled, "Medic! Medic!" into the dying sound of the slowing rotor.

The SWAT team deployed rapidly, covering the boathouse even as their medic helped Maji get Angelo onto a backboard and loaded into the chopper. She accepted a hand up into the bird, and as they took off she looked down at the scene. Two agents were cuffing Frank, now sitting up. Toward the house, two agents flanked Gino, who walked with his hands cuffed behind him. She pulled the headset on and spoke to the agent watching her. "The VA hospital. They're standing by for us."

Rose peered through the glass in the door to Angelo's room in the ICU. The sight of Angelo in the hospital bed, hooked to monitors and a drip line, pale and intubated, reminded her of Grandpa Stephano in his last days. But he wasn't dying, dammit. They just had to control the bleeding in his brain, keep him stable.

"ID, ma'am?" the deputy by the door said.

Rose frowned. "Oh, I…I don't have my purse."

The door cracked inward a few inches, and Maji's voice rasped, "She's family."

The deputy nodded and pushed the door farther open, allowing Rose to walk through.

The fluorescent lights overhead were mercifully dimmed, and the curtain between the beds was pulled back. The near bed was empty, its bedding rumpled. Maji limped away from Angelo's bedside toward her. Rose felt torn between embracing her and rushing past her to Angelo. His eyes were closed, a ventilator tube taped in place in his mouth. She stepped toward Maji, reaching for her. "Ri."

Maji stopped her hand before it made contact, limping over to the empty bed and leaning back on the edge. Rose gasped at the sight of her face, the left eye swollen nearly shut, the skin red, and the bridge of her nose bandaged.

"I'm fine." Maji turned her face away, so only the undamaged side showed.

"The hell you are." Rose stepped closer and slid her hand onto the back of Maji's neck, just under the braid.

Maji stiffened but didn't pull away. "Where's Jackie?"

"Still unconscious. Too much sedative."

The door shushed open, and a man's voice said, "Sergeant, I have the—"

Rose turned and looked at him, pulling her hand back to her side. A man in scrubs looked at her, then over to Maji.

Maji nodded, and he continued. "The papers for you to sign."

She held out her hand for the clipboard, face blank.

He stopped short of her. "Let's get that leg elevated again, okay?" His tone suggested it wasn't really a request.

Maji glared at him, but scooched back on the mattress and turned herself, swinging her legs up. Rose noticed for the first time that one pant leg was cut up the back from cuff to knee, an Ace bandage wrapped around the ankle. Maji hit the control buttons on the bedside table, and the back of the bed tilted her upright. She put her hand out for the clipboard, took it, skimmed through a few pages, signed it, and handed it back.

He took it back from her. "Ma'am." Then he simply turned and left.

Rose looked a question to Maji.

"They need to induce a coma. Until Jackie gets here, I have to sign off on his care. He gave me power of attorney."

"When?"

"Couple years ago. He has mine." She smiled grimly and moved her legs farther over, making room for Rose. "Sit. We need to talk before they come question me."

Rose perched on the edge of the bed, her hands in her lap. "How can I help?"

Maji leaned forward and took one of her hands. "I'm sorry. But I need to know who came to the house, what they asked you, and what you told them."

"Two FBI agents came. I didn't have much to tell them, but I begged a ride here." Rose had been desperate to see Angelo, and Maji as well. "Hannah gave me a message, though. She says your vacation is nearly over. And the firewall was never down. Does that make some kind of sense to you?"

Maji's eyes moved to the wall, then back to her. "Yeah. Thanks." She tilted her head toward the other side of the curtain. "Go talk to Ang, huh? Can't hurt."

Maji woke to the sound of Sander's raised voice. "I don't care about your list. Let me the fuck in!"

She made it to the door and cracked it enough to be heard. "He's family, too."

"Yes, ma'am."

When Ricky or Gino finally deigned to visit, she planned to withhold that line.

Sander looked like hell, and he didn't bother to hide his impression of her. "Jesus H. Christ on a raft." He looked past her. "I need to see him."

"You flew back? Just like that?" She held her ground.

"No. We rerouted to Newfoundland, and I got a charter back."

"We?"

"Me and couple of the guys, for security. Papa went on to Austria. But I couldn't leave Angelo behind."

Maji moved aside, and he slipped past the curtain to Angelo's bedside. Looking at him holding Angelo's limp hand, stroking his forehead, she almost felt sorry for Sander. "Stay as long you want."

"Rose says he's in a coma. We can fly him to somewhere better, make sure the surgery is a success."

"There isn't going to be a surgery. He's lost the part of his brain that controls autonomic functions. The machines are breathing for him, but he's gone."

"But…"

"I didn't know how to tell her. She loved him so much."

Sander was on his feet and holding her before she could wipe the tears. "It's not your fault."

Maji pulled back and blew her nose on a pocketful of damp tissues. "I tackled him, when the bullets were flying. He hit his head, and I didn't even know it. I let him down."

"So did I. But then, he loved you. He needed me—but he didn't love me."

Maji hopped to the chair by the sink and lowered herself into it. "Yes, he did. When I got to town, he was all about the money. Cagey about how he was going to get rich, but clear on that part."

"Okay. So?"

"So he changed a couple weeks in. He was still obsessed with that thing you two were cooking up. But he was all about proving his value, so you'd ask him to move to Vienna with you. The way he looked when you finally did—I've never seen him look like that."

"Like what?"

"Happy. Dude, he was in the closet since high school. He found guys to break a sweat with, sure, but he was never happy. Then you offered him a real life. Changed everything."

Sander sat and took off his glasses, putting his palms against his eyelids. "I am a curse on the men who love me," he said in Russian.

"Well, he didn't feel like that," Maji replied in English. "For what it's worth."

CHAPTER FORTY

Maji parked the bike in the shade of a maple at the end of the church parking lot. She pulled off the helmet and gloves, and pulled on the black beret that went with her green Class A uniform. She stood looking across the drive at the open front doors of St. Margaret's, willing herself to go in. The shiny new black oxfords pinched when she shifted from foot to foot, the starched shirt rubbed as she looked at her watch, and the wool of the beret was beginning to itch in the damp heat of the morning. Maybe she could just stand in the back of the church, in the cool dimness by the doors.

She stepped forward and stopped, seeing Frank emerge into the sun's glare wearing a slightly snug but immaculately pressed Marine Corps uniform. Noting the khaki shirt and tie, olive drab slacks, and shiny black shoes, she realized she had never asked his branch of service or rank, and he had never volunteered it. He turned his back to the sun and pulled a solitary cigarette from one trouser pocket, a lighter from the other. *Whatever gets you through the day, Frank.*

A taxi pulled to the curb, and a tall, middle-aged man in a dark gray suit got out on the road side, joined the cabbie by the trunk, and took two bags from him. He rolled them to the curb and opened the passenger door, extending a hand down to someone inside. For a second Maji stared at the woman on the sidewalk, wondering why Rose had only now arrived, and from where. Then she realized Frank was staring at the woman, too, his cigarette on the ground and his posture so erect he might snap a salute. The taxi pulled away and Maji could see the woman in black was slightly taller than Rose, slightly fuller in the hips, and her hair brushed her shoulders. *Bobbi diStephano. And that must be Gerald.*

Bobbi headed straight for Frank, who looked frozen in place, and took his face in her hands, shaking her head as she spoke to him.

Deciding to slip in while they held their reunion, Maji walked quietly past the trio, aiming for the sound of the organ indoors.

"Rios! Hey."

Shit, Frank. She turned halfway back toward Frank. He waved her over, earnest as that first night at the police station. Maji took a breath, straightened up, and walked toward them.

"Bobbi, this is Sergeant Rios. She's been looking after Rose this summer, saved her life more than once."

Maji extended her hand to Rose's mother. "Call me Ri, please. And Frank has a tendency to exaggerate."

"Bullshit," Bobbi said, taking Maji's hand and pulling her into a hug. "Thank you."

They stood back from each other then, each a little abashed. "Any chance we can sneak in without anyone noticing?" Bobbi asked.

Maji shook her head. "Doubt it."

"C'mon, then," Bobbi replied, putting her arm through Maji's. They walked through the towering doorway together, the two men following behind.

Rose turned in her seat near the front of the cathedral, between Nonna and Aunt Jackie, for the sixth time. "Where is she?"

"Your mother's not been back in thirty years," Nonna said. "If she don't show today, don't blame her."

Rose squeezed Nonna's hand. No point telling her that she didn't mean her mother—she meant Maji. She'd disappeared from the hospital while Rose was helping Jackie sign papers for the cremation people. And all Bubbles could tell her was that she wasn't at Hannah's, or her place either. That Rey had told her that the Army probably took her. That Maji might even be in the brig, pending an internal investigation. Apparently he had been an MP and knew these sorts of things.

The sound of wheels on the stone floor made Rose turn one more time. The organ swelled to life as she watched Maji walk down the aisle toward her. She looked stunning in her dress uniform, escorting…

"Mom," Rose whispered.

And behind them, her father. He and Frank made an odd pair, Gerald in a business suit and Frank in uniform. Looking surprisingly sharp, himself, and stoic. Holding himself together for Nonna, for Jackie, for her—so dependable, that way. And alive, thank God.

Rose caught Maji's eye and smiled at her, tearing up with relief at the sight of her. Maji didn't smile back, her eyes haunted above the purple and yellow residue of her bruises. She gave Rose a slow nod and turned to walk back down the aisle to an empty pew. Rose knew she needed to stay where she was and be strong for her grandmother and Aunt Jackie. But she wanted to get up and go comfort Maji. Or perhaps lean into her, and just cry.

Rose came back to the living room from Nonna's suite reluctantly. Gerald and her mother were staying back there, ostensibly to watch over Aunt Jackie. Mixing wine and those sedatives was dangerous, of course. But Rose couldn't help the feeling that her mother was hiding out, too. Unlike Nonna, upright in her black dress in that armchair, the Rose Kennedy of the New York Mafia.

The men in suits, so much more somber than they'd been just a week ago in this very house, filed by to have a quiet word with Mrs. B. On their way back out, they stopped and shook Gino's hand gravely, a hand on his shoulder to demonstrate heartfelt support. It was all such a charade, Rose wanted to scream.

A little stir in the room alerted Rose to Maji's arrival. Frank appeared beside Maji, and they shared a quiet word. Maji caught her eye and nodded almost imperceptibly, then headed directly for Nonna. With an up-nod to the suited men she passed, Maji limped over to the armchair and knelt on one knee. Rose moved behind the armchair and heard Italian flow between the two women.

Nonna squeezed Maji's hands and let her go, saying one last thing in Italian that made Maji almost smile. Maji winced as she started to rise, and Rose came around to offer her a hand. Standing face-to-face by the armchair, surrounded by strangers, Rose didn't know what to say. "Drink? Whiskey shots are the big thing."

Maji shook her head, but moved toward the sideboard laid out with whiskey, shot glasses, and pitchers of water. "Two shots, and there's no telling who I might deck."

Rose smiled and poured her a glass of water. "I know the feeling." She spotted Sander in the door, looking wound up, his gaze bouncing around the room until it landed on Frank. "Oh, dear."

They watched Sander say something to Gino, who looked angry in response and joined him in approaching Frank. Gino said something curt to Frank, and the three of them headed for the kitchen, Sander in the rear with his hand under his jacket. Maji followed them, saying as she went, "Block the door. Nobody else comes in."

"Got it." Rose let the door swing shut behind Maji and stood between them and the houseful of guests.

Sander's gun was already pointed at Frank. "Somebody let the Feds into your house." He said to Gino, "Papa could take your whole Family as an example, you know?"

Gino nodded. "No argument here. Just not in my house again. We got company."

Again? Maji thought, realizing why Ricky's absence still prickled at the back of her mind. Shit. "Hold on," she said.

Gino and Sander turned their heads toward her, alerted to her presence. Frank looked relieved that she had spoken up. "What's this about Feds?" she asked. "Should I be packing a bag?"

"This don't concern you," Gino said. "Walk away."

"No," Sander countermanded. Maji stepped closer, and he spoke to her directly. "Ricky was feeding intel to Sirko. But someone else let the Feds in. The caterers planted bugs all over the house."

"Jesus. I helped pick Cuba Libre—they had the best food, and music, too. You're telling me that was a front?"

He nodded. "And very well done. Angelo vetted them himself, and they held up. But the day after the party? Poof."

"So they must have been setting up the Benedettis for years—that's how they work. Why blame Frank?" She stepped in front of Sander, and he took a step back. And now the gun pointed at her. By now, she knew, Sander had seen the house video seized by the police, read the statements she'd given about what happened down by the water. "Besides, the Feds didn't kill Angelo. They don't sneak up with subs and Spetsnaz frogmen and shit."

Sander frowned, but tilted his head in acknowledgment. "Still," he said, "maybe Sirko had a Fed in his pocket. Maybe that's why he knew where to have his men."

"Or maybe your crew aren't as loyal as you think. Who was here that night, when we changed the plan? You, me, Ricky, Ang of course. And—"

"Sergei."

"There you go, then. His folks are dead, his wife died, what's he got to lose?"

"No way. Sergei's like family."

"So's Frank. Why would he possibly betray Gino?"

"Maybe he knows something the cops don't, about the accident," Gino said. "Max was his friend."

Maji turned so she could see all three men, and any movement of Sander's gun hand. Gino stood very still, across from her. "I'm not asking what you mean by that. I never poked my nose in Angelo's business, and I'm not interested in yours."

"Smart girl," Gino said. "But we'd feel better if you'd seal up all the leaks around here." He left the part threatening her loved ones unspoken, but it hung in the air nonetheless.

Maji nodded as Sander pressed the gun into her hand. It had been a long shot, trying to talk their way out. At least Frank wasn't on the ground yet. "Point taken. I'm sorry, Frank. It's not personal."

Frank looked at his feet. "I don't blame you, Ri."

At the door, Gino pulled on Maji's arm and leaned to her ear to speak so quietly she had to strain to hear. "Keep him close. He could try to run."

"I know," she said. "It's not my first rodeo."

She felt Gino pat her on the back as she went through the door to the patio, her free hand securely on Frank's elbow.

Rose moved aside as the kitchen door swung toward her. She expected to see all four of them, but only Sander and Gino came through.

"How's Jackie doing?" Gino asked.

"Resting," Rose said, irked to be distracted by his bland charm. "Where are Ri and Frank?"

"Having a chat," Gino said. "Nothing to worry about."

"Just business," Sander added. His jacket was off now, and the holster by his armpit was empty.

"No!" Rose roared as she pushed toward the kitchen.

Gino put an arm out to block her. "Look—"

"Let me through." She pushed against his arm, so that he stiffened up and pushed back against her. The amount of muscle in his portly body surprised her. But it tensed as she intended, and he stumbled forward when she released her hold.

Rose ducked under his flailing arms and ran across the kitchen to the back door, spurred by the sound of running dress shoes smacking the tiles behind her. On the veranda she looked frantically about. "Frank!"

"Stay away," his voice replied.

She ran toward it, and looked down over the parapet. On the grass below, Maji made a shushing motion at her. Frank blew her a kiss and waved her to back up. As what they were saying clicked, Maji yelled out, "Behind you!"

Rose whirled and faced off with Sander. From below and behind her, a shot rang out. "No!" she screamed.

Sander dashed to the rail, and Rose caught up with him there. Frank was running toward the front of the house, one hand clasped over the opposite shoulder. Maji chased after him, her bad leg slowing her down. Rose would have sworn she was genuinely trying to catch him.

Sander must have thought so, too, because he turned and barreled back through the house.

Rose followed as fast as she could, cursing her heels as she dodged the few men in suits still milling about the living room. Sander stood in the doorway, handing Gino another pistol. Rose palmed Sander's face, spinning him into the row of guests trying to watch the action.

As she took his spot in the doorway, Gino took aim at Frank, who had started down the driveway. "Gun!" Rose called out.

Maji, close on Frank's heels, dropped and spun, shooting back toward Gino. As he ducked behind an entryway support post, Maji dropped her gun, falling to her knees with her hands laced above her head.

Rose registered the blue and red flashing lights, the SUVs screeching to a halt only feet from Maji and Frank. Then she saw Gino move, and without thinking she swung her fist down on his arm. The gun clattered to the landing as he swore. She picked it up and pointed it at him, shaking all over.

"Rose." Sander appeared in the doorway, his hand extended. "Give me the gun."

"Drop the gun, ma'am," came an amplified voice, as a second SUV spilled forth a team of blue-jacketed agents. She looked at Maji, who was letting herself be cuffed next to Frank. Maji stiffened, looking frightened for her.

But the adrenaline kept pumping. "You killed him," Rose said to Gino, her hand shaking so hard, she had to steady it with the other. "I don't know how, but you did."

"Don't, Rose. He isn't worth it. Think of Ri," Sander said, still holding his hand out to her.

She looked at Maji again, and then at the row of agents with guns trained on her. She lifted her free hand in surrender and let the gun drop. Sander pulled her into his arms as the agents rushed forward.

Maji watched the agents shepherd everyone into the house, guns drawn and cuffs ready. She couldn't go in and check on Rose, even once they found her ID on the pat-down. They'd release her somewhere off-site, maybe into Rey's custody.

She looked over to Frank, who was docilely submitting to his pat-down. "Hey."

"Hey, yourself. Healing up okay?"

"Yeah. Listen..." She looked at the agent searching him. "Can we get a minute here?"

The agent looked affronted, but apparently did know who she was. "Two minutes," he said and went around to open the SUV's back hatch.

Maji spoke quietly. "They will set you up with a new life, as promised. But they will try to make you talk about more than Ang asked you to. Don't let them bluff you."

"Don't matter what they say. I know my script. Nobody's gonna get pissed at me but Benedetti folks—and they don't go after the women and kids."

"Thanks, Frank."

"Nah, it's me owes you again. But, Ri? Rose really, really likes you. Make her happy, huh? Don't make me come and find you."

Maji tried to smile, failed, and shoulder bumped him instead. "Happy isn't up to me. But I promise she'll stay safe." She caught his eye. "You want me to tell her—about you?"

The agent returned. "Time's up."

"Okay. Thanks," Maji replied, her eyes still on Frank.

"Someday, hon. When she's safe, and over all of this."

Rose watched the visitors file out quietly, respecting Gino's privacy by not looking at him. The teams of FBI agents spread through the house. She wondered if they would wake Jackie. Hopefully Gerald and her mother could help. *Welcome home, Mom.*

Asked to submit to handcuffing, Gino lost patience. "I was defending my home."

"We'll review the dash cams later, sir. Now, please put your hands forward and allow me to cuff you. Sir." The agent pulled a set from her belt, clearly ready to continue with or without his cooperation.

He put his hands out, grumbling. "You got no warrant to search. You got the shooter out there. Whaddya doing in my home, a day like this? You SOBs should be ashamed of yourselves."

The agent began reciting the Miranda rights, stone-faced. "You are under arrest. You have the right to remain silent. Anything you say may be—"

"Yeah, yeah," Gino interrupted. "Tell me when you got charges. Till then, don't waste my time."

She closed the cuffs with a sharp click. "Conspiracy to commit homicide, three counts, for the deaths of Maximillian Benedetti, Carlo Benedetti, and Angelo Benedetti. And fourteen felony counts under RICO—you want me to list them, sir?"

"Fuck you. None of that'll stick. DA's had me on the hook, what, a dozen times? Never one indictment, what's that tell you? What makes you think anything'll be different this time?"

"Evidence," Nonna said. She pressed herself up out of the armchair, and Rose gave her an arm. Nonna's grip was tight, and Rose took tiny steps as her grandmother shuffled toward her only surviving son.

"Ma! You don't believe a word of that, do you? You know how I feel about family."

"*Basta!*" Nonna reached up and slapped him hard, nearly stumbling forward herself. "Every time you open your mouth, you break my heart." She took the hearing aid from her ear, pulled out the transmitter pack from her pocket, and handed them both to the agent. "Take the damn thing. I'm sick of listening."

"Ma!" Gino blanched and wobbled on his feet. A male agent stepped up, putting an arm almost protectively on his back. They turned him toward the door, and the first agent began the Miranda rights from the top as they walked him out.

Rose spied her mother in the far doorway and wordlessly shushed her. Her mother nodded, face etched in worry as she looked at her own mother.

Nonna's eyes never left Gino's walk of shame. "We lost all the good ones. And Carlo."

Rose reached out for her grandmother, and they clung to one another as the door shut behind the last of the Benedetti men.

CHAPTER FORTY-ONE

Rose drove Aunt Paola's Mercedes to Hannah's house. If Paola missed it, let her report it stolen. She flipped on the wipers as drops began to spatter the windshield. *Now it can storm*, she thought. *Let it pour*.

Bypassing the white rental sedan out front, Rose pulled into the driveway and stopped short of the motorcycle. She headed for the back porch, stepping lightly toward the screen door. Inside the kitchen, the light was on and two women sat at the table.

"When is Ri coming down?" Iris asked. Impatient as always.

"She's grieving," Hannah replied. "Let's take this time to review the last steps."

"Right," Iris said, tapping her fingers on the tabletop. "Stage the articles. The first set are ready—my editor can pull the trigger anytime."

Rose winced at the wording. She shouldn't be eavesdropping, but so what?

"The last ones are here. They are key. The first provide context, but these—"

"Tell us why he got himself killed? Great." Iris paused. "Do we ever get the truth about Ri?"

Rose opened the screen door to Hannah's kitchen without knocking. She raised an eyebrow at Iris. "You cover mob killings now? Not your usual beat."

Iris opened her mouth in surprise.

Before she could form a comeback, Rose asked Hannah, "Where is she?"

"Upstairs. Are you all right?"

"Dandy. Nobody died today. Frank got arrested. Gino got arrested. Nonna gave the FBI a wire—she's been wearing it for months, apparently. And Ri disappeared again." In the back of an FBI van. But saying that in front of Iris? No.

A flash of lightning filled the kitchen, with a boom so close behind it the windows rattled. Rose jumped.

"Water? Tea?"

"No. I need to see her."

Hannah inclined her head in agreement. "Very well."

Iris stood, looking determined.

"Not you," Hannah said.

Rose took the stairs two at a time, as the skies opened up.

Rose found Maji on the balcony of Ava's office, stripped down to her underwear and tank top, drenched. Her face to the sky, arms uplifted, Maji didn't see Rose approach, didn't seem to hear her step out onto the balcony to wrap around her from behind. But she dropped her arms and hugged Rose to her chilled skin. Rose rested her chin on Maji's shoulder, her mouth by Maji's ear. "You left again."

"It's what I do," Maji mumbled, all the muscles of her back tensing against Rose's front.

Rose wanted to shake and to hold her, both. Instead, she stepped backward, pulling Maji with her into the room. Soaked now herself, she shivered. Maji twisted in her arms, slid her hands up Rose's front, and cupped the back of her head. And then they were kissing, melted together and pulling dripping clothing off.

As Rose pulled her toward the couch, Maji pulled back, looked at her with aching eyes. "I'm…" She paused. "I should have…" Maji seemed frozen, her face twisted in a knot.

Rose pulled her close again, kissed her eyelids gently. "Hush. Just hush." She kissed her face, forehead to chin to ears, until Maji finally sought out her lips.

Hannah and Iris both heard thumps from the room above. Iris looked up, alarmed. "Are they okay?"

Hannah tilted her head. "Time will tell." She stepped into the foyer and returned seconds later with a large manila envelope. "The rest of your story. All that Angelo had time to prepare."

"Well, that's it, then," Iris said. "All but good-bye." She looked up hopefully.

"It may be a while before they come down," Hannah said. "Would you like some lunch?"

From above came a sound like keening. Iris flushed. "No," she said, standing. "I need a smoke."

❖

Maji brushed the hair from Rose's face, luxuriating in the feel of her head against her shoulder. The couch cradled them and kept them close at the same time, Rose's warm length draped over Maji's aching body. The throb in her reinjured ankle kept time with her heart, slowing as it thumped against Rose's ear. Maji tilted her head down to kiss Rose's damp scalp, and Rose kissed her chest in reply. Maji wished they could lie like that forever, no language but touch between them.

"Thank you for helping Frank," Rose said.

Maji thought of Frank starting his new life, alone. "Thank you for not killing Gino."

Rose vibrated with what Maji hoped was laughter and pulled herself tighter against Maji's hips and chest. She slid one leg over and around Maji's stretched-out ones. *Pinned.* And not about to fight it.

"Mom and I are driving Nonna back to California in her car, that horrible old land yacht. Gerald's staying to help Jackie pack up a few things and deal with the insurance people. I'm not sure which of us pulled the short straw."

Maji smiled but didn't speak. She pulled the throw blanket down from the back of the couch. If they stayed on the couch any longer, they'd need to open it into its bed form. But she should be saying good-bye instead.

"You could come with us," Rose ventured. "If you have any vacation left." She trailed her hand from Maji's scalp down to her jawline.

Maji caught it and kissed the fingers, breathed them in, closing her eyes. "I can't."

"Okay," Rose said. "Then come out when you get a few days off."

Maji struggled for words she couldn't bring herself to say. "I can't, Rose."

"Can't what?" Rose said, trying to scooch up to look at Maji without disentangling. It didn't work, so she leaned back instead. Maji supported her with one arm, which began to shake. "Maji?" Rose asked, looking into her eyes.

Maji couldn't look into those beautiful eyes and hurt her one more minute. "I can't see you anymore."

"Dammit!" Rose gasped and twisted to catch herself as gravity took over. Maji sat up and offered her two hands. Rose took them and turned herself around, until she was perched on the edge of the couch, facing Maji. "Look. I know you do work you can't talk about. But you must have choices."

"Some."

Rose pulled the little blanket around her shoulders. "What are you afraid of, Maji? What is it you think you're protecting me from?"

"Me." Maji couldn't take those eyes anymore. She stared at Rose's shoulder. "I will leave you, and never tell you when I'll be back."

"But you'll come back."

Maji nodded. "I'd just show up again, and not tell you where I've been, or what I've done. You can't live like that. I can't plan vacations—I can't even own a pet. We'd make plans with your family or your friends, and you'd have to lie to them when I didn't show up. I'm not going to put you through that."

Rose turned away, then stood. "Whoa—back up the U-Haul, soldier. One, I have not named our children yet. And two, don't you think I get to decide how I can live?"

Maji hung her head. When she lifted it, the fight in Rose's eyes gave her strength. "Bubbles didn't tell me she's getting pregnant. Because she knows I won't be there when she needs me."

Rose opened her mouth to respond, reaching a hand out.

Maji turned her face toward the window, looking past her. "Don't. You don't get it. Ava didn't tell me she was dying, because she knew I couldn't come home to say good-bye. Hell, I almost didn't make it back for Angelo's funeral."

Rose put her fingers under Maji's chin and turned her face gently toward her. "I understand," she said.

The grief Maji saw reflected in her eyes made her want to punch something. "Understanding and living with it are different. Maybe you could do it. But I don't think I could live with watching you get hurt, over and over. And blaming myself for that."

EPILOGUE

Eight months later

Angelo slowed to a walk, enjoying the colors of the brightening sky over the Mediterranean as he finished his daily run. No wonder Maji called this the magic hour. What he wouldn't give to be able to share this with her. To share anything with anyone he knew. Well, not anyone. Just the handful that wouldn't want him dead again.

Inside the marina, he strolled down the dock he called home for now, waving to a few early risers, who greeted him by his new name. And in the cockpit of his little sloop, there was the first of six newspapers he would read today. Three in English, one in Russian, one in Arabic, and one in the new language.

ATTORNEY GENERAL INDICTS RECORD NUMBER OF SUSPECTS FOR WIRE FRAUD, RICO VIOLATIONS, the front page of the *New York Times* announced. The article went into some detail about Operation Rolling Thunder, giving the FBI credit for painstakingly setting up the sweep, with dozens of agents working together across federal departments for over a year. The article was light on details about how they had managed to identify the suspects and gather enough evidence to issue indictments, after years of floundering to secure even a few. Typical. Not that it mattered—the Feds got more than they'd hoped for out of his work.

Iris's series, released every few weeks over the fall and winter, was much more informative. The first article, published just a week after his funeral, capitalized on his death. The tabloids loved mob killings but never asked why the celebrity criminals killed each other. Iris intimated that her law enforcement sources confirmed that he was murdered for a program that improved organized crime's already pretty sophisticated money laundering techniques. He had to hand it to her—she knew how to throw out a hook. The next story went into some detail about how big an issue electronic laundering had become and pumped up the volume by pointing out how little national governments and commercial banks were doing about it. A nice dose of righteous indignation, for anyone who cared. The third gave average citizens a reason to care, tying money laundering to specific cases of terrorist cell and training camp funding.

By the time the virus kicked in, and trillions of dollars got sucked out of illegal accounts overnight, the public had forgotten about Angelo's death. Iris's piece, "NGOs: Surprise Beneficiaries of Untraced Funds," probably seemed a bit out of place in the series. But it was part of their agreement, and he appreciated the confirmation that the funds he'd worked so hard to remove from Khodorov's and Sirko's client lists were winding up where they might do some good. And he had chuckled a little at how flummoxed the banking authories were.

> *Funds show up with no source information in thousands of NGO accounts. Authorities are asking individuals or organizations who find unexpected electronic deposits to notify their banking institutions. What happens to funds with no known source? "This is an unprecedented situation," admitted Steven Wright, Chairman of the FDIC. "The Attorney General and OIG are researching the matter. Money which cannot be returned to its sender may lawfully belong to the recipient, once standard protocols are followed." The FDIC will be issuing a set of protocols for financial institutions to follow, to ensure that identification of the funds' source has been attempted using all current technology available.*

Iris had really come through, he had to admit. She'd kept publishing, even after the first attempt on her life, which she'd turned into a story that sounded likely to earn her a book deal. And the paper had just kept pumping out her articles, syndicating them to news outlets all over the world. Security at the office, and the editors' houses, must be hellacious.

As much fun as the media was having, speculating about who the Digital Robin Hood had liberated all that money from, it really blew up when Iris outed him. As little as Angelo wanted his old face all over the internet again, it had to be done. She used the statement he had given her, carefully crafted to protect the team while explaining why a Benedetti would give his own life to take on global terrorism. News of Yuri Khodorov's very public execution followed only days later. Angelo was relieved to hear nothing about Sander. Maybe he'd seen the tidal wave coming and used the last of Papa's hard currency to buy himself a life raft.

Only the New York papers covered Gino's indictment, a small matter overshadowed by the gravity of world events. The trial looked to go well, with Frank's testimony, and Gino having to use a public defender like any other broke criminal.

Angelo reached across the cockpit and grunted when his shoulder screamed at him. Maji hadn't lied when she said the scar removal process was worse than the burn itself. And his sinuses hurt whenever he leaned forward, thanks to the facial reconstruction. He wasn't as good-looking anymore, but maybe a good man wouldn't care so much. Of course, he'd have to master yet another language before then and get the whole life story for his cover ironed out before he could really date.

Where the hell was Sander now? Angelo looked at his shiny new laptop, then decided for the umpteenth time against opening it. He could find out so much, if he just went online. Not knowing how his mother, Maji, and Rose were doing drove him nuts, too. If he started hunting down any of them, he'd get carried away, maybe even leave a trail. No, he'd meant to be buried. And he would respect the risk Maji and the team had taken, against his orders, and stay gone. It was hard to be pissed at them on such a beautiful morning.

Rose sat front row center for Neda Kamiri's lecture. She'd driven all the way to Berkeley for it, nearly three hours in traffic slowed by March rain. It was worth it. In the wings, stage right, she could see a petite figure in the shadows, fitted out in black from head to toe—black cap, neatly pressed button-down shirt, BDUs, and, of course, running shoes. Under the cap, no doubt, chocolate and caramel hair pulled back into a french braid. She couldn't make out the look on Maji's face, just waited for her to pause while scanning the crowd of students and older fans in the front rows. Rose nodded, and got a single nod back.

At the reception, she saw Maji keeping a watchful eye on the room, close enough to her mother to reach her but far enough away to see everyone else. Rose saw Maji speak into a lapel mike, glancing in her direction, and she looked around to see who might be on the other end of the invisible line. No one else in the room stood out. But then, they wouldn't, would they?

"Hi," Rose said, offering her hand. "I'm Dr. RoseMarie diStephano, from Bonaventure College. And you are?"

Maji took her hand. Her eyes had their old spark back. "Maji Rios, Paragon Security. Nice of you to drive up. Did you want to meet Dr. Kamiri?"

"May I? I mean, yes, I'd love to. But I'm a little worried I'll start fangirling and embarrass myself."

"Just be yourself. I'm sure she'll appreciate meeting you."

Rose smiled. "Maybe afterward, you could tell me how I did? Over coffee, or something."

"Enticing as *something* sounds," Maji said, her cheeks dimpling, "coffee's all I can make time for."

The café in the student union was a little crowded, but Maji could see all the exits. If they leaned in, they could hear each other fine. She just hadn't counted on what seeing Rose again would do to her.

"Is this a safe place to talk?" Rose asked.

Maji made an effort to visibly relax. "Yes. And I'm on radio silent. If I run off…"

"I won't take it personally." Rose paused. "So, you're working for Paragon?"

Maji shook her head. "Couple weeks pro bono. My school break, before I present my thesis."

"Wow! That's great. I'm happy for you. And that's very generous for a student."

Maji shrugged. "A couple weeks' wages is enough to send one girl to camp next year. And what do I need it for? I'm getting ready to pay gift tax on five million. Aren't you?"

"No," Rose said. "I took the other option. I just couldn't leave the money in my account, knowing where it might have come from." She lifted one eyebrow. "And I recall you saying there was nothing you needed."

"Nothing money will get me. But I thought I might enjoy Robin Hooding a little. Anonymous gifts to strangers, you know."

"Now, that does sound like you."

The twinkle in Rose's eyes made Maji's chest hurt. "It makes me feel closer to him," she confessed.

Rose reached out and stroked Maji's cheek. "Don't you dare blame yourself. Surely now that we know what he was really up to, you understand why he didn't tell us. Especially you."

Maji inclined her head in acknowledgment. "I would have wanted to stop him. But if I did, you would have gotten hurt, for sure—killed. Probably your whole family."

"That's too hard a choice to ask anyone you love to make. And he did love you."

"I know."

They sat quietly a moment, sipping from the institutional white ceramic mugs. Not a very romantic reunion. But that was a good thing, right? Seeing Rose addled her brain enough, even here. Maji pulled an item from the back of her waistband. "I was going to send you this, but then Bubbles said you might be here, so..."

Rose felt the shape through the wrapping. "A book?" She ripped the shiny paper off with childlike anticipation on her face. She studied the cover of Vandana Shiva's *Monocultures of the Mind* with a wrinkled brow, but when she opened the cover, she gasped. "Maji! It's a first edition. And signed! Do you know how hard these are to come by?"

Maji laughed. "It's easier if you know somebody who knows her. I know you lost several books in the fire, but that one was your favorite, right?"

In answer, Rose leaned across the table and kissed Maji on the cheek. Her eyes said she wanted to do more, but she sat back into her own chair again instead. "I have a conference to attend later this spring. Traditional foods and cultural preservation by American tribes. You think you might have time?"

"You need a translator?" Maji teased. "Or a bodyguard?"

"Neither. Just company."

Real people time. With Rose. Oh, man. "Well, I never really know if I'll be free when I want to be."

Rose's face betrayed her frustration. "If you don't want to, just say so."

"No—I do. But this is just what I tried to explain, before. I could make plans, and look forward to it, and at the last minute get called away. I don't get to negotiate. If you retracted the offer, I'd understand."

"You'll make it, or you won't. *Je ne regrette rien.*" Rose stood. "When I have my itinerary, I'll send it, care of Paragon, US."

Her teammate's voice broke into the thoughts Maji struggled to put together. She keyed the lapel mike. "On my way." She stood and told Rose, with genuine regret, "They're moving out. I've got to go."

Rose moved around the table and gave her a soft kiss on the lips—a mere whisper. "Stay safe."

"You, too." Maji turned and headed back to her team. She really should have said no to Rose's offer, pushed her away and set her free to find someone who could make her happy. *Too late, Rios.*

About the Author

MB Austin, a mild-mannered civil servant by day, spends her discretionary time writing, training in a mix of martial arts, and working to end violence. She also enjoys cooking, eating, reading, dancing, and laughing as much as possible.

MB's first series, featuring Maji Rios, is inspired by real people, in and out of uniform, who work to make their communities and the world safer for all. And by the people who feed them.

MB lives with her fabulous wife in Seattle, an excellent town for coffee-fueled writers who don't need too much sun. Peek into daily life and upcoming stories at: www.mbaustin.me.

Books Available From Bold Strokes Books

A More Perfect Union by Carsen Taite. Major Zoey Granger and DC fixer Rook Daniels risk their reputations for a chance at true love while dealing with a scandal that threatens to rock the military. (978-1-62639-754-5)

Arrival by Gun Brooke. The spaceship *Pathfinder* reaches its passengers' new homeworld where danger lurks in the shadows while Pamas Seclan disembarks and finds unexpected love in young science genius Darmiya Do Voy. (978-1-62639-859-7)

Captain's Choice by VK Powell. Architect Kerstin Anthony's life is going to plan until Bennett Carlyle, the first girl she ever kissed, is assigned to her latest and most important project, a police district substation. (978-1-62639-997-6)

Falling Into Her by Erin Zak. Pam Phillips, widow at the age of forty, meets Kathryn Hawthorne, local Chicago celebrity, and it changes her life forever—in ways she hadn't even considered possible. (978-1-63555-092-4)

Hookin' Up by MJ Williamz. Will Leah get what she needs from casual hookups or will she see the love she desires right in front of her? (978-1-63555-051-1)

King of Thieves by Shea Godfrey. When art thief Casey Marinos meets bounty hunter Finnegan Starkweather, the crimes of the past just might set the stage for a payoff worth more than she ever dreamed possible. (978-1-63555-007-8)

Lucy's Chance by Jackie D. As a serial killer haunts the streets, Lucy tries to stitch up old wounds with her first love in the wake of a small town's rapid descent into chaos. (978-1-63555-027-6)

Right Here, Right Now by Georgia Beers. When Alicia Wright moves into the office next door to Lacey Chamberlain's accounting firm, Lacey is about to find out that sometimes the last person you want is exactly the person you need. (978-1-63555-154-9)

Strictly Need to Know by MB Austin. Covert operator Maji Rios will do whatever she must to complete her mission, but saving a gorgeous stranger from Russian mobsters was not in her plans. (978-1-63555-114-3)

Tailor-Made by Yolanda Wallace. Tailor Grace Henderson doesn't date clients, but when she meets gender-bending model Dakota Lane, she's tempted to throw all the rules out the window. (978-1-63555-081-8)

Time Will Tell by M. Ullrich. With the ability to time travel, Eva Caldwell will have to decide between having it all and erasing it all. (978-1-63555-088-7)

Change in Time by Robyn Nyx. Working in the past is hell on your future. The Extractor series: Book Two. (978-1-62639-880-1)

Love After Hours by Radclyffe. When Gina Antonelli agrees to renovate Carrie Longmire's new house, she doesn't welcome Carrie's overtures at friendship or her own unexpected attraction. A Rivers Community Novel. (978-1-63555-090-0)

Nantucket Rose by CF Frizzell. Maggie Jordan can't wait to convert a historic Nantucket home into a B&B, but doesn't expect to fall for mariner Ellis Chilton, who has more claim to the house than Maggie realizes. (978-1-63555-056-6)

Picture Perfect by Lisa Moreau. Falling in love wasn't supposed to be part of the stakes for Olive and Gabby, rival photographers in the competition of a lifetime. (978-1-62639-975-4)

Set the Stage by Karis Walsh. Actress Emilie Danvers takes the stage again in Ashland, Oregon, little realizing that landscaper Arden Philips is about to offer her a very personal romantic lead role. (978-1-63555-087-0)

Strike a Match by Fiona Riley. When their attempts at matchmaking fizzle out, firefighter Sasha and reluctant millionairess Abby find themselves turning to each other to strike a perfect match. (978-1-62639-999-0)

The Price of Cash by Ashley Bartlett. Cash Braddock is doing her best to keep her business afloat, stay out of jail, and avoid Detective Kallen. It's not working. (978-1-62639-708-8)

Under Her Wing by Ronica Black. At Angel's Wings Rescue, dogs are usually the ones saved, but when quiet Kassandra Haden meets outspoken owner Jayden Beaumont, the two stubborn women just might end up saving each other. (978-1-63555-077-1)

Underwater Vibes by Mickey Brent. When Hélène, a translator in Brussels, Belgium, meets Sylvie, a young Greek photographer and swim coach, unsettling feelings hijack Hélène's mind and body—even her poems. (978-1-63555-002-3)

A Date to Die by Anne Laughlin. Someone is killing people close to Detective Kay Adler, who must look to her own troubled past for a suspect. There she finds more than one person seeking revenge against her. (978-163555-023-8)

Captured Soul by Laydin Michaels. Can Kadence Munroe save the woman she loves from a twisted killer, or will she lose her to a collector of souls? (978-1-62639-915-0)

Dawn's New Day by TJ Thomas. Can Dawn Oliver and Cam Cooper, two women who have loved and lost, open their hearts to love again? (978-1-63555-072-6)

Definite Possibility by Maggie Cummings. Sam Miller is just out for good times, but Lucy Weston makes her realize happily ever after is a definite possibility. (978-1-62639-909-9)

Eyes Like Those by Melissa Brayden. Isabel Chase and Taylor Andrews struggle between love and ambition from the writers' room on one of Hollywood's hottest TV shows. (978-1-63555-012-2)

Heart's Orders by Jaycie Morrison. Helen Tucker and Tee Owens escape hardscrabble lives to careers in the Women's Army Corps, but more than their hearts are at risk as friendship blossoms into love. (978-1-63555-073-3)

Hiding Out by Kay Bigelow. Treat Dandridge is unaware that her life is in danger from the murderer who is hunting the woman she's falling in love with, Mickey Heiden. (978-1-62639-983-9)

Omnipotence Enough by Sophia Kell Hagin. Can the tiny tool that abducted war veteran Jamie Gwynmorgan accidentally acquires help her escape an unknown enemy to reclaim her stolen life and the woman she deeply loves? (978-1-63555-037-5)

Summer's Cove by Aurora Rey. Emerson Lange moved to Provincetown to live in the moment, but when she meets Darcy Belo and her son Liam, her quest for summer romance becomes a family affair. (978-1-62639-971-6)

The Road to Wings by Julie Tizard. Lieutenant Casey Tompkins, Air Force student pilot, has to fly with the toughest instructor, Captain Kathryn "Hard Ass" Hardesty, fly a supersonic jet, and deal with a growing forbidden attraction. (978-1-62639-988-4)

Beauty and the Boss by Ali Vali. Ellis Renois is at the top of the fashion world, but she never expects her summer assistant Charlotte Hamner to tear her heart and her business apart like sharp scissors through cheap material. (978-1-62639-919-8)

Fury's Choice by Brey Willows. When gods walk amongst humans, can two women find a balance between love and faith? (978-1-62639-869-6)

Lessons in Desire by MJ Williamz. Can a summer love stand a four-month hiatus and still burn hot? (978-1-63555-019-1)

Lightning Chasers by Cass Sellars. For Sydney and Parker, being a couple was never what they had planned. Now they have to fight corruption, murder, and enemies hiding in plain sight just to hold on to each other. Lightning Series, Book Two. (978-1-62639-965-5)

Summer Fling by Jean Copeland. Still jaded from a breakup years earlier, Kate struggles to trust falling in love again when a summer fling with sexy young singer Jordan rocks her off her feet. (978-1-62639-981-5)